QUEEN
FERRIS

Jack —

Happy Birthday!
Hope you like Queen
Ferris as much as Reiffe's
Choice. (I actually like
QF better!).
Thanks.

S.C. Butler,

December, 2007

TOR BOOKS BY S. C. BUTLER

Reiffen's Choice
Queen Ferris

QUEEN FERRIS

Book Two
of the
Stoneways Trilogy

S. C. BUTLER

A TOM DOHERTY ASSOCIATES BOOK
NEW YORK

QUEEN FERRIS: BOOK TWO OF THE STONEWAYS TRILOGY

Copyright © 2007 by S. C. Butler

Map by Elisa Mitchell

A Tor Book
Published by Tom Doherty Associates, LLC
175 Fifth Avenue
New York, NY 10010

www.tor.com

Tor® is a registered trademark of Tom Doherty Associates, LLC.

Library of Congress Cataloging-in-Publication Data

Butler, S. C. (Sam C.)
   Queen Ferris / S. C. Butler.—1st ed.
      p. cm.— (The Stoneways trilogy ; bk. 2)
   "A Tom Doherty Associates book."
   ISBN-13: 978-0-7653-1478-9
   ISBN-10: 0-7653-1478-9
   1. Kings and rulers—Succession—Fiction. 2. Wizards—Fiction. I. Title.
PS3602.U884Q84   2007
813'.6—dc22

                                                    2007024077

First Edition: November 2007

Printed in the United States of America

0 9 8 7 6 5 4 3 2 1

For Susan and Walter

Contents

BRIZEN

Mountains of the North

USSENE

KEEADIN

The Westing

The Easting

The Wetting

The Undram

Backford

The Great River

The Greenbank

The

Rimwich
WAYLAND

BANKING

Malmoret

The Edgwater

The Blue
Mountains

Grangore

The Ambare

Mremmen

REIFFEN

And one of her loves was a wizard,
a rhymer of light and death,
and though she knew
his chances were few,
she loved him with every breath.

And one of her loves was a soldier,
a hero throughout the land,
who sighed and pined,
but never could find,
the courage to ask for her hand.

And one of her loves was a king's son,
who bloomed like the swan once gray.
His wings, spread wide,
brushed his rivals aside,
and carried him off with the day.

−MINDRELL THE BARD

1

Sorrow and Stone

'm sorry, Mother."

His heart thumping, Reiffen watched Giserre's mouth open in wonder as the Tear dissolved around them. The silence of bookshelves replaced the rumble of the gorge.

"Where is this place?" she asked.

"Ussene."

Fear crept into the lines around her eyes. When Reiffen had taken her hand moments ago on the cold, wet stone of the Tear, Ussene was the last place Giserre had expected to find herself. She took a deep breath, her face hardening, and the wrinkle of dread was gone.

"The Three have brought you back?" she asked.

"I have brought us back."

"You!"

"Yes, Mother."

"The magic was yours?"

"No. Usseis laid the spell on me." Reiffen left off rubbing his itchy knuckle to show where the last joint of his left little finger had been reattached. The iron thimble that had capped it before was gone, though another remained on his right hand. "See? The body heals itself across any distance. The magic brought me back."

"And you knew this all along?" Giserre's anger rose. "You told us you had no idea what those things on your fingers were for."

"Their purpose only just came to me, Mother."

"And you used them to come here, to Ussene? After you had just been rescued? Have you lost your mind?"

"It was my only choice, Mother."

"Only choice? It was most certainly not! You could have remained in Valing. How could you possibly choose to return to the place from which Redburr and your friends just saved you?" Giserre drew herself up to her full height. Her robe rustled; the white of her nightgown flickered at her throat. "I refuse to believe you. This is some trick of the Three. My son would not be such a fool."

Reiffen's heart lifted. Perhaps he *was* under the Wizards' control. If that were true, then none of the responsibility was his. But this didn't feel like the other times he had been held captive by Usseis's will. His mind felt free; his heart remained open.

"It would have been worse had I stayed," he said.

"It would not."

"They changed me, Mother. Nothing is the same."

"I would have helped you fight them. We could have removed those . . . things." Giserre's mouth pursed with distaste as she gestured toward the remaining thimble. "Redburr would have cut them off quickly enough."

"Yes. And everyone would have been watching all the time for some sign I was doing the Three's bidding."

"That is not true! You were among friends. You should have trusted us. If your father were alive—"

"If my father were alive he would understand!" Reiffen's eyes blazed with conviction. "He died fighting them, and I will do the same if I have to. But the Wizards are not in Valing, Mother, they are here. Valing is done. I will not hide from them, or anyone else, any longer."

Mother and son stared angrily at one another. Never before had Reiffen spoken so roughly to her. He had not been the best behaved of children, but he had not quarreled openly with her either. He wanted to rush into her arms and beg forgiveness for speaking so harshly, but he knew he had to be strong. Always had his mother taught him that kings bore their hurts alone.

"Then why bring me?" she demanded bitterly. "Did Usseis order you to do that?"

"No." Reiffen closed the small gold casket that lay on the nearest reading table, hiding the thin streak of blood that marked the bottom.

"Then why?"

"Yes, Reiffen," asked a voice from the door. "Why did you bring your mother?"

Mother and son turned. Fornoch towered over them in his gray robes, his black eyes piercing the soft light. Whether he had entered normally, too silent for them to notice, or magically, Reiffen couldn't tell.

The Wizard inclined his head in the least deferential of bows. "My lady. Allow me to welcome you to Ussene."

Giserre moved closer to her son, her anger forgotten in the face of a common enemy. "Yours is no welcome," she replied.

"On the contrary, milady, mine is more welcome than either of my brothers'. Ossdonc, I know, would relish another wife. And Usseis has uses for everyone."

Reiffen pushed forward. "You might as well kill me, if you hurt her."

Fornoch smiled. "As long as she remains out of my brothers' way, she is unlikely to receive injury."

"Staying out of their way will be my pleasure," answered Giserre. "I have no wish to remain."

"It was not I who brought you, milady. Nor my brothers. But, if he who did bring you so prefers, I will send you back."

Reiffen started. "You would do that?" With sudden selfless-ness he turned back to Giserre. He had made the decision to bring her so quickly: what if he had been wrong? "Mother. You're right. I should never have brought you."

"You should never have come yourself. Will you return if I do?"

Reiffen met his mother's stare. His eagerness faded. "No. I have made my choice."

"Then I must stay as well. I will not leave you here alone, no matter what I think of your decision."

"I will offer no second chance," said Fornoch.

"I will ask none," replied the lady.

"Very well. I have prepared a suite of rooms for the two of you. Reiffen, you will find the arrangements much more satisfac-tory than on your previous stay, now that you have come to us freely."

The Gray Wizard led them out of the Library into the pas-sage beyond. Thick candles lit the gloomy way, smoke blacken-ing the walls and high ceiling. The dust raised by their passing settled behind them like dreary fog. A short walk brought them to a heavy wooden door that had not been in that particular hall the last time Reiffen had been in Ussene. He saw at once it had been fashioned like the doors in Valing Manor. Stout and dark, and seemingly stained with long years of use, the portal swung open easily at the Wizard's touch.

They found themselves in an ordinary sitting room. Dwarven lamps shone on the walls, brightening the sofas and chairs. Fornoch gestured toward two more doors in the far wall.

"Sleeping chambers lie beyond. I regret only one has a win-dow. Certain elements of this place are not particularly suitable for change. I presume, milady, you will prefer the windowed room."

The Wizard waited for her answer, but Giserre ignored him. Nor did she sit upon either of the pillowed couches beside the hearth, nor on the cushioned chairs. Fine tapestries covered the walls, the cloth glinting with thread of blumet, silver, and gold. A sewing basket topped a low table beside one of the couches, a hoop of fine linen near at hand.

"As you wish." Fornoch folded his giant hands into his robe's hanging sleeves. "You will have any length of time in which to acquaint yourself with your new surroundings. There is much to learn."

A slight tap interrupted at the door. A ragged servant shuffled in, the woman's eyes glued fearfully to the floor. Reiffen thought there was something familiar about her, and supposed he had passed her in the halls before his escape. A ratty shawl wrapped her shoulders; scraps of shabby dresses covered her from throat to ankle. Her filthy feet were bare.

"This is Spit," introduced the Wizard. "Perhaps she will provide you the same loyalty Molio once did."

Reiffen flinched at the mention of his former friend and hoped his mother hadn't noticed. He had told no one about Molio.

But Giserre seemed more concerned with Spit. "My son and I require no servant of yours, Wizard. We can care for ourselves."

One gray brow lifted, almost in amusement, but the rest of the Wizard's face remained unchanged.

"Very well. You may find Ussene trying at even the best of times, beyond the walls of this apartment. But, if this is what you wish, I shall leave you to your choice. Reiffen knows where the refectories are, when you feel the need to dine. I had thought you would prefer your meals alone."

The Wizard turned to Reiffen before leaving. "Tomorrow your training will begin," he said. His servant followed him out into the corridor.

When Fornoch was gone, Giserre ignored her son the way

she had the Wizard. Lamplight washed across the floor as she opened the door to the right-hand room, highlighting the color in the thick rug and the bright quilt covering the curtained bed. Another upholstered chair, a desk for writing, a chest by the footboard, and a tall wardrobe against the far wall completed the furniture. Giserre pushed aside the heavy draperies that covered the window and opened the casements; a breath of the outside world drifted in. Stars glittered in a narrow patch of sky, the shadows of tall cliffs sealing the darkness below.

Reiffen opened the wardrobe doors. Women's clothing lay piled neatly on the shelves.

"Fornoch is right." Giserre lifted the top of the chest, revealing more velvet, lace, and fine linen. "I will take this room. Unless you prefer it." The chest closed with a hollow breath as she dropped the lid.

"No, Mother."

She plucked at her homely robe. "Our hosts have thought of everything. I will not have to wear my nightdress for the remainder of our stay."

"I'm sorry, Mother, but this is what I have to do."

Rather than replying, Giserre traced her hand along the yellow and gold flowers stitched onto the light summer quilt, the royal hues of Banking.

"I embroidered a quilt like this myself, when I was not much older than you." The mattress gave softly as Giserre sat on it. "I doubt this is the same one, but they are as alike as two peas. Life was simpler then. We only worried about the war. Now, no more about your choice, my son. I have had mine as well. Tell me about Molio instead."

"I killed him, Mother," he answered softly.

Her eyebrows rose in surprise. "Had he attacked you?"

Reiffen shook his head.

"Threatened you? Did he hurt someone who had helped you?"

"He was my friend," Reiffen whispered.

Giserre pursed her lips and patted the quilted flower at her side. "Come. Sit beside me."

He did as asked. She took his palm in hers. Shivering, he squeezed her fingers.

"Usseis forced you, I suppose."

Reiffen nodded.

"Then you should understand it was not an act of yours. Penance is due, of course, to acknowledge that you were the vessel of this terrible deed, and remorse. But the guilt is not yours." With her free hand she brushed his hair back from his forehead.

His throat felt dry and tight. "You don't understand, Mother. It was worse than that. I chose the manner of his dying. Usseis left that up to me." He closed his eyes, which only made the memory of the falling man burn more brightly, and shuddered. His mother stroked his cheek.

"You would never have done it had Usseis not made you," she said. "It is the killing that is evil, not its manner. You cannot say what part of Usseis might have come into you along with his will."

Small tears melted along the sides of Reiffen's nose. He couldn't bring himself to tell his mother how easily the treachery had come to him.

"Is that why you brought me with you?" she asked gently. "Because the Wizards made you kill your friend?"

She lifted his hand, and together they looked at the pale end of his smallest finger. The weight of the remaining thimble hung heavily on his other hand.

"I was lonely." He spoke in such a low voice he hardly heard what he said himself. But his mother heard him plainly.

"Lonely? You could have solved that easily enough. You could have taken Avender back with you, or—" Giserre checked her thought. "No. It would have been wrong to take Ferris."

"It would have been wrong to take either of them, Mother. The Wizards would have made me kill them. Like Molio."

"But not your mother."

"No." Reiffen barely mouthed the word. His heart felt close to bursting. He had killed his friend, and now he had stolen his mother so he wouldn't have to be alone among the Wizards. He wondered again if she had been right, and everything he had done since arriving in Ussene months ago had been at the command of the Three. But he knew it wasn't true. At the very least, the Three had never asked him to bring his mother back to Ussene. That idea was entirely his own.

He flushed again at the thought of it.

"They won't kill you." He clenched his teeth so hard his jaw ached. "Ferris and Avender they might have killed and bound me all the same. But not you. Even they know that would be too much."

Giserre let go his hand and held him close. He hugged her tightly in return, and sobbed into the comfort of her shoulder.

"My son," she soothed. "I may disagree with your decision to return to this place, but in this other matter you bear no blame. It would not have suited to have taken your friends. I am with you now. We shall fight the Three together."

Reiffen wiped his nose with his sleeve. "But what if I'm wrong? What if Usseis makes me kill you, too?"

She pulled him closer. Through his snuffling tears he smelled Valing in her robe. The pine smoke from the hearth and the damp summer green of the roaring flume twined about him. He missed it all terribly. Valing was the only home he had ever known.

"We will take what they give us," she told him. "And when

they try to turn us to their purpose, we will fight them. In the meantime, we will learn what power we can."

They explored the rest of the apartment. Reiffen was glad his bedroom didn't have a window. His chest and cupboard were filled with clothes the same as Giserre's, though not so fine, and on his bed lay a quilt worked in diamonds of black and orange. "My brother's," said Giserre when she saw it. "Someone has been watching Malmoret for many years."

"Maybe Ossdonc remembers all this from when he was married to Queen Loellin."

"My aunt rarely visited our home. And Cuhurran, as Ossdonc styled himself then, was never with her when she did. When I saw him it was only in the palace, or riding through the streets at the head of marching columns. Always smiling and laughing, he was, as if the war with Wayland were a famous joke. But he was attractive, all the same. My brother Gerrit worshipped him nearly as much as the queen. What is this?"

Giserre pointed to a green pebble lying under a glass bowl on top of Reiffen's desk.

"That's the stone I told you about, Mother."

"The Talking Stone? The one Avender found?"

"No, Avender lost Durk in the dungeons when we escaped. This is the one Fornoch made for me. The Living Stone."

"The one that might protect you?"

"Yes. Fornoch said if I swallowed it nothing would hurt me, and I'd never grow old."

Giserre gestured toward the stone. "Perhaps you should use it, now you have returned."

"I don't want to stay thirteen forever, Mother."

He lifted the glass. The stone began to pulse and glow, its rhythm quickening as his hand drew close. Beneath his fingers its surface was smooth and cold. When he held it up to show his mother, it flashed in time with the steady beating of his heart.

"Take it," Reiffen said. "It won't hurt you."

Trusting her son, Giserre plucked the stone from his hand. He felt a sharp spark, as if his fingers had been pricked by a dozen pins, and his heart began to race. Giserre's face went white with pain. The stone glowed bright as a Dwarven lamp, then faded back to darkness as Giserre dropped it on the floor, where it rolled under the bed.

Reiffen gasped. His heartbeat slowed, but he could still feel its heavy thumping.

"It would seem Fornoch did not tell the truth." Giserre rubbed her fingers against her thumb. "That stone seems particularly unsafe to me."

"It never did that before."

Curious, Reiffen searched beneath the bed. The stone, dark again, lay just beyond his grasp. On hands and knees, he reached for it cautiously.

"Maybe you should leave it alone," warned his mother.

Reiffen was only half listening. He brought the tip of his finger close to the stone and felt nothing, not even the smallest spark. Nor did the stone begin to glow, which it had always done before whenever he came near it. Now it looked totally unremarkable, like any other polished rock. He closed his hand about it; the stone remained cold.

"Something's happened," he said as he stood back up. "The magic's gone."

"Perhaps you ruined it when you tried to give it to me."

Reiffen held it out in his hand. Giserre reached for the stone a second time, not expecting to be shocked again; but, as her hand drew close, the stone pulsed once more.

Reiffen looked at his mother. No longer did the stone throb in time with his own heartbeat. Giserre pulled her hand back slightly and looked with new fascination at the faint green glow.

"Something must have happened when I gave it to you," he said. "As if it switched to you from me."

Giserre said nothing. Her mouth parted slightly, she reached for the stone a third time. The throbbing brightness increased. This time there was no spark when she touched it. Reiffen felt nothing, either; his blood didn't stir. Giserre lifted the pulsing stone with the tips of her fingers and brought it close to her face.

"Is it beating in time with your heart?" Reiffen asked.

"Hmm?" Giserre did not take her eyes off the stone.

"The way it throbs, Mother. Is it in time with your heartbeat? It always was for me."

Giserre frowned thoughtfully. "Yes. I think it is."

"It must be set for you now."

"How do you think that happened?"

Reiffen shrugged. "I have no idea. I haven't learned any magic yet."

Giserre turned the small stone back and forth in her fingers as if she were candling an egg from the Manor henhouse. "What will Fornoch say when he sees the stone no longer works for you?"

"For all I know, he knew this would happen. That I'd give you the stone. Take it, Mother. It will keep you safe."

"No. It is magic."

"Everything is magic here. You can't keep it from you for-ever."

"Perhaps. All the same, I shall try to keep it away as long as possible. This stone can only protect one of us, Reiffen, and I would rather that be you."

"I'm not worried about myself, Mother. The Wizards want me alive. You're the one who might have an accident. Fornoch said so himself."

"I suspect, should the Wizards wish to harm me, they will

have ways to get around their own wizardcraft." Giserre held the stone up one last time, its green light winking rapidly.

"It's yours now," said Reiffen as she started to replace it beneath the glass, "whether you want it or not. You shouldn't leave it here."

"My taking it would be as much as telling Fornoch what we have done."

"I'm sure he already knows."

2

What They Thought in Valing

Far from Nokken Rock, Avender stood on the pebbly beach of Goosefoot Island and skipped stones across a lake as flat as glass. Rings welled out at every grazing touch, wrinkling the reflections of the mountains to the west and east. To the north, the windows of Valing Manor blinked drowsily from the top of the Neck in the hot afternoon sun, the rooms inside cool behind the heavy-lidded shade of long porches and high gables.

Skimmer flipped an inquisitive fly and splashed in the shallows beside him. "I still don't see why Reiffen left," he said, his whiskers drooping in the heat. "He just got home. I never even saw him."

Avender threw another stone. "Nobody understands it, Skim. Ferris has been up in her room crying all morning. And Redburr and everyone else are off trying to figure out what happened."

"But what did happen?" insisted the nokken. "I don't understand at all. You think they went back to those slimy Wizards?"

Avender's thoughts flicked back to the moment he and Ferris had discovered Reiffen was gone. Again. They had found one of Reiffen's iron thimbles lying on the Tear's cold stone, but nothing else, no trace of Reiffen or Giserre. Since then, everything had been an awful dream.

He threw another stone, and counted eleven skips across the dull blue water, the most he'd ever done. "Redburr thinks they went back to Ussene. Somehow the Wizards called him with their magic. Berrel isn't so sure, though. He and Ranner went down to the White Pool to look for any, um, sign of something else."

"Something else? What kind of something else?"

"Berrel thinks maybe Reiffen and Giserre were murdered."

Skimmer's long whiskers twitched.

"Well, maybe not both of them," Avender went on. "Maybe just Giserre."

"Why just her?"

"Because the Three aren't interested in her, that's why." Avender threw another rock. Too hard this time, the stone took one long, high bounce before plunging deep into the lake.

"Does Berrel think she was pushed into the gorge?"

"If she's not with Reiffen, or in the Manor, where else could she be?"

"Not everything that goes over the gorge gets found." Stretching his long neck, Skimmer sang in a voice as scratchy and broken as Avender's:

"Once there was a nokken fair,
Nokken fair, nokken fair.
Sleek her fur and white her hair,
White her hair, white her hair."

"What's that?" asked Avender. "I never heard that song before."

"'Whitespray's Fall.'"

"Whitespray? Isn't that the auntie who saved the rookery back in the old days? I never knew there was a song."

Drops clung to Skimmer's whiskers as he dipped his face in

the cool water. "We don't sing it much outside the rookery. It's too special."

"Did anyone ever see her again, after she went over the falls?"

Skimmer made a face, as if the very thought of going over the falls made him as uncomfortable as eating bad mussels. "No one can swim up a waterfall," he said. "Not even Longback."

Avender flung another stone across the water. Above the Hemwood on the eastern shore, a line of cows crept across the top of the meadow like brown and white caterpillars on a bright green leaf.

"What do you think happened?" the nokken asked.

Avender didn't like saying what he thought, though he was the one who knew Reiffen best. "I think it was Reiffen's choice to go back to the Wizards. And I think he took Giserre with him."

Skimmer squirmed farther into the lake across the stony bottom, cool water splashing across his back and sides. "Why would he do that? Wizards are nasty. The lake's much nicer."

Avender hefted the last two rocks in his hand. "You didn't see Reiffen when he came back. He wasn't the same. I thought he'd be his old self again once we got home, but I was wrong." It was just the sort of thing Reiffen would do, he told himself, especially if there was nothing to lose. Go back to Ussene to confront his enemies head-on.

"But why?" In deeper water now, the nokken rolled a few times to make sure he was good and wet, then swam slowly back and forth along the shore. His dark coat gleamed.

"For the magic. You know he hates giving up. He thinks magic is how he'll defeat the Three, I just know it. But he's wrong. The Wizards'll turn him, sure as anything. Unless they already have."

"I don't believe it."

"Neither does Ferris."

Avender threw another stone, but this time his aim was off

and the rock whipped into the water with a sound like a snowball burying itself in a snowbank. "Redburr thinks I'm right. He says Usseis would never have bothered to let Reiffen get all the way home. He would have brought him back the first chance he had. And only Reiffen would want to bring Giserre with him. Nothing else makes sense if we don't find her."

"So when are you going to rescue him again?"

"We're not. You can't rescue someone who doesn't want to be rescued."

Avender threw the last stone high and far across the lake. Like a swift moon, the rock rose and fell, finally settling far out on the blue with a small splash.

"I still think you should rescue him. I know I would, if I could. I helped last time, remember?"

"I remember. But rescuing him once was hard enough. And if Reiffen went back of his own accord, there really wouldn't be much point, right? Even Ferris sees that. The real question is what happened to Giserre."

A second dark head poked above the surface of the shallow bay and gave a barking call. "Skimmer!" the newcomer cried. "I've been looking all over for you. Longback's ready to lead us down Southway for the stickles. It's the first long swim for the pups, and he wants all the patrols out. Better flip and shake."

"Let me know if you hear anything more," Skimmer called back to Avender as he rolled into deeper water. Then he shot off beneath the surface like a swallow through a barn window and was gone, the lake rippling behind him.

Avender waded out to his boat and rowed sadly back to the Manor, where he was relieved to find there was still no sign of Giserre. For all Skimmer's talk of not everything being found that went over the falls, Avender was glad he didn't have to think about what it meant if Giserre had been murdered. His old friend may have chosen to follow the Three, to learn magic and spells and the dark ways of secret power, but at least he hadn't killed his mother.

A month passed, but the gloom in Valing didn't lift. Redburr guzzled his way through the berry patches on Baldun and the Teapot, but everyone else in Valing acted as if winter had already settled across the crisp, golden fall. Ferris regarded the bear's lack of concern as highly inappropriate, which was why she and Avender were in the Manor, and not picking sowberries with Redburr, when a column of riders emerged from Firron Pass one afternoon, their pennants' gay colors brighter than the orange and red leaves around them.

"A delegation from King Brannis?" asked Avender after Ferris told him the news.

"Of course that's who it is. I've been expecting them for weeks. The old thief wants to make sure Reiffen's really gone."

Hurrying through their chores, they climbed onto the wall beside the gate to watch the procession. Avender counted a dozen knights in two paired columns riding up the hill from the crossroads at Tucker's farm. Those on the left wore the bright silver of Banking while those on the right bore the dark brown tunics of Wayland. Long yellow and gold plumes tufted the steel helms of the Banking column; the brown tunics of the Wayland thanes bore the image of a tall keep. A pair of heavy wagons rumbled at the rear, a swarm of children following behind.

"That's a lot of knights," said Nolo, joining them on the wall. He stood on tiptoe, his lumpy nose poking above the battlement like a gall on the side of a tree.

"It's just Brannis showing off," said Ferris.

When they reached the far side of the Neck, the procession stopped. In front of them, a narrow bridge of land stretched to the Manor wall, a long fall to the lake on one side and a longer drop to the woods above the White Pool on the other. A herald approached and raised a golden trumpet to his lips. Sounding a short fanfare, he tucked his horn beneath his arm and called out in a loud voice:

"His Royal Highness, King Brannis, Lord and Master of Wayland and Banking, Suzerain of Grangore and the Lands Beyond the Blue Mountains, Marshall of the North and all the Forest Lands therein, Great Patron of the Keeadini, and Captain-elect of Cuspor, sends greetings from his throne in Rimwichside and requests the stewards of Valing entertain an audience with the king's messengers, Baron Sevral of Malmoret and the Duchy of Engui, and Sir Firnum of Chestnut Glen."

Straightening his helm, Dennol, accompanied by a pair of sentries, stepped out through the open gate. "Come on, now," he muttered to his comrades. "These southerners like everything official. Toddy, drop that drumstick. And don't wipe your fingers on your jersey, either."

With a gesture as formal as the herald's, Dennol gave the visitors a sharp salute. "Welcome to Valing, Sir Baron. And Sir Firnum, sir. Our house is yours."

Still saluting, the Valing sergeant stepped aside. The baron and Sir Firnum led their column in through the gate; dogs barked as hens fled across the muddy yard. Hern and Berrel greeted their guests from the top of the front porch as the teamsters found spots for their wagons along the wall.

"Welcome, brave knights," said Berrel. "As stewards of the Valing freehold, Hern and I offer you the best of our Manor's hospitality. Your throats must be dry and parched. Come, share our board."

The two captains bowed from their saddles and, with their squires' help, dismounted. Their hosts ushered them inside.

The crowd that had climbed the hill from Eastbay streamed in through the open gates. A crush formed on the porch as everyone tried to press inside; Avender and Ferris, knowing the Manor better than most, scooted through the barn and around to the lakeside doors to avoid the crowd. Inside they found the knights and their retainers standing beside one of the fireplaces in the Great Hall.

Ferris snorted in disgust at the sight of Tinnet Bulberry pouring wine from a flagon into glasses arranged on a tray. "I guess good Valing beer isn't fancy enough for Brannis's men," she said.

Before Avender could reply, Sally Veale ordered them off to fresh chores. With so many guests in the house, there would be twice as much work as usual. Avender found himself in the stables helping with the visitors' horses. The war stallions looked strong as plow horses but were much less pleasant, as Atty Peeks quickly discovered. There was a lunge and a gray mane flying, followed by a tearing sound as half of Atty's sleeve came away in the stallion's teeth. The younger boy nursed a red welt that might have been worse, while his older friends laughed. All the same, they stayed well away from the fronts and backs of the warhorses from then on.

That first night the delegation ate privately with the stewards in the Map Room on the second floor, Nolo and Redburr joining them. Despite much pestering from Ferris the next day, and a long hour by Avender spent grooming the bear, neither learned a word of what had been discussed.

"Not everything is about you," the Shaper told Ferris, after snuffling up the warm muffins she brought him.

"See if I ever bake you anything special again." Grabbing a half-eaten pastry right out of the bear's mouth, she flounced back to the kitchen.

The next day an official banquet was announced to welcome the guests. Invitations went out to Eastbay and all the towns downlake, but once again Ferris found she and Avender had been left off the list. This was too much but, despite Ferris's threats to run off to Far Mouthing that very night, Hern held firm. "This isn't a Feast," she said. "It's a formal banquet. A matter of politics and diplomacy. Children aren't wanted, especially the nosy kind."

Avender and Ferris were still skulking in the hallway when the guests arrived, which was where Nolo and Sir Firnum found them. Turning to the Dwarf, the thane asked brightly, "Mr. Nolo, these wouldn't by chance be the same two children who accompanied you on your brave mission?"

"That they are, Sir Firnum."

"And two such heroes as they haven't been included at tonight's board?" The thane gave them both a short bow, eyes twinkling above his beard. "We must rectify this matter at once. Ma'am!" he called to Hern, who left off giving Sally and Tinnet a few last-minute instructions to hurry over. "I have just learned this brave lad and lass are not to be included in tonight's celebration. I know I am only a guest, but it would please me greatly if you added them to the party."

Hern's eyes flickered suspiciously. "Very well," she said. "As long as they didn't put you up to it. I don't think it'll spoil them too much."

"Spoil them!" exclaimed Sir Firnum. "I wouldn't think you could spoil them enough. I haven't heard any songs yet in praise of their courage, but I'm sure there will be plenty by spring. And one of them a fair young maid, too." The thane winked broadly at Ferris, but his intent was hearty, and she took no offense. "You must tell me everything that happened. Prince Brizen talks about nothing else these days but how he wishes he could have gone with you."

Ferris fixed the thane with a doubting eye. "King Brannis's son wished he'd helped us save Reiffen?"

Sir Firnum's smile broadened. "For the renown, of course. To be sung about in every holding from Pennacutt to Rolling Hollow is a fine thing indeed."

At that moment the Mayor of Sothend arrived, breathless from his long climb up from the Lower Dock. He bowed to the emissary of the king with some difficulty. Hern took advantage of the opening to lead the children to the very bottom of the long table in the Great Hall. Sally appeared with a plate and cup for each as the steward sat them on opposite sides of the board. Mother Tucker and the Mayor of Low Spinney were their nearest companions, neither of whom had any wish to spend the evening talking to children they had known since birth.

"Be careful of the wine." Hern nodded toward the jugs on the table. "It's worth half a day's fishing. And stronger than what you're used to."

The dinner turned out to be less interesting than Avender had hoped. The food was good, but he had eaten already and could only manage another plateful. With Mother Tucker ignoring him in favor of the Malmoret knight on her right, he had no one to talk to. Ferris, craning forward to hear what was being said at the far end of the long table, waved him away irritably every time he tried to say a word.

The head of the table was much more lively. Hern and Berrel sat at that end, with Baron Sevral and Sir Firnum on either side. Without his armor Baron Sevral was a tall, thin man with short dark hair and a lingering look of disapproval, but the Wayland thane looked like a jovial Eastbay farmer. Occasionally the table stilled for a jest that Avender was almost able to hear, usually from Sir Firnum, but rarely did he catch what brought roars of laughter from everyone else.

Yawning, he settled in for a long evening. If he couldn't hear what was being said, at least he could watch Ferris, which was something he found he liked doing lately. And there was the wine to enjoy. Though not as filling as beer, it grew more pleasant with every sip. Each time he poured a fresh cup, the rest of the table drew farther and farther away. Not wanting her to catch him at it, he observed Ferris from the corner of his eye. He thought it lovely the way her dress bunched against the side of the table every time she leaned forward to try and hear Sir Firnum's jests.

And the way she kept asking Low Spinney's mayor what had been said, no matter how many times the woman told her to hush. Admittedly, Ferris was an enormous pest, but right now, Avender had to admit, he would enjoy any pestering he could get from her.

Closing his eyes, he remembered again how it felt that awful morning in the Tear when she had buried her face against his shoulder, once they realized Reiffen was gone. He hadn't paid much attention at the time, but he didn't think he had ever held her so close before. She had felt small, and oddly different. He liked it, but he was glad all the same that no one had seen them. It had been a long time before she pulled away and wiped off her tears on the back of her sleeve.

Blinking, he left off his dreaming and lifted his head from his hand. The table was quiet. Even Ferris was still. Nolo stood on the bench, the way he always did when he was making a toast, the eye of every guest upon him. Raising his cup, he asked the company to drink Giserre's health. Avender had to sit up and blink a few more times to make sense of what the Dwarf was saying.

". . . call upon you all to toast our fair princess. May she be alive and well."

Quiet extended the length of the board. Most of the guests were taken aback by the mention of Giserre in the midst of so much good cheer. Redburr, however, growled approval from his place beside the fire.

Baron Sevral glanced at Sir Firnum, who gestured generously for the Banking knight to proceed. Standing, the baron answered Nolo's request. "To the Lady Giserre," he said, lifting his goblet toward the chandelier above his head. "As noble and beautiful a Banking princess as ever graced the towers and ballrooms of Malmoret."

"Or Rimwich," added the thane.

"Or Valing," concluded Hern.

A chorus of ayes echoed among the guests. The thanes, except for Sir Firnum, were the least enthusiastic. The most ardent was Ferris, who leapt up, her cup held high, and answered, "To Giserre!"

Avender stood as well, his feet not quite properly set beneath him. Surprising himself, and everyone else in the hall, he decided that toasting Giserre wasn't good enough.

"To Reiffen!" he called. "A blessing to his mother and his friends."

A longer silence followed. Avender brought his cup to his lips but found it empty. Blinking once more, he put out a hand to steady himself against the table. His eyes found Ferris's; to his great joy she was nearly bursting with pride. Mother Tucker, on the other hand, looked as if she had caught him stealing eggs.

Delighted whoops from the children watching on the balcony broke the hush. The bear roared. Hern glared up at them but, for the first time in their lives, every child ignored her.

Eyes twinkling, Berrel rose in answer. "To Reiffen. A guest in our house as loved as any other."

Not every farmer and farmwife was as angry with Avender as Mother Tucker. Murmurs of approval brushed up and down the benches. Baron Sevral and Sir Firnum, bowing to the wishes of their hosts, raised their glasses as well. The knights and thanes followed their captains' lead. Sir Firnum gave Avender a quick wink, companion to the one he had graced Ferris with earlier, but the baron showed no emotion.

For Avender, the rest of the evening was a blur. He recalled the Shaper butting him affectionately, and the next day his shoulder ached from Nolo clapping it a little too hard. Sir Firnum had spoken to him as well.

"You're a bold lad," the thane had said. "Not many would pledge the enemy of the king in front of the king's own ambassadors."

Avender put a hand in front of his mouth to hide his hiccup. "Reiffen was my friend. He should be honored the same as his mother."

" 'Was,' you say. You think him dead?"

"No."

"Then what will you do if he comes riding down from Ussene at the head of ten thousand sissit?"

"My duty." A second hiccup caught Avender unaware. "Besides, that wouldn't be Reiffen," he continued. "That would just mean the Wizards had changed him."

"Aye. The Wizards change us all." Sir Firnum put a steadying hand on the boy's shoulder. "I wasn't much more than your age at the time, but I remember King Brioss when he was under Martis's spell. Not even my father noticed, and he was one of Brioss's closest friends."

Baron Sevral joined them. "That was well said," he told Avender, his silken beard poised above his chest like a dark dagger. "You have the courage of a soldier."

But the crowning moment of Avender's evening occurred when Ferris found him on the porch outside. "That was wonderful," she said, her face shadowed in the starlight. "Toasting Reiffen like that, even if you did drink too much. I'm so proud of you."

Like goosedown on a puff of air, her lips brushed his cheek. It wasn't the first time she had kissed him, but it was the first time he hadn't shied away. His skin grew hot, but Ferris was already through the door before he could say a word, her braids swinging across her back.

Avender touched his cheek and wondered why it had taken him so long to notice how pretty she had become.

3

Fingers

On their first morning in Ussene, Reiffen took his mother to the officers' mess. Spit arrived as they were leaving, with a tray of bread and tea, butter, cream, and jam; but Giserre insisted on breakfasting in the refectory all the same.

"Take this back to the kitchens and share it among your friends, Spit," she said. "Reiffen, it is not right that you and I should be served by the Wizards' slaves."

Knowing better than to argue, Reiffen led his mother out into the filthy tunnels. Already their apartment seemed a bright haven, separate from the rest of the fortress.

They heard the refectory before they saw it, and smelled it not much later. From the doorway they watched slaves struggle under trays of roasted meat and pots of ale as they wove among the cursing men: no bread and butter here. Sweat and smoke and the smell of sour beer wallowed in the heavy air. Noticing his guests, the senior captain snapped an order. The room went quiet; benches scraped across the floor. The officers came to their feet and bowed, knives and other weapons rattling. Giserre nodded in return.

With a grand gesture, the captain offered Giserre the seat

beside him. She made no reply, and didn't sit until he had cleared a place for Reiffen as well. Rich with fat and gravy, the meal arrived on gold plates with hacked and nicked edges, and required large drafts of bitter beer to wash down. Giserre ate no more than a bite, but Reiffen was hungry and cleaned his plate as quickly as the greasy lieutenant on his left, who squeezed a little farther away each time the boy's remaining thimble clicked against his spoon. A few of the diners winked at Giserre when they thought they caught her eye. Reiffen glared at them; his mother laid a cautious hand on his arm. The senior captain regarded her through slitted eyes while fingering the gravy in his beard. Even in the plain black dress she had found in the bureau in her room, Giserre stood out in that dingy hall like ebony gleaming in a bed of broken firestone.

Only when her son's plate was empty did she nod her thanks and leave. The air hung still as she and Reiffen crossed the room but, once they were past the door, roaring laughter burst out behind them. Giserre's grip on her son's arm tightened.

They found Spit waiting for them in the apartment. The breakfast tray was gone, but in its place the poor woman had brought a bucket filled with filmy water. Scrub brush and broom lay beside her as she kneeled on the floor. Hastily she scrambled to her feet as her new master and mistress entered, her head still bowed.

Giserre softened at once. "My son and I will be in the Library, Spit," she said. "Please mop the floors while we are away. You can start with the passage just outside the door. It will never do to have us tracking that filth into our parlor as we come in and out."

"You're coming to the Library with me, Mother?" asked Reiffen. "I thought you wanted nothing to do with magic."

"I presume there will be other books for me to read."

She paused at the door, as if making up her mind about one last thing. "And Spit, when you bring lunch, please bring it to the

Library. I have changed my mind about eating in the officers' mess."

Reiffen showed no surprise. Ussene was no place to stand on principle, no matter how firmly held.

"I hope I am right about there being other books."

"I'm sure there are, Mother. I remember some histories. And I think there are geographies, too, and books about birds and bugs. Stuff like that."

"Please do not use slang, Reiffen. Remember who you are. Even here, you must set the proper example, especially if we are to have Spit with us. I would like to see the histories, however, and perhaps the geographies also. And the volumes of natural history. I wanted to attend the College in Malmoret when I was a girl, you know."

"Why didn't you?"

"Girls are not thought capable of the higher orders of intellect by many of the learned in Malmoret. Not even when Loellin was queen were their prejudices questioned."

"That's dumb."

"Ignorant, Reiffen. Please use the proper word. Dumbness is an affliction of the unfortunate. And, yes. It is ignorant."

In the Library, Reiffen showed his mother everything he remembered about the room: the spider, the tall desks to read at while standing, the strange light that glowed from everywhere above their heads and cast no shadow. Quickly he found the volumes he had begun before, while Giserre examined the shelves. He was well into his first book, *Transposition and Binding,* by the time his mother picked out something for herself.

She noticed the Wizard first.

"Reiffen," she said. "Your tutor has arrived."

Looking up, he found the Gray Wizard bowing. A little deeper than before, but still not a gesture that was more than barely polite.

Giserre closed her book.

"Will you not stay for the lesson?" Fornoch inquired. "You would learn much."

"Precisely. Reiffen, I shall instruct Spit to bring your lunch to you here. I shall dine alone."

Her book clasped like a dark red badge against her dress, she paced out of the room. The heavy door swung silently shut behind her. Reiffen closed his own book eagerly when she was gone. This was what he had returned for, the reason he had risked their lives. The magic was about to begin.

"I know you are keen to start," said Fornoch, "but first we must pay our respects to Usseis."

His giant fist enclosed Reiffen's hand like a pike gulping a grayling. The Library disappeared.

Dim as a cave, the throne room of Ussene replaced the books. Usseis sat on his stone bench atop the dais; Ossdonc stood in ruffled finery behind him, a black sword at his hip. Fornoch's place was on the lowest step, his gray robes settling around him like decades of dust. From the distant gallery, rows of tall columns watched like mute courtiers at the edge of the enormous hall.

"You have returned," said Usseis, his voice thickening the air like clouds on a mountaintop.

Reiffen faced the White Wizard with only a little unease. "Yes."

"Why?"

"To learn magic."

Usseis showed no surprise. It was, after all, a part of what Reiffen had been offered. "And what do you bring us, that we would teach you magic?"

"I will be your king, and lead your armies into Wayland and Banking."

Ossdonc's quick protest boomed across the length and height

of the hall. "I will lead the armies," he insisted. "That is my pleasure."

"We are not concerned with your pleasure, brother," answered Usseis. "We will do what is fittest at the time. Your idiosyncrasies shall not interfere."

"I am not interested in leading armies," Reiffen told them. "You know what I offer, my claim to the thrones of Banking and Wayland. That was the bargain."

"It was." Usseis fastened the boy with his black eyes. Reiffen didn't look away. He was learning, now that he had returned freely to Ussene, that the White Wizard's threats meant less to him than they had before.

"Mark my words," Usseis continued. "I will hold you to your troth. Should your purpose waver, your pledge is forfeit. And I shall see to it that the minds and bodies of your family and friends are put to other uses than those which they would wish."

"I shall watch him," said Fornoch.

"And I," added Ossdonc with a ringing laugh. "And I shall watch your mother also. But only upon my return. There are other lands for me to play in while the rest of you diddle with potions and spells. Tell Giserre that Cuhurran looks forward to meeting her again, now she is grown."

Giserre showed less annoyance than Reiffen expected when he relayed the Black Wizard's message.

"That is his way," she said, arranging her embroidery in her lap. "It is the gallantry of the New Palace in Malmoret and does not signify in the least."

There was no longer any talk of Giserre taking her meals anywhere but in their rooms. Spit came freely with breakfast, lunch, and dinner, helped with the cleaning, and hauled firestone for the hearth and hot water. But she remained sullen from the start, much less eager to please than Molio, who had been so anxious for Reiffen to be his friend.

Reiffen preferred it that way, but Giserre took Spit's reticence as a challenge. As a princess of Malmoret, she had been accustomed to servants her entire life, much more so than her son, who had only lived in Valing. She understood that, if one took a personal concern in the well-being of one's servants, then one's servants might take a personal concern in one's own well-being as well. Even if one's servant was a slave.

At first Giserre asked questions. "Tell me about yourself, Spit," she asked. "You are not from this place, are you?"

Spit tucked her chin deeper into her rags and scrubbed more desperately at the floor.

"Are you from one of the river towns? Or the Great Forest? You are not a Keeadini."

Again the poor woman made no reply. Instead, she picked up her brush and bucket and tried to rush from the room. "I have not dismissed you, Spit," said Giserre. "If you insist on disregarding my authority, I shall request the Wizard supply myself and my son with another servant."

Spit stopped, halfway to the door. Reiffen, standing just inside his room, wasn't sure if the poor woman was more afraid of continuing forward or turning around.

"There is no need for fear." Giserre's voice softened once she had her servant's attention. "My son and I are not Wizards. You will find our treatment different from what you are accustomed to in this place. Come, my dear. Answer my questions while you pour the tea. You shall not find them difficult. Reiffen and I are not monsters. Would you care for a slice of toast?"

The offer of toast had the best effect. Spit turned around, her eyes still fastened on the floor. Slowly the poor woman's eyes crept across the narrow space between her feet and the tray.

"Reiffen. Make the toast, please."

Taking a long fork and the plate of bread from the tray, Reiffen followed his mother's instructions.

"Do you like toast, my dear?" she continued. "I imagine you do. I certainly enjoy it, especially while hot, with the butter melting on the crust. I must say, I was quite surprised to find butter with my breakfast here. Ussene is not a place I should expect to find anything so nice as butter. Here now, perhaps you should sit. That is quite all right, Spit, I have no wish that you remain standing in my presence, nor does Reiffen. Wizards may require it, but I do not. Yes, the floor will be fine, if that is what you prefer, though the chairs are more comfortable."

The first slice toasted, Reiffen handed it to his mother. He watched, astonished, as she prattled on. In the regular gossip of Valing, Giserre had rarely said a word, even to Anella. Indeed, Reiffen had always assumed she never even paid attention. Yet here she was, gadding on as if she had done so her entire life.

Tearing the buttered piece in half, Giserre shared her toast with the servant. "Do eat, Spit. I don't suppose Spit was your name before you came here, was it? Perhaps some day you might wish to tell me your real name. You must have had plenty of bread to eat when you were a girl. And rice, too. The wild rice of the northern woods is a delicacy in the south, you know. We await the coming of the long canoes every year with the harvest. It must be a terribly dangerous journey, coming down the River, waiting for the Keeadini to attack. Is that how you were captured?"

Spit spoke not a single word that first morning, but it was only a matter of time before she finally began to talk. Giserre's pressure was gentle, and relentless. Eventually Reiffen returned to the room one evening to find a fire crackling in the hearth and Spit on the floor sobbing into his mother's skirts.

"You should be careful, Mother," he said the next morning. "Friendship is more dangerous than hatred in Ussene. If the Three believe they can get to you through Spit, they will certainly try."

Finding a spot on her sleeve where Spit's dirty tears had dried into a brownish crust, Giserre flaked the filth away with the back of a nail. "Spit is not my friend. She is an unfortunate creature, deserving of our pity. While we are in Ussene we must make doubly sure not to forget who we are, or those who require our kindness."

So the days passed and, while Giserre was busy with Spit, Fornoch was busy with her son.

"The true power of magic," the Gray Wizard told him, "is to persuade something to deny its true nature. To make light in the dark, or dead flesh rise."

Fornoch held out his hand. A clump of grass appeared upon it, green stems pointed toward the ceiling, white roots stripped bare of earth. Without a word the plant burst into flame and was consumed. Wisps of gray smoke fluttered upward.

"Grass is simple," said the Wizard. "A plant will not fight back, if you call it to you. But I could not so summon even a new-born babe, not unless the child was close to hand. The principle, however, is the same. And objects that have themselves been enhanced can also have power, as with the Living Stone."

"I shall learn it all," said Reiffen avidly.

"You shall. And turn it against me in the end, no doubt. Yes, I am aware of what you plan. You need not pretend innocence. Why else would you return? Indeed, you did precisely as I hoped."

"You mean I've been under your control all this time?"

"Not at all. Power is not only about control, it is about understanding also. My brothers assume the promise of magic and kingship will be enough to bind you to them, but I know better. I warn you, however. You shall pass through many trials. Who knows how you will emerge from such black fires? Are you certain you will remain the same once I have taught you everything you are

able to learn? Who else will you have undertaken to kill besides
Molio, before you are through? Your mother? Your friends?"

Reiffen's newfound confidence in dealing with Wizards
drained away. Not only did Fornoch seem to know all his most
secret plans, but somehow the Gray Wizard had managed to un-
cover his worst fears as well.

"You would continue to teach me," he choked out, "even
knowing what I think?"

"Yes. Otherwise I should wish the services of a high priest."

Reiffen seized the opportunity to turn the conversation away
from himself. "What's a high priest?"

A smile creased the Wizard's massive face like cracks in the
earth. "Someone whose faith is stronger than his perception.
Very useful to the likes of me. Or you, perhaps, once you gain
more knowledge."

"I don't understand what you're talking about at all."

"Some day you shall."

That day seemed very far away, however, when Fornoch taught
him no spells. "Magic is an individual art," the Wizard said in
answer to Reiffen's pleas. "A true master fashions his spells himself."

It was another week before Reiffen determined to take the
Wizard at his word. Avender would have counseled caution, but
Avender had been left behind. Reiffen's first attempts were small,
spells that seemed obvious when described in the gramaryes and
grimoires. All the same, his incantations generally fell flat until
he learned that a quick and clever rhyme helped him focus. Even
simple castings raised improbable consequences. Trying a charm
of illumination, he set a spark to glow in his hand. His fingers still
burning painfully, he had the sense to cast the spell on the end of
a stick the second time.

Eventually the castings came more easily: spells of silence, spells of dark. Invisibility was surprisingly simple; it was all a matter of moving the light around until there was nothing there. It also helped to know from Fornoch's books that light was a thing as real as air.

He moved on to more difficult sorceries, but one spell eluded him, no matter how much he read. To travel as freely as Fornoch did, without any constraint of distance or walls, was what Reiffen wished to do more than anything else. To go anywhere in the world with a whispered word.

Then one evening, with great effort and after several days of preparation, he cast a traveling spell from the Library and woke to find himself being shaken by Giserre in his own bed. How he had come there he didn't remember, though memory, according to all the books, was the key to magical travel. Even Wizards couldn't go where they had never been. Memory of flesh or mind—some link was required to pass the restrictions of space and stone.

He woke gasping, his limbs thinned as if by famine. Had Spit not found him and summoned her mistress, there was no telling what might have happened. Fornoch appeared, and pushed the women aside. He cast quick spells and Reiffen's panting ceased. The boy's lungs grasped the air. Once again his flesh was firm and round.

"You left too much behind," the Wizard warned him. "Had I come less quickly you might have died. I have managed to return what you lost. But it is good that you are trying."

"It is not good at all!" Giserre pushed past the Wizard to Reiffen's side, her eyes flaring. "Certainly you have not gone to all this trouble just to let my son die!"

"I have not." The Gray Wizard regarded the Malmoret princess with the same grave dignity he gave his spider. "Your son will not die in Ussene, my lady, however close he may come. Are you feeling better?" he asked the boy.

Reiffen nodded. The helpless fog had lifted; he remembered his casting. Already he was sorting through his mind for what parts of the spell he could improve. He would do it better next time.

The following morning Fornoch met him again in the Library, his arms folded patiently into the sleeves of his robe.

"I have prepared talismans for what you will learn today, Reiffen, though you will have to name the spells yourself."

The spider watched jealously as the Wizard brought the boy to an empty table. Reiffen wondered what magic it was Fornoch wished him to prepare. A tight thrill crept through him, like the arrival of a long-awaited morning.

"This spell is most important," said the Gray Wizard. "With this spell you will always have an avenue of escape, no matter what is going on around you."

Insight stumbled into Reiffen's mind. He held the cold iron still soldered to his right hand up for the Wizard's inspection. "Are you going to teach me about this?" he asked.

"Yes." Approval showed faintly at the corners of the Wizard's mouth.

The boy struggled to control his excitement. "Why are there no thimbles on your fingers?"

Fornoch's eyes swallowed the question without an answer. A pair of iron caps, big as cups, flickered into existence at the ends of his fingers, then winked away.

"Wizards require no such assistance," he said. "Neither will you, when you come into your full power. But that is many years away. In the meantime, you must use such aids as you can to quicken the magic."

Opening his hand, Fornoch revealed a thimble that was just Reiffen's size. "You will have to change them regularly as you grow, or the magic will fail. Adolescence is an awkward time for mastering this art."

They began by enchanting the objects they would need for the operation. The iron thimble was first. "Iron holds magic better than other metals," Fornoch told him. "Of all the metals, iron was Areft's favorite."

"Is that why the Bryddin prefer blumet?"

"Blumet for men and Dwarves," the Wizard answered. "Iron for magic and Wizards."

Next he produced a small gold case similar to the one Reiffen had found in the Library upon his return. "Gold for purity," the Wizard said. "Properly spelled, gold will keep a thing unchanged, ever ready to rejoin the rest of you."

Last was the knife, silver as a moonbeam. Silver for light in the darkness, the moon's soft heart. Reiffen flinched as he recalled Usseis wielding just such a blade in his workshop, removing the ends of Reiffen's little fingers without a word.

Fornoch held the knife up to the light, twisting the blade back and forth, small as a toy in his enormous hand. "You will find it difficult to keep silver sharp. A dull blade, however, will cause you greater pain. I recommend the sharpest knife. But it must be silver. Silver is the metal of night and shadow, and can sometimes pass unseen. A silvered cut keeps fresh the memory of your flesh."

The Wizard laid all three instruments upon the table.

"We will begin with the cap."

In Fornoch's palm, Reiffen's thimble appeared no larger than a pea. The Wizard held it out before his pupil's face. "What magic would you recommend, Reiffen, to seal this to your bone and skin?"

Reiffen shivered at the thought of iron frozen to bone and skin, but answered confidently, certain he was right. "A spell of binding."

"Yes," the Wizard agreed. "A spell of binding. Have you such a spell?"

Reiffen nodded. Could such simple magic really work for something so complicated?

"Perhaps you should try it now."

Carefully, Reiffen plucked up the thimble between thumb and finger. Placing it in his own palm, he chanted the words. The magic lingered in the air after he was done, like snow in a dark forest.

"Flesh and blood be sealed within,
Iron thimble bind my skin."

"Now the case," said Fornoch.

The magic wavered as the Wizard spoke, but didn't wither. Reiffen took the golden case from the table. It was heavier than he expected, but then he had never handled much gold.

"What sort of spell do you think is required here?" Fornoch asked.

"Protection." Again, Reiffen was certain he was correct. What could be more natural than a spell of protection to guard a finger?

Fornoch nodded, and waited for Reiffen to cast the spell. This time the boy had to think awhile; protection was harder than binding. Binding was internal, a connection; but protection was a spell that, by its very nature, must react with the outside.

"Bubble rises from a stream;
Inside, skimbug, like a dream,
Caught within the airy ball,
Waterskinned against a fall."

"Very good, Reiffen." Fornoch smiled, but his empty eyes seemed to give his approval the lie. "A bard could scarcely do better."

Reiffen swallowed and tried to imagine what sort of spell the knife would require.

"Yes," continued the Wizard, his understanding of what the boy was thinking as thorough as ever. "The knife will be difficult. A sundering, but a joining as well. What sort of spell will allow your finger to be severed, and yet remain attached?"

Reiffen racked his brain as he lifted the gleaming blade, but couldn't come up with an answer. What had the Wizard been teaching him since his return? Magic was understanding the connections in the world. Know the connections, the ties that bind everything together, from rock to leaf to bird, and all would come to the discerning mage. The strength of the rock, the purpose of the leaf, the freedom of the bird: the power of each could be captured by one who understood how and where to look.

Somehow, in that rule of magic, Reiffen was supposed to find what he was looking for, the means to maintain the end of his finger, or any other piece of him, as part of himself, no matter how great the separation. The answer, however, wouldn't come. Nothing he thought of was any use. His training had gone quickly thus far because, as the Wizard had told him, he had been lucky enough to grow up around a Shaper and a Dwarf. "From the children of Ina there is always much to learn." But his own understanding, however enhanced, wasn't up to this latest task.

He threw up his hands. "I don't know. I haven't the slightest idea which spell to use."

"Then you will never be much of a Wizard, will you?" Fornoch's smile still limned his face. "Despite this library I have fashioned for you, Wizardry remains a process of the mind. If you cannot solve the problem, you cannot cast the spell. Think again."

Reiffen did as he was bidden. What, he asked himself, could be reattached to itself after separation?

He thought of Giserre planting roses on the south side of the

Manor. The long stems rose toward the sky like swans' necks but, sometimes, especially when Hern joined her, the two women would combine the roses, tying sticks from one plant onto another, binding them fast, new shoots onto old. And Berrel did the same in summer with the apple trees, and the pears along the Eastbay road.

But that wasn't quite right. It was more than that: it was the essence of attachment in all things. The children of Ina, Fornoch had said. That was the key.

He paused, his long hair falling across his face as he crafted a verse. When he was satisfied he knew what to say, he began.

"In stone and water, beast and earth
The Ina each have given birth.
Connected all with living wonder,
No distance vast can ever sunder.
As twig is switched from tree to tree,
A finger cut, returns to me."

Like the box and thimble before it, the dagger trembled at the spell. Reiffen felt the blood throb in his hand. His fingers curled around the hilt as he readied himself for the final task.

"There will be pain," murmured the Wizard.

Reiffen didn't ask if there was a spell for stopping pain. Setting his jaw, he cast about for a place to begin.

"Place your hand upon the table." Fornoch nodded toward the nearest desk. "Where there are no books. It would not be wise to spill blood among these volumes. There are so many different things in Ussene that might show interest."

Unable to control the shaking in his hand, Reiffen laid his left palm on the table. The wood felt as it always did, warm and smooth. But, with his hand spread on the tabletop, his other fingers were in the way. It would be impossible to cut the little finger without severing another digit as well. The edge of the table was much better, his knuckles jammed against the side, his little finger the only one extended.

Awkwardly he shifted the knife in his palm. The Wizard offered no further advice. A fast blow would hurt least, but Reiffen wished to make no mistakes. Finding the joint would be difficult however he went about the operation. Hoping he got it right on the first stroke, he set the point of the knife against the table beside his finger. Like a joiner measuring wood, he brought the blade down. Bone crunched. Blood pooled.

Gasping, Reiffen worked the silver blade through his finger. He could hardly see through his tears, but nothing dimmed his sense of touch. The smallest twist sent hurt stabbing up his arm. Each bit of muscle and tendon seemed to require a separate stroke. Warmth dripped past his fingers to splatter on the floor.

He knew he was done when the blade ground solidly against the wood. His finger burned like fire. With a moan, he opened his eyes. Fresh blood seeped from the stump of his finger like water at a tiny spring. His entire body ached.

"Finish the spell." The Wizard's voice flooded across his neck and ears, thick as the blood puddling on the floor. "Otherwise your pain will come to nothing."

Reiffen wiped his forehead and eyes; his head spun numbly. The thimble felt cold between his fingers, not at all like the blood. Awkwardly, as if his hands were three or four rooms away instead of at the ends of his arms, he jammed the iron cap fast against the broken end of his little finger. A shiver of warmth swarmed back into his bones. The agony eased.

Blinking, he regarded the room around him. The books emerged from the well of darkness he had fallen into. He remembered when Usseis had performed the spell, cast under a gleam of sickly light in the dungeons deep below. That time Reiffen had felt no renewal when the magic was done, but this was different. This time he had cast the spell himself; the power in the thimble returned to him as blood and iron mixed. His finger ceased bleeding, his knuckles stained dark as a tub of wine.

Left hand still throbbing, he picked up the severed end of flesh from the bloody table and placed it in the golden casket. "What about the blood?" he asked.

"Do you have a rag?"

Reiffen produced a handkerchief from his pocket, large enough to wipe up little more than the spots on the floor.

The Wizard brought a towel out from within his drooping sleeves. When Reiffen finished cleaning the floor and the table, towel and handkerchief were stained dark red. "Burn them," the Wizard advised. "No pool in Ussene is clean enough to wash them. Burn them in the fire in your rooms. I will make certain nothing happens to the smoke."

There was a great deal more to do. Before he left, Fornoch made Reiffen cast spells of preservation on the small gold casket, wardings and shrouds to hide the box from prying eyes, and charms and enchantments to attune both box and flesh inside with the memory of his voice and thought, no matter how far away. By the time the Wizard finally allowed him to stumble off, filthy towel and gold treasure gripped firmly between his thimbled hands, Reiffen was exhausted. Not wanting a drop of blood to splatter on the stone, he held his burdens close to his chest and hurried out of the Library into the cold stone hall.

A drizzle of wind pierced the sitting room through his mother's open doorway when he reached the apartment. Even on the coldest nights Giserre was reluctant to close her shutters, for fear of losing all contact with fresh air and the outer world. At the sight of Reiffen's arms full of bloody towel, she dropped her embroidery hoop with a frown. "More vivisection?" she asked.

"No." Reiffen draped the soggy mass carefully across the back of the fire. The coals hissed; black tendrils steamed upward through the flue. With the poker from the hearth, he stabbed at the damp cloth. Tongues of flame licked the bloodstains from below, lightening the color from dark to light red, the difference between a deeply welling wound and morning sunlight shining through his fingers.

Giserre rose from her seat. "Look at you," she said. "You will make a mess of the hearth. Let me do that."

But as she came closer, her concern switched from the fire to her son. "What is the matter with you? You look white as a sheet. Was that your blood?"

She noticed the second thimble on his hand.

"What has the Wizard done to you now?"

Reiffen shook his head, unable to restrain his pride despite his fatigue. "I did it myself. Fornoch cast no magic. The spells were mine."

Giserre took her son's hands in her own. Reiffen felt the concern in her touch, her fingers playing across his like the inquisition of a cat. Her eyes flicked upward, from hands to face. Reiffen didn't look away.

Letting him go, she sat back on the couch. "You appear unchanged," she said. "Do you feel different?"

Eagerly Reiffen showed her the small golden case. "I feel stronger. The pain is practically gone. I even felt the magic when I placed the thimble on my finger."

"And the box?"

"We must find a safe place to store it. The last joint of my finger lies inside."

Giserre picked up the small container. Reiffen wondered if she would open it, but she did not. "I shall keep it in my room," she said. "Unless you would rather keep it in yours."

"I think yours is best."

"And the other?"

Reiffen looked at Giserre in confusion. "What other?"

Giserre nodded toward his right hand. "The other finger. You will need to persuade Fornoch to give it back, you know."

"Or I could just pull the thimble off and cast the spell," answered Reiffen with quick insight.

"I had not thought of that."

"Now that I know the magic, I can do it anytime."

Giserre put out a cautious hand. "I would be in no hurry, if I were you. We have no idea where you might arrive, should you do so."

"Wherever I end up, I can always use this one to come back." Almost giddy, Reiffen waved the new thimble on his left hand.

The golden casket glowed red from the fire as Giserre tucked it inside her reticule. "We are in no hurry, my son."

He slept uneasily that night. The memory of cutting his finger gnawed at him as he lay in bed, the covers kicked aside despite the chill. In his dreams, gulls swept down from the Neck, chased off by cawing crows. He woke to a summer morning in his room with Avender beneath the highest gables, only Avender's bed was empty. Going to the window, he saw Molio tumbling down through the air. He reached out to grab him, but found the little man just out of reach, spinning round and round like a leaf in a whirlpool. Only it was no longer Molio: the falling figure was Spit.

The wretched woman began to scream.

"Reiffen! Wake up!"

He opened his eyes. Giserre gripped him on the bed. Hearthglow from the outer room blurred the black and orange diamonds on his quilt.

"Is it morning?" he asked hopefully.

Giserre shook her head. Her long night braid bobbed across her back like a girl's. "It's a long time yet till dawn."

She caressed his forehead, then brushed the back of her hand across his cheek. Her touch made him feel better at once. Nestling his chin into the blanket after she left, he thought again how happy he was, now that he was no longer alone. His thimbles clicked as he folded his hands above the covers and went back to sleep.

4

Giserre at Home

The months passed. Winter came. Snow fell lightly on the hills outside Giserre's window and never stuck. Inside, the stone-wrought chill remained the same.

Ossdonc's return was the only change.

Coming home early one day with a new spell to show his mother, Reiffen found her sitting in the front room with a large man dressed foppishly in a frilly black ruff and vest. Reiffen recognized Ossdonc at once, despite the Wizard's transformation to human size.

"Cuhurran has come to pay his respects," said Giserre.

"That's not Cuhurran, Mother. That's Ossdonc."

"He prefers to be addressed as Cuhurran when human-sized. As guests in Ussene, it becomes us to address him in the manner he prefers."

"Thank you, milady."

The Black Wizard inclined his head in the most respectful of small bows. Even man-sized he looked far more dangerous than anyone Reiffen had ever met, despite his ruffles and the ornate obsidian brooch nestled among his frills like an egg of polished stone. His dark eyes, sporting white around the pupils while he masqueraded as human, gleamed.

"Your mother was a child when last I saw her," said the Wizard. "It is most delightful to see her again in the fullness of mature beauty."

He bowed again, deeply this time, his face dropping to Giserre's. Reiffen found himself wishing his mother had the sense to slide further down the couch. Instead she bent forward to retrieve her knitting from the table. Ossdonc stepped back to avoid being knocked in the face by the top of her head and retreated to the hearth, his graciousness exceeded only by the mockery in his mouth and eyes.

"I would not wish to keep you from your duties, sir," she said as Reiffen came to stand at her side. "I am a mother now, and nothing like the young girl you once danced with at the Queen's Ball."

"We danced more than once, milady." The Wizard's rich, deep voice filled the room like dark wine. "You were a stunning girl. Well do I recall it, the gardens of the New Palace ablaze with lamps, Loellin's hall glittering. Baronesses scarcely less lovely than yourself advanced in ranks across the polished floor. Banking was a noble land when it was ruled by its own."

"Perhaps it shall be so again, sir."

Ossdonc threw back his head and laughed. Reiffen winced, but at least he didn't feel the need to cover his ears now the Wizard wasn't so large. And he was glad to learn his mother knew to play up to the Wizard's vanity. Mindrell had taught him that trick, on a green hillside deep in the High Bavadars. He supposed Giserre had learned it on her own as a girl in Malmoret.

"Plainly, milady, your son gets his spirit from you."

"Reiffen is much like his father."

"But more alike to his mother, some would say."

The Wizard's eyes glittered, relentless as rain, but the uncomfortable audience was brought to an end when Spit arrived with the laundry. Humming a happy song, she stopped midnote at the sight of Ossdonc by the fire. Her hamper spilled to the floor.

"It has been kind of you to visit," Giserre told the Wizard, "but I have some domestic affairs to see to with Spit, now she has returned. I do hope you will excuse us."

"Of course, milady. I should not think to intrude, charming though your company may be. I look forward to the day the two of us ride with your son down the Street of Kings. No doubt the cheering shall be magnificent."

With his deepest bow yet, his right leg stretched well forward and his left arm tucked behind his back, the Wizard took his leave. Deferent he appeared, but his insolence remained bright as a rat's eye.

The son turned to his mother as soon as the Wizard left. "Are you all right? Did he hurt you? You know Ossdonc is the worst of the Three."

Giserre's tension wound out of her in a long, heavy breath. "I am fine, my son. As he said, he came to renew old acquaintance. Spit, if you think you can manage it now the Wizard has gone, you might pick up those things you dropped on the floor. We can put them away later. I think the sight of the Black Wizard was worse for you than it was for Reiffen or me."

Nodding, the serving woman got on her knees on the hard stone to pick up the scattered garments.

"You shouldn't trust him," said Reiffen, dropping onto the couch beside his mother.

"I would not dream of trusting him," she answered, returning to her knitting.

"Was he here a long time?"

"Long enough."

"What did he say?"

"You heard most of it."

"His insolence is intolerable. I almost struck him."

Spit gasped.

"I am glad you did not," said Giserre.

"I know. But I wanted to."

They sat quietly for a while, allowing the Wizard's presence to drift away. Spit laid her basket beside the couch and found a sock to darn. Now that she lived with them, her hair was clean and her face washed. She had found a cat to bring with her as well, a scrawny scrap of dirty gray like the sleeve of a torn sweater. It wandered in from Giserre's bedroom to lick its paws at the edge of the fire.

Giserre's needles clicked softly in the silence. For a moment, even in Ussene, it was almost a drowsy afternoon.

"Here, Mother." Reiffen remembered why he had come back early from the Library in the first place. "I want to show you something."

The fire cast bright ribbons across Giserre's dark hair as she looked up. "What is it, dear? Did you find something interesting in the Library? A new book?"

"It's not a book, Mother."

Dropping her work to her lap, Giserre frowned. The small lines slanting above her eyes met at the bridge of her nose. "You know how I feel about magic, Reiffen."

"You'll have to give in eventually, Mother. It's all I do now. And I think you'll like this spell."

Lifting her work from his mother's hands, Reiffen spread the needles and yarn flat on the low table. Spit scooted out of the way around the side of the couch; the cat stalked across the ruddy glow of the fire.

Reiffen took a step back. "What are you making?"

"A sweater."

"A sweater? You already made me a sweater."

"I am not making it for you, Reiffen. This one is for the child Spit and I discussed the other day."

"The one in the kitchens whose mother died?"

"Yes."

Reiffen refocused on the needles and readied his rhyme. Spit peered over the top of the couch behind Giserre, her face flush with fear and interest. But Giserre's eyes scarcely flickered as Reiffen intoned, in a voice slightly deeper than usual:

> *"Simple spell for simple task,*
> *Needles dance to what I ask:*
> *From this yarn please knit and purl,*
> *A garment warm to please a girl."*

Like sparks popping from a log, the needles hopped straight into the air. Hovering impossibly, they began knitting swiftly, clicking and clacking like a box of tacks spilled down a stair. A new row of stitching appeared almost immediately above the first.

Spit clapped her hands and laughed. Giserre's mouth tightened. The slack yarn drew taut as new rows were added, until the skein rolled off the side of the couch and across the floor. The cat pounced at once, toying with the skittering thread. Finished fabric spilled across the table.

"When did you learn how to knit?" Giserre plucked a snag free from where it had caught beneath a book. "And I told you I was making a sweater. Where are the arms?"

"I can't manage sweaters." Reiffen, his face crumpled in concentration, spoke from the side of his mouth. "Only scarves. You could make a sweater. Once I teach you the spell."

"I am not letting you teach me the spell. Besides, your way does not seem relaxing at all."

"It's not supposed to be . . . relaxing." The boy struggled to speak, his eyes never leaving the needles. "It's supposed . . . to help . . . you do it . . . quicker."

"I am not a drudge, Reiffen. I have no wish to knit more quickly."

"You could make more sweaters . . . for more children."

Giserre sighed patiently. "There is certainly much more I could do for Ussene's poor slaves, were I to devote my life to them. But I suspect eventually I should reach a point of lessened returns. Knitting is about more than the finished work, my dear."

"Maybe I'll teach Spit then."

Spit gripped the back of the couch tightly.

Giserre frowned. A fresh fold of black yarn tumbled to the floor. "Yes, the Three would like that. A slave knowing magic. Really, Reiffen, I know you want to show me what you have learned, but I do think you could find a more appropriate manner. And how long do you intend to make your scarf? Already there is enough for three."

Reiffen raised his hand; the needles collapsed in the fluffy pile. The cat continued batting the skein across the rug, hoping the yarn would start wriggling once more.

Giserre retrieved her needles. "Now I shall have to start again from the beginning."

Reiffen bowed, a little put out that his mother had neither accepted his gift nor admired his growing talent. "I trust you shall at least find it relaxing."

"Now you are being ridiculous. And you behaved so well toward Cuhurran. Do stop sulking. It is unbecoming."

"I am not sulking. I am thinking of what I will do to Cuhurran once I know enough magic to challenge him."

Spit shrank back behind the couch, as if expecting the Wizard's fist to burst out of the ceiling and smash them.

"Spit, please get up. Reiffen has no intention of fighting

Wizards." Giserre scowled at her son. "Really, you should not say such things in front of her. Do you want to frighten her to death?"

Spit looked suspiciously over her shoulders before she rose. "You can't hurt Wizards," she said. "You shouldn't even talk about it."

"That is not true," Giserre replied. "Wizards can be harmed, though not easily. Why, even Areft was killed. It stands to reason his children can be killed as well."

Spit's eyes went wide. "His children?"

"Do you not know the Wizards are Areft's children?"

The poor servant shook her head, overcome with amazement.

"Well then, it is time you learned the tale. Reiffen, please fetch the small red book from my bedside. I have been meaning to read this story to you and Spit since I first came across it several days ago."

"I already know *The Tale of Areft,* Mother."

"This version is different from the one you learned at school."

Returning from his mother's room, Reiffen handed her a thin volume. The spine of the old, dry book crackled as she opened it; small edges of yellowed paper fluttered to the ground. Settling back against the couch, Giserre began to read.

"'I, Andiss, here set forth the true tale of the world, as I have learned it from Redburr himself, and others among the Oeinnen. I write these words knowing the College in Malmoret has chosen to ignore the truth; but some record of that truth must be preserved and, for that reason, and that reason alone, I here set out the true wisdom of the past, and the true nature of the world as it has been given forth. For Areft did not make the world for humankind, but for himself. . . .'"

Reiffen allowed himself to be caught up in a tale he had heard many times before, though perhaps never with such a tone of presumed authority. How Areft had separated himself from his fellow Ina to fashion the world; how he had raised the mountains and dug the deeps. How some among the Ina took pity on the humans he made from sand and clay, once Areft began to hunt them across his barren world.

". . . Then did Issing thrust herself into Areft's world. And she did collect those of his children nearest her, and gather them from the rocks to keep them safe. And they cowered from her, though she had made herself different from Areft, until they felt her gentle touch, and the softness in her hands. And Issing carried them far away, across the deep places of the world.

"Then did Areft, after he had killed all the children about him, look up and search for more. But there was nothing that could hide from Areft within his world, and he saw the trace of Issing's footsteps in the stone. Great was his rage as he realized he was no longer alone and that another had dared enter his world. And Issing hid his children from his approach, and met Areft at the edge of the deep, with the land sloping up behind her.

" 'Do not kill your children!' she cried. 'Know that they think and feel. For I have taught them words, and they want only your honor and praise.'

"And Areft frowned, for this new thing was not of his devising. Now his children might speak among themselves, and carry tales beyond his knowing. And so Areft came upon Issing and smote her. And Issing fought back against him, but the world was his, not hers. And as he struck her she fell upon her knees and wept. And her tears swelled out across the emptiness, filling the bottom of the world. And behind her the children looked on in wonder as the waters rose and the seas formed. And Areft grew yet angrier, and struck her great blows from his fists, until finally Issing sank beneath the surface and was lost. And Areft, thinking she had escaped him, searched wildly through the water, and great storms rose up, and rain poured down upon the land and across the upturned faces of his children.

"The watching Ina wept, for Issing was no more. Her spirit washed only in the waters, rain and storms the spoil of her sorrow and Areft's wrath. And never can the sea be still; always must it roll from tide to tide, seeking peace. But even so, there were among the Ina three who saw the truth in Issing's fate: that Areft's world was not his alone, and that it could yet be changed. And though they pitied Issing and feared for themselves, still did they follow her into the world and leave all Ina behind.

"Bavadar, Oeina, and Brydds: these were the names of the Ina who came into Areft's world. And they came separately, in different ways, that Areft might not catch them all at once. And Bavadar rose up from the ground, and brought with him the green of grass and trees, watered with Issing's tears. And Oeina came forth from the waters, washed in the spirit of Issing, and brought forth with her all the birds and fish and beasts. But Brydds burst out in great light in the sky above, and for the first time all the world perceived the beauty of the sun.

"And when Areft saw that new challengers had come to his world, his rage increased. And the tops fell off the mountains and the oceans quivered in their beds. Nor was his wrath lessened by the golden light that showed new creatures flying and running and swimming around him. The cold and emptiness were gone, and in their place the bursting of warmth and light and life. And Areft reached up to drag the sun from the sky and smash it on the rocks below, but Brydds was too quick for him, and spun his creation beyond Areft's grasp. Then did Brydds drop down to the land below and hide himself among the jumbled caves.

"In his anger Areft pulled great swaths of grass up from the earth to feel the dead stone. And he chased Bavadar and Oeina across the world, but Bavadar was too quick, and escaped among the mountains. But Oeina was not so lucky and Areft fell upon her and thrust her beneath the sea. And a second great storm rose around the world, and the land was flooded, and great streams poured down through the caverns of the earth. And many children drowned.

"Then did Bavadar, seeing the danger to his companion, rush back across the world. And the storm grew fiercer, and the rain beat down upon the earth until the birds were washed from the sky and fish swam across the land. And Areft reached up and took Bavadar with his right hand, and forced him down beneath the ocean beside Oeina. Great was the struggle between the three of them, with the sky as wet as the sea and the winds carrying waves across the world. But Areft's strength was too great even for Bavadar and Oeina together, and their struggling soon grew weak as Areft sought to quench their lives in Issing's sea.

"Then did Brydds spring out from his hiding place brandishing a great sword of stone fashioned with his own hands from the rock of Areft's world. And into the sword he had given something of himself as well, so that the blade would be hard enough to pierce the spirit of Areft. And Brydds ran out across the water to the heart of the storm, where the mist and fog rose thickest.

"But Brydds had never held a sword before and his first stroke was unsure. He cut a great gash across Areft's back, but that was all. Bavadar and Oeina sprang away as Areft howled in anguish; then Areft, quickened in his agony, struck Brydds. Blade and Ina spun across the ocean to the shore, but Brydds lost the sword in the surging mist and fled.

"Then did Areft come ashore and decide that, rather than share his creation, he would destroy it. For he could always build anew, while the others were lost in the darkness. With a laugh he raised his foot and stamped upon the ground. Great cracks opened across the world, shattering the earth like a bowl broken on the floor. And the Abyss opened up and the world began to fall.

"Areft's laughter was overwhelmed by the crash of rock and stone. He danced lightly from block to block until he came to Brydds, who clung to a falling boulder in despair. And the Ina wept again as Areft seized Brydds and thrust him through the world and into the Abyss. And then Areft turned to Oeina.

"But Bavadar did not despair. He crawled down among the falling rocks and reached out with all his strength to join the stone together. And Bavadar became one with the stone, though the work was Areft's, and added his strength to the strength of the stone. And his heart beat for the stone, and his blood boiled in pockets of fire through it. And his bones stretched out and became the stone's bones. And the world stopped falling.

"Then did a great shudder pass through the earth, and Areft and Oeina were cast upon the ground. And both were overwhelmed by their struggle. And after a time the children who were still alive came down from their mountaintops and out of their caves and crept back across the world. And the storm ceased and the birds dried their feathers and the fish returned to the sea.

"And this is what they saw. For Oeina and Areft had fallen close together, and the world lay jumbled around them. And mountains grew from the sea, and lakes had grown among the mountains. And near to Oeina lay the sword.

"But before the children could reach it, Areft awoke. And he shook his mighty head and looked about, and saw Oeina close beside him. And the children shrank back among the rocks as Areft came upon Oeina by the shores of the sea and thrust his last enemy's face deep within the water. And the sea bubbled and boiled as the last of Oeina's breath departed and the children were left alone.

"But there was one among them who threw aside his fear. Nor is it remembered who he was, no matter how many kings claim his kinship. And he came up behind Areft as Oeina's life was ending and seized the sword from where it had fallen among the rocks. And the power of the sword was such that, even though it had been fashioned by Brydds for the shape of Brydds's own hand, so did it also fit the hand of the nameless hero who

took it. Light as the air it was, yet hard as stone and sharp as cold-
ness as well. And braving all things, the human came up behind
Areft and swung the sword in a great arc against him. More fortunate than Brydds before him, or perhaps because he could see
clearly now that the storms and fog were gone, the human's blow
when it descended cleft Areft at the waist and severed him in two.
And Areft howled, and his blood boiled on the ground, blacken-
ing the sword, even as his slayer brought the weapon down upon
Areft's neck in a second blow. Then did Areft lie in three parts
upon the earth, and black mist rose up around them. And the
hero stood resting on the pommel of the sword as Areft's head
erupted in pale lights that laced across the sky. And Areft's body
glowed, and melted into the ground. And a great chittering rose
up out of the world as a swarm of vermin skittered and fluttered
out of the blackened earth and away. And three shadows followed, racing across the sea.

"Then did the rest of the children come out of their hiding
places and look in awe at the mark where their enemy had lain.
And they laughed and sang, as Issing had taught them, and danced
upon the ground. And they cheered their hero and asked him to
be their king. But he said there could be no kings after Areft and
walked away. And some of the people went with him, while others remained in celebration on the shore. And great was their astonishment as Oeina, whom they had thought dead, rolled over
upon her back, gasping in the air, and called to them, and told
them she would leave them with one last gift before she followed
Areft beyond the world. And as she spoke she fell back into the
ocean, and her body fell apart, and the Oeinnen emerged, crawling and running, leaping and jumping, flying and soaring across
the land. And they taught the children of Areft many things. And
among them was Redburr, who himself told me this tale. And to
him I dedicate this work, and to Oeina, and Brydds, and Bavadar,
who have rescued us from the hand of our maker, who meant for

us no joy. And the sun set and the stars rose, and the world went on as it never had before, for the love of all the creatures in it, and not he who thought to rule them."

Giserre finished and closed the book; the cat looked up from the ball of yarn.

"I like that Brydds was the one who made the sun," said Reiffen. "I never heard that before."

"There is much about Brydds we never knew before the coming of the Bryddin." Giserre turned toward Spit, who had completely forgotten to finish her folding, so enthralled was she by the tale. "Tell us, Spit, what do you think of the Wizards now? You see, they are Areft's children, and can be harmed just as he was, if one has the proper tools."

"Begging your pardon, milady, but I must have missed the part about the children. Sounded to me like he got killed before he had a chance to sire children. And a good thing for us, too, or we'd be even worse off."

Then Giserre explained to the poor woman how the three shadows that had fled Areft's corpse were each one of the Wizards: Usseis from the head, Fornoch from the torso, and Ossdonc from the waist down. But Spit just shook her head stubbornly and said she didn't see that at all.

"It's the same story as my old gran used to tell me, milady. Only she said it was Pittin slew Areft, and that's why there's been feudin' ever since."

"That's how we learned it in Valing, too." Reiffen tossed a few fresh lumps of firestone on the hearth. "Except for the part about the feuding."

The cat pawed at the whispering yarn as Giserre began to rewind the skein. "It is said, Spit, that Reiffen and I are descended from Pittin."

"Redburr says the first kings of Banking just claimed that to strengthen their hold on the throne."

"Redburr?" Spit's eyes went nearly as wide as her mouth. "Is that the same Redburr as in the story?"

"It is," Giserre acknowledged.

"And you talked to him?" Worry crept into the poor woman's face. "Is he . . . a spirit?"

Reiffen smiled. The idea of an insubstantial Redburr was a good one, even in gloomy Ussene. "He's alive."

"Redburr is old, Spit," said Giserre. "Like the Bryddin."

"And the Wizards," added Reiffen.

"What's a Bryddin?"

"Spit, don't tell me you've never heard of Dwarves?"

"Spit has been in Ussene a long time, Reiffen." Giserre pulled the last of the yarn away from the cat and dropped the skein in the basket on the table. "Longer than Dwarves have lived on the surface of the world."

The slave looked down at the floor. "If you hadn't come along, milady, I'd still be Downstairs, muckin' out after the stinky, slippy bats."

Gathering the folds of Reiffen's long black scarf, Giserre added it to Spit's basket. "You are safe with us, Spit. Or as safe as anyone can be who spends too much time with Wizards. Now, what would you like me to tell you about the Bryddin?"

5

Prince Brizen

ook, there's Brizen."

Ferris ducked behind the parapet at the back of the castle wall. The last thing she wanted was to spend the morning answering any more of his admiring questions about Valing and Ussene.

"Don't let him see us," she said.

"Oh, come on, Ferris. He's not that bad." All the same, Avender crouched down beside her.

"Maybe not for you. He's not following you around the castle like a lost gosling."

Leaning around a corner of the stone, Avender peered once more across the courtyard at Rimwich Keep's tall tower.

"Did he see us?" she asked.

"Not yet. He's still looking, though. You know, if he comes out onto the wall, we'll never get away from him. All he's got to do is start up the stairs and there'll be nothing we can do."

"We'll start crawling the other way if he does."

"You can do that, but I'm not going all the way around the keep on my hands and knees. Uh-oh. Here he comes. If he asks the guards, they'll tell him we're out here for sure."

Ferris resisted the urge to peek over the parapet. Already they had attracted the notice of the sentry stationed nearest them on the wall.

"He's stopped. Now he's leaning out over the wall and looking in the courtyard. No, we're not there." Avender chuckled, his interest in Ferris's game increasing. "Now he's standing on tiptoe, scanning the wall one last time. I think he's going back inside. Yes, that's it. He'll probably be up and down the tower another half dozen times before he gives up."

Ferris started to rise, her skirts getting filthy from the stone. Avender caught her arm with his hand.

"Don't get up," he said. "Let's make sure he doesn't come back out first."

"He's not that clever."

"He's not that stupid, either. Really, he's much nicer than we thought he'd be. You don't have to be so mean to him."

But the prince didn't return, so the two lurkers got to their feet. Sighing, Ferris turned to the town, whose narrow streets cut through the houses like deep gullies in a bank of brown clay. At the bottom, where things began to flatten out, a high Dwarven wall stretched all the way around Rimwich from one bend in the river to the other. "Designed the defenses myself," Nolo had told them when they marched in through the main gate two days before. "These Wayland masons didn't do a half-bad job of work on it, either."

Beyond the gate, a road passed the houses of the outer town, then split west and south. Golden fields stretched across the level plain to forest and more hills. Right and left the fields gave way to long commons along the river, where cattle and horses spotted the lush green grass. Small boats plied the water beside them, disappearing occasionally around the end of the upstream wall where it ran out a third of the way across the channel to guard the docks on the other side.

"I wish we could go into town." Ferris leaned over the edge of
the parapet, the wall sheer for five or six fathoms to the cobblestoned square below. Surely Hern hadn't let them out of Valing
for the first time since Reiffen's capture the year before just so
they could loiter like gargoyles on top of the castle wall.

"You know Redburr said we could this afternoon."

"If Brannis wants us to meet with him, he should just say
when and where. This hanging around is a pain."

"You know kings are used to having people hang around
waiting for them. And stop calling him Brannis." Avender glanced
at the guard who had been watching them. "What if he heard
you?"

"What if he did?"

Turning from the town, she looked up at the keep. It was an
impressively tall tower, though not nearly as spectacular as the
unnerets in Issinlough. At the very top, above the gray pigeons
and brown doves fluttering like bees around a hive, a crown of
trees clustered like green blooms atop a single giant stem. Thin
windows pitted the dark stone below.

"All Brizen has to do is look out one of those windows to find
us," Avender pointed out.

"Yes. But we'd be gone by the time he got back to the wall."
With one hand shading her eyes, she glanced up at the top of the
tower. "The only good thing about having an audience with
Bra—I mean the king, will be that we'll finally get to see what it's
like up on top. It's a great view from here and all, but Redburr
told me you can see Malmoret from up there on a clear day."

"Today's the day to prove it," said Avender.

They wandered back to the tower and went inside. A pair of
sentries guarded the stairs leading up to the apartments of the
king, but the wide stair down to the main hall and the rest of
the castle was clear. They had already started for the kitchens
when footsteps echoed from the upper way. Ferris feared Prince

Brizen was about to catch them on the landing until she realized more than one pair of feet were scuffing the stone. The guards drew back; Sir Hinnder appeared, leading two soldiers carrying a large wicker basket. A third brought up the rear. Nodding to Ferris and Avender, the king's steward led his small party across the floor to the next section of winding stair. The children bowed in return.

"Do you think that was a hisser?" Ferris asked Avender before the sound of footsteps died away. In Grangore she thought she had caught glimpses of thin, forked tongues protruding from similar, smaller baskets. Maybe in Rimwich she would get to see even more.

"It looked like one."

"What would a hisser be doing in Rimwich?"

"How would I know?"

Further speculation about the basket ended as a second, heavier tread sounded on the stair. The guards stepped aside once more. Redburr, in human form because a town and castle were no place for a bear, descended the last few steps. In one hand he held half a loaf of dark bread, a goblet of something even better in the other.

"There you are." His cheek bulged as he shifted his mouthful to one side so he could speak. "Your turn next. Nolo spotted you on the battlement."

"Was that a hisser Sir Hinnder was escorting down the stair?" asked Ferris as the Shaper led them upward.

Redburr filled his mouth with wine to sweeten the bread and swallowed loudly.

"It was."

"What's it doing here?"

"None of your business, girl. The king doesn't need to explain himself to you."

"I still don't understand why we're even here. Why should we talk to Brannis?"

"You wanted to come to Rimwich more than anyone." The Shaper's growl was much less threatening when he wasn't a bear. "I told you the king would want to see us if we came. And so he has."

"He already saw us at dinner last night."

"That was a banquet. This is different. A personal audience."

A window in the outer wall flushed the stair with light. The river glistened far below, curving around the town like a dark snake.

"For all you know, he's hired the hisser to murder us in our beds tonight," Ferris complained.

"I hadn't thought of that." The Shaper took another bite from his loaf as he plodded heavily up the stairs. "But, to tell the truth, I don't think he'll bother. Hissers are generally hired as spies, not murderers."

"Who knows what Brannis might do."

The Shaper turned around, his woolly red hair almost golden in the light of the window behind him.

"You know, Ferris," he said, "the situation with Brannis is more complicated than you think."

"Complicated? How can it be complicated? He stole Reiffen's throne."

Dust swirled in the light above the Shaper's head. "Yes, but you've only ever heard Giserre's side of the story. It's always looked a little different from Rimwich."

"Hern and Berrel agree with Giserre."

"Giserre's their friend."

"She's our friend, too," said Avender loyally.

"Even Brannis knows what he did was wrong." Ferris pressed her advantage now that Avender had joined her. "Why else did he try to murder Reiffen? He wouldn't have done that if he didn't think Reiffen's claim was real."

"True." Redburr held Ferris's gaze with his small, dark eyes, his wide body filling the stair as he loomed on the step above. "But Brannis has never admitted to being behind that."

"Why would he?"

"He wouldn't, but that still doesn't prove his guilt. Ask yourself, who had the most to gain by an unsuccessful attempt on Reiffen's life? Brannis had to know any attempt was bound to be unsuccessful with Nolo and me watching the boy. So why even try?"

"It would help the Wizards," said Avender thoughtfully.

The Shaper grunted, glad someone had finally seen the obvious.

"But the men you caught said Brannis hired them," argued Ferris.

"They said an agent of Brannis's hired them," Redburr corrected. "But there was never any proof. Anyone can claim to be Brannis's agent."

"It's just the sort of thing the Wizards would do," said Avender. "Look how we all thought it was Brannis who kidnapped Reiffen last summer."

"If Mindrell had gotten clean away," said Redburr, "we would never have been any the wiser. Everyone would have said Brannis had taken him. And then, when the Wizards showed up with Reiffen years later, they could have said anything they wanted to make themselves look better. They might even have claimed to have rescued him from Brannis. And who would have been there to deny them? Now come on. We've talked about this enough. We're going to be late. And it's never a good idea to be late for an appointment with a king, no matter what you think of him. Or his son."

Redburr accompanied this last remark with a sharp look at Ferris, then headed up the stair. The light soon grew brighter, much brighter than from any window, until their last steps brought them out on top of the tower.

They entered a garden edged about with sky. Battlements and cherry trees walled off the clouds. Roses and snapdragons bloomed in stone flower boxes that filled much of the open space between, lending an extra air of unreality to an already insubstantial perch. Even from the middle of the tower, with no long drop in view, Ferris felt exposed. At the first slight brush of wind she braced herself for swaying in the stone below her feet. But it never came and, after a while, she learned to appreciate the roof garden's quiet calm. Though the nearer hills clearly rose taller than the tower, she still felt as if she were standing at the top of the world.

She was disappointed she couldn't see Malmoret, however.

Not quite at the middle of the roof, the king sat on a stone bench, a grapevine drooping heavily from an arbor above his head. Other, empty benches circled a bank of red and yellow roses. Sir Firnum and several other members of the Rimwich court stood beside their liege; Prince Brizen was there as well.

The prince came forward first, a clumsy smile lighting his hopeful face. "I was so happy when Redburr told me on the stairs that Father was having an audience with you. Now we can spend the afternoon together."

Ferris bobbed a curtsy in reply. There was no escaping the trap now, but Redburr was going to catch it the next time she was alone with him. Nolo emerged from the foliage to join them as the Shaper brought his charges before the king. Acknowledging the introduction with a nod, Brannis gestured for his visitors to rise.

Now that she saw him up close, Ferris found her original impression of the king at the banquet, when she had only seen him from a distance, confirmed. He was not what she had expected. She had always pictured a cruel man with a thin face and a hard laugh, something like what Reiffen had described in meeting the Three. Instead she found herself regarding someone who looked both quiet and sad. The lines in his face led from his mouth to his eyes, where they dissolved in weary pools. But there were currents beneath the pools, and other things, perhaps, adrift in the currents. He studied her closely, and Avender also, and when he was done Ferris doubted he would ever forget either of them. As she would not forget him.

His melancholy reminded her of the weariness they had found in Reiffen after rescuing him from Ussene.

Gesturing to the bench beside his own, the king bade them sit. "I wish to hear your tale," he said. "Baron Sevral and Sir Firnum have told me what you told them, but I believe it's always better to hear things firsthand. So please, speak to me of your quest."

Ferris did most of the talking. Prince Brizen listened with rapt attention. She told them everything, with Redburr nodding for her to continue every time she glanced his way. She spoke of Issinlough and the Abyss; of the *Nightfish* and sailing through the darkness to Cammas; of the long trek through the Stoneways and the discovery of Durk; of sneaking into the dungeons of Ussene with Delven and the other Dwarves; of Reiffen's rescue and the attack of the mander, when Redburr went berserk and Durk was lost. Last, she described returning home only to have Reiffen stolen away from them once more. Avender only spoke when Ferris asked for his opinion or confirmation. And neither he nor Redburr said a word when Ferris explained how she was certain the Wizards had called Reiffen back with the thimbles, no matter what anyone else believed.

When she was finished, the king called for wine. Ferris would have preferred cider or plain water and sipped at her cup sparingly, one eye on Avender to make certain he did the same. The day had turned hot, though the breeze at this height was soft and cool. Pale fruit thickened on the branches overhead.

"You are my nephew's friends," said the king at length. "It is only right for you to take his side in any quarrel. At another time

I might well have had you killed. No doubt that is why Redburr has brought you here now, when he knows you are safe. Reiffen may be more a threat than he ever was before, but that threat has fallen beyond my reach. What is done, is done."

A dove cooed from the feathering branches. Regret, or a shadow from the trees overhead, drifted briefly across King Brannis's face.

"I never wanted my brother's crown," he continued. "Redburr can tell you that. I was Brioss's faithful servant, his strong right hand. I was the one who should have led the flanking force beyond the Wetting, not Mennon, when Martis in his slyness suggested there might be a way to attack Cuhurran from the rear. But Brioss wanted me to remain in the town, in case anything should happen to him. And when Cuhurran slew Mennon on the fields of Rimwichside, before the truce was called, it was I who led the sortie from the city to avenge our brother. It was I who stayed behind when Brioss took Ablen with him to see the Sword.

"When he and Ablen died, the crown came rightfully to me. There were no other heirs. By the time I heard of Reiffen's birth it was too late to go back, even had I believed it. We had come through years of strife and, when it was revealed who Martis and Cuhurran truly were, I doubted everything but the evidence of my own eyes. Were the stories of a wedding true, what assurance had I that the child wasn't some fresh trick of Cuhurran's? So I chose to rule my kingdom instead, as justly as I might. The Three will find no traitors in Wayland—the thanes agree with what I've done. Only in Banking, where a few barons chafe at Wayland rule, is there any real grumbling. I have ruled both kingdoms fairly. On occasion my hand has been heavy and my justice harsh, but there will always be hostility from a conquered enemy, no matter how open the hand of the conqueror.

"I tell you this now so you don't misunderstand me. There is no malice in me toward Reiffen. Had his mother not been so loud in her son's claim to the throne, I might well have welcomed him to be a brother to my own son, the way I was brother to his grandfather. But Giserre resisted my overtures, and now the world is as it is. The Three have a weapon in Reiffen far stronger than anything we have ever faced from them before. Now they can act openly, claiming they have the right. Everyone will know Reiffen is a puppet, but there will always be those who prefer convincing themselves that such is not the case. It is because of them that I will forever be Reiffen's enemy. And his friends will be my enemies as well, should they ever seek to aid him again."

The king looked among his guests, from Redburr to the children, passing over Nolo as someone beyond human affairs. "Even if that person is my own friend," he said, his gaze settling on Ferris. "Or the friend of my child."

Ferris flushed. She wanted to say something clever, but King Brannis's manner cowed her.

Prince Brizen coughed into his hand. The king smiled and gestured broadly beyond the tower's walls.

"My son reminds me I promised to be brief, as he wishes you to be his guests for the remainder of the day. Please, it is my privilege to have such brave heroes in Rimwich Keep. You honor us all. I regret having spoken so bluntly, but I have found plain speaking to work best when I wish to make myself clear. I am certain you understand."

The prince bounded forward, tugging at his ear. "Um, what shall we do first?" he asked.

Ferris decided the problem with Brizen was that he was like a too affectionate puppy, with the disadvantage that, unlike the puppy, he couldn't be smacked on the nose.

Chattering away, he led them down the stairs. "Are you sure you don't want me to take you out to show you the farms? Or we could go for a sail on the river. I'm quite a good sailor, you know, especially where the current slows at the bend around town."

A malicious glint started in Ferris's eye as they filed past the guards on the landing. "I'll tell you what you can do, Your Highness, if you really want me to remember your lovely keep. You can take me to see the hisser."

"The hisser?" Brizen's eyebrows rose nervously. "Um, I can't do that."

"Why not? You're the prince. You should be able to do whatever you want."

"But hissers are dangerous."

"I fail to see how a snake in a basket can be dangerous."

"There are guards."

"Don't the guards in your father's palace do what you tell them?"

"Um. Actually, no." The prince pulled awkwardly at his ear again, his eyes falling back and forth between Ferris and Avender without actually settling on either.

"Come on, Ferris." Avender reached for her arm. "Stop being so difficult. I'm sure His Highness would show us the hisser if he could."

"I suppose. But, if I can't see the hisser, I'm not sure I really want to do anything. I am a little tired after the banquet last night. There were so many speeches."

With a hand to her forehead, Ferris pretended a twinge of fatigue. What Avender had said was true, but she really found Prince Brizen completely annoying. He meant well, and didn't put on airs or anything, but she couldn't stand to think how Reiffen's crown would fall into his feeble lap some day. And while Reiffen suffered in Ussene, too. It wasn't fair. Why should Brizen get everything?

She turned to go. Prince Brizen continued tugging at his ear. Avender stood between the two of them, torn between following Ferris, despite her bad mood, and remaining with the prince.

Ferris was almost through the door when Brizen finally spoke.

"There is a way," he said. "I think I might be able to manage it. We'll get in an awful lot of trouble if we're caught, though."

"Who said anything about being caught?" asked Ferris as she started back into the room.

Avender threw up his hands. "This is exactly why Reiffen and I never used to let you come with us on any of our raids."

"Raids?" asked Brizen.

"Of Mother Spinner's sugar house," said Ferris. She fixed Avender with a withering stare that would have made Hern proud. "Really? And I suppose you're going to tell me I was a nuisance in the Stoneways? Or Ussene?"

Brizen nodded, his chin bobbing. "She has you there, Avender. Ferris has already proven she's just as brave as you."

"Bravery's not what I'm talking about."

"Oh, come on." Ferris looped her arm through Avender's, knowing he was just as likely to go off and sulk if she didn't stop arguing with him. Being alone with the prince was not what she had in mind. "You know you want to see the hisser as much as I do."

Unable to disagree, Avender let himself be carried off. Brizen led the way into the heart of the castle, up and down stairs and through long hallways, some busy with the business of the kingdom, others completely empty. Other than the fact that everything was made of stone rather than wood, there was much about Rimwich Keep to remind Ferris and Avender of their home in Valing. The same rambling halls, with odd rooms and stairways encountered when least expected; the same sparse furnishings. Instead of cupboards at the ends of otherwise empty halls the castle held suits of armor, and far more portraits of kings with dogs and dead stags, and queens with cats and embroidery hoops, than Ferris could ever imagine hanging anywhere.

They came to a door where two soldiers stood guard. Ferris

thought she recognized them as the ones who had carried the basket on the stair, but wasn't sure. They bowed to the prince as he passed, and Brizen nodded to them in turn. Ferris felt a tingle of anticipation but, rather than ordering the guards to let them in, the prince led his new friends away down the hall.

"Wasn't that the hisser's room?" she demanded the moment they rounded the corner.

Brizen nodded, his eyes bright with brazen glee. "Yes. That's it."

"Aren't we going in?"

"We can't go that way. Even if the guards let us pass, they'll report it to Sir Hinnder. And he'll tell my father."

"Is there another way?" asked Avender.

Pleased with his own cleverness, the prince went on. "I know the castle pretty well. Much better than the Old Palace in Malmoret. We only go there in winter, or for special events."

"Well, don't just tell us about it," said Ferris briskly. "Show us."

The eager prince led them on. A set of short stairs ended in the kitchens, which were nearly five times the size of the one in the Manor, and with ten times as many cooks. Ferris smelled bread baking in the ovens, and someone peeling onions. Pots bubbled on a dozen stoves. Judging from what she saw hanging from the ceiling, Rimwich Keep's collection of saucepans was enormous.

Through a side door nearly blocked with baskets of potatoes, Brizen escorted them into a small courtyard. Several chickens squawked and half flew up to the roof of their coop against one wall. Pigeons swooped down to peck at the hens' unguarded grain.

"Up there." The prince pointed to a window above the chicken coop. "That's Ssiliss's room."

"Ssiliss? Is that the hisser's name?"

"Um, yes."

Ferris's eyes narrowed suspiciously. "Have you met it already?"

"Um, no."

"Then how do you know its name?"

"I heard my father call her that."

"Why does it matter if he's already met her?" asked Avender.

Ferris answered with a prim smile. "If he'd already met her, then there really isn't any need for sneaking around like this, is there?"

"Um, Sir Hinnder says she's dangerous."

Avender sniffed at the barnyard beneath their feet. "I want to know why such an important guest has a window looking out over the chicken coop."

"This way," answered the prince, "if she gets hungry in the middle of the night, she can get herself a snack without scaring anybody."

"What I want to know," said Ferris, "is how we're supposed to get up there."

"The last time I was here there was a ladder. But that might have been because they were working on the windows on the other side."

"Well, there's no ladder now," said Ferris. "Any suggestions?"

The prince pulled at his ear for a second, then clambered on top of the coop. The roof creaked but held, as if it had been built with just this sort of alternative use in mind. Hands over his head, Brizen reached for the windowsill above, but was still an arm's length short. He gave a little jump, afraid of the roof collapsing when he came back down.

"Maybe we can climb," he said, eyeing the rough stone.

"Have you ever tried to climb in a skirt?" asked Ferris.

"I'll give you a boost." Avender clambered up onto the coop to test its strength. More creaking, but nothing gave way. Hopping back to the ground, he helped Ferris up, then joined her.

"Um, don't you think I should go first?" A hint of pleading

lurked in Brizen's eyes as he asked the question. "I mean, it is my castle. And you are, um, wearing skirts, Ferris. Like you said."

Frowning, Ferris removed her foot from Avender's cupped hands. Avender offered the makeshift stirrup to Brizen.

"How will you get up?" asked Ferris, as Avender grunted and heaved the prince up the side.

"I'm taller than Brizen. I can reach the window."

Brizen's clothing scraped the stone; for a moment he scrabbled at the sill, almost losing his grip. Avender gave both the prince's boots a hard shove with his hands and propelled him up and into the room.

Ferris followed more easily. Though she was shorter than the prince, she was much lighter, too. Avender's first boost sent her flying halfway over the sill. She rolled the rest of the way in and landed atop Brizen in the dark.

"Ow," said Brizen.

"Shh," said Ferris. This wasn't nearly the same as creeping through the dungeons in Ussene, but she still didn't want to get caught.

Quietly she got to her feet. Beside her the prince stumbled against something but managed to catch it before it hit the floor. Ferris glared at him in the gray, dimly lit room. Not a lot of light came through the window.

They were in a small chamber, much smaller than her own in the castle. A narrow bed lined one wall, a small fireplace on the other side. In between stood the basket.

Something moved. Ferris's heart nearly jumped out of her throat, but it was only a rabbit creeping in the corner. She and Brizen exchanged a glance; yes, Brizen had seen it was only a rabbit, too. She put a finger to her lips in case he forgot himself and asked the same question she was thinking. Then the answer came to her, making her frown at the ridiculousness of her fright. She hadn't expected a snake would eat its rabbits stewed, had she?

Now that she found herself in the hisser's room, she wasn't sure what she had expected. The snake coiled up in the fireplace? Hanging from a chandelier? She looked up and, with some relief, saw there was no chandelier.

Brizen tapped her on the shoulder and pointed toward the basket. Carefully they both stood up. It occurred to Ferris that, no matter how much they tiptoed now, the hisser had already heard them come crashing into the room. Nonetheless, she didn't stop tiptoeing.

They were still a couple of steps from the basket when the lid popped open and a very large head, much larger than Ferris had imagined, rose out of the shadows inside. Diamond-shaped, the head floated just above the level of Ferris's nose. Its eyes glowed, the same color as the setting sun. The body below was thicker than her arm.

"Greetingss, guesstss," said the hisser. "What a pleasant ssur-prisse."

Ferris thought of the rabbit hopping timidly on the floor. The hisser's tongue, much longer than the one she thought she had seen in Grangore, flickered out of its broad, snubby mouth. She realized she was close enough to count the scales between its eyes. Holding back a shudder, she asked herself why she had wanted to look upon such a creature. Had it ever really been about the hisser at all? Had teasing the prince been worth it?

Softly the hisser began to sing.

> "Pleassant food, sso good to eat
> Ssing a ssong and have a treat."

"Come again?" asked the prince.

The hisser's eyes flicked from Ferris to her companion. The thought occurred to her that she ought to look away, but, before she was even halfway to acting on the idea, the hisser had fastened its orange-gold eyes on hers once again. In a soft voice, slick and dry as scales, the hisser chanted a second time:

"*Sslither and sswim,*
 Ssquiggle and ssquirm
 A sspeaking ssnake iss not a worm.
 Sso pleasse don't run
 And pleasse don't fly
 A ssneaking ssnake will help you die."

Ferris hardly heard the words. It was the sound that held her, not the sense. The hiss of Ssiliss's voice reminded her of the first murmur of a kettle on a winter day, the whisper of wind-stirred leaves in fall. Like the hum of summer insects, the song suggested she relax. There was no tension in her neck or shoulders. No worry in her mind. Only the snake holding her with its eyes, its great head, attractive as a flower on a vine, bobbing back and forth between her and Brizen.

Something crashed. The hisser shot high above the basket, its head nearly to the ceiling, its song cut off. The eyes turned fiery orange. Something clunked against Ssiliss's body and dropped to the floor. An instant later Avender threw himself against the basket, sending snake and wicker tumbling.

"Get out!" he cried. "She's trying to eat you!"

Ferris snapped back to the castle, remembering the hisser's words. She was trying to eat them! Beside her, Prince Brizen gaped at the snake writhing on the floor.

Avender scrambled to his feet, still shouting. "Quick! Before it gets all the way out of the basket!"

Ferris, seeing the prince still wasn't moving, grabbed his jacket and pulled him toward the window. That was enough to wake Brizen from his trance. Together they clambered over the sill.

"Ssweetmeatss, why are you here?" called the sibilant voice behind them. "Are you not for eating?"

Holding herself up with her arms, Ferris looked back. Avender held a chair before him, guarding the window. The snake swayed in the middle of the room, its tongue questing. Its coils writhed on the floor. With a last, long hiss, its broad head darted forward. The chair rammed against Avender's chest. Back he flew out the window. Letting go of the sill, Ferris and Brizen dropped to the roof of the chicken coop. A great crash followed as all three landed together and smashed through to the nests inside. Chickens rose squawking in the air, wings beating as fast as Ferris's heart. Straw and splinters exploded across the tiny courtyard.

Ferris lay briefly stunned, wondering if she were dead. Opening her eyes, she saw the jagged edge of the smashed roof above. Something wet seeped through the seat of her skirt. Straw prickled her face and neck.

"Um, are you all right?"

Brizen's worried face appeared above her.

"I think so."

She sat up, pulling bits of straw from her mouth and wrinkling her nose at the smell. An egg that had somehow survived rolled off her lap. She caught it before it hit the ground.

"How's Avender?" she asked.

"I can't tell."

Avender lay between them. He had fallen the farthest, breaking through the floor of the coop to the stone below. Splintered boards and feathers spread beneath him. Not until he groaned were his friends convinced he was alive.

By that time the kitchen staff had all pushed through the door and were staring at their prince in amazement. Ferris and Brizen helped Avender to his feet, but he was still having trouble breathing. His mouth hung limp as he tried to force the air back into his lungs. Just as Ferris was becoming concerned, he coughed and took a great, gasping breath.

"Prince Brizen." The chief cook stepped forward, his towering white cap marking his rank. "Are you all right?"

"Yes, Gridlin. I'm, um, fine."

"Might I inquire what Your Highness has been doing?"

"I was, um, showing my friends, um, the, um . . ."

"I wanted to know where you got your eggs," said Ferris. She lifted her chin confidently. "His Highness was kind enough to show me."

Gridlin grew more confused. "But Your Highness, you know we get our eggs fresh from the market. These are for the snake."

"Which was just what His Highness was telling me when Avender here felt he had to climb on the roof. Now, if you don't mind, His Highness and I have to take our friend somewhere he can lie down." Ferris waved her hand. The crowd of cooks and scullions parted to let them pass.

"That's, um, correct," said the prince, tugging at his ear.

"He's missing one of his shoes, sire." One of the kitchen girls pointed at Avender's bare foot with a wooden spoon.

"If you find it, um, please bring it to the tower."

By the time they reached Avender's room, Avender was urging them to find Redburr and tell him everything. Ferris, however, insisted they wait till they were actually caught.

"That's what you and Reiffen always did," she said. "We'll have plenty of time to confess then."

Which was why she didn't hesitate when Redburr turned up at the door with Avender's shoe dangling like a muttonchop from his hand. "Any reason why I found this in the hisser's room?" he asked.

"I threw it," said Avender. "To distract—"

"It was my fault," Ferris interrupted. "I told Prince Brizen I wanted to see the hisser. I made him do it."

"That's not true," Brizen protested. "I didn't have to show her."

Raising his bushy eyebrows, the Shaper turned to the first of the three companions. Avender accepted the return of his shoe.

"Well, it was Ferris's idea," he said. "But I suppose I should have stopped her."

"Avender saved us, Sir Redburr," added the prince.

Crooking his finger for them to follow, Redburr led the three miscreants back up the tower. Ferris, despite her contrition, couldn't help but ask questions.

"But why did it try to eat us?"

"Why wouldn't she?" Redburr answered. "I'm sure she's tired of rabbit and eggs. There are tribes in the Blue Mountains known to feed their prisoners to hissers."

"You'd think she'd know better. She is in the middle of a town."

"It's precisely because she doesn't know better that King Brannis has two soldiers guarding her all the time. And to think I thought Avender would keep you out of trouble now he's on his own."

Even Ferris's defiance disappeared in the face of Redburr's reminder of what had happened to Reiffen. Whatever Brannis decided to do to them couldn't possibly compare with the suffering Reiffen was going through. What was the worst the king could do to them? Order them to clean the stables?

Which was precisely what he did. With a stern face he lectured them on the importance of guests behaving themselves, especially around other guests. What would their mothers think? Ferris almost pointed out that Avender hadn't had the advantage of a mother for a long time, and how he should be forgiven. After all, he had saved the prince. Who knew what might have happened had Avender not thrown his shoe?

But the king reserved the worst of the lecture for his son. At some length he explained, in front of everyone, that this was hardly the sort of behavior he expected from the heir to the thrones of Wayland and Banking and how, if Brizen couldn't learn to conduct himself in the proper manner of someone who had to think of all his subjects, and not himself, then perhaps the king should call a gathering of the thanes to discuss the subject of selecting another heir. Ferris's eyes went wide. She knew that a gathering of the thanes was a very rare occurrence. She could only imagine what it must be like to be told you have misbehaved that badly.

At the end it looked as if only Ferris and Avender were going to be sent to the stables. Prince Brizen, however, his jaw set stubbornly, faced up to his father and insisted he be punished, too.

"Very well." The king turned to his steward. "Sir Hinnder, if you please. Send for the whipping boy."

"Immediately, sir."

"Whipping boy!" Ferris almost raised her voice above a whisper in her disgust.

"Don't you know what a whipping boy is?" asked Avender. "That's some poor fellow who has to take Brizen's punishment for him."

"I know that," she hissed in reply. "And just when I thought he might amount to something, too."

She was still fuming after Hinnder led them all the way down the tower and around the back of the castle. Rimwich Keep's stable was much bigger than the Manor barn. Even with the whipping boy to help, a husky lad almost as large as Avender, they would be lucky to be done by midnight.

"It's not such a bad job," said the boy when Ferris apologized for having gotten him into trouble. "Better pay 'n any other job I can find. I almost make as much as my mom does washing. An' sometimes there's tips, too."

They hadn't been at the work five minutes when a fourth figure slipped into the long, smelly building. Ferris thought she saw a flash of silver as Brizen clasped his whipping boy's hand. Then the other tipped his cap and, casting a quick glance about to make sure no one was watching, dodged out to the courtyard and away. Brizen fumbled with his shovel for a moment, then fell in beside his friends without a word.

After that, Ferris never tried to hide from Prince Brizen again.

6

The Green Stone

nother year passed, and even Ussene grew routine. The rest of the world drifted away. Giserre, with Spit's help, began seeing to the needs of the fortress's slaves with more than just sweaters and scarves. Reiffen helped by mixing salves and potions, though his mother still refused any magic for herself. Somewhere in her room she had hidden the green stone but, as far as Reiffen knew, she hadn't yet availed herself of its power.

In the meantime he studied with Fornoch in the Library every day, and also with Usseis on occasion, in other parts of the fortress, examining things he would have preferred never knowing about at all. From Ossdonc, however, he learned nothing, no matter how often the Black Wizard came to call.

One day in the Library, as Reiffen pored over his books trying to decide just what was meant by the phrase "the twisted knot of lust's unborn," he noticed the Gray Wizard looming beside him.

"Have you been here long?" asked Reiffen without bothering to look up.

"Not very. Do you fear what I might have seen?"

"No. I assume you know everything about me. It was unsettling once, but I'm used to it now."

Unwrapping his hands from his sleeves, Fornoch gestured to his pupil. "Come. You have advanced greatly in your skill. It is time for more than books."

Without a thought, Reiffen accepted the Wizard's proffered palm. The Library whisked away, replaced by a dim cavern where a red fire glowed in a deep hearth. Frogs croaked in the shadows; lamps flickered on the walls.

"Your own workshop," the Wizard said.

At first glance the cave looked to be a smaller version of Usseis's own laboratory, lacking only creatures chained to the walls. A small pool gleamed at the end opposite the hearth, its dark surface reflecting the nearer lamps in wriggling eels of light. Three stone tables lined the space between. The first supported a scaffolding of pipes and alembics, crucibles and retorts, while the second carried jars of glass and stone stacked in a wide pyramid at the center. The third was empty.

"I'll need more light," Reiffen said, looking forward to having a more appropriate space than the Library for his experiments. "I can't work in the dark like Usseis."

"You know the spells."

Reiffen gestured toward the ceiling. The darkness lifted. Small things scuttled back into the cracks in the walls.

"Where is this place?" he asked. Now that the edges of the room were better lit, he saw there was no exit.

"Away from Ussene," replied the Wizard.

"We're not in the fortress?"

"No." Fornoch picked up a jar from the second table. Something thick and wet sloshed inside, dripping slowly down the glass.

"Where is it?"

"Does it matter?"

"What if I can't use my magic? Then I'll need to know where this place is to get here."

"Magic is the only way to travel to this chamber."

Reiffen looked about the room once again. The stone walls looked thick and strong; he guessed the workshop was buried deep within the earth. Only a Dwarf could ever find it. But Reiffen had perfected the traveling spell now, even without thimbles. Once this place was fixed in his memory he would be able to come and go whenever he wished.

"This would be a good place for a reliquary," said the Wizard. "Usseis does not know it. Far safer for you to carry yourself here than back to the Library, or your apartments in Ussene."

Opening his gigantic hand, he revealed the companion to the golden casket that housed Reiffen's little finger, the one Fornoch had previously kept to himself.

"Both are yours now" he said, placing the case upon the empty table. "Even Usseis trusts you will not run away."

The Wizard departed, and Reiffen spent the next several hours closely examining the chamber and all it contained. He found the pots and jars filled with every substance he had ever heard or read about, and quite a few others besides. From ratwing to earloam, fleabite to wortwattle, jellied nimbus to nail parings of the freshly dead, everything was there. And the collection of vessels on the other table was complete, though they showed all the tiny scratchings and dullness of having been heavily used. The frogs croaked in their pool; the flames twisted in the hearth. Reiffen's shadow watched him from the walls.

When he was finished, he selected his ingredients and prepared a traveling spell. Lying atop the third table, small pots smoking at his feet and head, he readied his memory for his return. The table suited his purpose better than the floor because, if the casting took too long, he didn't want any of the small things his light had scared away to interrupt his concentration.

He closed his eyes. One had to be relaxed for the traveling spell to work, which was why emergencies required a connection, finger joints or an ear. Fornoch had told him that Usseis, when committing a servant to return, always preferred removing something more important, but that was not the sort of thing to think about if Reiffen wanted to relax. Composing himself, he settled his back against the hard table and allowed the smoke to fill his mind. Close to sleep was when the spell was easiest.

He concentrated on his room, on the black and orange coverlet, and the lines in the stone ceiling. The world had become so much sharper since he had started learning magic. Now he knew how colors smelled, and the shapes of sounds. What figures laughter formed, and the textures of the air. His own room, thick with his own odor, but also of his mother and Spit, two oddly similar fragrances like a pair of crossed roses. And the trail of the cat as well, dragged across the other scents like an earthworm wriggling in the hoofprints of an ox. Flickered memory, touched with the barbed tails of the dust lingering in every hall and cavern of Ussene.

The stone beneath him turned soft as a mattress. Reiffen remained still a moment longer to make sure he had left nothing of himself behind. Like spun sugar, the line between this place and the one he had left stretched and sagged. Gently he pulled. The tethered end came free.

He opened his eyes as his door squeaked open. Spit jumped in surprise, the loose hair around her ears frizzing in fright.

"Reiffen! Oh, you gave me such a shake! One of these days it's going to kill me, you popping out of the empty air like that!" Fanning herself with both hands, the poor woman rushed from the room. "Milady! Milady! He's doing it again! Please say something to him for me, won't you?"

A few days later he was returning to the apartment in the more regular way when he heard the rolling boom, like boulders tumbling down a mountainside, of the Black Wizard's voice. Scowling, he quickened his pace. He preferred to have his mother to himself when he came home and was growing weary of the Wizard's endless visits. Spit was one thing: Reiffen had grown up in the Tear with Anella as well as his mother, and Spit wasn't much different. But he had no wish to share his mother with a Wizard.

He stopped when he could hear both voices clearly. "I tell you again," Ossdonc was saying. "Your life will be much easier."

Anger lanced Giserre's reply. "My life does not require easing."

"I will make your son's life easier as well."

"Reiffen requires relief no more than I. He shall follow the path he has chosen."

"Paths can be rough or smooth, milady. You would not want your son to stumble."

"I will not pamper him."

"Most humans are not so hard upon their offspring."

"Most children will not have such purpose placed upon them as mine. Believe me, sir, your offer is unattractive any way you make it."

"My offer, my lady, is likely to be the most attractive you will ever have."

"I assure you, Cuhurran, I am uninterested in offers of any sort."

"Perhaps if I permitted some others within the fortress to make their attentions known, your preference would change. One of my captains? A sissit?"

Hands clenching, Reiffen wished he had a sword. Better yet, he wished he had mastered a few more spells. No doubt magic would prove more effective on a Wizard than plain iron.

"You demonstrate your vileness, sir, in even alluding to such things. I would have you leave."

"There are other ways, milady. Usseis is not the only one who can compel."

"I do not fear your compulsion, sir. That is the way of a coward. You have committed many crimes against many people, but no one has ever accused you of cowardice."

The passage echoed with Ossdonc's heavy mirth. "My lady, your temper is as charming as your aunt's. I have never regretted anything so much as when my brother killed her. Have you yet taken the Stone? I know all about it, you know, and urge you to take advantage of a boon so offered. It would be a shame if your own gifts were lost as foolishly as Loellin's."

A note of uncertainty arose in Giserre's voice. "I have not, as yet, decided what to do with the Stone."

"I suggest you choose quickly. We both know your son would be lost completely, should you cease to be by his side. Not to mention my own feeling in the matter."

Giserre's voice firmed. "As I said, I have not yet made up my mind." Reiffen, who knew his mother better than the Black Wizard did, understood she had made her choice in the moment of speaking.

"Very well then," continued Ossdonc. "I leave you to your decision. Understand, however, you and I are not finished. Not by many days and years."

The voices ceased. Reiffen took a step forward, wishing to comfort his mother, but stopped as the thought occurred to him that Ossdonc might be already coming down the corridor. It was one thing to tell Giserre he had spied upon her conversation, but he preferred Ossdonc not know. Hurrying back toward the Library, he retraced his steps as far as the first bend in the passage. Even so, when Ossdonc passed, the Wizard gave Reiffen a broad wink and a short laugh, as if to say he understood it all.

He found his mother at her usual place on the couch, her knitting in her hands. Small lines of anguish lingered in her face as she smiled.

"Reiffen. I did not think to see you until supper. I am glad you have returned early."

"So am I. I heard you and Ossdonc from the hall."

"I would rather you had not. Our talk was not suitable for you to overhear."

"He is the vilest of the Three."

"He is certainly the most human."

"If he hurts you in any way, I will kill him."

"Thank you, Reiffen." Giserre nodded modestly. "For my part, I shall do my best to make certain your vengeance is unnecessary."

She held out her hand. Reiffen, though he thought he was too old for holding hands, took it just the same.

"I heard what Ossdonc said about taking the Stone," he confessed. "How do you think you would do it?"

"The Stone is not so large it cannot be swallowed entire. A glass of wine to oil my throat would not be amiss, either."

"Do you have it?"

"I do. In the sewing box."

Reiffen found the box on the low table before the couch. Beneath the pincushion, needles, and thread lay the Stone, dark and still.

"You've made up your mind, haven't you," he declared.

"I have."

"When are you going to do it?"

His mother dropped her work in her lap and looked up. "Now, if you want. I suppose I can put it off no longer. You told me yourself I should do this when we arrived."

"I would never have brought you, if I hadn't thought I could keep you safe."

"There is no safety now, Reiffen. Only boldness."

The green stone gleamed among the tangled threads as soon as Giserre's fingers approached the sewing box. She picked it up like a jewel from the nest of a jealous bird and held it in her hand. Its pulse quickened.

"I am more nervous than I would have hoped," she said.

Reiffen poured his mother a glass of wine. Thanking him, she took a small sip. With her other hand, she slipped the stone like a large green grape past her lips. Her cheeks were pale; her dark hair topped her face like a spreading crown. Taking a fresh mouthful of wine, she swallowed with some effort. Her eyes teared, her throat struggled with the thickness. When she was finished, she coughed delicately behind her hand.

Reiffen's heart pounded in his chest.

"That was not so difficult," said Giserre. "I feel no difference."

"You look no different, either."

"Perhaps the effects take time."

"Can you feel it? In your stomach, I mean?"

Giserre shook her head. The color returned to her cheeks. "I feel nothing at all. It passed down my throat more easily than I would have expected; I believe the wine was an excellent idea."

Reiffen settled back on the couch without taking his eyes from his mother. "I suppose there is no way to test it."

"No, there is not."

"You could prick yourself." Reiffen offered his mother a pin from the pincushion.

"Prick myself? Why should I want to do that?"

"Fornoch said the Stone would make you live forever. I wonder if he made it so nothing could hurt you, either."

"If you insist."

With a shrug that suggested she would never have done such a thing had her son not proposed it, Giserre accepted the pin. Pausing to give Reiffen one last view of her hands, she jabbed her left forefinger.

"Does that satisfy you? I certainly felt the pain." She held her finger out to her son's gaze, a crimson dot welling at the tip.

Reiffen's eyes narrowed. There was something odd about that drop of blood. A slight, sparkling sheen glimmered green in the light. He could barely see it, and for a moment he thought it was a trick of the Dwarven lamps in the room. Then it was gone, his mother wiping her finger clean with her handkerchief.

"Did you see it?" he asked.

"I saw nothing but a drop of blood."

"You didn't see the green?"

"No." She gave him a sideways look. "Did you see something?"

"I think so. There was the tiniest hint of green, almost a glow, really."

Giserre looked back at her finger, but the blood was gone. She squeezed it and a fresh drop appeared. Frowning, she said, "I still see nothing."

"I do. It's right there." Reiffen was even more certain than before. The slightly green hue was plain to him; he didn't understand how his mother could miss it. "Maybe if you held it closer to the light."

But, no matter how his mother looked at her finger, she couldn't see the green hint in the drop of blood. Blotting her finger a second time with her handkerchief, she held the sheer fabric up before the lamp, but still found nothing in the stain. Reiffen, however, saw it clearly, even after the blood had dried.

Her brow furrowed. "How can I not see it, if you do? My sense of color is excellent."

"Maybe I'm more attuned to the magic. My spells are coming much more easily now that I have my workshop. Watch."

"Light reflects, and burns and turns.
Bend its beam so none discerns."

At the end of the last word, he disappeared completely. Even he couldn't see his hand before his face.

Giserre cried out, "Reiffen! What have you done?"

"I'm right here, Mother. On the couch beside you."

Her eyes darted back and forth along the cushions. "Reiffen, this is far worse than the blood. I cannot see you at all. Come out at once!"

Leaning forward, he tapped his mother's knee. Giserre started as he popped back into view beside her. Never had he seen her so flustered.

With a deep breath, she put a hand to her throat. "You frightened me. And touching me like that was almost as bad as the disappearing."

"I'm sorry. I didn't mean to scare you. It's not a very difficult spell. If I could do it well, nothing would make me reappear until I spoke a word of recall."

Giserre took a second breath, not so deep as the first. "Your expertise seems quite sufficient. But perhaps you are correct. If you can effect such magic so easily, with only a simple rhyme, then perhaps you did see something in my blood unavailable to my untrained eye." She looked once more at the pinprick on her finger, as if she might be able to perceive what Reiffen had seen now she had a firmer belief in his power.

"I'm getting stronger," he said. "Would you like another demonstration of magic knitting?"

"No thank you." Giserre's mouth pinched. "You have frightened me quite sufficiently for one evening. I shall, however, require more substantial warning the next time you wish to demonstrate your skill."

It wasn't that night, but several days later, when Reiffen dreamed again that he was back in Valing. It was springtime, and the ice had melted on the lake. A heavy curtain of cloud rose above the falls to mingle with the snow-shouldered mountains. He was in the Tear, the roar of the gorge echoing dimly through the misted glass. Avender was with him, and Ferris. And Skimmer, too, though Reiffen couldn't remember how Skimmer had managed to waddle all the way up the long stairs from the lake. They were eating mussels by the fire while waiting for Giserre to join them. The humans took turns tossing shelled meat at the nokken, who caught their presents in his whiskered mouth before gulping them down.

Despite the blazing hearth, Reiffen shivered with cold. His mother was bringing the blankets, he remembered. Beyond the windows the fog raced quickly around the hanging tower. Where was she?

The door opened. Giserre stood on the doorstep, a single blanket in her arms. Reiffen watched as the Tear separated from the stone bridge connecting it to the Neck and fell into the gripping fog. Giserre screamed.

He woke shivering, his quilt kicked to the floor. The room was dark, but the cracked door let in a wedge of light from outside.

His mother screamed again.

Leaping from the bed, Reiffen rushed into the sitting room. Spit, eyes wide in terror, clutched her blanket by the fire. Reiffen raced on into his mother's room, where he found Ossdonc gripping Giserre tightly by the shoulders. She slapped him; the Black Wizard laughed. Blindly, Reiffen raised his right arm and called out words he'd only recently learned. A flash of light, and a bolt of fire struck Ossdonc in the back. Giserre collapsed on top of the wrinkled bed; the Wizard rolled across the room. The smell of burnt clothing hung on the air.

"You dare use magic on me!" The Wizard pulled a dagger from his belt and sprang to his feet, enraged. "I shall take far more pleasure from you than I ever would have from your mother."

"You shall not."

Reiffen stiffened as Fornoch's voice sounded from behind his shoulder.

"Stay out of this, brother," said Ossdonc. "The boy attacked me. He is mine."

"He was provoked."

The Gray Wizard's words coiled easily around the room, comforting in their cold assurance. Reiffen glanced toward his mother lying motionless on the bed, her dark hair unbound.

Ossdonc took a step forward. "None may strike me and live. You know that. You cannot protect him."

"I can. And Usseis can, as well. Put away your blade. You know we have other plans for this one."

"Singularly useless plans, if he prevents my taking what I want."

"You are too short-sighted. You forget the promise of the future in the grasp of present desire."

"You are an old woman and a coward."

"There is wisdom in old women and cowards that is lacking in an intemperate child."

Brushing past Reiffen, Fornoch entered the room. Unlike Ossdonc, he had not made himself human-sized, and had to stoop to fit through the door. He stood with his gray robes shielding Reiffen from his brother's ire.

But not Giserre. With a sudden leap, Ossdonc bounded forward and plunged his dagger into Giserre's breast. She gasped, a bubbling in her throat. A crimson stain spread across her white nightdress and dripped upon the bed. With a cry, Reiffen fell upon the quilt beside her, his eyes fixed in horror on her spreading wound.

"Imbecile!" Fornoch raised an angry hand: Ossdonc flew across the room, his weapon in his fist. "Leave now, before you cause more harm!"

"Do not think this is ended." The Black Wizard wiped his knife blade with his hand.

Giserre coughed as her attacker strode from the room. Drops

of bright blood scattered across the top of her gown. Gently Reiffen slipped a pillow beneath her head. He felt so helpless watching her die.

"I apologize for Ossdonc's conduct," said Fornoch, his great head bowed beneath the ceiling. "Had I known he had grown so lacking in self-control, I would have watched him more closely."

Rage and bitterness welled out from Reiffen's heart. "I don't want your apology. My mother is dying."

Fornoch's eyebrows rose. "Is she? Can you already have forgotten what I told you about the Living Stone?"

"I don't care what you told me." Reiffen gritted his teeth and tried not to sob.

"She is not dying." The Wizard wiped the blood from Giserre's lips with the edge of his gray sleeve, but there was no tenderness in his touch, nor in the hard cast of his enormous mouth.

She coughed again, but no fresh blood welled at her lips. Spit appeared at the door, her concern for her mistress finally overpowering her fear of Wizards. Reiffen couldn't bear the thought of his mother dying, but he couldn't bring himself to hope Fornoch was right, either. It was so much easier to wallow miserably in between.

"Get back from the bed," ordered the Wizard. "Give her room to breathe."

Reiffen scrambled away. Fornoch bent over Giserre. Her chest rose and fell weakly. Before Reiffen could stop him, the Gray Wizard grasped the collar of her nightdress and ripped it open. Spit gasped.

"Look," Fornoch commanded his student. "See what you already should have seen. The wound heals."

Torn between his wish to cover his mother and his need to learn, Reiffen leaned forward. At first he thought her entire chest had been split open: dark blood smeared her pale skin. Forcing himself to focus, he noticed a narrow wound running across her chest. Ossdonc had struck upward as he thrust, to pass between the ribs. As Reiffen watched, the wound began to shrink, the skin closing. Already the blood had ceased to flow.

"Fetch water, Spit. Giserre will want washing when she wakes."

The poor woman hesitated at the door.

"Spit. Bring us water. Now."

Reiffen felt the compulsion in Fornoch's voice. Spit blinked and shook her head, then hurried from the room.

Reiffen remembered the washbasin Giserre kept atop the dressing table. By the time he had brought both basin and a clean cloth back to his mother, her wound had closed completely.

"But how . . . ?"

"Think. Or have you lost your wits entirely?" Fornoch sat on the edge of the bed and seemed suddenly larger, now that he no longer stooped beneath the ceiling.

Wetting the cloth in the basin, Reiffen wiped the blood from his mother's pale shoulders. There was no trace of the wound at all; her healing had left no scar. His fear eased, and he was able to pay closer attention to what had happened. For the first time he noticed the same green shimmer to his mother's blood he had seen before.

"It worked," he breathed. "The Stone worked."

"Why would it not? Did I not say the Stone would allow you to live forever? That would hardly be true if a simple knife thrust, even from so deft a hand as Ossdonc's, were enough to end it. What I should like to know is how you broke the charm."

"Charm?" Reiffen looked at the Wizard blankly.

"Ossdonc placed a warding around the apartment. Otherwise my own alarums would have revealed his presence far earlier."

"I felt no charm."

Fornoch's black eyes pressed Reiffen flat as parchment. "My brother must have cast his spell around the outside of your suite,"

he mused after a moment. "You seem to have broken it in your attack. Ossdonc's concentration has never been the best."

"I was angry," said Reiffen. "He shouldn't have touched her."

"No," said the Wizard. "He should not. As he has learned.
But it is late, and you need your rest as much as the Lady Giserre.
You have spent more strength than you know in your casting.
Seek your bed. We will continue this discussion tomorrow."

Reiffen looked at his mother breathing peacefully among the
bloody bedclothes. The pain in her face was gone. "I don't want
to leave her alone."

"She will not be alone. I shall remain until Spit returns."

"And Ossdonc?"

"Ossdonc will not return."

"Maybe I should stay and help Spit change the sheets."

The Gray Wizard waved his hand. The bloodstains on the
covers disappeared. A second gesture, and Giserre floated a few
inches above the bed. The covers unrolled as if under the touch
of an invisible hand. Giserre descended gently to the mattress;
the sheets and blankets rolled back across her sleeping form.

Reiffen rubbed his temples. "I still don't think I'm going to be
able to sleep. Too much has happened."

"You will."

The Wizard raised his hand a third time. Reiffen yawned.

"You do that too easily," he said, trying to stifle another.

"In time that power will be yours," said Fornoch. "If you remain diligent. You have already done well. Tonight's casting had
force and power, or Ossdonc would never have been affected. Finally you have learned not to muscle the magic through on will
alone, but to release it naturally, like blood spilled from a
wound."

His fatigue overpowering him, Reiffen stumbled back through
the sitting room, where he met Spit returning with an ewer of

water in either arm. Yawning, he collapsed into his bed's thick softness. His last thought before he fell asleep was how strange it was that he was willing to leave Fornoch alone with his mother, though he would have killed Ossdonc for taking the same liberty.

The next morning he woke strangely invigorated. He had knocked Ossdonc down! Though he knew he would have received much worse in return had the Gray Wizard not come to his rescue, it was still a splendid feeling. Some day he would need no one, Wizard or human, to stand beside him. The strength would be his alone.

At breakfast he assured himself his mother was fine, then proceeded to the Library. Fornoch was waiting for him with a new Stone, red as blood, beneath the glass bowl.

"Perhaps you will not be so quick to give this one away," said the Gray Wizard, "now you have seen Ossdonc's temper."

"Perhaps some day I shall make my own Living Stones," Reiffen replied, still flush with last night's success.

"Perhaps you shall," said Fornoch. "Though that sort of magic may prove more challenging than you realize. Death requires little from the conjuror, but life is another matter entirely."

7

A Ball in Malmoret

ou're sure Ferris is going to be there?"

Avender looked closely at Redburr as they neared the King's Gate. The outer town's stalls and bazaars, fat with melons, summer squash, and the first golden ears of corn, tugged at them like greedy beggars. Dark roe spilled from the plated bellies of oldfish almost as long as a man.

"She'll be there." The Shaper scratched his belly where it threatened to burst free of his shirt and ogled the gleaming fish. "There isn't a woman in Malmoret—or Valing, either—who'd pass up an invitation to the prince's coming-of-age celebration."

"And Nolo?"

"Nolo's in Issinlough. Taking a vacation from humans."

Flipping a heavy coin to the nearest fishmonger, Redburr scooped up three bowls of the salty roe and gobbled them down before he and Avender were halfway to the gate. In two years of traveling together, Avender had seen no sign of the Shaper's appetite ever abating.

"Come on." Redburr gave a loud, savory belch. "We're going to be late."

The King's Gate rose before them. Evening light splashed brightly against the lofty walls, making the pale stone look more like the sides of a yellow barn than the first defense of the wealthiest city in the world. Inside, deep carvings covered the cool, dark rock with scenes of triumphant kings. But beyond the wall the city teemed.

Avender sniffed the air. No place else smelled like Malmoret: all odors drifted here eventually. Awful at first, because of the slaughterhouses by the river, but gradually improving. Bread was baking somewhere, and washing hung to dry. A few steps down the road the scent of a scholar's ink clung to the air like words on parchment before being scratched out by the sharp tang of an apothecary's herbs. Smoke of all kinds whirled and spun from fires seen and unseen. Birch and cedar burned, and the matted press of cow pies, and firestone, and gumwood from the Wetting, and incense thick with midnight meetings, and the bones of horses and the piercing fetor of the tanneries upriver. Best of all, as far as Avender was concerned, were the smells of a thousand meals being cooked around him: lamb and goat, soup and stew, eggs and beans. If he enjoyed it so much, he could only imagine the temptation to Redburr's much more easily distracted nose.

"Are we going to the Ox and Plow?" he asked as they shouldered their way through the crowd.

"Not this time, boy." Redburr turned sideways to avoid a conk on the head from a milkmaid's yoke. "We've better lodgings to look forward to tonight."

They headed south and east toward Edgewater and the New Palace. Houses stood straighter and gutters ran cleaner as they moved into the more prosperous parts of the city. Fewer people jostled on the path. Shade and fruit trees stretched green branches over courtyard walls. The scent of the river joined the medley in the air.

"So, where are we staying?" demanded Avender as Redburr

led them out of Pucker Street and onto Newkin Way. On their right, pennants fluttered from the villas lining the banks of the river.

"You'll see."

The mansions grew more magnificent as Redburr led them farther east. Most impressive of all, the New Palace loomed at the end of the avenue like a great cream-colored cat sleeping at the bottom of a thick hedge, its terraces bright with vines and flowers. Few lights gleamed in the wide windows: the ball that night was to be held in the Old Palace in the center of the city. King Brannis preferred the thick stone of the older keep to the dancing fountains and terraced gardens of the new, where Queen Loellin had once held court with her Wizard consort.

Before they reached the New Palace, however, the Shaper led Avender into the last, and grandest, villa. A crested flag marked the entrance, where a pair of guards in Dwarven armor stood at strict attention. Avender recognized the standard at once: three white swords crossed on a black field. Only three people in all the world might fly that flag and two of them, if they still lived, were in Ussene. The third was Prince Gerrit, Lady Giserre's brother.

A bowing footman led them inside. They hadn't half crossed the front hall when a whoop sounded from the stair. Ferris bounded down in a dressing gown, two and three marble steps at a time. Avender caught a glimpse of Hern as well before Ferris caught him and the Shaper in hugs the equal of any bear's.

"Finally you're here! We've been waiting for days! Not that it's been boring, of course. We've had picnics on the river and Brizen's been by and I'm teaching Pattis and Lemmel how to sail. Why weren't you here yesterday? Did you forget the ball's to-night?"

"Ferris, please calm down." Hern joined them on the orange and black paving in the hall. "The prince and princess gave up all hope of your arriving on time, Redburr, and are off preparing for the evening. Which is what Ferris and I should be doing, and you two as well."

"Mother's already ordered baths for you," laughed Ferris. She pinched her nose delicately between thumb and finger. "Redburr, you smell like you've been at the slops again."

The Shaper gathered himself majestically: a button popped off his vest and rattled across the marble floor. "You will not believe the transformation I am about to undergo," he intoned.

Hern waved a hand in front of her face to scatter the oldfish fumes spreading through the hall.

Upstairs, Redburr and Avender had adjoining suites with views of the Edgewater where it met the main stream. The curtains in their wide windows fluttered in the evening breeze. Off his room Avender found a second chamber with a copper tub, filled and steaming. He enjoyed his soak, but turned up his nose at the scented soap set out for him. The warmth dredged the road from his bones, and he only climbed out when the water was nearly as tepid as the air.

Back in his room, he found a magnificent set of clothes laid out on the bed. The jacket was a little tight, but it had been several months since the steward had last seen him and he was still growing. Scowling, he discovered the breeches only reached the tops of his calves, with pearl buttons to fasten them tight below the knee. At least the shirt wasn't too ruffled. He had to unfasten the breeches again when he realized the long white stockings were supposed to fit inside, then squeezed his feet into fancy shoes that wouldn't last a quarter mile on a muddy lane.

Ferris and Hern were waiting on the terrace when he went back downstairs. Evening had fallen, and stars sparkled in the darkening sky to match the dance of light upon the water. But Avender had eyes only for Ferris. Her figure was still slight, and her hair the color of mud, but when she smiled or spoke there was nothing plain about her at all. Leaning over the wide banis-

ter, she pointed across the garden at the boat she had taken Pattis
and Lemmel sailing in, one foot lifted girlishly for balance.

Hern pulled her daughter back from the rail. "Remember
what I told you, Ferris. This isn't Valing. No jackrabbiting."

"We're not at the ball yet, Mother. Allow me to have some
fun."

Bathrobes billowing, Prince Gerrit's daughters raced down
the terrace to meet the new guests, but Ferris was the person they
really wanted to see. Sweeping the two girls up in her arms, she
kissed them both before the governess arrived in their wake, red-
faced and puffing. The prince and princess followed, beside whom
Hern, in what Avender knew to be her most special gown,
looked like a brown hen caught beside swans.

Dowdy though she seemed, Hern retained the full measure
of her dignity. "Prince Gerrit, Princess Arenne. May I present
Avender of Valing."

To Avender's surprise, Prince Gerrit dropped to one knee and
bowed his head. Beside him Princess Arenne dipped in a deep
curtsy, and the children and their nurse as well. Blushing to the
ears, Avender bowed in answer.

"Welcome to Malmoret," said the prince graciously as he regained his feet. "We are honored to host such a hero in our hall."

Though it still embarrassed him, Avender had learned over
the years how to receive such praise. He bowed a second time
and said humbly, "You honor me too much. Reiffen was my
friend."

Prince Gerrit's face contracted, reminding Avender of Reiffen
when he was angry. "You believe my nephew dead?"

"Reiffen will always be my friend," replied Avender, recovering as best he could. Evidently Prince Gerrit, like Ferris, refused
to recognize what must have happened to Reiffen in the three
years since he had been gone.

The prince relaxed. Even when he smiled, he bore more than

a passing resemblance to Reiffen in a temper. But he was as gracious as Giserre.

Princess Arenne stepped forward, slim and tall as her husband, with the golden hair of southern Banking. "Welcome to Malmoret," she said, extending a delicate hand. "How do you find our city?"

"It's very beautiful," Avender stammered, somewhat overcome by the woman's resplendence. It was almost too much, like spooning sugar on top of Mother Spinner's maple candy.

"Have you visited Malmoret before?"

Avender nodded. "We never stayed in a palace, though."

"You have been in Malmoret previously?" The sharp look rose once more in the prince's eyes. "With Redburr? And he has not brought you here so that I might pay my respects?"

"Usually we stay at the Ox and Plow."

The prince frowned, looking more like Reiffen than ever. "Wine-bibbing and gluttony are ever the Oeinnen's favorite pursuits. However, he has been prompt this evening. I believe he is waiting by the carriages. Madame Steward, if I may?"

Hern accepted Prince Gerrit's offered arm. Avender was afraid he, as the only other male present, would have to escort Princess Arenne out to the carriages, but she was busy kissing her daughters good night. Instead Ferris placed a green-gloved hand in his and laughed.

"There's one more surprise," she said. A thin chain gleamed beneath the lace shawl around her shoulders, a borrowed jewel dazzling at her throat. "I only saw him because he came to our rooms so Mother could let out his jacket."

They found a tall, stately baron waiting with his back to them at the door. One hand fiddled with a black-ribboned monocle as he examined a portrait in the hall. His tight velvet breeches and snow-white stockings showed off his muscular calves to great effect; his long blue coat covered a towering frame. Ringlets of red hair cascaded down his back beneath his fine beaver hat. Although he seemed a trifle heavy, his heaviness bore the look of prosperity and dignified age rather than gluttony and sloth.

"Redburr?" asked Avender in astonishment as the baron turned around.

His little finger arched, the Shaper screwed a monocle securely into his eye. "Ah, Avender. I was wondering what had become of you."

"Isn't it amazing?" Ferris laughed merrily. "Have you ever seen him so clean?"

"Not unless one of us was doing the cleaning. How'd his hair get so long?"

"It's a wig, silly."

Redburr's eyebrows rose. Clearly he thought Avender's question both presumptuous and uncouth.

"It's not polite to mention a gentleman's wig," said Prince Gerrit.

"It is all the rage," said the Shaper. "You shall see for yourselves tonight at the Old Palace."

"Wigs and girdles can't hide a glutton, if you ask me," said Hern.

"I think he looks quite civilized." Princess Arenne graced the Shaper with a small, approving nod as she came in from the terrace.

"But where'd you get the clothes? And the hat?" Avender rubbed the fine fabric of Redburr's jacket between his fingers.

"Although he has not seen fit to bring you with him," said Gerrit, "this is not the first time Sir Redburr has been our guest."

"You should look at the trunk in his room," said Ferris. "It's filled with all sorts of fancy clothes. The next time he turns into a bird I'm going to ask him to be a peacock, now I know how vain he is."

"Vanity, my dear, is the least of my sins," advised the Shaper gravely.

Ferris snapped a finger against Redburr's tight jacket. A hint of the same soap Avender had refused wafted sweetly from the back of her neck as she stood beside him. "I think Hern might have let this out a little more. Avender, be a dear and fetch my sewing bag from upstairs, will you? Just in case he loses a button on the way."

Hern tapped the reticule on her arm. "I'm ready for him, Ferris. Now, let's get going."

They traveled in two carriages, the prince and princess in one, Redburr and the Valingers in the other. The Shaper moved stiffly and, by the time he had settled into his seat, small beads of sweat dampened the roots of his artificial curls.

"What's wrong with you?" Avender regarded the Shaper with concern. "You look like you're about to have a fit."

"He's wearing a corset," confided Ferris.

"A corset?"

"I'm waiting to see how long it takes before he explodes."

Hern glared at her daughter. "You behave yourself. He's only doing it for you. Do you think any of us want to be here? Hmph. I'd rather be knitting by the fire."

Avender tugged at his starched collar, and checked to make sure none of the buttons on Redburr's shirt had burst from the effort of climbing into the car.

Other carriages joined them as they wound their way through the streets to the Old Palace. The horses' hooves clattered like a parade; the carriage wheels hummed. Avender had never been in such a well-sprung vehicle in his life and decided there could be few better ways to travel on a lovely summer night. Overhead, the stars drifted past houses and trees in time with the spinning wheels.

Passing through the wall of the Old Palace, the coaches stopped one by one in the crowded courtyard to let off their passengers. Though the grounds and entrance blazed with light, the high towers remained darker than the starlit sky. Hern and her charges followed the prince and princess inside to wait their turn in the receiving line.

"Ferris!" Brizen exclaimed when he saw them. "And Avender, too! Welcome. Hern, I'm so delighted you and your daughter were able to attend. And is this Redburr? I should never have recognized you, old fellow."

The heir to two kingdoms clapped the Shaper on the arm. Redburr grimaced politely in return. Although the prince had grown taller and less boyish since Avender had last seen him, his guileless face remained clear and open. He shook all their hands, but lingered longest over Ferris. Avender watched them so closely he almost missed Baron Sevral's greeting.

The baron's severe face pinched even more sharply. "My wife, the baroness."

"Very pleased to meet you, milady," said Avender.

The baroness's limp hand inside her pale beige glove matched her smile. Avender bowed and moved on. Brizen followed Ferris with his eyes as the party ascended the broad stairs to the King's Hall. A peculiar look passed over the prince's face, as if he had just stepped into a bucket of ice cold water and not even noticed.

The new arrivals found themselves in a looming hall. On a balcony at the far end, musicians sent a soft song swirling above the crowd. Below them, on a raised dais covered in dark red cloth, sat King Brannis. Thick pillars ran down either side of the hall, dividing the room in three. The middle portion was for dancing, which hadn't yet begun, with the outer aisles reserved for watching and drinking punch. Garlands of white lilies dripped from the arches, and bouquets of gladiolas and mums and dogwillow covered the pillars, but the effect only increased the gloominess of the high, vaulted ceiling. Ravenously, the tall darkness swallowed the torchlight.

Hern sniffed. "They haven't done much of a job making the place cheery, have they, Ferris."

"Look at the people, Mother, not the decorations."

More extravagant than flowers, the guests filled the room with bright fields of color. The men looked as brilliant as the women, though the women, with their twirling gowns, took up more space. In their tight pants and stockings, the men revealed more leg, but the ladies, their gowns cut low in front and behind, showed far more shoulder. Ferris's face fell as girls younger than she twirled by in dresses twice as ornate, their busts trussed like the prows of sailing ships, their hair packed with jewels. Settling her shawl more thoroughly over her shoulders, she retreated to the nearest pillar.

"I think you look beautiful," said Avender gallantly.

"Of course she looks beautiful," scolded Hern. "She looks like a real girl, not some trumpery good-for-nothing bedsheet like the rest of them. Ferris, anyone who looks at you can tell you know how to pluck a chicken and beat a rug."

Ferris glared at her mother, who returned the look exactly. Avender couldn't hide his smile, which caused Ferris's scowl to shift his way, his compliment forgotten.

Redburr gathered the last of his strength and wheezed. "Hush, woman. You'll ruin your daughter's good time."

Hern's eyebrows rose. The Shaper took an uneasy step backward. Redburr would pay for that remark the next time he came to Valing, but here in Malmoret the best the steward could do was glare.

A stick thumped loudly on the hard stone floor. The King's Hall fell quiet. In a loud, clear voice that carried the length of the room, a herald announced, "His Majesty requests the ball begin!"

A space cleared in the center of the room. Skirts rustled; new shoes scuffed on worn stone. The king descended from the dais, Princess Arenne's hand held above his shoulder. Except for a long purple plume extending from his wide-brimmed hat, his outfit looked dull beside the princess's reams of silk and buttered gems. They bowed, then stood for a moment side by side, their fingers barely touching. The chief musician snapped his baton forward. Music filled the hall. The king and the princess began the dance.

It wasn't at all the sort of dancing Avender was used to. Neither participant was doing the brisk hopping, head bobbing, or heel kicking he recognized as dancing. Instead they looked as if they were uncertain they had ever been introduced, stepping toward and away from one another with trim, measured paces, their heads and shoulders barely moving. They spent as much time standing still as they did dancing.

Prince Gerrit approached Hern and bowed slightly. "Madame Steward. Would you honor me?"

"I would be delighted, my lord." She held out her skirts in an old-fashioned curtsy.

Ferris rolled her eyes. Her mother paid her no mind. Avender watched the couple proceed out onto the floor and wondered if he was supposed to follow with Ferris. Before he could make up his mind, someone else jumped in before him.

"Um, Ferris, would you care to dance?"

Her face glowing, Ferris placed her hand on Prince Brizen's arm. He led her onto the floor beside his father, where her bright smile tamped the brilliance of every other woman in the room. Avender sighed. His chance had come and gone. He looked around for someone to talk to, but Redburr had vanished in the direction of the nearest punch bowl. With Hern and Ferris dancing, there wasn't another soul in the place he knew.

But not for long. A soft voice startled him and he turned around.

"How well do famous slayers of manders dance? I would be very interested in finding out."

Out of the press of piled hair and glittering gowns came the prettiest girl Avender had ever seen. Although not quite so plain as Ferris's, her lemon-colored dress was far simpler than the billows and buttresses of her peers. Her eyes were dark but her hair was fair, a combination Avender couldn't remember seeing in anyone before. Her bare shoulders were round and smooth.

Accepting his silence as assent, she slipped her gloved fingers into his.

"I, um, I don't know how to dance," he finally managed to say.

"I can teach you."

Other couples followed them onto the floor. Though intricate, the dance was slow enough that Avender recovered easily from his missteps as he learned. He suspected his partner was an excellent teacher.

"Don't you want to know my name?" she asked as he began to catch the pattern.

"Don't you want to know mine?" Vainly, he thought a little cleverness might offset his earlier awkwardness.

"I already know yours." Tiny dimples danced at the edges of her mouth. Avender blushed. Of course she had known who he was. Hadn't she already called him a famous slayer of manders?

"I suppose you'd better tell me yours, then," he said. "Just to make us even."

"My name is Wellin, Avender."

She noticed him glance toward Ferris as the other couple paraded close by. "Your friend is very lucky to be dancing with the prince. Every woman here wishes she were as fortunate."

Avender gathered himself bravely for another try at wit. "Would you believe me if I said I'm luckier than the prince?"

Wellin laughed, a rich laugh for a girl, filled with good fortune for her partner. "No, but you learn quickly, for a country boy. I suppose that's only natural. They say you were raised by Lady Giserre alongside her own son. Is that true?"

"Reiffen was—is my friend."

The music stopped. Wellin regarded her partner with eyes that seemed to observe much more than the brilliant dresses and jewels that filled the hall.

"I have never met Giserre," she said. "But, if she is anything like her brother, I expect she is a stern taskmaster. Come, I claim this next dance with you as well. Do you see, Prince Brizen is ignoring Lady Reiss's mute pleading, to dance again with your friend. Which means I may get no further opportunity to dance with him myself than you may get with her."

Before he had a chance to protest, Wellin whirled him away on the galloping tune. The room spun round, much as the Bavadars did when one rode a tray wildly down the Shoulder on hard-packed snow. Avender caught sight of Ferris and Brizen twirling nearby, their faces brighter than the candles on the walls.

He examined Wellin more closely. She appeared to be his own age, though she sounded much older. But there was no time for talking as the couples bounded round the hall, especially not for beginners trying hard not to tromp on their partners' toes or careen into the other dancers. When they were finished Avender found himself out of breath, his face flushed, and his legs eager for more.

Wellin's shoulders rose and fell; her eyes sparkled. "Look," she said, "your friend seems exhausted. Perhaps we should join them."

Pulling him behind her, she bore Avender off the floor as fresh dancers advanced to pace off a new pavan. Her yellow dress brushed through the other guests like the tip of a fox's tail in a thicket.

Beyond the pillars they found a station where white-gloved servants poured cups of bitter red punch. A crowd had already gathered round the prince, who was busy with a glass in either hand, one for himself and the other for Ferris. Avender despaired of getting any closer than the outer ring, but Ferris spotted him at once. Laughing, she called, "Avender! Come join us!"

He didn't see how he could: the crowd was disinclined to let anyone else near the prince on the word of some chit from the mountains. But Brizen, noting Ferris's desire, opened a narrow way. Avender bulled his way in. Wellin tightened her grip on his hand and allowed herself to be dragged behind him.

"Brilliant musicians, don't you think?" The prince handed glasses round to the new arrivals. "No one plays so well in Rimwich. Though our bards are good, you know."

"I don't like bards," said Ferris, sipping.

"You don't? I love them. Oh, but that's right. The fellow who kidnapped my, um, cousin was a bard, wasn't he? So sorry to have mentioned it."

Avender found the punch far stronger than the cider favored at the Ox and Plow. He thought about how Brizen, who was two years older than Ferris and he, sometimes seemed younger. Following the same line of reasoning, he wondered if that meant Wellin, who seemed so much older, was actually the youngest of them all.

"I am so glad Your Majesty has found something to enjoy in Malmoret. You visit us so rarely." Wellin cupped her glass carefully in both hands, hardly drinking.

Prince Brizen turned reluctantly from Ferris. "Rimwich is the seat of government. You know that, Wellin. As my father's heir, I have to learn my statecraft at his side."

"But do you have to be there all the time? Many of your subjects would adore seeing you more often in Malmoret."

Ferris smiled prettily. Avender saw she had taken an instant dislike to the other girl.

"Why don't you go to Rimwich?" she asked.

"Me?" Wellin looked enchanted at the thought, then sighed

regretfully. "Mother would never permit my going alone. Nor can she take me, as she finds the climate terribly uncomfortable. Too damp in summertime, too cold in winter."

"The Barony of Lansing is in the south, you know," Brizen informed Ferris.

"How unfortunate for you." Ferris gave Wellin a pitying look, then laid her hand on Avender's arm. "Avender, I saved the next dance for you, just as we arranged. I think I'm recovered from that gavotte." She drank the last of her punch and handed her glass to the prince.

"When did we ar—"

"You remember." Her fingers tightened on Avender's arm. "On the way over in the carriage. We discussed it all."

"Dis—"

With an elbow to his ribs, Ferris pushed him away with her through the crowd.

"What was that all about?" he asked as they lined up with the other couples. "Why'd you hit me?"

"To make sure you remember better next time."

The music began. They found themselves in another slow dance that involved a great deal of parading and changing partners. Chances to talk came frequently, but didn't last.

"Remember what?" he asked when he next held Ferris's hand.

"To know when I need rescuing."

"Rescuing from what?"

They changed couples again. Avender found himself dodging the massive coif of his new, shorter partner. Ferris had her own troubles with the woman's doddering husband.

"From the prince," she answered a minute later.

"I thought you liked the prince."

"I do like him—"

His next partner was a matron who wondered whether summer ever came to Valing, and was it true the people lived in huts made of ice that melted every time they tried to have a fire? She didn't seem to care whether Avender answered or not before he was paired with Ferris once again.

"—but he's in love with me," she finished.

"That's plain enough."

"I don't want to encourage him."

Another change. Another round. This time Avender never even noticed his partner.

"Why not?" he asked.

"Because I'm not in love with him, that's why."

"You look like you're enjoying yourself."

She whirled away once more. Avender's heart raced faster than his feet, but neither was swift enough to bring him back to Ferris as quickly as he wanted.

"Of course I'm enjoying myself. It's a ball. But I'd like to have more than one partner for the evening."

"I'll dance with you."

She laughed, her voice rising gaily above the somber music. She meant no harm, but Avender understood it all. Dance with a childhood friend when princes and barons were lining up for the opportunity? Every eye in the hall was fastened on her: Brizen had chosen her over all the rest.

And, when their dance finished, there was the prince waiting for another turn. Ferris cast an imploring look at Avender, but he really didn't know what he could do. It was Brizen's ball. Wistfully he looked for pretty Wellin, but she was already in the arms of a handsome officer. With a smile and a wave she whirled away. Avender turned from the floor and found himself face-to-face with a woman almost as tall as he, and at least as broad-shouldered. Clearly she had come for her turn with the hero from the north. Other girls and women waited behind her. Careful not to show his regret, he bowed and led his tall partner out into the press. By the time they were done he felt as if he had just finished an all-day hike to the top of Whitetooth, banging his shins on every stone along the way.

The music stopped. Another young beauty appeared before him. Ferris glowered from across the floor, but all Avender could offer was a helpless shrug. No doubt his arm would ache as much as his feet by the time Ferris stopped punching him in the carriage.

He had finally begun to get the hang of it when the musicians took a break. Wellin had slipped in as his last partner, which almost made him regret the music's stopping. Gratefully he brought her back to where Hern stood beaming at the side of the pillar. Ferris and Prince Brizen joined them, but there was still no sign of the Shaper. Never had Avender seen the steward look so proud, not even the time Ferris's quilting had managed third prize at the Eastbay Fair. Quilts were one thing, but the son of a king was something else entirely.

"Your Highness," said Wellin as Brizen reached them, "Avender was just telling me he has something important to say to Ferris. Perhaps if you could fetch me a fresh glass of punch." Without waiting for an answer, she wrapped her arm around that of the good-natured prince and escorted him into the aisle behind them.

Hern turned dagger eyes on Avender.

"I never said that," he protested, but his face grew hot because he wished he had.

The steward shifted her irritation toward Wellin, whose back might have begun to bleed had she not already disappeared into the crowd. "Devious little schemer."

"Well, if you didn't say it, I'm glad Wellin did," said Ferris. "I like her much better for it. The next time Brizen makes me dance with him, I'm going to talk about nothing but gorgeous, sensible Wellin."

"Ferris!"

"I want to enjoy this party, Mother. I'm sure we won't be having one like it in Valing any time soon."

"You can be sure Prince Brizen won't come chasing after you, if we do."

"I'm not so sure of that at all."

"Why you have to be so willful, I just don't know." The steward opened her fan with an angry flip and attempted to cool her temper. "It's not as if he isn't nice."

"He's *too* nice, Mother." Ferris tapped a finger against her cheek and studied the room. "He might even be handsome if he'd stand up a little straighter. But look at that tall guardsman over there, and the cavalry officer with the attractive sideburns, and that one with the good-looking legs—"

Hern smacked her daughter with the fan.

"Mother!" Ferris rubbed her shoulder angrily. "What is wrong with you?"

"You were being flip." Hern waggled the fan menacingly under her daughter's nose, reminding Avender of more than one encounter between steward and bear. "I am still your mother, you know. Dance with as many young men as you like, but I'd have thought any daughter I raised would have enough sense to come in out of the rain."

"I'd rather catch cold."

"Say, where's Redburr?" asked Avender, trying to change the subject before mother and daughter came to actual blows.

The musicians began to play again before Hern could answer. There was a quick rush for Ferris, with the guardsman beating out both the cavalryman and the baron with the good-looking legs. Avender, lacking the experience to pick up the musical cue as quickly as the others, found himself last in line once more. Wellin, on the other hand, reappeared with Prince Brizen still attached to her arm. Avender wasn't sure whether he was more jealous of the prince or the guardsman as the young woman soared, light as a feather, across the floor in Brizen's arms.

He had already made up his mind to be jealous of the guardsman, when a husky voice said, "Excuse me, ma'am," from behind his shoulder. He hoped it wasn't the tall, awkward girl again, though her voice hadn't been quite that deep, but she was already dancing with a tall, gaunt baron old enough to be her father.

Turning, he found a footman bowing to the steward.

"If you would follow me, ma'am."

Hern's eyes narrowed. "Where?"

"To the kitchens, ma'am. You are needed."

Neither Hern nor Avender waited to hear more. Redburr had been missing too long. They followed the footman to the far end of the crowded hall, bowing respectfully to Brannis as they passed the dais. Torches lit the gloomy passage beyond, filling the corridor with a sharp, smoky odor. Servants hurried by with fresh trays of food and drink, or brought away the old.

In the kitchen bedlam reigned. Redburr had taken the high ground, perched on top of a tall cupboard. An army of cooks shook their rolling pins and saucepans at him from below. His clothes were in tatters; the buttons on his front had all burst and great swaths of red-haired belly bulged through the rips in his corset. In one hand he held a half-eaten pie, most likely blackberry from the color and consistency of the filling dripping onto the cooks below; in the other was a large slab of cake. The ruined tower that marked the rest of the pastry was now topped by a red wig and broad-brimmed hat. Splotches of custard and cream covered the walls.

"What's going on here!" Hern pushed a pair of cooks out of the way and waded into the scrum. "Redburr! What are you doing up there! Get down this instant!"

The Shaper lolled forward on his perch, his eyes glazed from a surfeit of flour and fruit. Quick as a diving hawk, he heaved his handful of cake at Hern, her plain brown dress suddenly conspicuous in the field of white cookwear. But Hern was quicker and, with a snap of her wrist, caught the flying dessert on her open fan.

"That does it." She shoved the remaining undercooks out of the way and advanced to the foot of the cupboard. Smashed crockery crunched beneath her shoes. For the first time a dash of fear appeared in Redburr's face.

"Get down from there at once," she ordered. "You've had your fun."

The Shaper looked uneasily from side to side as understanding gathered in his eyes. At the back of the room a young scullion, still caught up in the excitement, launched a muffin that burst in a shower of crumbs against the wall beside the Oeinnen.

"That does not help." Hern picked bits of muffin off the front of her dress and glowered into the crowd. The cupboard creaked ominously as Redburr took the opportunity to slide closer to the door.

Hern's attention shot back to the wall. "The only place you're getting is down, mister. I mean it. Unless you want to ruin Ferris's good time completely, Avender is taking you home."

The Shaper could only handle the steward's glare for so long. Setting his pie gently on the cupboard beside him, he set about climbing to the floor.

The head chef, who had worked his way from the back of the crowd to the front once it was apparent that Hern had the situation under control, spoke up at once. "But, madam, my cake! What shall I serve the king?"

"I'll deal with the king." Hern waved the poor man's objections aside. "You must have something here for dessert. We can always make pancakes. And an extra barrel of beer usually helps, too."

"Pancakes!" Aghast, the chef raised his hands to his cheeks, leaving small frosting smudges behind.

"Yes, pancakes. Folks like them in Valing and I'm sure they'll like them here, too. If you want them fancy, we can spread jam on them and roll them up into little tubes."

"Ah, you mean crepes!"

"No, I mean pancakes. Just get me an apron and I'll show you how it's done."

The chef drew himself up stiffly, the tuft of beard at the end of his chin quivering like a pastry brush. "I assure you, madam, crepes are something we can take care of ourselves."

"Really? The same way you took care of him?" Hern nodded over her shoulder at Redburr, who had made little progress trying to reach the ground. Every time he lowered a careful foot, the whole structure tilted dangerously, sending the last unbroken bowls smashing onto the heads of the undercooks below.

"I think he needs a ladder." Avender handed a bowl he had caught to the scullion beside him.

"Someone get a ladder," snapped Hern. "And I still want that apron."

A stepladder was fetched; Redburr transferred himself gingerly from the cupboard. Avender and two footmen held the ladder steady as he descended.

"I hope you're ashamed of yourself." Hern poked the Shaper in the chest with a long spoon once he was safely on the floor. "Now you know why I told Gridlin to send for me if there was any trouble."

The Shaper hung his head and eyed an untouched tray of cupcakes lying temptingly near to hand.

Avender stepped neatly between Redburr and the cakes. "Why do I have to take him home?"

"I have to help here." Her apron tied around her waist, the steward began to roll up her sleeves. "Besides, you don't expect me to let you chaperone Ferris, do you? That's my job." She tapped her chest with her spoon. "Yours is him."

The Shaper sighed. Avender led him toward the door, only to have Hern call them back at once. "Not that way." She waved her spoon in the other direction. "The back door for you. And don't go taking our carriage, either. I don't want Ferris spoiling her dress with blackberry filling. You'll walk if you have to."

A potboy guided them away. They came out of the keep at the side of the courtyard, away from the front of the house. A good-sized tip from Redburr bought them passage in one of the waiting carriages, though the coachman made sure to spread a horse blanket across the seat before he allowed them inside.

Redburr refused to talk at first. Instead he picked grumpily at the bits of cake and frosting in his beard. But he cheered up immensely when Avender brought out the cupcakes he had stolen just before they left.

"It's not like we wouldn't have had a couple anyway when they were served."

"No need to explain yourself to me, boy."

"If you had more self-control, we wouldn't have had to leave."

"True. Then again, maybe I control myself better than you know." The Shaper turned a beady eye on his companion. "But why are you so interested in going back to the ball? It couldn't have been all those young ladies flocking to dance with you, could it?"

"It wasn't so bad," he admitted.

"Of course it wasn't. You should have seen me in my day. Nothing like summer in the woods, especially if the strawberries are out early. Cuff a few rivals, chase a few sows. Of course I'm too old for any of that now."

"Good. Because I really don't want to hear about it."

"No, I don't suppose you would." The Shaper settled comfortably into his seat as the carriage rattled off King's Road into

Nibling Street. "But you know what I'm saying. And Ferris, too. Brizen did have his eye on her, didn't he? Not that she seemed too interested."

"She told me she wasn't interested at all."

"That's probably just the reason he likes her."

"Why would he do that?"

"Sometimes the tastiest honey's in the hardest tree to climb."

"Ferris is different," Avender grumbled.

"As different as Lady Wellin?"

Avender snorted, a little more than necessary, perhaps. "Lady Wellin? She's not like Ferris at all."

"You and Brizen may be the only people at tonight's entertainment who thought that. Though Wellin might have been a lot less nice if she thought Ferris was interested in the prince."

"She should have done a better job of keeping him out of the way then, if she's so interested in him."

"That's the spirit, boy! Have you told her?" Redburr's small eyes twinkled.

"Told who? Ferris? Told her what?"

"You know what I'm talking about. Being coy only works for girls. Males have to come right out and say it. Stand up, boy. Tell Ferris how you feel."

His ears burning, Avender hunched deeply into his seat. "I might have said something tonight," he confessed, "if Brizen hadn't gotten in the way."

"You'll get other chances." Redburr looked past the driver as the carriage pulled through Prince Gerrit's gate. "It's not as if you'll never see her again. Just don't wait too long. And make sure you time it right. I think Hern was afraid Ferris was going to take a swing at the prince tonight, if the fool had said what was on his mind."

A footman helped them from the car. He looked twice at Redburr, not quite certain if this was the same person who had left earlier in the evening. Redburr paid him no notice and, settling his torn jacket more properly around his shoulders, ascended the steps to the villa.

"Aren't you going to clean up?" asked Avender as the Shaper walked past the stairs toward the terrace.

"I'd rather take a dip in the river."

"You know you can't go traipsing through this house all wet, don't you? It's not like swimming in the Hartrush. You're going to need towels and a robe."

Redburr scratched his hairy belly where it rolled out over the top of his pants. Sloppiness was so much less unattractive in a bear. "So bring me some. I'm going swimming."

Grumbling, Avender climbed the stairs. Sometimes it seemed all he ever did for Redburr was fetch and curry. To think he could have been dancing with Ferris instead. Or Wellin.

He had only just started to hunt for a robe in Redburr's room when the Shaper appeared dripping at the door. Somewhere along the way Redburr had lost his jacket, his stockings, and his shoes, and his shirt and breeches were dripping wet. His round stomach was the only thing keeping the torn corset in place.

"If you think Hern was mad at you before," Avender began, "just wait till she hears—"

"Hush, boy."

His broad feet slapped wetly on the floor as Redburr crossed to the window. Separating the curtains with his hand, he peered down toward the river. Avender waited for the Shaper to explain what was going on.

"It's too late now." Redburr let the curtain fall back across the glass. "They've already gone inside. We'll have to see if we can catch them on the way out."

"Catch who?"

With a sly wink, Redburr fell to changing out of his wet clothes. "That's just it. I don't know. But while I was swimming a rowboat started in toward the dock. It stopped when whoever was rowing heard me in the water, but the boat's tied up at the end of the dock now. I only came up so they'd think I hadn't seen them. I'd guess whoever was in it is meeting with Gerrit right now."

"But Prince Gerrit's at the ball."

"So were we, boy. But a man on horseback can go back and forth without being missed at all."

Without bothering to towel himself dry, Redburr pulled on the dirty clothes he had arrived in that afternoon and asked Avender how well he could move in his fancy dress.

"It's only the jacket that's tight," said Avender.

"Then take it off. And your shoes, too."

Barefoot, Avender followed the Shaper out the window. He found the big man sitting on the ledge outside, quietly shaking the leafy vines growing up the back of the house. A thick green scent tickled at his nose.

"This won't hold me, but you're light enough. I'll have to find another way down."

"You want me to climb down the outside of the house?"

"You've done it often enough at the Manor. And there aren't any vines to help you there."

"Then what?"

"Get as close to the dock as you can. I'll be there as soon as possible. But don't do anything but watch, whatever happens."

Avender crawled out the window onto the ledge, his bare toes gripping the rough stone. Climbing down the vine was easy, though the ruffles on his shirt kept catching on the leaves. Too much rustling for a night bird or sleepless squirrel, but no one was around to notice. At the bottom he darted across the wet grass to the river. He was certain it was too dark for anyone to notice him among the flower beds and sculpted shrubs unless he made too much noise, but that meant it was too dark for him to see anyone either. What little light glittered on the dark water came from the brightly lit hall of the prince's villa, still awake for the guests' return.

The Edgewater lapped at the dock posts; a night heron squawked from the reeds. The scent of jasmine and river filled the air. Worming his way closer through the shrubbery along the bank, he wondered how long it would take Redburr to follow.

As Avender's eyes adjusted to the darkness, he saw the boat as an empty smudge at the end of the dock. Nervously he waited for the Shaper to join him. He had no idea what to expect, though he supposed it was some sort of secret meeting. Prince Gerrit had always been suspected as being the leader of the rebel barons, but no one talked much about them anymore. Except for a few pirates in the Toes, King Brannis had rid Banking of all the malcontents in the last few years. Or at least that's what everyone said.

Shoes scraped on the terrace; voices whispered in the air. Avender had no idea whether five minutes or half an hour had passed since he clambered down the vine. His heart raced. Where was Redburr? Three figures, two cloaked from head to toe, appeared on the steps to the garden. The uncloaked man was Gerrit, his fancy dress glittering in the light from the house. The other two figures were unrecognizable, though they looked like men from their height and bearing.

Their footsteps crunched on the path. At the edge of the dock they stopped, not five feet from Avender.

"I look forward to seeing you again, Uncle," said the smaller of the cloaked figures, his voice muffled. Prince Gerrit grasped his hand warmly in both his own.

"And I you, Reiffen," he replied.

Broad fingers clamped over Avender's mouth before he could cry out. "Hush," whispered the Shaper in a voice softer than down. His rough beard scratched Avender's ear. Strong as Avender was, he remained helpless in Redburr's heavy grip. He could only fume, and worry desperately why the Shaper didn't want to try and rescue their old friend. No one knew they were there: surely the two of them could handle Prince Gerrit and the second cloaked figure.

With Redburr's knee jammed into his back, Avender watched helplessly as Reiffen and his companion walked out on the dock. The stranger climbed into the boat first, while Reiffen unfastened the moorings and followed. The blade of an oar flashed briefly in the light from the house; the dark smudge of the rowboat, taller now with two more shadows seated at the oars and stern, pulled slowly away toward the darkness at the middle of the river.

Prince Gerrit returned to his villa. Avender panted savagely against the Shaper's palm.

"Will you be quiet if I let you go?" Redburr allowed the young man enough room to nod. "Good."

The hand and knee were removed. Avender turned on him in quiet fury.

"We could have rescued him!"

"No, we couldn't."

"All we had to do was grab him!"

"He was with Fornoch, boy. The Wizard would have slain us both before we had taken two steps. He may be a coward, but he fights when he has to."

Redburr rose, his broad feet squishing against the soft ground. The sound of oars had disappeared. Avender's anger flailed uselessly at the night. They had been so close.

"We were lucky," said Redburr. "Had I known Fornoch was on the river, I would never have left the house."

"Are you going to tell anyone?"

The Shaper scratched his chin. "It's hard to say. Maybe Brannis.

It's not as if we learned anything new. Everyone knows this was bound to happen sometime. It's why the Three captured Reiffen in the first place. Gerrit is the obvious contact."

"We have to tell Ferris."

"Do we, boy?" The Shaper gave Avender a curious look. "Why does she need to know, above everyone else?"

Avender wondered himself why he had been so quick to think of telling Ferris. "So she finally understands Reiffen is gone."

"And why does she need to understand that? You think that'll make her happier?"

Avender made no reply. The heron cried again, low and throaty like a frog. No one wanted Reiffen back any more than he did, but at least he knew that was no longer possible. The sooner Ferris understood . . .

He didn't dare think any further. Even if Ferris did finally accept the fact that Reiffen was gone, she probably wouldn't think of him any differently anyway.

All the same, he wished he were still dancing with her.

8

The Woodsman

y love is like a woodsman
Who strikes both straight and true
And when he struck my heart was when
I fell in love with you."

The song rang through the trees, the last line cut short by the chop of an ax biting wood. Somewhere a blue jay heckled. Reiffen's boots sank slowly into the soggy moss at his feet as he tried to place the singer in the forest. As easily as he was able to cast the traveling spell now, after nearly four years of practice, he still needed a moment to set himself properly when arriving in a new place.

"The time has come for the pup to prove his mettle," the Black Wizard had said the day before.

"Yes," Usseis had agreed from his plain bench in the spacious throne room. "We have shown enough patience. Now we require proof of progress before continuing. Greater matters will emerge in a year or two, and my brothers and I wish to assure ourselves of your commitment before investing you with further portions of our time."

"It is my intention to fetch an assistant," Reiffen said. Fornoch had warned him a test was coming, and the young man had come to the audience prepared.

"You wish to try your hand at compulsion?" asked the Gray Wizard.

"I do not. Compulsion is a weak tool, and requires too much handling. You show the preference yourself by asking me to take an active part in your affairs."

"Go then," Ossdonc commanded. "Fetch your servant. But do not be gentle."

"Yes," the White Wizard agreed. "We will consider the manner of your obedience as much as its substance. Do not let us down."

Reiffen had hastened immediately to his workshop to prepare the proper spells. Now, at the back side of the Great Forest, he pulled his feet from the clinging mud and started toward the singer, his long cloak brushing the ground. On the other side of the marsh a gray pond glinted through the scrubby pines.

> "My love is like a hammer
> That drives the straightest nail
> But crooked brads still break and bend
> Though measured blows prevail."

Reiffen's goal lay to the right, around the pond. He couldn't see it yet, but he knew it was there. The map of this place lay plain in the memory of a bird's bright eye. And he had examined it briefly from the ground as well, or he would never have been able to use his memory to return in human form. The smell of woodsmoke told him the dogs would not catch his scent because he was downwind. Not that it mattered. Either way, the dogs would be the easiest to kill.

Beyond the marsh he came to a path. Another ax stroke

creased the air. He continued on, knowing what he would find. Halfway to the house a woman's voice skirted through the trees. The chopping stopped. Reiffen halted, preferring to approach the woodsman alone. Voices rustled as the hidden couple spoke; a baby laughed. The blue jay answered noisily. A moment later the sound of the ax carved the woods once more.

In a small clearing at the side of the pond Reiffen found a cabin fashioned of split logs and sod. Thin smoke peeled from the top of its stone chimney. Near the trees a tall man raised his ax for another blow. Firewood, the split sides white as the inside of a fresh apple, gleamed in a pile beside him. A single dog reclined on the ground close by.

Deciding he was too close to the house, Reiffen stepped back into the woods. With a quick *thock,* another log split in two. Reiffen thought for a moment then, with a murmured word, pointed a long finger at the raised ax. The axman swung; the iron head whistled off through the bare trees. The headless haft banged hollowly off its target; the axman dropped the shaft and wrung his hands.

The dog stood, sensing something wrong. Tail high, it sniffed the unsplit log. The woodsman examined his ax handle. Frowning, he peered off into the woods. "Come on, Cooey," he said. "Let's go find that ax head." He offered the shaft to the dog who, after sniffing it, trotted into the forest.

Leaves crackled. Like a small twist of wind, the dog snuffled through the autumn undergrowth. As soon as it came into sight, Reiffen cast his spell. The animal froze, mouth caught in the beginning of a snarl.

The man, already into the woods behind his hound, looked up as the noise of its passage ceased. "Found it, Cooey? Give a call there, will you? I can't find you if I can't hear you."

He stopped when he saw the stranger in his woods. Reiffen

got a clear view of the fellow's face for the first time, but he already knew who the man was.

"Hello, Mindrell," he said.

The woodsman's face tightened. He still held his ax handle, but otherwise was unarmed. Reiffen remembered the bard was very good with a sling, and assumed Mindrell could probably hit him with the ax handle at that short distance if he chose.

"Who are you?" Mindrell asked.

"Don't you remember?"

The man studied him without expression. No sign of recognition appeared in his face, not even when he spoke.

"Reiffen. You've grown, Your Majesty."

Reiffen couldn't help but smile. "You're the same as ever, harper. Insolence before all."

"I find no reason to change. What have you done with the dog?"

"Look to your left. At the foot of the ash. If you move too suddenly I'll do the same to you. And then where would that leave your wife? Or son?"

A grim smirk split Mindrell's face. "I see you've been watching me awhile. I should have known the Black Wizard would give me away. Ossdonc likes treachery even more than killing."

"Ossdonc didn't give you away. The gold hidden in your chimney carries his touch. That's how I found you."

Mindrell snorted. "I should have spent it all. That's what comes from tying yourself down, Your Majesty. Take my advice, never marry."

"It was a melancholy air you were singing."

"I'm a melancholy man." Mindrell shrugged, the easy smile returning to his face. "I suppose you've already picked the way you'll do it. Lightning bolt from the eyes? Turn me into a worm and toss me in the pond?"

"Why would I kill you?"

The bard's arrogance flushed away. Reiffen had said something he hadn't expected. Gathering himself, he forced a final weak grin.

"Is it another song you want? I have to warn you. Except for lullabies and love songs, I'm a bit out of practice. And I left my lute back at the cabin."

Reiffen shook his head. "You can work on your singing in Ussene."

"Ussene?" This time Mindrell didn't bother to conceal his understanding. "You really do intend to pay me back in kind."

Reiffen nodded.

The bard gestured back over his shoulder. "I don't suppose you'll let me take the wife and child."

Reiffen shook his head. A pair of late mallards skittered across the pond, racing for the sky.

"Then there's no reason I shouldn't attack you."

"If you fight me," said Reiffen, "it will go badly for your family."

"What do I care?" Crudely, Mindrell waved away the thought of his wife and child. "You can do what you want to them."

"I can do what I want to them regardless." Reiffen fingered a small pellet from one of the pouches inside his cloak. Now was the time the bard would be most dangerous. Unlike the dog, he would be expecting Reiffen to cast some sort of spell.

The harper tossed the ax handle with a quick, underhand motion that sent the wooden shaft spinning wickedly in Reiffen's direction. At the same time he turned and dashed back toward the house.

"Marte! Marte! Take the boy and run!"

Reiffen stepped to one side and threw his stone. The ax handle spun past him into the trees. Catching Mindrell behind the shoulders, the pebble exploded with a loud bang and a puff of smoke. The blue jay darted upward with a shrill cry; the bard pitched forward on his face at the edge of the forest. A woman appeared at the cabin door, a baby in her arms.

Reiffen strode through the trees. Pausing at the side of the frozen dog he pulled a knife from his belt and slit the stiffened animal's throat. Hot blood gushed across his wrist as the creature collapsed to the ground.

The woman started, and stepped back behind the door as Reiffen appeared in the clearing. The child rested its head on her shoulder.

"Where's my husband?" Her voice wavered.

"Mindrell leaves with me." Reiffen wiped the knife and his bloody hand on his cloak and remembered the other dog was still loose.

"Who's Mindrell? Rowen is my husband's name."

"Know his real name, Marte. Mindrell."

"Why would he go with you?" The woman leaned cautiously out the door and looked from side to side for sign of her husband.

"Because I asked him."

The woman shook her blond head. She was very pretty. Prettier than Ferris, in a soft sort of way, though not nearly as striking. "That's no reason for him to leave."

"Suit yourself." Reiffen crooked his nose at the faint smell of sulfur drifting out of the trees. The bard should remain senseless for a while yet, but there was no sense in dawdling. It was time to go. From another pocket he extracted a lump of poisoned meat for the second dog, and dropped it on the ground.

As he pushed back into the woods, Marte took a step past the threshold of her home. "Rowen?" she called, softly at first, then louder. "Rowen!"

She was still calling when Reiffen grasped the finger on his left hand and, Mindrell draped over his shoulders like a fallen deer, removed the thimble. "Return," he breathed, grunting beneath his burden.

The bard came to his senses shortly after they arrived. Reiffen rubbed his itchy finger and slipped the small gold casket into his pocket.

"Where are we?" Mindrell rubbed his temples, his usual quick irony hammered flat.

"In Ussene."

As his head cleared, the bard took in the books on the shelves around him. With a practiced glance he measured the distance between himself and Reiffen.

"If you kill me," Reiffen said, "you'll never leave this room."

"What did you do with Marte?"

"Nothing."

"Nothing? She won't last the winter without me."

"Not necessarily. They have food and shelter. And I left the dogs to look after them. You can return after you have finished your service."

"When will that be?"

"A year or two."

Mindrell shook his head. "They'll be dead by then. Marte doesn't know the life."

"You should have thought of that before you brought her to the north woods."

The bard looked at Reiffen more closely, as if noticing something new in the cast of the young man's face. "This has come easily to you, hasn't it? Killing my wife and son."

"As easily as drowning Avender came to you."

"Your friend was in the wrong place at the wrong time."

"As were your wife and child."

Mindrell's shoulders drooped. "What is it you want from me?" he asked wearily.

"I need you to guard Giserre."

The harper laughed. "Me? You want me to guard your mother? After what you've done to my wife and boy?"

"I think you'll perform the task admirably."

"I should kill her at the first opportunity."

"Slaying Giserre gets you nothing. You don't strike me as a man who works without pay. Nor one who would allow himself such a dainty as revenge."

Mindrell's voice turned deliberate. "What would you pay me?"

"When the time comes I'll release you from my service. With gold, of course."

Bitterness edged back into the harper's voice. "What will I want with gold if my wife and child are dead?"

"You told me before you didn't care. And I know you only took them to the Great Forest because you owed money to every dicer in Far Mouthing. How long before you would have left them yourself?"

"I admit I was beginning to grow tired of being tied down—"

The bard's face froze unnaturally in the middle of his sentence. Reiffen looked up. The spider hung stone-still by its thread beside the Gray Wizard, who had arrived and cast a spell to hold his pet and Mindrell fast, just as Reiffen had done to the hound in the forest.

"An interesting choice," said Fornoch. "I had thought you would select Avender."

"Mindrell has fewer scruples. Avender would get himself killed much too quickly."

The Wizard picked his way along the wall, the spines of the books flowing behind his gray robe like a rainbow hiding behind a cloud. "He left no one behind?"

"He left a wife and child."

"He left them?"

"I left them."

Fornoch nodded thoughtfully, as if he were learning of this for the first time. Reiffen wasn't fooled.

"There were others to care for them?"

"No. I made certain there was no one else. I even killed the dogs. I didn't tell him that, though."

"Good." The Wizard ceased his pacing and turned back toward the center of the room. "No doubt they shall have a cruel winter before they die. Mistreating Mindrell is one thing, slaying innocents something else entirely. Usseis will find your originality refreshing."

A slow smile spread across Fornoch's face, like blood welling from a wound.

"You have done well. You used Usseis's command for your own purpose, impressing him and furthering your own plans with one stroke. My teaching has fallen on fertile ground. My brother may believe in animating clay, lifting deadness back to an imitation of life, but he has been blind to other methods. If the pupil is taught well enough, and early enough, he may yet surpass the master. And bring forth further masters still. I had worried that you came to us too late, but you have learned well and thoroughly.

"Your reward shall be the freedom to come and go from Ussene whenever you want. Before, your spells would have been blocked. Usseis and I have always watched you. Now that you have proven your worth, you will be left alone. This is even better than that small task you performed for me in Cuspor. Those women never knew they were with child. Mindrell, however, will know his loss."

With a last crooked smile, the Gray Wizard disappeared. Reiffen was left alone with the motionless spider and bard, and what almost felt like a father's blessing. Briefly he toyed with the idea of walking away from Ussene and never coming back, but it was far too late for that. Too much blood was on his hands, and he knew there would be more. Ossdonc and Usseis would never be satisfied with only one trial.

With a word he broke the Wizard's spell. The spider dropped

on its line; Mindrell came unfrozen without ever knowing any time had passed.

"—but even if I had left, I wouldn't—"

"Enough," said Reiffen to his prisoner. "I have no doubt you will do as I ask. It's time you met the rest of our household in Ussene."

"My love is like a barrow
  Where light and life are done
  Without my love there's nothing left
  For me beneath the sun."

The next night, when he was more rested, Reiffen tested his new freedom. After the trials of the previous few days he felt ready for a special treat, one he had been waiting four years for. He thought of traveling full-bodied, as he had to Mindrell's steading, but decided against it. There was no need to shock Ferris too much. And he hadn't yet tried dreamtravel beyond Ussene.

No incantation was needed, no scented room or senses reconstructed. The magic lay in the dreaming. And a moonlit visit would be best anyway. Pulling his sheets and blankets up to his chin, he reached for the memory that was easiest and best.

He woke in a round, dark room. Dust lay thick on the ledges around the empty hearth. Had his footsteps made noise, they would have echoed across the empty chamber like bats dashing between the misted windows. He was home. In the Tear.

The heavy doors creaked as he opened them; he didn't know the magic well enough yet to ignore their presence. Across the half-bridge and up the stairs he strode. The sky opened out above him as he climbed above the wreathing mist, so much more spacious than the sliver of stars glimpsed from his mother's window in Ussene. The gorge rumbled in his legs and ears, throbbing like the heartbeat of a mander.

Pale as a moonbeam he shimmered past the Manor. The path rippled beneath his feet. Windows and porches loomed like the layers of a cake above his head. Round the scullery, along the alley between the kitchen and the stables, he followed the night to the front of the yard. He knew the route well. Avender and he had perfected it before they were ten, after Ferris had demanded they find a way to bring her with them on their late-night forays to the kitchen, or down to the lower dock for a moonlight swim. The handholds were exactly as he remembered them on the trellis by the front porch. His ghostly hands paid no attention to the late-autumn thorns.

He crossed the shingles on the porch roof without a sound. This was always the hard part, inching around the corner of the stewards' bedroom without waking them, to Ferris's room beyond. Empty as moonlight, Reiffen knew this time that would be no problem at all.

The trees in the orchard swayed; something white flickered through the darkness at Ferris's window. Reiffen's heart jumped at the thought that someone might have crept up before him, Avender perhaps. Well, he'd show Avender. The white shape waved again: not Avender at all, but only curtains. Reiffen inched out along the ledge and, grasping the edge of Ferris's window with his left hand, lifted himself inside.

Indecision seized him. He wasn't supposed to be here. Hern had made that quite clear to all of them: sneaking into Ferris's room would not be permitted once they reached a certain age. Lurking in the corner beside her wardrobe, he listened for some sign that someone had heard him. But sneaking around the Manor was nothing like sneaking around Ussene; the only sound was Ferris's soft breathing in the deeper shadow of her bed.

Panes of moonlight squared the bare wood floor. As Reiffen stepped through the glow his body brightened. The shimmer in his form went still. "Ferris," he called softly.

Her nightgown peeped out beneath her quilt, white as the outline of his arm. Her dark hair fanned the pillow beneath her cheek. She was so beautiful. Had he not long since hardened it, Reiffen's heart would have broken then over all he had left behind.

"Ferris," he called again.

The girl stirred dreamily. Her lips were fuller than he remembered, her cheekbones higher in her face. He decided that dreaming was the best way for her to think she was seeing him. Pressing her shoulder gently, he called her name a third time.

"Ferris."

"Mmmmm." Ferris rubbed her cheek more deeply into her pillow and stretched. "Not now, Mother," she murmured in a voice older than he remembered. "It's too dark."

"It's Reiffen, Ferris. Not Hern."

Her lashes fluttered like moths beside her nose. "Reiffen?" she said sleepily. "You're not supposed—"

She sat up sharply, the quilt sliding from her shoulder. A tremble of fear lifted across her face. "Reiffen?"

"Shh." Reiffen lifted a pale finger to his lips. "It's just a dream. I'm not really here."

"You look like you're here." Ferris pulled the covers back across her nightgown and shrank into the bed until her back was against the wall.

"I'm dreaming, just like you are. I'm asleep in Ussene and dreaming. Here." He held out his pale arm. Away from the moonlight the lines of his shape flickered once again.

"You look like a ghost," said Ferris, reaching a fearless hand to touch his arm.

"I'm not a ghost. I'm as alive as you. Just not here."

Her fingers passed through the spot where Reiffen's arm was supposed to be. Instead of recoiling, she waved the top of her hand back and forth through his empty form. He wondered how it was he could press her shoulder to wake her, but she couldn't touch him.

"You are a ghost," she said, leveling him with her eyes. "I'm going to call my father."

"Don't." Reiffen drew back to the other side of the room. "If you call Berrel, I'll go away. I didn't come to see him."

"That's obvious. If you'd come to see him you wouldn't be sneaking around my bedroom. You know you're not supposed to be here." Her eyes narrowed and she pulled her blanket more tightly around her throat. "And how do I know it's you, anyway?"

"I knew how to climb up here, didn't I?"

"Fornoch could easily have sent you flying in through the window. I don't know much about ghosts, but if I can't touch you, how were you able to climb up here?"

Reiffen shrugged; milky ripples flowed up and down his body, bumping into one another and finally shuddering to a stop around his waist. "I don't know much about ghosts either. This is the first time I've ever been one."

Even in the shadow by the wall, Reiffen could see Ferris's face grow curious. "The first time? It really is you, Reiffen, isn't it? No Wizard would say that. Are you learning a lot of magic?"

Reiffen knew he couldn't tell her everything. "Lots. Most of it's not very nice. But I know how to move myself here and there around Ussene, and how to listen to mice talking. I can even throw a fire bolt."

"Can you teach me?" Without dropping her quilt, Ferris leaned forward from the wall.

"Not here. Not like this. And I'm not taking you back with me."

"I should hope not. Is it horrible?"

Reiffen nodded. This time the ripples faded not much beyond

his shoulders. Somehow, despite there being nothing there to feel with, a lump formed in his empty throat.

"Is Giserre all right?" Ferris asked.

"Yes. If I'd left her in Valing she'd have been more miserable than I."

"Have you taught her any spells?"

"Mother doesn't want to have anything to do with magic." He didn't mention the Stone. "She's helping the slaves instead."

"I'd rather learn magic."

"Some day I'll teach you."

Gathering her quilt around her shoulders, Ferris shook her head and settled against the wall. An open window was good for sleeping in late autumn, but not for sitting up in bed in the middle of the night. "No, you won't. When you come back it will be with armies and swords. The Three have you now. I don't want to learn magic from you."

"It won't . . ." Reiffen began. Then he stopped.

"Won't what?" asked Ferris.

"Nothing." But it had occurred to him that, no matter how much he might want to, telling Ferris about his plans would be the wrong thing to do. She would never be able to keep the secret. She would tell Avender, at the very least, and then one of them would tell Redburr, and then it would be just as if the whole world knew.

"Tell me," she insisted, clasping her folded knees as she leaned forward once again. "It sounded like it was important."

"It wasn't."

"I don't believe you."

Reiffen shrugged again. It was no use arguing with Ferris, but that didn't mean he was going to tell her.

Recognizing that Reiffen was shut tight as a mussel, Ferris tried another tack.

"So, why did you come here, if you're not going to tell me

why I should learn magic from you? Why'd you visit me instead
of Avender?"

"Because I miss you more than him. I miss you more than
anyone."

"That's because you took Giserre with you."

Ferris, seeing she had scored a hit of her own to match Reiffen's unwillingness to finish what he had started saying, lost most
of her irritation.

"Avender and I went to a ball in Malmoret last summer," she
went on. "It was wonderful. I danced with everyone, even your
cousin. He's not such a bad fellow, you know, though he is terribly moony."

"I wish I could have danced with you."

Ferris's chin dipped shyly in the face of Reiffen's admiration.
"I'm glad you came to visit me," she said. "Even if it is only a
dream."

"Yes," said Reiffen. "A dream is all it is."

"Will you come back again some time?"

"I hope so."

Ferris hugged her knees closer. "We can pretend you never
went away."

"It would only be pretend."

"I won't mind. I'll even pretend, when you come back for
real, that it won't be with armies and swords. Everyone else be-
lieves you're lost. But not me."

He almost told her everything then, all his hopes and plans.
She was better than his mother: Giserre had to believe in him because he was her son. Ferris believed because she wanted to.

But he didn't. Kings must bear their own burdens, he told
himself, especially if they never become kings.

The moon passed behind a cloud.

"Good-bye," he said.

No longer having the heart to make his way back through all

of Valing, Reiffen allowed his dream to die away. His moonbeam outline faded. Ferris leaned forward on her knees, her dark hair falling across her shoulders. The Manor disappeared.

He slept late the next morning and woke to the sound of Mindrell singing for Giserre and Spit in the next room, the bard's voice mournful as a loon's.

> *"My love is like an oak tree*
> *That thickens round with age*
> *And when you cut it down the stump*
> *Shows rings for every stage."*

AVENDER

She found herself in the Wizards' lair
In the cold and the filth and the sickly air
With her son who was caught in the Wizards' snare
Alas for the fate of Giserre.

Her only friends were a slave named Spit
And a bard who was known for his crimes and wit
Oh can you imagine the shame of it!
Alas for the life of Giserre.

—MINDRELL THE BARD

9

A Whiff of Danger

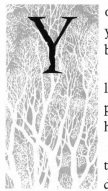ou know," said Avender three years later, "I like you a lot better when you're almost anything but a dog."

"Really?" Redburr sniffed at a dead bush and lifted his leg. "Why's that? I think I make a pretty good dog. And it's a lot better than being human."

Tail wagging, the Shaper trotted on through the dry brush. To the right a steep slope led down to a dusty road; on the left the hillside rose to a ridge just above Avender's head. Two days' march to the south, a Banking troop waited for them to bring back news of the enemy's activity. But the Wizard's patrols had withdrawn, and Avender and Redburr had been forced to push ever closer to Ussene to learn what was happening. Another few leagues would bring them to the gates of the fortress itself.

Another bush caught the Shaper's attention. Avender waited as Redburr sniffed right and left, and right and left again.

"Soldiers?" The young man peered at the low ridges of the hills around them.

Redburr shook his head, his pink tongue swinging back and forth beneath his jaw. "Jackrabbits."

"We're not scouting for jackrabbits."

"If I caught one, I could ask it lots of questions."

"We already know you can't catch jackrabbits, or any other kind of rabbit. You're too fat."

Exactly like a dog, Redburr went back to what he was doing. He crisscrossed the trail, covering two and three times as much distance investigating the dusty ground as Avender did scanning the scrubby slopes on either side. These northern hills, and the higher crags looming beyond, were far different from the peaks the young man was used to. Where the Bavadars were white and green, each color waxing and waning with the season, here in the north everything was always brown and dry.

For another hour they crept deeper into the hills, finding nothing but the occasional quail bursting from the brush and the tracks of last night's mice in the sand. Three ravens, wings working heavily, rose past the shoulder of the hill ahead and into the low, gray sky. Avender dropped to the ground.

Redburr froze. "Rowrr. What do you see?"

"Three ravens. Flying toward us along the road."

"Did they see you?"

"I don't think so."

The birds winged away south between the hills, their flight slow and deliberate. Redburr sniffed the air. His pointed ears lifted.

"Anything?" asked Avender.

"Not enough wind for smelling. And the hill's in the way for listening. But I'm sure there's something coming."

Avender crawled forward to a point where he could see the empty road. Sensing movement at the top of the far ridge, he examined its crest. Nothing. But, as soon as he looked back at the road, the movement returned at the edge of his vision. Yes, there it was, a man walking just below the edge of the hill. Another followed over the rise.

"Two men on the far hill," he whispered to the Shaper. "Scouts by the look of them."

Redburr licked his sharp yellow teeth. "It's about time we found someone. What about on this side? If they're flankers, there should be a patrol over here as well."

Avender scanned the slope above but was too low to the ground to see anything. Carefully he rose to a crouch, well aware that any sudden movement would draw the attention of the men across the valley as surely as he had been drawn to them. From the vantage of his knees he still saw no one on their side of the road.

Redburr growled softly. "I don't like it. If it's just a patrol, they wouldn't be watching the road. They'd either be on the road or in the hills."

"Maybe you should investigate." Avender dropped back down slowly beside the dog. "You can get up the hill without being seen more easily than I. And if you don't find anyone, you can see what's on the other side."

The Shaper slunk off into the bushes. Avender snaked down to a spot that commanded both a good view of the road and the other side of the dry valley, then settled in to watch from behind a brittle bush. Rocks prodded his ribs and knees.

A third man joined the two on the far hill, the feathers in his hair standing out against the gray sky. Stretched out in a line, the Keeadini patrol worked its way along the side of the ridge. Avender readied himself to lie there all day, if that's what it took to learn what might come down the road behind them.

No sooner had he dug himself in than he heard voices on the hill above. They spoke in the lilting cadence of the tribesmen, whose language Avender had learned only a little of on previous trips with Redburr to the Waste. But there were many tribes and dialects in the plains and, though he thought he heard them say something about a dog, he understood nothing else. He didn't dare move to see where they were, but it was only a matter of time before they crossed his trail and began to hunt him down.

His attention shifted to the dusty highway. Something was approaching around the side of the brown hill. His hands gripped the dry earth as two horsemen bearing black banners rode into view. Behind them a horde of sissit mobbed the valley, their mattocks and spears spiking the air like a weedy field. The tramp of their feet and the jangle of their metal harnesses rang clearly down the narrow valley. Avender wondered if he would have the chance to see how many there were before he was flushed from his hiding place. Already it looked like the vanguard of an entire army.

A shout pierced the air behind him. Avender decided the time for hiding was over. Like a startled buck, he leapt to his feet and raced toward the top of the ridge. A second cry followed the first, and he caught a quick glimpse of two Keeadini scouts unslinging their short bows as he bounded up the slope.

Five quick strides, his back feeling more exposed with each one, and Avender darted off at an angle to the right. Almost at once he changed direction again. An arrow burrowed into a bush beside him. He shifted direction a third time, pounding uphill all the while. Two more shots whistled past his legs. The ground grew steeper. Leaning forward, he used the bushes to pull himself along. The short Keeadini bows had little range; if he could only keep up his speed for a few more yards they would have to chase him. He hoped there wasn't a third scout to head him off on the other side of the ridge.

Another short valley opened before him as he stumbled to the top of the rise, a higher hill beyond. Speed was all that mattered now. He needed to put enough distance between himself and the scouts to be out of reach of their arrows by the time they topped the hill.

He raced down the other side. The slope was steep enough

that every step threatened to send him head over heels into the ragged gully at the bottom. Leaping bushes and dodging stretches of loose rock, he kept to the flatter sections as best he could, angling south. A straight descent after the first few strides would have been suicide. His footsteps ruffed rapidly against the dirt; his breathing huffed. He heard nothing of his pursuers, but knew they had not given up the chase.

At the bottom of the hill he took a quick glance over his shoulder, but saw no one. Other scouts and sissit would be joining the hunt, trying to cut him off to the north and south. Thighs straining, he bore off up the next hill. With a final burst of effort, he scrambled the last few yards over the crest. Chest heaving, he crouched against the side of the ridge and looked back.

He spotted the first two pursuers easily. One was following his trail closely, but the second had angled down the valley, already cutting off his retreat to the south. As Avender watched, the one immediately below him slowed, wary of any trap Avender might be preparing on the other side of the rise. But the man was farther away than Avender had expected. Like a good hunter, he was willing to let his quarry exhaust itself while he and his partners conserved their own energy. What they didn't know was that Avender had spent most of the last five years following a bear around every forest and mountain in the three kingdoms. It would be a long time before he was exhausted.

He surveyed the rest of the ravine. He still couldn't find the third Keeadini he supposed was working with the first two, but he did notice three sissit top the ridge behind them. Their pale skin gleamed like bones against the dry brown hillside. Avender guessed a company had been dispatched south to make sure he was driven farther north and west into the hills. When a third group of trackers crested the ridge to the north, Avender understood it was time to go. Ossdonc, or whoever else was in charge, was making every effort to prevent his escape.

He turned north. A small cliff blocked the ridge in that direction. If he got behind it, anyone pursuing him from the other side would have to loop farther north, or double back to the south, to regain his trail. That would put them as far behind him as the scouts who had flushed him out in the first place. The only question was whether or not the third Keeadini was already on the other side of the cliff.

Either way, it was his best chance. There was still no sign of Redburr. Avender rolled back from the edge of the hill and wondered if the Shaper had gone north or south. Not that it mattered. The dog could circle all of them three or four times without anyone knowing the difference. It was up to Redburr to find Avender, not the other way round.

Crouching, he worked his way back up the ridge until he was sure no one could spot him from the other side. He made no effort to hide his trail. The Keeadini scouts would see him anyway once they came over the hill. Unslinging his bow as he jogged along, Avender fitted an arrow to the string, just in case he found the missing scout. Already he felt better for his short rest.

A shout from behind told Avender the Keeadini following him had come over the top of the ridge and discovered his change in direction. He had expected that. What he hadn't expected was to find the third scout sprawled across the brush in front of him at the same time. The man lay awkwardly across a patch of open ground, the earth darkening at his throat. A low snarl came from a clump of bushes nearby.

"Redburr?"

The hidden dog growled. "Go on up the ridge, boy. I'll lie here. If the next one comes by alone I'll take care of him, too. Then we'll really have a start on the rest of them."

With a last look at the dead tribesman, Avender started up along the base of the cliff. He had seen dead men before but wasn't yet so hardened that the sight failed to bother him. He concentrated on his running, keeping his pace as fast as possible without any real strain, wanting to keep a reserve of strength for any sudden need. His heart thumped; his breathing came steadily and full.

Several minutes passed before he heard growling and fresh shouts of alarm. He didn't bother to turn around. The Keeadini would be all the more eager to catch him now, having lost two of their number. But they would also be more careful, which would slow them down.

From the top of the ridge he descended westward. There were no paths, but the coarse sage was sparse enough that any way was easy. If he went north he would likely run into more sissit sent to cut him off, and south was the direction they expected him to take. Only by pushing deeper west could he be sure of getting farther away. Redburr would let him know if he thought they should follow another plan.

He found the Shaper waiting for him at the top of the next ridge. The dog lay in the thin shade of a shrub, his pink tongue dangling. Bounding to his feet, he trotted along lightly beside the man.

"You can slow down a bit," he barked. "They've settled in for a long chase. You're starting to pull away."

"Isn't that what we want?"

"No need to overdo it. You'll never outrun them completely. Just keep up a steady pace for about an hour while I run on ahead. By the time you reach me I'll have shifted into something else. I'll think of what by the time I get there."

"What if I can't find you?"

"Follow my tracks."

"The Keeadini will be following them, too, you know."

"That's what I want them to do, boy."

With a wink from one of his dark eyes, Redburr quickened his gait and pulled away. His red coat darted through the bushes and disappeared over the top of the hill. By the time the next valley opened up in front of Avender, there was no sign of his companion except paw prints in the dry earth. He took a moment to scan the hills behind him for Keeadini and found three descending the far ridge. Other bands would be widening the net to the north and south, traveling in groups now to avoid being picked off by the dog.

He continued on. The northern mountains smudged the distance, gray peaks blurred by the hazy sky. Around him the hills grew longer and steeper. To focus on something other than his aching legs and chest, Avender tried to guess what shape Redburr would take when he found him again. He really hoped it would be a horse. Then he could get off his tired feet and leave their pursuers behind. But, if Redburr thought they were going to have to fight, he might switch back to being a bear. His natural state was always best for fighting. Even manders had problems with Redburr when he was a bear.

Certain he had gone well past Redburr's hour, Avender finally reached the end of the Shaper's tracks. He found himself on the back side of another ridge, perhaps twice his height below the crest. Except for a tuft of red dog hair on a yellow sage, and an area that looked as if it had been brushed by a dog's tail, there was no sign of the Shaper at all. Frowning, Avender wondered if he should continue on. Had Redburr changed into a bird and flown away?

He started on down the hill.

"Psst! Not that way."

Avender looked back toward the spot he had just left. "Where are you?"

"Under the bush by the flat rock. How close behind are they?"

"The same as before."

"Good. We won't have long to wait."

Avender took a step forward. "What have you turned into? A rock?"

"You know I can't do rocks. If you can't see me, it means they can't either. Now listen, this is what I want you to do."

Avender listened patiently as Redburr described his plan. "What if they shoot as soon as they see me?" he asked when the Shaper was done.

"They won't," Redburr's voice assured him from the bush. "They'll want you alive, for questioning. You watch, they'll be very cautious when they approach. Just make sure your knife is close to hand."

Hardly convinced, Avender nonetheless did as he was told. Redburr had, after all, survived more generations than Avender could count. He found a suitable rock and lay down beyond it, twisting his leg as much as he could to make it look injured. Knife in hand, he lay with his right arm caught awkwardly behind his back, his eyes open just enough to allow him to peer through his lashes.

Gradually his breathing slowed. His heart, however, pounded as hard as ever. Sweat muddied the dirt beneath his ears. A minute passed, and another. The longer he waited, the more his nervousness increased. A scorpion scuttled out from under a rock and crossed the ground beside him, its tail coiled.

The first nomad appeared on the ridge, silhouetted against the dingy sky. An arrow notched to his bow, he stopped short at the sight of Avender lying on the ground and held up a warning hand for his comrades. For a long time he studied the brush around his fallen quarry. Then, motioning for his companions to follow, he started down the slope.

"Watch out for the dog," he said in Keeadini clear enough for Avender to understand.

Avender tightened his grip on the knife behind his back. The other two scouts followed their leader over the crest of the hill. Certain his slightest move would result in an arrow to the chest, Avender hardly dared breathe. The first tribesman came right up to his fallen quarry and kicked him hard, an arrow still pointed at Avender's heart. Avender groaned at the blow and opened his eyes.

He wasn't sure what happened next. Something rattled in the brush behind the first Keeadini. The other two looked to see what had moved. Avender heard two quick hisses, almost like a nokken spitting water. The trailing scouts screamed and dropped their bows to claw at their eyes. The one in the lead turned to see what was the matter and in that same instant Avender lunged forward, burying his knife in the man's chest. The Keeadini scout grabbed weakly at the blade and pitched forward to his knees. Avender pulled his knife free, his jaw clenched against the rasp of metal on bone. The dead man fell facedown in the earth. The other two nomads writhed on the ground, their hands still scrabbling at their eyes.

"Finish them," ordered Redburr. "I can't do it myself."

Avender's nose told him why. He burst into a fit of coughing even as he unshouldered his bow. Trying hard not to think about what he was doing, he put an arrow into each man. At his feet a large skunk marched back and forth, its black and white tail still upright.

"Well done," said the Shaper. Avender stepped back from the bodies and took several quick gulps of fresh air, more than he might have needed just to clear his nose of the skunk's burning spray. He had never killed a man before and now that he had he wanted to get down on his knees and retch. But there wasn't time. Thrusting his blade into the earth, he wiped it clean on his thigh.

The Shaper started back up the slope the way they had come.

"Let's go," he said. "Our best chance is to double back again. We can slip south between the road and our pursuers before they figure out what's happened. Don't stand up! The whole point is to make sure we're not seen."

"Won't the others have heard the shouting?"

"Not unless they're already on this side of the ridge. Which they aren't. Now come on."

Avender crawled up the hill behind, and a little to the side, of the skunk.

"You made me lie there out in the open when all you were was a skunk?" he whispered.

"It worked, didn't it? You can't do everything with brute strength."

"But what if you'd missed?"

"I perfected that technique a long time ago, boy. There wasn't a chance I'd miss."

Avender was still shaking his head incredulously when they reached the top of the ridge. Pausing, they looked right and left for any sign of other pursuers. Another three men were visible to the north, but it took Avender a while to find anyone south of them. Neither party showed any awareness of their fellows' fate.

"Do you think that's all there are?"

Redburr wiggled his small black nose. "There might be more to the south. But that's the way we have to go. We have to get back and tell Worrel the war's begun. And Brannis."

"Are you sure that's what this is?"

"Yes. I had a good look at that column before the Keeadini scouts flushed you out. Five thousand spears, at least. You didn't leave me time to see the end."

"I didn't have much choice."

"I know." Redburr scratched at the base of the nearest shrub but pulled up nothing more than dirt and twigs. "Our choices are likely to keep lessening for some time. Right now we need to concentrate on getting out of here. We'll lie low a little longer. Tell me what you see."

"It would have been a lot easier if you'd just turned into a horse. Then we could have outflanked them in no time."

"Yes, and be caught when I had to rest. This isn't horse terrain, boy. Now they'll never figure out what happened back there. They'll be wondering for a month how you managed to get a skunk to help set up your ambush. And it'll make them think twice about what you're capable of, too. Besides, if I were a horse, I'd have to carry you. This way you can carry me."

"That's not going to happen. You're a lot bigger than the average skunk."

"True. But I can't run any faster than the average skunk. If we have to run for it, I trust you'll make sure I escape."

Avender snorted, but didn't reply. After all, Redburr could have run off on his own as a dog any time. They waited a little longer, but found no sign their pursuers had figured out what had happened. Satisfied his plan was working, Redburr led them south along the ridge, their path just below the crest of the hill. That way Avender could watch the hills around them for any sign that the enemy had found their trail again. Often Redburr used his fluffy tail to brush away the signs of Avender's passage, just to confuse the Keeadini even more. It would be some time before the scouts noticed their quarry was heading south through country the hunters believed they had already scoured, if they ever noticed it at all.

They hadn't gone far when they realized the skunk really couldn't keep up. Avender's long strides ate up the distance even when he wasn't running. Reluctantly, he lifted Redburr onto his shoulders, where the Shaper soon fell fast asleep. His purring was oddly soothing and, as evening rose and the air cooled, the young man was glad of his fur collar. Despite his fatigue, he knew he would be moving south all night. In the darkness, as long as he kept below the ridgeline, there was little chance of being spotted. With any luck they would be back on the plains by the next afternoon, well ahead of the Wizards' army.

The land, so lifeless during the day, came awake at night. Small creatures rustled through the sere brush. Night birds called across the darkness. Near midnight Redburr woke and nipped at his friend's fingers, telling Avender to put him down. Not as nimble as a cat, the skunk thumped awkwardly against the cold ground and stretched. Avender stepped out of the way, wary of possible accidents.

After learning there was still no sign of pursuit, the Shaper called a halt. Avender found himself a stretch of ground without too many rocks and settled down to rest. The skunk padded softly toward him, his white stripe gleaming in the starlight.

"What do you think you're doing?" asked the Shaper.

"Taking a nap. Isn't that why we've stopped?"

"No. I have to make another shift. You have to stand watch. What do you think I should be this time?"

"I don't suppose you'd consider becoming a horse?"

"I hate being a horse. Might as well be a slave. The choices are bear or eagle."

"If you're an eagle you'll be able to get the news back to Sir Worrel faster."

"True. But I'll also be leaving you alone."

"I'm sure we're well past the enemy's patrols by now."

Redburr snuffled along the ground, tracing the trail of some roving beetle in the dark. "True. But I still don't like the idea of leaving you."

"It wouldn't be the first time. I'll be okay."

"Ferris would skin me alive if I lost you, too."

"It wouldn't be your fault any more this time than it was with Reiffen."

"It's not the guilt that worries me, boy. It's the skinning. Crossing Hern was bad enough, but I'm afraid Ferris is three times worse."

"Prince Brizen can worry about that."

Redburr cocked a glittering eye. "Now, you know that's your own fault. I told you to speak up years ago. You need a good talking-to, but this isn't the time. You have to keep watch while I change."

Grumbling, Avender got back to his feet. He could hardly keep his eyes open, but that wouldn't matter to the Shaper. All the same, he was glad this wasn't the time for a talking-to. It wasn't his fault Ferris didn't like him the way he liked her. She didn't like Brizen, either, but everyone assumed she would give in eventually. Especially now the war was about to begin and Reiffen would have to show his true colors. Avender remembered the last time he had seen his friend, cloaked with Fornoch in Prince Gerrit's garden. No one could live seven years with the Three and come away unaffected. Not for the first time, he wished Redburr would let him tell Ferris what they had seen. At least that way she would be warned.

Taking a few steps into the brush, Avender looked out at the night. The rising moon peeped thinly through a cleft in the clouds. Except for the shuffle and grunt of Redburr settling himself, the sounds of the darkness remained as regular as breathing.

Half dreaming, Avender thought of home. Memories like windborne leaves whirled through his mind. The lake breeze curling Ferris's hair. The way her cheek glowed red beside a fire. Sighing, he turned and picked his way back through the shadowed brush toward the Shaper. He had never witnessed Redburr shift and knew of no one who had. Usually the Shaper changed privately, which was only natural. At no other time was Redburr so vulnerable. Thousands of years into his life, it was safe to assume the Oeinnen had not grown so ancient by taking chances.

The moon's dim radiance dipped lightly across the land. At first Avender made out nothing in the shadow where the Shaper lay, only vague lumps that seemed to shift and move, as if two or three small children were playing beneath a blanket. The light wasn't strong enough to make out any detail. Whatever he was looking at was already much larger than a skunk, or even a large dog. And it was hard to tell where Redburr's lumps ended and the bushes around him began. For a while longer he peered into the gloom, hoping to see the reflection of moonlight in an eye or even a long claw.

An owl's wings flapped heavily in the dark; the scent of sage wafted up the hill in the stillness. But from Redburr's recess came no sound, no matter how hard Avender strained in the darkness.

When he finally did hear something he backed away, quickly alert. The last time he had greeted Redburr shortly after a change had been a near disaster, and he had no desire to repeat the experience. Patiently he waited for some clearer sign the Shaper was done, the screech of his eagle voice or the sight of the bird waddling out of the bushes. Instead there was a loud cracking, as if something heavy had just rolled over a tree, and a large shape appeared against the sky. Shrubs shook as the bear waddled forward, his eyes gleaming in the moonlight like small stars.

"So. You decided not to turn into an eagle after all," said Avender.

"You still think like a cub," came the gruff reply. "Even if you are full grown."

"You just figured out there's nothing around here tall enough to get a really hefty eagle into the air, didn't you?"

"I could always have turned into a pigeon, boy. But don't thank me. I'm just a friend."

"I'd have gotten back to camp fine on my own."

"I'm not saying you wouldn't. But my mind'll be easier, this way. An extra few hours won't change the world."

The bear turned, his massive backside blocking out half the night sky. Even in the moonlight there was something comical about the way his heavy fur rolled back and forth on its cushion of fat with every step he took. All the same, Avender had to stretch his own legs to keep up as they resumed their journey, the low hills finally starting to flatten before them.

10

Across the Waste

A thin rain was falling when they met the first of Sir Worrel's outriders the next afternoon. The horseman galloped forward when he saw them, his jaw dropping at the sight of the bear. Water dripped from his unshaved chin as he pulled his mount to a stop, leather harness creaking. Avender remembered his name was Keln, one of the younger troopers.

"What happened?"

"I had to do some shifting," said Redburr, his fur matted and wet as the grass beneath the horse's hooves.

"The sissit are on the march," added Avender.

The rider's eyes lit up. "Sissit? How many?"

"Keeadini scouts found us before we had a chance to count them."

The rider nodded and gestured toward the west. "The tribes are on the move, too. Borne's patrol rode in yesterday with news they've crossed the Westing."

"The battle begins," growled the bear.

Keln spat on the grass. "Let them come. We're ready."

They left the trooper to continue his circuit and walked on to camp. Neither tents nor fires marked the trampled grass, only a line of picketed horses and a circle of men and saddles at the bottom of a shallow swale. The horses cropped the turf contentedly; the men huddled stoically under cloaks and blankets.

Every dog in camp bounded forward as they scented the wet bear, their tails wagging furiously.

"Rowr," greeted Redburr.

"Woof," answered the dogs.

"None o' them ever gonna be any good for huntin' now," remarked a trooper.

The dogs nipped and snapped like playful puppies at the return of their sire; the Shaper broke into a series of barks and howls.

> "Ruff grr growl!
> Arf yip yowl!
> Woof bark bow!
> Bow wow wow!"

"What was that?" Avender draped a blanket over his head as the dogs yowled joyfully.

"Dog poetry," said the bear.

"Dog poetry?"

"That's what I said." The Shaper cuffed a mongrel tugging too affectionately at his ear. "It's one of my favorites, 'Hound in the Manger.'"

Sir Worrel came forward, his weathered face more creased than usual. More than Keln, he knew Redburr's appearance as a bear signaled change, and probably not for the better. "Borne's returned," he said, after the Shaper finished describing what they had learned at the edge of the mountains. "And Affen came in just before you."

"Keln gave us Borne's news," Redburr replied. "What of Affen's?"

"Affen found nothing. Not a single hunting party despite wissund herds all along the Easting."

"Wissund and no tribesmen?" Redburr shook his shaggy head, spraying the excited dogs. "They must all be headed for Backford."

"They are." Sir Borne pushed forward among the gathered men. "I never saw so many tribes, not all at once like that, and no feuding either. They sense this is their time." The troopers around him nodded agreement, their manner easier with their officers this far out on the frontier than it ever would have been in Malmoret.

"Which it will be, if I don't get word to Brannis quick enough."

"Backford has already been warned, Sir Redburr," said Sir Worrel. "I sent riders the moment I heard Borne's news. Your tidings won't help the baron ready his defense any quicker."

"How soon do you follow them?"

The captain glanced thoughtfully at the sky. The clouds weren't dark, but the rain from the low, gray roof was steady all the same.

"We'll leave now," he said. "We can ride all night, if the clouds clear. How far behind do you think the sissit are?"

"At least a day. But they won't move nearly as quickly as you."

"All the same, I don't want my retreat cut off by the tribes. Not if this is an all-out attack."

"It is." Absently, the bear furrowed the dirt in front of him with his heavy claws. "But the Keeadini are as wary of the Three as anyone. Usseis was stealing their children long before he stole any of yours. They'll make no move on their own."

"The tribes have little love for us, regardless of their relations with Ussene," answered Sir Worrel. "Even if they don't join with Usseis, they'll flock across the Tumbling like crows on corn if Backford is breached. They've been waiting generations for an opportunity like this."

"Then hurry home and make sure they have to wait another dozen." Redburr's massive shoulders rolled as he started forward. "In the meantime, I'm for Rimwich."

The circle of men parted to open a path for the bear.

"Hold on," said Avender. "I need to get some fresh provisions before we go."

The Shaper turned his heavy head back toward his companion. "Did I say you were coming with me?"

Avender started in surprise. "You're going alone?"

"I am. Neither you nor anyone else will be able to keep up with me. I'm not going far as a bear. Don't worry, though. I'll meet you in Backford before the fighting starts. I figure it'll take at least a week."

Accompanied by the dogs, the bear trotted up out of the swale and off into the prairie. The horses started nervously as he passed, but their hobbles kept them from bolting. Several troopers hurried out to calm them and call back the dogs. Avender remained in the hollow, the rain trickling down his face. The possibility he and Redburr might be separated had not occurred to him. Though he was older now, and had seen and done many things in his years with the Shaper, he still felt empty and alone at the sight of the retreating bear. He was an outsider here, even if he might soon be fighting battles beside these men. And all his training had been for solitary scouting, not battles on horseback or in stony keeps.

Keln clapped a friendly hand on Avender's shoulder. "We'll ride together, you and I," said the trooper. "With any luck, we'll even kill a Waster or two."

"It's not tribesmen I'm worried about." Avender nodded back toward the north. "It's what's behind us. The Wizards will bring magic with them. And other things."

Keln followed Avender's gaze. "Let them come. We've beaten them before and we'll beat them this time, too."

Avender made no answer. He kept his eyes on the north, but the rim of the nearest hill cut short his view of anything other than the wet, gray sky. Somewhere out there, he was certain, Reiffen rode with the marching sissit.

The horses were saddled. Sir Worrel ordered a ration of dried wissund meat handed round the troop. Keln found a mount for Avender among the extra steeds. The trooper also asked among his companions for any spare gear and, before they left, Avender found himself decked out as a regular member of the troop, from iron helm to wooden shield, short sword slapping at his thigh.

"No extra armor, though." Keln frowned and tapped his leather breastplate. "But that shouldn't matter. The Keeadini are raiders, not fighters. Unless they outnumber us ten to one, they won't attack. Their idea of a good fight is to ride up, shoot all their arrows, and ride away. Or sneak up in the dark and knock you over the head."

The fifty-odd troopers headed off south and west, their dogs trotting beside them. The rain didn't lessen as the day wore on, but it didn't strengthen either. Small herds of wissund dotted the hollows, their humped backs like brown hills in the grass, but there was no sign of any Keeadini. The troopers walked their horses, preferring to keep them fresh for any sudden need. Only the outriders remained mounted at all times, and they were changed every hour.

Avender took his turn riding picket, but mostly he marched with Keln in the middle of the column. The trooper wanted to know all about Valing and the nokken, Issinlough and the Dwarves. Avender answered every question, but somehow Keln did most of the talking.

"Have you ever seen Backford?" he asked. "No? That's right, you came across the Easting from Rimwich when you joined us. Well, it's built up in the hills beyond the Wetting, on the only dry patch of ground between the swamp and the Blue Mountains. There's no other way into Banking from the north. And there's the Tumbling to get across, too. It's not very wide, but it's fast and deep. And cold. You and I could hold the bridge against a hundred. Well, maybe you and I and a couple of friends. You'll see. We've kept the Keeadini out of Banking for hundreds of years. I suppose we can stop Ossdonc, too. Notice he came in disguise the last time, pretending he was human. Afraid to try the main gate, if you ask me."

Avender hadn't asked, but kept his thoughts to himself.

They saw no sign of the tribesmen until the next morning, when one of the western pickets galloped in to say he had seen a scouting party of Keeadini to the north. Ordering the entire troop to mount, Sir Worrel sent more riders out to patrol. For an hour the nomads kept their distance, studying the column, until they finally rode away. The Banking scouts followed for a mile or so across the rolling grass, to be certain another, larger party wasn't close behind. Though the rain had stopped, the grass remained wet, and even a galloping troop wouldn't stir up enough dust to attract notice. The column dismounted after the patrol's return, but Sir Worrel doubled the number of outriders just the same.

"Are we going to make a run for it?" Avender asked.

Keln shook his head. "We're still too far away. And we've got nothing to worry about as long as it's light. It's hard to ambush anyone out here in the open. Most likely they'll try to catch us off guard tonight, if they attack at all. Probably near dawn. Their other trick is to get us running so they can pick off stragglers, but the captain's too smart to fall for that old chestnut."

Morning passed, and afternoon as well. The horizon remained empty as the sea. Sir Worrel would have kept them marching all night, but once again clouds covered moon and stars. Only when there was no point in the darkness left to steer by did he finally bring the column to a halt.

Wrapped in their blankets, the troop lay on the damp grass in groups of three and four around the sides of a low hill, the saddled horses tethered in the middle. The deep night reminded Avender of the Under Ground, where darkness surrounded even the brightest light like crows above a dying lamb. A dog settled beside him, its head jerking at any sound other than that of the horses cropping at the grass. Avender scratched it between the ears.

Only after he heard the third grouse call in a row did he realize something was up. The dog beside him growled.

"Did you hear that?" Avender's whisper cut across the darkness like a sharpened knife.

"They're out there," Keln answered softly.

His heartbeat quickening, Avender felt for the sword at his side and the bow across his back.

"Do you still think they'll wait for morning?" he asked.

"They can't see in the dark any better'n we can."

"So we're just going to wait for them?"

"No." Keln's whisper crept quietly along the slick grass. "If I know the captain, he'll lead us out just before dawn. No sense waiting for them to charge and maybe drive off the horses."

The night dragged like plow horses in the heat of the day. Avender listened to the breathing of the men around him and imagined he heard the thumping of their hearts. But it was only his own, slow and strong.

Eventually a soft whisper sounded behind them.

"Mount up, you lot. It's time."

Crouching, Avender followed Keln back through the soaked grass. The horses snorted and snapped, their heavy teeth biting blindly. Avender took a moment to say a few soothing words into his mount's ear, smoothing its velvet muzzle with his hand. Then he was in the saddle, pulling hard at the reins to keep the animal aligned with the others on either side. This was the most dangerous moment: if the Keeadini charged now the troop would bolt, scattering in all directions. Then it would be an easy matter to hunt them down by twos and threes. But the darkness was even more confusing to the tribesmen, who couldn't see what the troop was doing. Unless they were already prepared to charge, the Banking column would be off across the plain before the tribes could stop them.

A horn sounded. Avender's horse stiffened. More grouse called in the night. A second winding followed the first, a long and wailing note. Jostling and stamping, the horses started forward. Avender gave his animal its head, hoping instinct would lead it to follow its bolting fellows.

They took off. Not being the most skilled horseman, Avender clutched his horse around the neck. Water and bits of grass sprayed his face. Other steeds bumped against him. Faster and faster they ran, hooves pounding the earth. Avender's horse struck something in the dark and stumbled. Avender held on for dear life. The wind tore at his face and hair; jingling weapons and harnesses rang time with the galloping herd.

It was over more quickly than he expected. The pace of the stampede slowed; Avender no longer felt the strain in his horse's stride. The troopers called back and forth among one another and praised their steeds. Before he knew it, and without any horsemanship on his part, Avender was cantering along in the middle of the crowd.

"Avender!" Keln's cheerful voice rose up close beside him. "Are you still with us?"

"I'm here." Realizing he was still clutching his horse's neck, he groped for the reins. A pale pink color limned the east, like a giant slowly opening an eye.

A good-humored chuckle rose from the nearest riders. "You're one of us now, lad." Avender recognized the voice as coming from one of the senior sergeants. "If you can stay on your horse in a dawn charge, you can ride through anything."

A laugh rolled across the troop. The excitement of the ride, and their successful escape, had put them all in good spirits. Above their heads the sky lightened in front of the rising sun; the riders emerged from the darkness like fishing boats coming out of a fog.

Sir Worrel called a halt once it was clear there was no pursuit. The horses steamed in the gray light, their heads bent to the wet turf. Counting off, the troop discovered two of the spare mounts were missing, but none of the men. The dogs trotted in out of the grass one by one, their tongues pink as the morning.

A vee of geese winged east through the breaking clouds as the column headed south once more. Closer than Avender had expected, the Blue Mountains rose ahead of them in a line of low hills. Like the northern range, these crags weren't capped with snow, at least not in early summer. Their tops gleamed reddish purple as they caught the end of the sun's long reach. Avender wished they were already in the mountains, where he would feel much more secure than he did out in the open plain.

By midmorning the tribesmen were back. At the rear of the column, perhaps half a mile away, a low black cloud crept across the grass. It took Avender a moment to understand he was looking at a mass of closely packed horsemen. Like flies circling offal, the tribesmen's outriders dashed forward on either side.

"It won't be long now." Keln winked at Avender, much more confident than his companion.

"Shouldn't we be running?" Avender was hard-pressed to resist urging his horse forward on his own.

"No point in that. We can't outrun them. Keeadini travel lighter than we do. Running would only tire out the horses. But they won't dare attack unless they have overwhelming numbers."

"That looks pretty overwhelming to me." Behind them, the

advancing horde had already covered a third of the distance to the column.

"That's about half of what they think they need." Keln squared his shoulders confidently. "Even if they do attack, they'll give up once we've killed a few. Wasters don't know much about real warfare. Why, we might even be able to ride all the way to Backford without them getting up the nerve to attack at all. They'll shoot arrows at us, of course, but that's why we've got the shields."

Avender doubted their retreat would be so easy. A mile or so later, when one of the pickets raced back toward the column, he was certain he was right. Another group of Keeadini had ridden around to bear down across their path. Avender and Keln could see them sweeping forward from the right at the top of the next rise: a second, smaller swarm of riders, not much larger than their own troop.

Keln remained as cheerful as ever. "We'll see some action now. Those fellows up there must have talked themselves into a fine state to think they can turn us. If only we had our lances we'd really show them something. But they never do let us take lances out on these long patrols."

The horn sounded again at the front of the troop. Outriders galloped back to the column. A second call rang out and the ranks of riders quickened. Avender didn't think they were going as fast as they had in the dark, but then he couldn't really tell. Casting a quick glance to the rear, he found their pursuers only a long bowshot behind. The Keeadini kicked their steeds into a full gallop and waved their swords, their howls drowned in the rush of wind and hooves.

A third call sounded on the horn. Avender followed Keln's lead and unsheathed his sword. No longer able to keep up with the galloping horses, the dogs scattered into the long grass on either side. Avender had never fought on horseback before, but he guessed the weight of the horse would add strength to his blows.

If he figured out the timing. Before them the enemy disappeared into a fold in the earth, only to reemerge much closer a moment later. Avender tightened his grip on the reins. The exhilaration of the charge coursed from his flying horse up his legs and into his pounding heart.

The line of Keeadini wavered. The Banking troop, instead of turning aside, charged straight toward the nomads. One bold chief brandished his feathered spear. His fellows shook their heads and turned aside. Spotted ponies whisked their long tails and bolted as the heavier horses of the massed column struck. Sir Worrel's sword flashed in the morning light. The daring chief fell at his stroke and disappeared. By the time Avender and Keln passed the spot where the two groups had met, there was no one left to fight. Tribesmen and ponies had fled to east and west. A nomad lay twisted in the trampled field. Avender had a quick glimpse of blood and bone and broken weapons strewn across the bright green grass before he was into the open plain beyond.

The charge continued. The horses strained. Avender clung tightly to his mount with hands and knees. Looking back, he saw that only a few of the Keeadini were still pursuing. The riders behind them had run head-on into their scattered fellows, and the resulting confusion had brought most of them to a stop.

A fresh blast of the horn rang out. The galloping horses slowed. The nearer Keeadini shouted terrible insults in the Banking tongue, but none of them dared approach any closer until they had reformed their attack.

"Column, halt!" called the Banking sergeants. "Dismount!"

Avender, his chest heaving, slipped off his horse. Its flanks were thick with sweat. The air wheezed with the snorts of winded animals. Avender was about to say how easy it had been when he saw a trooper lowered motionless from his saddle. That was when he also noticed a few horses with arrows in their shoulders and thighs. The troopers broke the shafts off close to the skin, but there wasn't enough time to remove the points. Even Keln's face fell as he saw that not all of their comrades had made it through the charge.

"If we're lucky," the trooper said, scowling through clenched teeth, "they'll try that again."

They walked their horses longer than Avender thought possible. Noon had passed by the time the tribesmen gathered to attack once more. This time, instead of another bold assault, they galloped their light ponies alongside the column, remaining just out of bowshot. Every once and a while a single rider raced in, set himself, and flung a shot toward the troop. Usually their arrows fell short, but enough came close that the riders remained vigilant with their shields. Roving squads of five or six troopers chased the daring bowmen off before they had a chance to do real damage.

There were no more halts. Sir Worrel kept the column moving at a steady pace. However, until fresh danger emerged, everyone remained on foot. As the day wore on the ground grew rougher and began to slant upward to the south and west. Long stretches of grass were replaced by stony ground; low heather covered the rising hills. Small paths had been worn everywhere between the brush, the tracks of innumerable years of wissund. Now and again Avender spied one of the heavy beasts grazing alone on the hills beyond the Keeadini.

He soon saw they had come to terrain where the nomads might be able to use their numbers to advantage. The column crossed a number of deep gullies that cut sharply through the hills; should they ever be forced into one for any length of time they would be easy prey to ambush. Already he could see the tribesmen trying to push the troop off its chosen path and toward the rougher ground.

"Not much farther to go now, at least," said Keln.

Almost as he spoke the sergeant's horn sounded again at the front of the column. "Mount up!" Wearily Avender pulled himself back into his saddle. He was sure he had walked at least five leagues since dawn. The Keeadini rushed in to launch another round of arrows. A horse in the line ahead reared, its rider struggling to hold it in place. Avender could see the arrow that had pierced its neck angling wickedly against the sky. The horn called again and the column started forward. This was their final dash.

A pain like the sting of a dozen hornets pinched Avender's leg. He looked down and found an arrow lodged in the top of his thigh. Wincing, he tried to snap the shaft with his hands. White pain filled him; his leg felt like it was tearing open. He let go of the arrow and the pain eased. Though the jolting of the horse stung his wound at every hoofbeat, it was still bearable compared with the agony of trying to break the shaft. Gritting his teeth, he began to worry whether or not they would make it through to Backford. Every tribesman in the west appeared to be riding the Waste beside them, the steady *plink* of shafts striking shields as annoying as a growing rain.

He covered as much of his right side with his shield as he could, knowing Keln was doing the same on his left. The flights of arrows ebbed and flowed. Sometimes the air seemed as full of flying shafts as a hive is full of bees. At others an arrow seemed as sudden as the strike of a lone hawk. In the brief lulls Avender peered out from behind his shield, but always the rough hills around them were thick with hunting Keeadini. He didn't see how they could ever cover the final stretch to safety.

A man tumbled from the horse before him. Farther up the line a stallion stumbled, an arrow in its neck. The column flowed around each fresh casualty like a brook rushing over fallen trees. Avender didn't dare look behind to see what happened to the men who fell. He had heard tales of what Wasters did to prisoners unlucky enough to fall among them. Even so, he supposed being captured by the Keeadini was better than being taken prisoner by the Three.

An arrow glanced off the top of his helm. Another struck quivering at the top of his horse's shoulder. The animal's eyes widened with pain and fright. Avender gripped the reins tightly, prepared for the worst. But all the horse did was flatten its ears and pick up its pace until its nose bumped the back of the steed ahead. The steadying touch of its companion did more to calm the animal than Avender holding tightly to the reins.

From up ahead the horn wound one last time, a long, triumphant note that marked no signal or command. Another rush of arrows buzzed and stung.

"Look!" cried Keln. "The lancers!"

"It's the baron!"

"Hurrah!"

Avender looked up, hope ready in his heart. At first he saw nothing but Keeadini, the same sturdy ponies effortlessly paralleling their own heavier horses. Then he saw many of the Wasters pulling back hard on their mounts, turning the horses' heads in the opposite direction. The rain of arrows ended. Nomads hurried back the way they had come; in a moment they were gone. But the troop kept riding, their slow gallop widening the gap between them and their enemies. Up ahead, where before the land had been filled with whooping Keeadini, now stretched a long line of riders, each with a lance pointed toward the sky. The rescuers hadn't begun their full charge, before which even Wayland's strongest pikemen had been known to flee, but already they were comfortably in control of the field. Before Avender had recovered from the shock of their arrival the lancers had rumbled past, the threat of the baron's spears driving the enemy before them into the plains.

Ahead, a small tower crowned the top of a steep hill. Above it white gulls wheeled. Out of the long, dull waste of Keeadin, the Backford column came limping home.

11

Lovers and Swains

Ferris frowned at the awkward figure approaching through the orchard. It was just like Nod Woolson to hike up to the Manor the morning Prince Brizen was expected to arrive. Of all her suitors, he really was the worst. From his rough hands to the spot under his chin he always missed while shaving, he was the exact opposite of what she wished for in a swain. Even Hern knew better than to press his suit. Other young women in Valing might think him a catch, with his broad shoulders, fine pastures, and stone house close by Forning Spring, but Ferris wanted nothing to do with him. She dreamed more grandly, and Nod Woolson represented exactly what she wished to leave behind.

Sighing, she sliced the top off another strawberry from the bowl in her lap and reminded herself it had been a while since Reiffen had visited her, even in her dreams.

There was no escape once the farmer found her, so Ferris resigned herself to another round of tedious wooing. As Nod patted his flat yellow locks into place and joined her, she told herself that sharing a kiss with him in the moonlight would be only slightly more romantic than sharing one with Mother Peek's prize bull, Dewlap King.

"Here. I brought you these." Nod handed Ferris the bouquet he had brought abruptly, the same way he might hang a pitchfork on a wall. "Picked 'em myself from Ma's garden."

"You shouldn't have." Ferris dropped the flowers on the rock beside her since the strawberries were already in her lap.

"Oh, yes, I should." A pair of yellow butterflies fled over the edge of the cliff behind them as Nod sat heavily on the other side of his present. "Ma tells me I need to treat you nice if I'm ever goin' t' bring you round t' my way of thinking."

Ferris made an effort not to sigh a second time. "I've told you before, Nod, I'm very flattered, but I think you might find the girls in Eastbay more to your liking."

"You're the one I fancy," he said stubbornly.

"But I don't fancy you, Nod."

Sullen disappointment flooded the farmer's ruddy face. Ferris almost regretted her inability to be any nicer when turning her suitors down. But it was just too annoying. How many times did they have to be told? His long face almost plowing the ground, Nod picked a stalk of grass and stuck it between his large, square teeth. Noticing a fresh scuff mark on his boots, he rubbed at it with a broad thumb.

"You've got to stop pestering me some day, you know," she went on. "I'd never be happy milking cows and making butter, and that means you'd never be happy, either."

"Hern says you churn a good tub." The farmer's tone was determined, but he lacked the courage to look his heart's desire in the face as he spoke.

"Being able to do a good job doesn't necessarily mean I like it."

"Sour heart makes sour butter, Ma always says."

Ferris rolled her eyes. "I'm not your grandmother, to be

swapping old saws with by the hearth. I've seen more of the world than just Valing."

This admission of the basic difference between them brought a pained sigh from the lovestruck farmer. "I wish you hadn't o' gone off an' done that. You an' I might be livin' cozy as hatched chicks by now. Why don't you go an' marry that Prince Brizen, if you like the outside so much. I know I'm just a dub of a farmer, but I love you as much as him. An' I'll bet his sheep don't shear near as thick as mine. Nor his cows have sweeter milk, neither."

His long speech finished, the longest Ferris had ever heard from him, Nod tucked his chin back into his chest and nursed his sore-heartedness along with his stalk of grass. Ferris would have pitied his misery had she not been sure it would pass once his practical side took over and he settled down with one of the girls who could truly love him.

"Prince Brizen is not your concern," she told him.

"Well, if it isn't him, it's Avender. I know it isn't Norby Brad. Even my sis knows Norby's a moony tup. But Avender don't care for you no more'n a milk stool, the little time he spends in Valing these days."

Ferris straightened haughtily. Brizen was one thing, but Avender was another matter entirely. Nod should know better than to think Avender had anything to do with it. "I'll have you know I got a letter from Avender a month ago. He and Redburr were on their way to the Waste, to ride with the Backford troopers."

Nod frowned, his heavy chin narrowing sulkily. "Fine, then. You run after your worldly friends while you're breakin' the hearts of honest farmers."

"I've never broken your heart, Nod Woolson. You're doing that job yourself." Now she was just irritated enough not to care how hard she sounded. "You have any number of girls longing to marry you. Why, Renny Punter would take you tomorrow if you thought long enough to ask. And she'd make you a better wife than I ever would, too, because she'd want to. Here, give Renny these." She thrust the bundle of pink and yellow blossoms back into the farmer's rough grip. "She'll like them a lot more than I ever will."

Without giving Nod the opportunity to say another word, Ferris popped to her feet and strode off with her strawberries to the Manor. Glimpsing her mother's face in the kitchen window, she decided to wait awhile before returning to the house. Prince Brizen wasn't expected before late afternoon at the earliest, so she didn't have to get ready right away. For him she would condescend to take off her apron, even if he was as foolish as Nod in his own, more considerate way.

Setting the bowl of strawberries on the porch railing, she took a left turn and followed the long gallery the length of the Manor. It had been a wet spring, and the plume of midsummer mist rolling up out of the gorge looked like a white column supporting the sky. The ground thrummed as she cut back across the damp grass at the end of the house and gazed into the chasm at the western end of the Neck. The Tear peeped up through the veiling fog like a mother playing peekaboo with her child.

To most of Valing the Tear was a cursed place. Nolo had built it as a refuge for Giserre, and no one had lived there since she left. "Shows what happens when people take on airs," Mother Spinner had sniffed on more than one occasion. All the same, Hern made certain the half-bridge and the round room beyond remained clean and free of mice and squirrels.

Ferris followed the stone stair down. Inside the Tear she circled the ring of mullioned windows, tracing her fingers along the glass. Outside, the mist swirled as the lake threw itself down the chasm in a frothing rage. Memories of visits with Giserre, both as a small, awestruck child and as a young girl accustomed to such privileges, filtered through her mind. She had always admired Giserre and had tried to learn whatever the elegant woman, so much younger than her mother, would teach her.

The dark oak doors at the entrance opened. "I thought I'd find you here," said Hern.

Ferris descended the circling tiers to the center of the room, where the hearth lay cold and bare. Her mother followed down the steps from the door.

"Did Nod ask you to marry him again?" she asked.

"I didn't give him the chance."

Hern's forehead wrinkled. "I know you're not interested in Nod, dear, but you really should let him have his say. If only for practice. Some day someone you like will come along and, if you're so used to being a bear, you might scare him off before you know what you've done."

"I practice with Brizen."

"You certainly do, and I'm surprised he keeps coming back. He won't forever, you know. That pretty Lady Wellin will catch him one of these days, and that'll be a good chance missed. You won't find princes knocking on your door every day."

"Who says I'm looking for a prince?" Ferris plopped down among the cushions on the lowest bench and fingered the embroidery. A flock of nokken raced a fleet of canoes across a blue velvet background.

"Please, dear. We all look for princes. You've just happened to find a pair of real ones."

"I never thought of Reiffen as a prince."

"Oh no?" Hern's eyes widened suspiciously. "Then you're the only one. Perhaps I should have had you scrubbing the kitchen floor a little more so you'd been able to tell the difference."

"If I marry a prince I'll never scrub a floor again." Ferris brushed her fingers across the rich fabric, enjoying the softness. "Princesses don't work in kitchens. They lie around all day eating plums and chocolate cake."

Trying hard not to show her curiosity, Hern sat on the bench beside her daughter. "Is it really the prince you prefer? I always thought it was someone else."

Ferris wondered if her mother had figured it out. Hern's next words proved she hadn't.

"Avender's been away a long time. He only comes home once or twice a year now. If that's been your hope, Ferris, he certainly hasn't given any indication that his is the same."

"Avender's my oldest friend, Mother, and knows I've never thought of him that way. Unlike most of the geese that pass for men around here, Avender has the sense not to dream about what he knows is impossible."

"Impossible? Why should it be impossible? You've always liked him. And Reiffen's been gone a long time. We all know where your heart was headed then, Ferris. But that's impossible now. Even you know that. We don't always get our first pick off the tree, dear," she added in her kindest voice.

"I know, Mother. Which is why I'd appreciate it if you'd leave me alone and let nature take its course."

"That's just what I'm not going to do." Hern smoothed her apron. "If I leave you alone, you'll be off traipsing around the world, nursing your sore heart just like Nod Woolson, and never settle down. Why do you think I haven't pushed harder for you to take the prince? It's because I know you don't love him. But you like him, and that's a start. And don't think your father and I aren't proud he loves you. Our grandchildren, the heirs to Wayland and Banking? We may be Valing folk, but we like to see our own do well the same as anyone else. Better you than those pieces of fluff that pass for ladies in Malmoret. If you did marry Brizen, your children could spend every summer with us. That way we'd be sure they had some sense in their heads."

Ferris eyed her mother sternly. "You'd call Brizen's children heirs to Wayland and Banking? Really, Mother. As much as anyone, you know who the true heir is. You were there the day he was born."

"Yes, but Reiffen's gone now." Hern stroked her daughter's hair gently with the back of her hand. "Even if he comes back, and the Wizards manage to set him up as king, we both know it won't mean much."

"That doesn't matter." Ferris pushed her mother's arm away stubbornly. "Either way, Reiffen's the true king. Not Brizen."

Hern returned her daughter's stern look with one of her own. "You're a splendid child, Ferris, and all a parent could ever wish for, even if you are sometimes too clever for your own good."

She sighed, undoubtedly remembering every scrape Ferris had ever gotten into. "But even you're going to have to understand some day that a true king's not just a matter of blood. There've been strong and good rulers of Wayland and Banking who stole the throne from their betters. And there've been poor rulers whose bloodlines were clean as the Hartrush. Reiffen's gone, king or otherwise. He wasn't the same boy when you brought him back seven years ago, and he'll be even less the same if he ever shows up again. It's time you thought of other things."

"I know, Mother." Ferris took a deep breath and stared at the empty hearth, remembering again how long it had been since Reiffen had last visited her.

"Prince Brizen's a good enough fellow, especially from what I've heard about princes. He loves you quick as a duckling, too. Think about it, dear. You could be queen some day. I happen to think you'd make a fine one."

"That's just it, Mother. I do think about it. But then I'd be against Reiffen, and that's what I can't do. Not while there's still hope."

"Then I'm sorry for you, dear." Tenderly, Hern put an arm around Ferris's shoulders. "And I won't ask you to go against your own heart anymore, even if I do think you're being foolish. You'll see, though. If Reiffen does come back, there won't be anything left but the memory we keep right here, in these pillows and stone." Hern patted the nearest bolster. Dust puffed out around her to fall ghostlike to the floor.

"Hmm. Remind me to take these cushions out for a good airing the next time Anella and I come to clean."

Lovingly, she kissed her daughter. "Don't worry, sweetheart. Marriage is a bigger change for a woman than it is for a man. They get to keep on doing what they've always done, but our lives are never what they were. Children change more than your body."

The water rumbled through the gorge. Mother and daughter both looked as if they wished they had something to do with their hands. Reluctantly, Hern let go of her daughter and stood.

"Well, now. I've been gone long enough. There's still a lot of work to do before the prince arrives. He may be an easy guest, but his people are nearly as much trouble as Redburr. Stay here if you want, but tomorrow I'm going to need you to help Myrtle and Renny with the washing. We can't have what happened last time, when Myrtle lost the prince's linen in among the tablecloths."

With no wish to remain sulking in the Tear, Ferris followed her mother back to the Manor. For a few hours the day passed as had so many in her childhood, in cooking and cleaning and talk. Ferris had nothing to worry her but the work of her strong, deft hands.

As expected, the prince arrived later in the day. A more devoted lover might have charged more quickly over the pass, but a more devoted lover would not have had to travel with an esquire, a herald, a valet, and a dozen knights in shining mail, none of whom shared his hurry. For them Valing was a backwoods billet where there was nothing to do but fish. Unless one of the farm girls let you take her out on the lake in the moonlight, where she was as likely as not to laugh at you and tip you both over in the canoe.

The prince, as he greeted his hosts, was less awkward than he once had been. He would never be as tall or good-looking as Avender, but his hesitant manner had transformed into a charming deference. When Hern and Berrel and everyone else in the Manor bowed formally in greeting, Brizen shocked his escort by bowing in reply. It really was too bad, thought Ferris, that Brannis was his father.

"It is so nice to be back," he declared with a winning smile. "They tease me for it at court, but I do believe Valing is the most beautiful place in the world."

"You're too kind, Your Highness," answered Hern. "Though you only say what we think ourselves. Welcome. This is an unexpected treat."

Brizen stole a quick glance at Ferris from the corner of his eye. "Thank you, ma'am. You know how hard it is for me to stay away."

That first evening, and most of the next day, the prince all but ignored Ferris, for which she thanked him silently. Too much attention was too much of a good thing, even for her. Instead he renewed the goodwill he had earned on his last visit by bringing gifts to his old friends. Had he been less gracious about it, Ferris would have called them bribes. The thought did cross her mind when she saw him give Sally and Tinnet's son a bright silver rattle, and Old Mortin a pouch of fine Lansing tobacco. But, when he brought nothing for her parents, she understood Brizen's gifts had come from kindness alone, and not from any other motive. And she liked how he knew that her parents would consider presents an insult to their hospitality.

He found her alone the next morning. During her break from the washing she had gone out to the pine woods behind the house, where the rumble of the waterfall was softer and the drop to the river below twice what it was to the lake. Laundering was hot work, and the north side of the Manor, where paths led through the white pines to the edge of the cliff, was cooler than the south. Finding a seat on a ledge of flat rock, she looked out on the Whitewash, plunging northward through the mountains toward the distant forest.

Brizen must have been waiting for her to leave the washroom, or he never would have found her among the thick trees. He came hesitantly along the path, fending off the sweeping branches with his arms, his boots crunching the needle carpet. Ferris folded her red hands in her apron as he came up beside her.

"This is a nice view," he began.

"Not as nice as the lake." Ferris decided against making room for him to sit on the rock beside her, knowing he would only take it as a wider invitation.

"No," Brizen agreed. "But it's wilder. The gateway to the northern forest."

"It's not much of a gateway." Ferris nodded toward the white line of the river rushing among the hills. "You'd never get a boat through those cataracts, not even a canoe."

"Still, it's not that far to the Great Forest." Brizen anchored himself with a hand on a small hemlock and stepped closer to the edge of the cliff. "And it's the same river that winds through the forest, past the Waste to the Wetting, all the way to Far Mouthing and the Inner Sea. I wonder." The prince leaned forward and gazed down at the White Pool frothing at the bottom of the cliff. "If you sent a barrel through the gorge, how long would it take to reach Malmoret?"

"It would never make it through the gorge."

"I wouldn't imagine anything could make it through the gorge," Brizen agreed. "Or the White Pool, for that matter, or any of the next twenty leagues to the forest. Still, if it could, I wonder how long it would take."

"Years. Maybe we can get Redburr to ask the fish."

Brizen kicked a pinecone into the green gulf. "Sometimes, in Malmoret, I think about how marvelous it would be if I were a fish myself. If I were, you know, I'd turn my fins upstream and swim up here to Valing as fast as I could."

"You'd have as hard a time getting up this last bit here as the barrel would getting down."

"I know that." Brizen glanced briefly at Ferris, then looked off into the trees. "I was just dreaming. I do that a lot these days, you know."

Not wishing to encourage him, Ferris made no reply. He would come to the point quickly enough on his own. A wood dove darted out from the pines on their right and plunged into the valley. A second followed close behind. Ferris and Brizen watched until the birds grew too small to spot against the trees.

"I am sorry, Ferris, but I did want to see you again. I hope you don't mind."

"I don't mind, Brizen. You're my friend. Hern and Berrel love seeing you. You honor us greatly every time you visit."

"I wish it was more than just your parents who loved seeing me."

Ferris folded her hands in her lap and stared straight ahead. Brizen, getting no response to his declaration, sighed for both of them.

"I do love you," he said, stepping back from the edge of the Neck. "I wish there was a way I could prove it. Monsters to slay, or someone to rescue. As it is, it's hard enough just finding the time to come up here. You're the lucky one, getting to see the Pearl Islands and the Stoneways. I have too many towns to visit and barons to dine with. Not to mention all the time I have to spend with the army."

Ferris dug a pebble out from a crack in the stone and nudged it over the cliff with her foot. "You know, you could go to Issin-lough, if that's what you really wanted to do."

"I will some day. But right now Father says there's no time to waste in gawking."

"You come here. Your father doesn't approve of that at all."

"I'd rather come here than Issinlough any day. Father knows there are some things about which I won't answer to him. Besides, the Seven Veils can't possibly be as beautiful as you."

"That's sweet, Brizen, but it doesn't change anything. I'm not in love with you. If I were, it wouldn't matter what your father thought. I'm sure you love me very much. Nod only has to sail down from Bracken and climb a hill to see me, but you have to come all the way from Rimwich or Malmoret. It's very flattering, but it doesn't change anything."

"Most girls like flattery. The ones in Malmoret think I'm going to marry them the first time I say something nice."

"I like flattery, too. Just not as much as the girls in Malmoret."

"You're not anything like the girls in Malmoret. That's why I love you." As he spoke, Brizen looked her full in the face. Ferris couldn't help but turn away before his show of sweet, earnest ardor.

She brushed off a pine twig that fluttered into her lap. "You were in love with me before we even met, Brizen, though I can't say I blame you. I think if I'd met someone my age who was a famous hero when I was fifteen, I'd have fallen in love, too. But it's not very flattering. It's not me you're in love with, but the girl you thought I was before we even met. If you'd just pay more attention to the girls who already like you, like Wellin, for instance, you might have more success."

"Wellin is beautiful, but I'm not in love with her."

Ferris couldn't help herself. Even if she didn't love him, it piqued her pride to hear Brizen praise another woman while he wooed her. "Fie, sir!" she chided, in her best Banking manner. "You talk about how beautiful another woman is, even when you say you love me?"

"You know I didn't mean it that way." Brizen stepped forward manfully. For a moment Ferris thought he might grasp her hand or shoulder.

"I know," she apologized. "I was just teasing. And Wellin *is* beautiful. More queenly, too."

A thin line hardened along the prince's jaw. When he was most determined was when he looked most like his father. And Reiffen. "Wellin wants to be queen too much," he said.

"Maybe so, but I like her the more for it. I don't know why, but of all the fine ladies in Malmoret, she's the only one I ever felt much in common with."

Brizen's mouth fell open in astonishment. "You and Wellin? Why, the two of you couldn't be more different."

"I'm not talking about the way we look. Or about whether we could be friends, which I'm sure we couldn't. But I like the way Wellin speaks her mind and the way she goes after what she wants. She's the only woman I ever met in Malmoret, at least among the ladies, who would let a pat of butter melt in her mouth. Though there was that Lady Breeanna, too, come to think of it, who married the baron twice her age. Now, if you'll excuse me, I think I need to get back to the laundry."

Before she could stop him, the prince took Ferris by the hand and helped her to her feet. She waved him away, but he only let go after they were a couple of steps back from the cliff. He didn't seem to mind the rough redness of her hand at all.

"Now that you mention it . . ." He stared thoughtfully at the ground while mulling this new idea. "You two are a bit alike. I can't believe I never noticed it before. You're both tenacious. And intelligent. And beautiful. How could I not have realized it?"

"Probably because you've known Wellin your entire life." Ferris set off back through the wood to the Manor, the pine boughs dappled with light and shadow. "You only met me when that sort of thing began to matter."

200 | S. C. BUTLER

"I suppose that's true." His eyes still thoughtfully on the ground, Brizen followed. They emerged at a small, green lawn beside the house.

"You know what that means, though," he continued. "That means Wellin's about as likely to give up pursuing me as you're likely to give in."

Ferris pulled up short in the middle of the path. "Excuse me? Did I just hear you say you finally understand I'm not going to change my mind?"

"Not at all." Brizen drew himself up to his full height. An attractive confidence glittered in his eye. "I just realized I have to be as tenacious as you are. I don't suppose Wellin will give up on me until I'm safely married to someone else. Well, you'll just have to assume the same about me. That is, of course, unless I really start to annoy you. In which case I'll do whatever you ask. But at least I have one advantage over Wellin."

"What's that?" Ferris frowned as she realized that Brizen, far from understanding he had to give her up, was more determined than ever.

"You don't have anyone you're pining for," said the prince. "Wellin knows she doesn't stand a chance as long as you're in the picture. But there's no one you're in love with the way I'm in love with you. If you were in love with Avender, I think I would know, though Wellin tells me he is the handsomest man she has ever met. And I don't think there's anyone else around you really like any more than you like me."

Ferris bit her tongue, remembering what her mother had said about not getting one's first pick from the tree. Not that she was ready yet to stop reaching. The prince was correct in one sense, however.

"You're right about that, at least," she said. "There is no one else around. But I still don't love you."

"You didn't even like me, the first time we met. Now you do. I shall never give up hope until I have to."

Thanking her stars that men were so incredibly obtuse, especially when they were in love, Ferris shook her head. But there was a lot to think about as she went back to the washroom. Her mother was right. Reiffen would be changed if he ever did return. And how long would she be willing to wait to find that out? No, she really wasn't ready yet to give up either of her princes.

After lunch, Brizen took his troop off to Bracken to inspect the flax ponds and dine with the mayor. Though there were no kings in Valing, any representative of the higher nobility was very much in demand for formal banquets. Brizen and his guard wouldn't be back until the following afternoon. Guests gone, Ferris ate a peaceful supper with her parents and Anella in the breakfast room, while Tinnet and Sally enjoyed their own quiet family evening. Hern asked no questions, though Ferris was certain her mother knew everything that had occurred. *She* certainly would, should she ever have a daughter. Instead they discussed the next day's events over their soup and bread, their spoons clicking softly in time with the crickets beyond the window. Outside, the summer evening fell late to darkness.

The stewards' apartment was in what was supposed to be the oldest part of the Manor, and the old oak planking on the floor was certainly dark enough for that to be true. Other stewards had added to the rambling house over the years, and no one was really sure which parts of the Manor had or hadn't been rebuilt, but Ferris always felt the most at home here, even if her parents had never managed to fill the rooms up with brothers and sisters for her. Her thoughts strayed briefly to the pair of small graves on the Shoulder, not far from the plots of Avender's and Reiffen's fathers. A boy and a girl her parents had lost before Ferris was born. No wonder her mother wanted her to settle down.

In her own room the mattress sighed as she sat on her bed to remove her shoes. Hern had already opened the window; the curtains rustled like loose dresses in the breeze. Ferris looked up at the twinkling lights of the Throne and the Bear. Something in the sky made her think back to the Minabbenet in Grangore, where the Dwarves' small jewels sparkled in the stone roof to echo the world above. She wondered, as she did in almost every quiet moment, about her friends so far away. Avender with Redburr. Reiffen with his mother. She missed them both all the time. At least Brizen wasn't an oaf, like Nod. He was at least as nice as Avender, and without all the melancholy. There were worse things than being a queen. She wasn't about to take her heart back so easily, though. Not yet.

Not even for a crown.

The moon had risen when she thought she woke. Silver ribbons striped the floor. She rubbed her eyes and wondered what had disturbed her. Judging from the height of the moon, morning remained hours away. She was about to snuggle back against her pillow when she noticed a shadow shimmering beside her window. It had been a long time since she had last dreamed of Reiffen, at least a year. She had taught herself to believe it was because she was growing up, and no longer needed to pretend her old friend had never left. All the same, she missed his visits, few though they had been. But this was how the dreams always began: a shadow by the curtains that seemed no different from the curtains themselves. Until it stepped forward and said, "Have you missed me, Ferris?"

Her heart leapt. Even if it was just another dream, she would take what she could get. Throwing off the blankets, she twisted round until she was sitting on the edge of the bed. Shivering, she reached for her robe.

"Where have you been?" she asked, not bothering to answer his question.

The ghostly image shrugged. His moonlight body rippled like a reflection in a pond. Ferris knew her hand would feel nothing if she tried to touch him, but he did seem more substantial this time than he ever had before. Though that might just be her excitement at dreaming of him once again.

"The Wizards have kept me busy."

"Have you tried to escape?"

"There is no escape. Mother and I have to stay where we are."

"Why?"

Reiffen didn't answer. Ferris hadn't expected him to. He had never told her before, and there was no new reason to tell her now. Since it was only a dream, whatever he might have said wouldn't have mattered anyway.

"Have you accepted Nod yet?"

Ferris's eyes narrowed. It was one thing to have Hern bothering her about Nod, but quite another for a phantom Reiffen to be so nosy.

"As if you don't know the answer to that."

"What about Brizen?"

"I'm sure you know that answer, too. What do you care, anyway? It's not like you've been paying me any attention. Even if you are just a dream."

Reiffen smiled. "You know I'm not a dream. But I'm glad you haven't accepted him. I didn't think you would. Mother thinks you'll marry Avender."

"Avender! Please tell your mother I'll marry whom I want when I want, and not a minute before."

"As long as you don't marry Brizen. Neither Mother nor I think he's good enough for you."

"His father thinks I'm the one who's not good enough for him. But if you really want to know, it's Hern who's most interested in the idea of my becoming a princess."

A quiet moment passed. Ferris studied the patterns of silver on the floor, trying to guess which ones were from the waving curtains and which from her ghostly guest. Reiffen crossed his legs and seemed to lean against the window frame.

"Is that all you came for?" she asked. "To find out whom I'm marrying?"

Reiffen shook his head in that decided way he had that Ferris remembered well. He was taller than when she had last seen him, and his shoulders had broadened also. She thought him very handsome, though most would pick Avender as the handsomer. Handsomer, stronger, and nicer, too, when you came right down to it. But Reiffen was the one she loved.

"I was just checking to see if we're still friends. You know, you're the only friend I have left."

"That's not true. We're all still your friends."

"I don't think so. If Redburr saw me now, he'd kill me with one swipe. He wouldn't even give me a chance to explain. Nolo might let me talk, but I don't think he'd understand."

"Avender's your friend."

"Maybe. I'd have to test him first."

"Why test any of us? Just come home. You know you're welcome here. Redburr will have to answer to me if he lays a paw on you. And he and Nolo aren't here now."

"They'd be here soon enough if I showed up." Reiffen uncrossed his feet and straightened. Once more his silvered form rippled in the air. "But I can't come home. Not yet. The worst of what I have to do is going to start very soon. Even you may have doubts."

"Don't be ridiculous." Ferris pushed her hands firmly against the bed and scowled. "I'll never have doubts."

Reiffen bowed solemnly. "I thank you for your faith. All the same, the world is about to change. I would have one person remain my friend, regardless of what I do. And even if you cannot understand it, I hope you will understand that I remain myself.

And that what I do, I do because I must. Because there is no other way."

Though Ferris knew she would feel nothing, she reached out for her friend's hand. His silver fingers curled toward hers, but the air was empty at their touch. Like passing fog, his hand wrapped hers in moonlight.

"I will always be your friend," she whispered, wishing he had asked for more.

He closed his shadowed eyes. Not for the first time, she thought he was about to say something more. Instead he nodded slightly, his nose flaring with a deep breath. He shimmered, as if his reflection had been shaken, and vanished. Ferris found herself sitting at the edge of the bed, her hand brushing the curtains in a draft of wind.

She returned to her pillow, wrapping herself in quilts and covers. It had felt so real, just as it always did, but it had to be a dream. What else could it be? Reiffen was hundreds of miles away, in that horrible fortress. Ferris shuddered as she recalled the long, dark tunnels, where terror had plucked at her with a creeping, wretched touch. That's where Reiffen was. It was only her imagination that called him to her dreaming. She missed him terribly. Everything would be different if Reiffen were still in Valing. She wouldn't have to bother about Nod or Prince Brizen, for one thing. And Hern would have approved completely.

A gust of wind blew the curtains into her room like arms, the ends twisted into long white fingers. Lightly they trailed back against the wall as the breeze failed. Her chin tucked deep into her softest blanket, Ferris didn't fall back to sleep for a long, long time. And when she did, it wasn't Brizen she dreamed of.

12

Lady Breeanna

vender nearly fainted when Keln went to work on the arrow sticking out of his thigh. Fresh blood darkened his trousers as the trooper broke off the shaft close to the skin.

"There," said Keln. "Now you can ride without poking yourself in the eye. The surgeon can cut out the rest in Backford."

Avender was one of the lucky ones. Anyone else in the column not badly wounded was walking the last half league home, and there were a few soldiers whose bodies were lashed to their horses' backs. All the same, the troopers' spirits were high. They joked and laughed about their close escape, and boasted of what they would do to their enemies the next time they met.

The officers were more subdued. "They'll be back," Avender heard Sir Worrel tell the baron. "Ossdonc is on the march."

"Have they joined forces with the Keeadini then?" asked one of the Backford lieutenants.

"It's hard to say. So far the tribesmen only seem to be taking advantage of the situation to do a little raiding. But we'll find out soon enough."

Soldiers saluted the passing column from the squat stone

tower as they filed past Watch Hill. On the other side, cattails and sedges as tall as horses blocked the view of Backford Pool. Men were already at work filling the gap in the dike that blocked the narrow spit of land between hill and marsh. Avender clung awkwardly to his horse's neck as it scrambled down the trench in front of the wall and up the bank on the other side. His teeth ground at the pain.

Past the dike they entered a broad pasture that stretched back around the side of the hill. Scattered horses and cows grazed the lush grass. Beyond them the ground rose steeply westward toward dark forests and tall mountains. Reeds stubbled the lakeshore on the eastern side, a fringe of beard around the water's smooth face. A stone bridge marked the end of the meadow, a single broad pier anchoring the span to the middle of the river and the town beyond. On the slope above, Castle Backford hunched beside the rushing water like a giant squatting with hands on knees.

Cowherds ran up to ask for news of the battle. The baron paid them no attention, but behind him his men were happy to call out greetings, especially the captain's troop, which had been gone many weeks. One boy ran straight to Keln, who returned the youth's joyful salute with delight.

"Perret!" the trooper cried. "Have you missed me?"

"Has his sister missed you, that's the real question," called another soldier.

Keln joined in his comrades' laughter. Tousling the boy's hair, he pulled a long black and white feather from his saddlebag. "This is for you," he said. "Took it off a Waster myself."

"Hope you've got something better for the sister," added the jester, and everyone laughed again. They were all so delighted to be back home with sweethearts and wives, children and comfortable beds. Avender almost felt as if he were coming home himself.

The baron led them on across the grass. Nearing the bridge,

Avender saw the meadow side was marked by a high stone wall, where a crowd had gathered to welcome them home. At the front stood a large woman in a tall, conical hat, a long yellow veil fluttering from the tip, her ladies ranked around her. She waved a tiny handkerchief enthusiastically in a hand almost as large as Redburr's. Avender realized she was the baroness at once, but it wasn't until she had taken her husband's horse by the bridle and was leading him into town that he remembered dancing with her in Malmoret years before. For the life of him, he couldn't remember her name.

The prettiest of the baroness's attendants lingered behind long enough to blush at Keln. He met her glance with a wink as broad as the noon sun. Bending her smiling face to the ground, she hurried off after her mistress.

"Perret's sister?" asked Avender.

"Aye," replied his friend, his face still shining.

On the other side of the bridge Avender found himself helped down from his horse and led off with the other wounded. A blacksmith lent him a broad shoulder to lean on. They entered what looked like the town's best inn, at the corner where the main road continued south and a side spur ran up the hill to the castle gate. Inside, the baroness herself took a look at him, her high hat and veil put aside.

"Welcome to Backford, Sir Avender." Her strong fingers shredded his trouser leg to get a look at his wound. "I daresay you don't remember me."

Avender winced. Strong she was, but not gentle. "I do, my lady," he answered through clenched teeth. "We danced four years ago in the Old Palace."

The baroness gave her patient a teasing push. Avender only just avoided falling by grabbing on to the bench beneath him.

"How flattering of you to remember," she said. "I know I was

thrilled to dance with the Hero of the Stoneways. The baron
proposed to me that night, you know." The baroness winked
like a blind rattling down a shop window in Malmoret. "I believe you made him jealous."

"It wasn't my intent, ma'am."

"Oh, go on with you. I know that. The baron and I were the
talk of the town, you know. Now, let's have a look at your leg. I
don't suppose it's poisoned."

The baroness pushed at his thigh with three thick fingers.
Fresh blood welled from the cut.

"Doesn't look poisoned."

Perret's sister peeked around her mistress's back. "Do you
think he needs the surgeon, Lady Breeanna?"

The baroness mopped Avender's leg with a clean sheet. "It's
not deep. I'm certain I can do it myself."

"Are you sure the surgeon shouldn't check it first?" asked
Avender as her ladyship jabbed him with her heavy fingers for the
third or fourth time. "Just in case?"

"Nonsense. This isn't the first arrowhead I've ever removed,
Sir Avender. The baron tells me I have the softest touch in the
north. Hold still and I'll have you fixed in a jiffy. Marietta, if you
could bring me a clean knife and another sheet."

Avender watched as the ladies prepared to deal with the arrowhead in his leg. Around them other women, and several men,
busied themselves among the wounded troopers. Most were
hurt more severely than Avender, which made him suspect that
having the baroness attend to him was not a mark of any particular honor. With some apprehension he watched as she took a
small, sharp knife from her assistant and applied it to his thigh.
Avender breathed deeply through his nose. Marietta wiped away
the fresh blood. But what the baroness lacked in delicacy she
more than made up in quickness. Like a milkmaid at her stool,

her movements were deft and sure. A squeeze and a pinch, and a quick flick of the knife, and the small black barb came free. Avender felt suddenly faint.

"He's all yours, Marietta." The baroness patted her patient roughly on the knee. "The wound's clean. I'll go see whom we can help next. And you, sir, must be our guest in the castle this evening. It would never do if someone of your stature spent the night at the inn."

Avender nodded, his mouth too dry to speak, and lay down on the bench. Closing his eyes, he found Marietta's touch much lighter than her ladyship's. Except for a few slight tugs, and the odd sensation of thread being pulled through his skin, he felt nothing of her nursing at all. No doubt she was better at embroidery than her mistress, too.

He woke with the disoriented feeling of not having slept for nearly as long as he needed. Sitting up, he found his leg bandaged, his trousers still torn all the way to the top of his thigh. Gingerly, he lifted himself to his feet and wondered if he could persuade Marietta to mend his pants. His wound ached when he put weight on it, but not nearly as badly as when the arrowhead was still lodged inside.

Holding fast to the backs of the tables and chairs, he hobbled to the door. The inn was no longer full; most of the patients and physicians appeared to have left, including the baroness and Marietta. Outside, however, all was confusion. Horses and wagons jammed the streets. Clouds of dust thickened the air. Avender looked about for someone he recognized but saw no face he knew.

Remembering the baroness's invitation, he gazed up the hill. Castle Backford was barely a furlong away, though several switchbacks lengthened the road. He was saved from trying to clamber aboard one of the wagons with his bad leg by the reappearance of Keln from the crowd.

"Avender!" his friend called, cheerful as ever. "You are a limp-kin. What are you waiting for? Every drover in town would be honored to carry the Hero of the Stoneways to Backford Keep. Just remember to remind her ladyship who it was found you. Marietta will be your friend for life if you do." With another of his broad winks, the trooper stopped the nearest cart and, helping Avender onto the back, jumped up beside him.

"We've got to make sure you don't strain yourself. Otherwise you'll be in no condition for the battle."

"I'll be okay. It's really nothing more than a deep cut. Look. I'm not even bleeding."

Avender pointed to his bandage, already dusty from the street, but otherwise clean.

Keln clapped him on the shoulder. "Good. I'll be disappointed if you're not by my side when we sweep our enemies from the field."

Avender wished he shared the trooper's confidence as the wagon jerked them up the side of the hill. Wanting to think of something else, he studied the town below. The higher they went, the more sense he made of its hurry and bustle. Their wagon, and most of the others toiling up the road, was filled with fodder. Other wagons trundled loads of brown dirt toward the dike at the far end of the meadow.

Avender peered north toward the watchtower and the edge of the reedy lake. "How long do they think it'll be before they attack?" he asked.

Keln shrugged. "The Keeadini won't dare enter Banking on their own, no matter how many of them there are. But if Ossdonc is truly on the way, it'll be another two, three days before his army arrives. They won't be able to make anything like the time across the Waste we did."

The wagon hauled them through the thick castle walls and into the busy courtyard beyond. Avender's leg was stiff but, with

Keln helping him along, he had little trouble reaching the inner keep.

The baroness met them at the door. "Sir Avender. I can't tell you how delighted I am to have a hero like you come to us in our hour of need."

Avender bowed. "To the extent my sword and wounded leg can be of service, Your Ladyship, they shall be."

"Tosh. You shall assist my baron to great victory, I'm sure. I hope you had no difficulty climbing the hill. I sent a man to fetch you, but I suppose you must have passed one another along the way. I've been frantic with worry." The baroness tossed her hands with a gesture of helplessness that might have thrown a young ram over a five-foot fence.

"Keln was good enough to help me hail a passing hayrick."

"Was he? Hmph." The baroness frowned primly at Avender's companion. "No motive of his own, I suppose. I should tell you, trooper, Marietta is still down in the town."

"I know, ma'am." Keln, with two good legs, bowed much more deeply than Avender. "She sent me after Sir Avender herself."

"I suppose you're telling the truth. Well, since you're here, you might as well come to supper. The Bryddin are joining us, and the baron wants to hear all about Sir Avender's adventures in the Stoneways. Now, if you would lend our guest your shoulder, I can show him to his room. Of course, Sir Avender, if you're too tired to dine with us this evening, I can have a meal brought to you there."

Avender had no intention of dining alone if there were Dwarves in Backford Keep, and wondered if he knew any of them. He hadn't seen Nolo in months. "Thank you, ma'am. You said you have Bryddin in the castle?"

"Oh yes. Three of them. They've been supervising the strengthening of our fortifications. But you know all about

Bryddin, don't you. You've been to Issinlough. You've seen the Seven Veils, and flown in one of their strange contraptions. And fought manders, too."

Her shining eyes, as she led the Hero of the Stoneways up to his room, showed she was every bit as interested in his adventures as her husband.

With Keln's assistance, the baroness brought him to a large chamber with a view to the east. Evening had crept well forward across the town, and lamps glowed in the windows below instead of the setting sun. Beyond the Wetting a line of early stars fanned forward from the bottom of the sky. Avender imagined Ferris far away in Valing, the same stars spilling over the tops of the Bavadars as she watched from her bedroom window. Tired though he was, he still managed to catch himself before sighing sorrowfully in front of his new friends.

He fell asleep the moment they left, the Bryddin completely forgotten. Later he woke to find the baroness and Marietta fluttering like moths around his room, candles cupped in their hands. Not sure whether he was awake or dreaming, he pulled his pillow over his head and slept on through morning, as deeply as Redburr on sunbaked stone.

Daylight booming in through the window finally roused him. His sore leg had stiffened during the night, but at least it no longer felt ready to tear at the slightest strain. His clothes he found cleaned and mended on a small table, a tray of breakfast beside them. He was dressed and well into his second buttered roll when a heavy knock sounded on the door.

The baroness poked her cheerful face into the room. "So, you are up!" The door swung wide as the rest of her followed. "I was just telling Marietta there was no telling how long you'd sleep. Our mattresses and pillows are famous through all Banking, you know. Made from our own goosedown. With the Wetting so close, it's a matter of course that Castle Backford is known for its soft beds." She blushed, as if the very mention of beds was too pleasant a memory for mixed company.

Avender spent most of the day in his room, but the baroness did permit him to take the air on the battlement, where he watched Backford's preparations for the coming siege. The dike rose higher between hill and marsh; the lancers practiced charges across the field. But the real question was how many Wizards would join the attack. Redburr had once told him that Ossdonc was the only one of the Three who liked to fight. Fornoch preferred to talk, and Usseis to skulk in his workshop's shadows, fashioning armies instead of leading them. But even one Wizard might be more than Backford could handle. And Reiffen might be with the enemy's army, too.

That night Avender dined at the baroness's table, along with Sir Worrel, several other officers, and their wives. He wondered if the Bryddin were coming later.

"Ah, Sir Avender! I was about to send a page up to see if you had fallen asleep again."

"I'm a little slow still, milady," Avender apologized. "And I regret not having more appropriate attire."

"Nonsense!" The baroness dismissed him with a flip of an arm. Her fine silk dress swept round her like a bedsheet in a high wind. "Dress signifies not in the least here on the frontier. Why, the baron has hosted Prince Gerrit himself while still wearing his spurs. Come, allow me to introduce you. Despite Sir Worrel and the baron's triumphs in the field yesterday, you remain the Hero of the Hour. Everyone wants to hear your tale."

His host was older than Avender expected, standing as straight as he rode, a tall, thin man with a curling, carefully groomed mustache and eyes the color of cold water. He received Avender's bow with a gracious nod, then resumed listening to Sir Worrel describe the day's progress in strengthening the town's defenses.

The baroness placed her guest in a large, high-backed chair by the fire. A pillow, plumped nearly to death by her own hands and presumably filled with the local down, was set upon his seat. The rest of the room went silent as Avender told his tale. The baron stroked his long mustache, while his wife smothered his other hand in both her own. Though smaller than the Great Hall in Valing, the heavy stone walls and lack of chandeliers made Castle Backford's hall seem gloomier and more mysterious.

"A talking stone?" The baroness clapped her hands delightedly when Avender was done; the flame gusted in the fire. "I should dearly love to meet your Durk."

"I'm certain he would have enjoyed meeting you, Your Lady-ship. Durk shines when he has a good audience."

"And that awful mander," said one of the other ladies. "To think that you killed it!"

"Only wounded it, my dear." Sir Worrel nodded gallantly as he corrected his wife. "As I understand the tale, not even the Oeinnen was able to slay the monster."

The baroness sighed. "It's too bad the Oeinnen had to fly to Rimwich to warn the king. I so would have enjoyed having him as a guest at the castle. He cut a splendid figure that time I met him in Malmoret. That was when Avender and I first met, you know. And that charming girl the prince is so enamored of."

"Isn't she also from Valing?" asked one of the other matrons.

"Quite," answered the baroness. "A slip of a thing, full grown by now, I'm sure. She and I were great friends before the baron and I were married. I thought her absolutely lovely, but there were others who were appalled by the way she threw herself at Prince Brizen. People in Malmoret aren't always so gracious as we are here on the frontier, you know."

All the ladies nodded. Avender recognized the baroness's great liking for Ferris despite her careless words, and guessed that every lady in the room had been snubbed some time or other in the capital. None were great beauties, nor was it likely that any of them were rich.

"I'll be sure to remember you to Ferris, the next time I see her, Baroness," he said.

"Oh, she won't know me as a baroness. That was before the baron swept me off my feet." Avender pictured just the opposite as the baroness startled her husband with an affectionate pat. "Please tell her you met Lady Breeanna. That's the name she'll recall."

"I hear the prince is quite smitten," said Lady Worrel. "And that she actually turned him down."

"I should be very surprised to learn the prince has been so incautious as to propose." Lady Breeanna looked about the company with knowing primness. "He knows better than to cross the king."

"They say the king prefers Lady Wellin."

"If there has been a proposal," said the baroness, "you can be sure Ferris would never have turned him down. Unless, of course, all the swains in Valing are as charming as yourself, Sir Avender."

"You honor me, Baroness."

"Though I should never have picked you over my baron, mind you." Lady Breeanna gazed adoringly at her husband, who dipped his long nose gallantly in return, like an egret in Backford Pool.

Heavy feet clomped on the stone floor as three Dwarves barreled into the room, dust and dirt trailing behind them. Lady Breeanna curtsied deeply in answer to their bows, her chin high above their heads.

"Welcome, friends," she said solemnly. "I trust your day has been productive. Have you finished your tunnel?"

"Not yet, my lady." The first Dwarf scratched his chin, sending a fresh shower of dirt to the floor. "But we've almost reached the tower."

"I'll lead a sortie myself when the way is opened tomorrow," declared the second, lowering a heavy sack to the floor. He was an odd-looking Bryddin, with a sword at his side instead of the usual tool belt. He was also shorter and slimmer than any Dwarf Avender had ever seen. If not for his tangled beard and hair, he might almost have looked like a lad of ten or twelve.

"Splendid, Findle!" The baroness beamed at the shortish Dwarf. "You must be famished. And thirsty. I've brought another barrel of the West Todding up from the cellars, but you'd better ration yourselves a little more carefully than before. It's the last."

A smile cracked Findle's beard. "We'll do our best, Baroness. But your hospitality is hard to ignore."

Avender thought he recognized the third Dwarf, but it had been seven years since he had seen the fellow and wasn't sure his old acquaintance would remember him. "Nurren? Is that you?" he asked.

The Dwarf looked up, a glass of the West Todding already in his hand. "Aye, I'm Nurren. Who are you?"

"Why, Sir Nurren!" Lady Breeanna galloped over to her guests, anxious to make the proper introductions. "I thought all Bryddin knew Sir Avender of Valing."

Nurren's eyebrows huddled. "Avender? That's not Avender. He's half again too tall and has whiskers on his chin."

Avender rubbed his slight beard self-consciously. "It's me, Nurren. I was a boy the last time we met. I've grown, but you haven't changed at all."

With a sound like hammered rocks, Nurren smacked himself on the forehead. "What a blockhead I am! I forgot you humans grow, like fish and mushrooms. Avender, it's good to see you."

"How marvelous!" exclaimed Lady Breeanna. "Old friends meeting again in Castle Backford. It's like something out of a story. Baron, dear, isn't it wonderful?"

The baron acknowledged his wife's glee with a regal tip of the head. His eyes, however, twinkled above his mustache.

Everyone took their places at the long table in the center of the room as the servants brought in the meal. Except for the attendants and the fact that there were individual chairs rather than benches for the guests, it was not that different from a high meal in Valing. Her ladyship presided over a roast pig, briskly carving out much larger slices than needed for her guests. In front of the baron two large fish, their skins crinkled and brown, lay head to tail on a bed of leeks and parsnips.

"What brings you to Backford?" asked Avender when he found himself seated beside his old companion.

Nurren wiped his mouth on the back of his sleeve and helped himself to the mashed potatoes. "Nolo thought we could be useful."

"Nolo sent you?"

"He didn't send us, mind you, but he thought we might be interested. Especially after we finished digging the new way. We've been here a couple of moons. Worked on the castle, and the bridge, and the dams upstream."

"There's a new way?"

With a quick glance around to make sure no one was listening, the Dwarf moved closer to Avender. "The Sun Road's not the only way into Bryddlough anymore, you know." He put a finger to his nose and gave the young man a quick wink.

"Nolo told me about the Valing road," said Avender, "but I didn't know there were others."

Nurren nodded. "The one we just finished's not too far from here. It's very secret. Only the baron knows. But I don't think Nolo and Dwvon will mind my telling you. I'll take you out tomorrow and show you the new tunnel we're cutting to Watch Hill at the same time."

When the meal was finished Lady Breeanna asked Marietta to sing. Her dark hair gleamed in the torchlight, and Avender couldn't help but think, though she was more beautiful than Ferris, with a figure like a sheave of wheat, she seemed a trifle dull. She sang better than Ferris, too, but that wasn't saying anything at all.

> *"In Backford when the moon was full*
> *And summer lay on ram and bull,*
> *Starlight glistened on the stream*
> *As Keeadini crept.*
>
> *Across the meadow, deep with hay,*
> *They lay in wait, until the day*
> *Rose up from the edge of dream,*
> *As Banking soldiers slept . . ."*

The baron closed his eyes. The only sign he hadn't fallen asleep was the occasional stroking of his mustache with a single finger. The baroness sat beside him, her back straight as a washboard, nodding beatifically, although a little out of time with the tune.

When Marietta's song was finished the first Dwarf, whose name was Garven, approached the baron with Findle's sack. "Dwvon and Nolo sent these," he said. The bag clanked heavily as he lifted it onto the table. "Nolo told us we would know when to bring them out."

The Dwarf removed something long and thin, wrapped in soft cloth, from the bag. Unfolding the fabric revealed a long, white sword. Among the humans, only the baron kept his aplomb. Avender and the officers marveled at the sight of a weapon fashioned from a single piece of pale stone.

"Magnificent," said Sir Worrel.

"What's it made of?" asked the baroness, craning forward.

"Inach," answered Garven. "Heartstone, in your tongue."

"Heartstone? Isn't that what the Sword of Valing was made from?"

"It is, my lady."

"Only heartstone can harm the Three, they say," said Findle, his fingertips grazing his own sword's grip. "This is a proud weapon."

Holding the gift at hilt and blade, Garven presented it to his host. Bowing, he said, "Baron Backford, I offer you a sword of Inach, crafted by Dwvon himself in Issinlough.

"Bone of Ina,
Long asleep,
Has strength to strike its children."

The baron bowed in turn and reached out to accept the offering. His arms gave slightly under its sudden weight. Clasping the hilt with both hands, he held the weapon up against the candlelight. The pale stone didn't so much cleave the illumination as bend it like a rock in water, forcing the light around its edge on either side. Gently, the baron swung the blade above his head, then down across his body in a slow, slashing arc.

"This is a mighty weapon," he said, laying the sword carefully on the table before him. Behind him, Breeanna beamed. "It shall be an heirloom of my house. I thank you. And I thank Dwvon, and all the lords of stone."

Garven bowed a second time.

"There's more." Findle pulled a handful of arrows from the bag. "Give these to your best bowman. There aren't a lot of them. Every shot has to count."

Five arrows rattled onto the table, each half as long as Avender, with solid, goose-feathered shafts and stone points. Reaching for the nearest, Sir Worrel weighed it in his hand.

"Wysko won the last tournament," he said. "He'll make the best use of these. They feel heavy in the tip, though."

"There's no heavier stone than Inach." Garven picked up an arrow and eyed its line from fletching to head.

"Maybe you Bryddin should keep them." Sir Worrel's arrow rattled as he dropped it back on the table. "You might be able to get more tension on the bow."

"We make poor archers," said Findle. "Our arms aren't long enough for your long bows, and we break anything smaller. Crossbows, though, are another matter."

"Is this all you brought?" asked Avender. When Nolo had first found the heartstone deep in the High Bavadars, he had talked about making swords and spears enough for an army. "Aren't there any more?"

"It takes time to cut Inach," answered Garven. "Dwvon is still learning the art. Of the swords he's fashioned so far, Brannis and his son each have one, and Prince Gerrit another. And Berrel has a fifth in Valing."

"Your gifts are great treasure." The baron gave Avender a stern glance before continuing. "But the friendship and strength of the Bryddin are worth far more. Singly, our enemies might stand against us and prevail. When we take arms together, they surely will fail."

The next morning the baroness insisted on examining Avender's leg before he left his room. She pushed and poked at the wound with her ungentle fingers but, short of prying the stitches apart, was unable to make it bleed. Despite herself, she had to admit he was healing nicely. Rewrapping his leg, she reminded him not to overdo it.

Nurren was waiting for him in the main hall when she was done. The eastern windows, high above the floor, showed patches of blue like bright fabric hanging on the opposite wall, though the room was dim and cold. Through a small door beneath the stone stair, Avender followed the Dwarf into the lower levels of

222 | S. C. BUTLER

the castle. Unlike the Manor, where a torch was always handy for any descent into the caverns in the Neck, here he followed the Dwarf into musty blackness. The stair ran straight down, the steps narrow and rough. Avender went slowly, not trusting his leg to any sudden need.

"Watch the wall." Nurren's voice rumbled close in the darkness. "The passage turns to the right."

Avender raised a hand just in time to catch the stone in front of him. His eyes grew used to the gloom. Beyond the turn a gray glimmer shone at the bottom of the stair. A stump of candle burned in a niche in the wall, barely illuminating a chamber almost as wide as the hall above, though the ceiling was much lower. Casks lined the walls, with smaller barrels and baskets filling the rest of the room. Dark mouths of tunnels led off to other places. Nurren led Avender to one of these, rougher than the others, their footsteps scuffing on the flagstones.

"We'll put a stout door here, when we're done." Nurren paused at the entrance to pluck a Dwarven lamp from his pocket. The clear stone gleamed between his fingers like cold fire as he fitted it into the socket at the front of his iron headband. Motioning for Avender to follow, he ducked inside the passage.

They walked in single file along the narrow tunnel, the ceiling high enough for Avender to pass without stooping. Nurren's lamp revealed walls unfinished by Dwarven standards, though quite smooth by any other.

Stopping, the Dwarf pointed to the left-hand wall.

"Look here," he said.

At first Avender saw only bare rock. Then a thin line began to show in the stone, gold as the light from Nurren's lamp. As Avender watched, the outline of a low door formed. Nurren placed his hand on the rock inside the line and pushed. Slowly the door swung open to reveal a second narrow passage.

"Is that the way we're going?" asked Avender.

Nurren shook his head, his lamp batting light and shadow across both tunnels. "That's the back door."

"Back door?"

"There should always be a back door. In case something gets stuck in the front."

"Where does it go?"

"Up the hill. Where it comes out isn't far from the way to Bryddlough."

"I thought that was what you were going to show me."

"Not this time. Garven says the baron told him there are too many spies. Someone might follow us and find the way. I'm taking you to the watchtower instead. I can show you where the way begins just as well from there and no one will notice."

Seizing the edge of the stone door, Nurren pulled it closed. "You'll need one of these to find it, though." He tapped his lamp with a thick finger. "This door will open without a lamp, if you know where to look. But the other needs a key."

"I have a lamp." Avender patted his shirt. Close to his chest he carried his most precious gift in a small, soft pouch: the lamp Uhle had given him on his first visit to Issinlough.

They continued on down the main passage. A sharp right turn brought them to a long set of stairs running into deeper darkness. To ease the strain on his sore leg, Avender braced his hand on the ceiling in front of him.

At the bottom of the stair the tunnel flattened and turned left. The air seemed damper than before, and the rock shone wetly in spots. A second set of steps led upward.

"Are we under the river?" asked Avender.

"We were. Now we're on the other side."

Avender hadn't counted the stairs as they descended, but it seemed they were going up even farther than they had gone down. His sore leg began to ache. He didn't think they had gone nearly far enough to reach Watch Hill, though.

"Are we coming out soon?" he asked.

"Coming out? On the surface, you mean? No, this road runs all the way to the watchtower. How could it be a secret way if it didn't?"

"But the meadow's much lower than the castle." Avender was confused. The shortest distance to the watchtower was through the meadow.

"Too wet for tunneling beneath the meadow," answered Nurren. "We'd need too many pumps. No, this road runs along the shoulder of the hill all the way. Much better cutting that way. Good, solid olath."

"You cut through solid rock all the way from the castle to the watchtower in two months? Why, it must be at least a mile."

"Point seven three four miles, as I understand your measure of a mile. But we'd have done it quicker if we hadn't been working on the castle and the dams and everything else around here."

The steps ended. Nurren led them forward through a flat passageway once more, while Avender marveled at how quickly the Dwarves could mine. He knew the hardest rock, except heartstone, was not much more than butter to them. But still.

Avender's boots clicked against the stone as they padded through the narrow way; Nurren's bare feet slapped softly. Avender supposed the tunnel curved with the side of the hill, but there wasn't enough light to see far enough to tell. When a light finally did appear ahead, the road ran straight toward it. They found Garven at the top of a short flight of stairs, putting the finishing touches on a stone door similar to the one Nurren had shown Avender at the other end of the tunnel.

"Another back door?" the young man asked.

"No. This is the entrance to the tower." Garven pulled the door open as he answered. His and Nurren's lamplight washed over a clutter of old casks, baskets of withered apples, and sacks of what looked like potatoes. In the middle of the room a wooden ladder led to a trapdoor in the ceiling.

"Where's Findle?" Avender looked around the tower cellar for the third Dwarf.

"Hunting."

"Hunting?" In all his years with Nolo, Avender had never heard of Dwarves hunting, except perhaps for manders.

"Hunting Keeadini," said Garven.

"Findle has killed more manders than anyone," added Nurren.

"What do Keeadini have to do with manders?"

"Nothing." Nurren scratched his chin. "But Findle likes to hunt. Since there aren't any manders up here, he's taken to hunting what you humans hunt."

"Each other," pointed out Garven.

Avender decided Findle was the oddest Dwarf he had ever met. Odder even than Grimble, who at least was strange in ways that seemed normal for a Dwarf.

Garven ran his hand along the edge of the door, smoothing the stone beneath his palm, then led them into the cellar. Climbing the ladder, he rapped on the trapdoor and, after a brief interval, flipped it open. Dim sunlight seeped into the chamber, enough to drown the lamps' pale gleam. The outline of the Dwarven door disappeared. Avender gave the spot where it had been a push; the slab swung open easily as a curtain.

"Anyone might find this," he said.

Nurren looked back, his hands and one foot on the ladder. "There'll be locks and bars when we're done. But first, I have to show you the entrance to the way. And it's a fine view up top, too."

Avender followed the Bryddin up several ladders and through several floors to the top of the turret. The strong summer sun, still east of noon, beat upon their shoulders. The Blue Mountains glowered like a row of old men needing shaves. The soldiers on watch nodded cheerfully as they arrived, well used to the presence of the Dwarves.

Nurren was right. The view from the tower was much better than from the castle. Watch Hill thrust out toward the lake like a peninsula in the grass, away from the hills and mountains. Three directions opened up to view: the Waste rising in long waves to the north; Backford Pool and the long marshes of the Wetting glittering to the east; and Banking proper to the south, a land of homely green.

At the foot of the hill the height of the earthen wall had doubled across the road; sharpened stakes protruded from the northern side. Carts rumbled across the meadow with fresh dirt to build the wall still higher, but the long meadow itself remained unobstructed all the way to the river. "For the lancers' charge," Keln had told him when he asked about it the day before. "If the tribesmen manage to get across the wall, the baron himself will drive them back to the Waste."

Having seen the Keeadini melt back into the plains before the leveled spears of the Banking heavy cavalry once already, Avender had not doubted his friend. The question was, what would Ossdonc and his sissit do? And Reiffen, if he was with them.

He looked to the north. Bands of Keeadini trotted back and forth across the open ground, not caring who saw them. Twists of smoke rose into the blue sky from many campfires. For once the great plain was filled with people instead of wissund herds.

"Who'd have thought there could be so many humans?" wondered Nurren, peering out between the notches in the wall.

"Aye," said the nearest soldier. "And no hope of friends of our own unless Duke Arrand shows up."

"He'll come," said a second.

"Not that it matters," replied the first. "We can hold them ourselves. No one crosses the river without the baron's say-so."

"I still say a good charge through their camp would be just the thing. Scare the filthy Wasters right off when they think they're settled."

"Can't do that without tearing down the wall." The speaker looked toward the carts tipping fresh dirt on the dike at the bottom of the hill. "The baron's made up his mind to make them come to us. Fight them at the wall, then mow them down in the meadow."

Nurren tapped Avender on the arm and led the young man to the other side of the tower. Across the meadow the white on blue of the baron's pennant fluttered in the breeze.

"See that knob of olath up the hill?" The Dwarf pointed at the slope above the castle, his voice low so none of the soldiers would overhear. "That's the entrance to the Backford road."

Only after Nurren stopped telling him to look for the olath and pointed out a slab of grayish rock like a scar on the side of the mountain was Avender able to see what he meant.

"But how will I find it?" he asked.

"Head straight up the slope after you leave the back door. It's three hundred and seventeen paces. Though maybe fewer of yours." Nurren glanced briefly at his companion's longer legs. "You won't miss it, once you see it. You'll have to climb up the loose stone at the bottom to get to the door, though."

"You said there was a key."

"Right. I almost forgot. You'll see the keyhole when you shine your lamp on the door. The lamp's the key. And you better take someone else strong along with you. You'll never get it open on your own."

Avender took one last look at the spot on the side of the hill to make sure he would recognize it. "Hopefully I won't be using it any time soon," he said.

They were turning back from the wall when one of the soldiers cried out from the other side.

"Here. What's that?"

"What's what?"

The other soldiers turned to see what their fellow had found. Avender and the Dwarves looked as well. A dark smudge stained the rolling plain in the distance.

"Just another band of Keeadini."

"No, it's not. Keeadini don't travel packed so close together."

"They do when they're bringing the whole tribe."

Avender leaned forward above the wall, straining to see in the distance.

"What's that with them?" asked one of the soldiers.

"Looks like a siege tower," his companion answered.

"A siege tower? How do they think they're going to get that across the river?"

"Whatever it is, it's not Keeadini."

The sergeant made up his mind. Crossing to the castle side of the tower, he took the horn from his belt and blew a long, hard blast. The note echoed across the hills. By the time the sergeant blew a second, the nearest ducks were dashing across the water toward the sky. By the time he started the third, a troop of horsemen were spilling across the bridge and into the meadow at a full gallop.

"You finish that tunnel back to the castle yet?" asked the soldier nearest Nurren.

Avender, staring hard into the distance, was sure he saw the tower lift a massive arm. A Wizard, definitely. After all the time Reiffen and he had spent as children imagining themselves as great warriors, it was hard to believe that now, when the moment had finally arrived, they were going to find themselves on opposite sides.

13

Fog and White Spray

Ferris woke to a clap of thunder. Leaping from her bed, she dashed to the window to close the shutters before the room was drenched, only to find there wasn't any storm. Pale dawn crested the mountains. Mist covered the lake like a herd of huddled sheep, without a breath of wind.

Fog wasn't unusual at daybreak in Valing, but who ever heard of lightning in a morning fog? Leaning farther out the window, she searched for storm clouds in the mountains. A flash from the lake regained her attention. Thunder followed, brief and muted. Another flicker lit the fog.

Grabbing her robe, she rushed to fetch her parents. Their bedroom faced the courtyard, and there was every chance the faint thunder hadn't woken them.

"There's something happening on the lake!"

Berrel just barely beat Hern out from under the covers. "What is it?" he cried, the tassel on his nightcap bobbing in front of his anxious face.

Three more thunderclaps rumbled through the house. Berrel pulled the tassel away from his eyes and leaned out the nearest window.

"Where's the storm?"

"On the lake. In the islands, I think." As she spoke, Ferris remembered Reiffen's appearance in her room the night before. Dream or not, he had said something was about to happen. And he hadn't sounded as if it would be good.

"Maybe it's magic," she added.

In nightgown and nightshirt, Ferris and her father hurried downstairs. Hern paused to gather cloaks before following. Outside, the wet grass chilled their bare feet as they ran through the orchard to the edge of the cliff. Bursts of light still stirred the fog, accompanied by feeble strokes of thunder. Slowly the flashes moved north through the mist.

"Whatever it is," said Berrel, "it's coming this way."

"I'm sure it was over the islands before," said Ferris.

"It's past the Bottle now."

"Can you tell what it is yet?" Hern came up beside them, wisps of gray puffing out beneath her nightcap, and handed out the cloaks.

"It's magic," said Ferris, not bothering to put hers on. She was warm enough already. "It has to be."

"Then it must be dangerous."

Ferris hadn't seen her mother so anxious in a long time, not since the morning Reiffen and Giserre had disappeared.

Berrel started back to the house. "We have to find out what's going on. They can probably hear it in Eastbay and Spinner's, but we're the only ones high enough for a clear view of how odd this is."

"You won't be able to see a thing on the lake," warned Hern.

"It'll burn off. Besides, if I can't paddle a straight line from here to the Bottle, fog or no, I'll know the reason why."

As they came out of the orchard they found Sally hanging out of her upstairs window, her husband peering over her shoulder. "Hern!" she called. "What's going on?"

"Everything's under control!" Hern waved Sally back inside. "Berrel's just on his way down to the lower dock to find out. Come on down to the kitchen and we'll get some breakfast ready."

Dennol met them at the house, a pair of sleepy guards lumbering behind him.

"Snug, Fells," Berrel ordered. "You two come with me. Dennol, you're in charge while I'm gone unless Ranner shows up. Keep a watch from the cliff, but make sure the gate stays manned. Eastbay'll probably send a runner to find out what's going on. If they do, send him back to tell the mayor to get a couple of long canoes out with the Home Guard."

"I'm going with you," said Ferris.

"No you're not," said Hern.

"Yes I am." Ferris had never told anyone about her dreams and wanted to make sure there was a connection before she said anything now. "Four paddlers are better than three."

"You can come, Ferris." Berrel ignored his wife's nasty look. "Four paddlers *are* better than three. But if you don't meet us at the lower dock in five minutes, armed and dressed, we'll leave without you."

Knowing her mother was too stout to catch her, Ferris raced up the stairs. The dread she had felt the moment she woke followed at her heels. What else could those flashes and weak thunder be but magic? Coming as they had the morning after her dream, they must be more than simple chance. Maybe Reiffen had found a way to escape finally, after all these years. The lightning could be a signal he needed her help.

She tried not to think about the alternatives as she pulled on her clothes. By the time she returned to the kitchen, Hern and Sally were firing up the stove. Her mother gave her a short look, which Ferris knew was meant both for reproof and good luck. Armed with a bow and quiver from the stock in the unlocked section of the armory, she hurried down to the cellar and the long stair leading to the bottom of the Neck, her knife already tucked into the sheath at her belt.

She found Snug and Fells already on the quay. The sight of their shadows flitting through the dim light that filtered in from the entrance to the cave reminded Ferris of Reiffen in her dream. Chains creaked as Fells turned the wheel that raised the gate. Water dripped from the portcullis in loud splashes that echoed hollowly off the stone.

Old Mortin hobbled out from his small room beside the dock, his candle casting a soft light across the chamber.

"What's going on?"

"Just an early start, Mortin," answered Berrel as he emerged from the stair. "Go on back to bed."

Snug jumped down to the floating wharf and began to untie one of the canoes as Ferris picked four paddles from the rack and joined him. The dock swayed beneath her feet.

They slipped out onto the still lake, ducking as they passed under the stone entrance because of the high water. The gorge drummed distantly, its direction twisted by the fog. Behind them the Neck disappeared in a matter of strokes. Snug paddled bow, with Berrel in the stern and Ferris in front of her father. Pulling together, they drove the canoe through the water faster than a man or woman could walk. Small waves surged out from the canvas sides.

After a while, Ferris realized they hadn't heard any thunder at all since leaving the cave.

"I know," replied her father to her question. "Whatever was happening has stopped."

Anxiously she peered into the haze, but it was Snug, in the bow, who saw something first.

"Island to starboard," he called.

A low shadow loomed in the mist to their right. Ferris couldn't tell if it was a small island near at hand, or a large one farther away. Fells glanced nervously at the lake and the unseen sky.

"Cease paddle." Berrel's voice was muffled in the fog. "Is it Bottle?"

"Can't tell. What do you think?"

The slow current pulled them closer.

"It's Bottle," Fells confirmed.

"We'll check it first, though the last flashes were beyond it." The canoe rocked slightly as Berrel straightened and peered around at the rest of the lake. "Until the fog lifts and we can see, we'll have to check each island. Easy now. Everyone paddle light and slow."

Ferris matched her stroke to Snug's. She kept her eyes and ears open as they slid forward, the current pulling them along as much as their paddles. The island grew as they approached, darkening from smoky gray to dull brown and green. Its neck pointed south, away from the falls, a narrow beach on the eastern shoulder. Small and stony, the island was not usually worth pasturing even a single sheep.

"What's that?"

Ferris ceased paddling and pointed as something large and brown moved on the beach.

"It's a nokken," said Snug from the bow.

"What's the matter with it?"

The nokken lay on its stomach with its nose on the stony shore. It flopped suddenly as the humans drifted close, its flippers splashing weakly.

"Icer, is that you?" Ferris thought she knew that gray muzzle.

The seal replied with a short bark, his whiskers fluttering at the effort. Ferris slipped out of the canoe into cold water as deep as her waist before her father could stop her. With lunging steps she plowed up the shelf to kneel by the injured seal. A long, ugly burn stretched from shoulder to flipper along Icer's right side, the skin blackened and raw. Just the sort of burn a bolt of lightning might leave behind. Thin wisps of blood curled out into the clear water; small fish nibbled at the ends.

Ferris tried to pull Icer farther up onto the beach. "Help me get him up on dry land!"

"Don't . . . don't waste time," gasped the nokken. "Pups . . . still in the water."

Exhausted at the effort of speaking, Icer's head flopped back down on the stony shore. His quivering whiskers broke Ferris's heart. Snug and Berrel held the canoe steady while Fells jumped out to help Ferris. Together they pulled the heavy nokken farther up the beach, ignoring the uneasy feeling that whatever had hurt him might still be lurking nearby in the heavy fog.

"Pups." The nokken barely lifted his head as he tried to speak once more.

"What happened? Who did this to you?"

Icer closed his eyes wearily. "Don't know . . . have to save the pups . . . too much current . . . the gorge."

Ferris understood at once, her anger increasing. Harming a pup was as bad as harming a human baby. She looked back at the canoe. "Icer says there are pups still in the lake. We have to find them before the current drags them over the gorge."

"In this fog?" Snug gestured toward the thick mist. "We'll be in the White Pool ourselves before we find a one of 'em."

"We have to try."

"Ferris is right." Berrel's mouth pursed grimly. "We have to do what we can to save the pups. Icer, we'll be back for you, but probably not till the fog clears."

Leaving the old nokken on the beach, Fells and Ferris climbed back into the canoe. Berrel steered them around to the west side of Bottle Island, where the current rippled along the shore. For a long way north the lake was safe, but there was a limit to how close they could come to the gorge, especially when the lake was high. Ferris tried to remember where the rippling that showed the start of the heaviest current began. Had it been a stone's throw from the head of the gorge? Two? Either way, if they found themselves in that part of the current it would be too late. The key would be to recognize where they were long before that.

The island disappeared in the mist. The only sign they were moving was their wake; the current's pace couldn't be told without landmarks to measure their progress. Eyes alert for nokken in the water, especially the bobbing heads of pups, they pressed forward into the fog. Nor did they forget to watch for whatever had wounded Icer. Ferris took some comfort that the nokken hadn't known what had attacked him. Had it been Reiffen, Icer would have recognized him for sure.

Minutes passed. The roar of the gorge and the waterfall beyond grew louder. Above their heads the mist began to thin.

"If we don't find something soon," said Berrel, "I'm taking us back."

They came out of the fog into a patch of sunlit lake. Mist surrounded them in stealthy banks.

"There's something to starboard," said Snug, pointing.

Ferris peered across the canoe, but saw nothing.

"It just went back in the fog," said the bowman.

"I saw it."

Berrel guided the canoe back into the cloud. Ferris shivered as the damp air kissed her cheek. Then she saw it, a small brown head struggling feebly in the water. Small waves stuttered around it. They paddled fiercely, ignoring the rising roar of the flume. Leaning forward, Snug plucked the wriggling body out of the lake and dangled him over the canoe by the scruff of his neck. One shoulder was black and burned, though without the raw wetness that had marked Icer's wound.

"Let me see him," said Ferris.

Fells took the pup from Snug and handed him over. Ferris

cradled him in her arms, trying not to hurt his shoulder. The pup squirmed and spat but, without any water in his mouth, he couldn't really give her much of a spraying. She saw at once he was too small and scared to tell them what had happened, which might have been the reason whoever had burned him hadn't bothered to finish him off.

Laying the pup gently in the bottom of the canoe, Ferris took up her paddle again. "Icer said there was more than one."

"First let's find out where we are," said Berrel.

Once more the canoe glided out of the fog. Green mountains soared up against blue sky. They recognized where they were at once, just beyond the northern entrance to the bay outside Spinner's Farm, about as far north as they wished to go. A puff of wind widened the lane of air around them, bringing the Neck into view on the other shore. Threads of mist washed clear against the dark stone like a spent wave, small figures watching from the cliff above.

"There's another!" called Fells, pointing east.

Berrel frowned. "I don't know if we can get that one. It's awful close to the cut."

Ferris gripped her paddle. "We have to try."

His face set, Berrel agreed. All four paddlers bent their backs to their strongest stroke yet. Ahead of them, a long plume of cloud rose up to the sky behind the Teapot's spout. The small black blur they were pursuing followed the retreating mist toward the gorge.

At first Ferris thought they were going to reach it in time. But even as they closed quickly on the bobbing head the current around it quickened. Ferris gritted her teeth and forced her paddle through the water as powerfully as she could, wishing she were stronger. If they could just have a few more strokes.

"That's enough." The canoe slowed only a little as everyone

ceased paddling. "Snug, hard turn toward Spinner's. We can't risk going any closer. Best to get out of here while we can."

Her heart breaking, Ferris took a last sad look at the nokken. Its small muzzle rose and fell as the pup struggled amid the growing waves.

"Paddle, Ferris," ordered her father sharply. "We're not free yet."

She bent her back once more, hands and shoulders aching. Berrel guided them at an angle across the current, racing for the slack water of the bay. The water tugged at the canoe like a large dog, dragging them toward the gorge. For the first time it occurred to Ferris they might have gone too far.

But Berrel knew his lake. The pull of the current weakened. No longer did the western shore slide so quickly across their bow. Exhausted, they coasted into calmer water. Ferris leaned forward, gasping with fatigue, her paddle athwart the gunwales as an eddy spun the bow back toward the north. Her chest burned. Before them the mist had cleared almost all the way to the mouth of the gorge, leaving a clear view of the dark blue water as it thickened at the top of the flume.

"There's another nokken to port," said Snug, panting hard. "A big one. Must be one of the bachelors."

Like the shadow of a diving bird, the large nokken darted forward a stone's throw from the canoe. Though the pup looked as if it had already drifted beyond help, the pursuing nokken kept up the chase all the same. Often he leapt clear of the water, his sleek brown body arcing above the current like a leaping fish. Quickly he gained on the struggling infant. The race was going to be very close.

Ferris gave a little cry the second time the nokken leapt. She had seen Skimmer soar back and forth across the bows of too many boats not to recognize him in midflight. Her hands tightened fearfully on her paddle as bachelor and pup hurtled toward the lip of the gorge.

He was going to be too late. Already the pup was at the edge of the wild chute, spray mingling with the fog. Skimmer remained two or three canoe lengths away. Ferris imagined she heard a terrified squeal as the pup vanished into the rolling waves. Skimmer leapt clear of the lake one last time and plunged into the spray behind it. The white mist swallowed them both.

Ferris threw her face into her hands and wept. At her knees, the pup they had saved whimpered on the wooden planking. Berrel waited until the last hope of Skimmer's return had died, then gave the order to paddle back into Spinner's Bay. As they rounded the southern flank of the Teapot the gorge disappeared behind them. Quiet replaced the tumbling roar, but Ferris felt Skimmer's loss even more keenly. Her only consolation was that it hadn't been Reiffen who had attacked the nokken, or Icer would have told them.

They paddled straight to Spinner's dock, where everyone clung to the rough wood for a much needed rest. The dogs trotted out onto the pier, their friendly barking the signal to Mother Spinner and her sons that the visitors weren't a threat. Ferris gasped, her throat too dry from paddling for further tears.

"Nokken'll do just about anything to save a pup, lass," said Fells kindly.

"I'm thinkin' he knew he couldn't beat the current, but kept on anyway," said Snug.

Berrel climbed out of the canoe and looked back toward the Bottle, one hand shading his eyes against the morning glare. Two of Spinner's dogs stood beside him, their tails wagging briskly and their noses pointed in the same direction.

"Looks like Eastbay sent the two canoes I asked for." His eyes scanned the rest of the lake. "But there's still no sign of what

QUEEN FERRIS | 239

caused all the ruckus. We'll have to go back and talk to Icer. Fells, go get some bandages from Mother Spinner. And a pot of salve, too. Icer will talk better when we patch him up."

"The pup needs patching, too." Ferris took a long, halting breath and wiped her eyes.

The steward looked down at her as she brought herself under control. "I'm sorry, Ferris. I wish you hadn't had to see that. I'll send a party down to the White Pool to look for the bodies this afternoon. But first we've got to learn what happened."

The pup at her knees whimpered again. Ferris felt for a handkerchief in her pocket and, finding none, dipped her hands into the lake. Gently she poured cool water onto the small nokken's wound. The pup flapped his fins; Ferris couldn't tell if she'd made him feel better or worse. Suddenly tired, she wiped the back of her wet hand across her forehead. The worry of what they had yet to find tugged at her like the last wisps of current on the canoe.

Fells didn't have to go far on his errand. Enna Spinner met him at the foot of the dock but ignored him entirely. Her son Elm followed close behind her.

"What's going on here?" she demanded as she hurried out to the end. "Was that you makin' all that racket this morning, Steward?"

Berrel ran a hand through his half-gray hair. "I don't want to scare you, Enna. But it seems someone's attacked the nokken."

"Attacked the nokken?" Mother Spinner peered across the lake at the islands, the wrinkles crinkling around her eyes. She didn't look scared at all. "That's a fool thing to do. Did Longback drown 'em?"

"We don't know yet. We've been rescuing pups."

Berrel nodded toward the canoe. Ferris leaned back to make sure Mother Spinner got a good look at the small brown nokken lying in the bottom.

"Something burned it," said Ferris. "I was wondering if you could bring some clean cloth for bandages."

Mother Spinner cocked her head at her son. "Elm, go tell Min to bring out one of the old sheets. And some of that ointment I mixed up last time your brother burned himself in the sugar house." The spry old woman turned back to Berrel. "How'd they get so burned? There's no smoke I can see out there on the islands."

"That's what we still have to find out. We only pulled in to your dock to get out of the current. We lost another pup to the gorge."

"And Skimmer, too." Ferris didn't imagine she would feel any worse if it had been Avender who had been lost over the falls.

Mother Spinner clucked grimly. "It was bad enough the time that Mindrell fellow came through. Now folks are attackin' nokken. I suppose we'll have Wizards hauntin' us next. When I was a girl this sort of thing didn't happen in Valing, Steward."

"Well, it's here now, Enna," said Berrel, "and we have to find out what it is before we can stop it. Ferris, bring that pup up out of the canoe. You can nurse him here while we go back to Bottle."

"I'm going with you." Carefully Ferris picked up the nokken, its wet fur dampening her sleeves. "Mother Spinner, if you could watch him for me, I'd really appreciate it. I have to go back to the island."

"Well, now, Ferris. I've my morning chores to see about. And there's breakfast—"

"Skim always loved your candy better than anyone else's, ma'am. All the nokken do."

The old woman's frown deepened. "Well, if it's for the nokken. I suppose I can manage. Just make sure you send one of the aunties round for him when you're done."

Min Spinner's shoes clattered as she hurried onto the dock with an armload of clean sheets for bandages and a pot of salve.

Ferris took them all, knowing there would be more at the farm-house. Climbing back into the canoe, Berrel and his crew pushed off from the dock and paddled rapidly uplake toward the islands. Ferris took a last look behind her as they left; Mother Spinner cradled the pup in her apron, her head bent as she looked to see how badly the small seal was hurt.

The sun had topped the Low Bavadars by the time they reached Bottle. All fears forgotten, Ferris was out of the canoe even quicker than before, bandages and jar of salve in hand. Berrel looked back to Nokken Rock to see if the Eastbay men would follow them over. Sure enough, once they realized the steward wasn't coming to them, the farmers and fishermen of the Home Guard piled into their canoes and continued on to the smaller island.

Ferris was nearly done with her bandaging by the time they arrived. She had found Icer right where they had left him and, shooing the flies gathering on his flank, set to work smearing ointment on the raw burn. The nokken's whiskers trembled.

"You find the pups?" he asked, before Berrel could question him about what had happened.

"We found two," said Ferris.

"That's all was missing. Firrit came by while you were gone. Told me they'd found everyone but Longfin and Rollby. But a lot of them are burned like me. And the aunties, too."

Ferris looked up at her father, who shook his head. Later they could tell Icer they had only been able to save one of the two pups they had found. And that Skimmer was gone, too. In the meantime, better not to shock him.

Sniffling, Ferris wiped the ointment off her hands and brushed away her tears. "We'll have to tell Firrit and Longback to bring anyone who's hurt by the lower dock for medicine. I don't think you nokken know much about burns, living in the water like you do."

"I'll tell 'em myself when I get back."

"I'm afraid you're not going anywhere, Icer. If you want this to heal properly, we're going to have to keep it dry."

Icer's long neck curled forward; he winced as his exertions stretched his burnt skin. "Not go back! What do you mean! I have to go back. The aunties'll take care of me."

"The aunties don't know anything about burns, Icer." Ferris laid a comforting hand on the nokken's shoulder. "We'll bring you to the Manor. You can keep Old Mortin company. And I'll make sure you get maple candy every day. Unless you'd rather stay in Eastbay."

The nokken eyed Ferris and her father suspiciously. Berrel he had known his entire life, and Ferris only a little less. Never had he known either of them to be anything but trustworthy.

The steward, sensing his fear, squatted down beside him. "It'll be okay, Icer," he said cheerfully. "The troop can come visit every day. Not even Longback's ever lived with humans. You'll be the first."

"They'll sing songs about you," added Ferris. "And about how you got your wound."

The nokken's suspicions dimmed as he weighed the attractiveness of the humans' offer.

"Speaking of which." Berrel pointed at Icer's raw side. "How did you get that?"

"Let me finish bandaging him first." Ferris picked up the strips of cloth she had torn from Mother Spinner's sheet. "If you can lift him from the front, I'll be able to wrap these all the way around."

Icer looked remarkably better once his wound was dressed, and had just settled back comfortably on the rough beach when the two canoes from Eastbay arrived. Another score of men tumbled out onto the shore.

"What's wrong with Icer?"

"Scratch yourself on the rocks chasing aunties, did you?"

"You found out yet where all that racket was comin' from this mornin'?"

"That's what I'm hoping to learn right now." Berrel hushed the Home Guard and turned back to the nokken. "Are you ready to tell your story?"

"Hmm," began Icer, his voice a rasping bark. Ferris scratched behind his ears with soothing fingers, his head pillowed on her lap. "We were after pike today. Longback left me in charge of the pups and aunties round Bottle. Would have taken them to the Rock to catch some sun, only the fog was too heavy. That's probably what helped us, though, in the end. The Wizard might have killed us all if he'd been able to see."

"Wizard?"

Ferris's fears came rushing back as Berrel repeated the terrible word. What if it had been Reiffen attacking the nokken after all? Hushed gasps and anxious glances filtered through the Home Guard; a few looked around nervously.

"Which Wizard?" Ferris asked, trying not to show her unease. Instead she smoothed a patch of fur on the top of Icer's head, careful not to touch the bandages on his neck.

The nokken's whiskers quivered. "How would I know which Wizard? I never seen one. Only heard you humans talk about 'em. I don't even know their names."

Ferris relaxed again. To be sure, it was horrible the nokken had been attacked, but at least it hadn't been Reiffen doing the attacking. As she had told herself more than once already, Icer would have recognized him.

"How were you wounded?" asked Berrel.

"The Wizard didn't get me right away, you know. I saved more than a few pups before he finally caught me." A small shiver rippled through Icer's damaged coat at the memory.

"Maybe if you started from the beginning," suggested Berrel.

Icer settled his muzzle more comfortably on Ferris's lap. "It was terrible," he said. "There we were, watching the pups on Bottle, when, boom! we were in the middle of a storm. Lightning crashed, thunder bashed. No rain or wind, though, which should have given us the scent. But we were busy getting the pups away from the island—everybody knows lightning always hits right next to islands. Then I saw it wasn't lightning at all, but fire hitting the water around us."

"Fire?" asked one of the Eastbay men.

Icer nodded, and winced as his skin tugged painfully beneath his bandages. "That's what it was. Bundles of fire, only with no wood. Don't ask me how the Wizard did it. But they hissed like fire when they hit and the water got hot, same as it does when you humans poke it with burning sticks."

"How'd you know it was a Wizard?"

"Who else would know how to make fire without wood?"

"Did you get any sense why he was attacking you?" asked the steward.

"Not at first." Icer rubbed his hind flippers against the ground like a dog trying to scratch an itch it couldn't reach. "Just thought he was trying to kill us. Didn't stop to ask why. Like I said, if the mist hadn't been so thick, a lot of pups and aunties might a' died. Lucky for us the fog only got thicker each time one of them fireballs hit the water. Most of 'em hit between a pup and an auntie, and it wasn't long before he'd driven the pups out around the bottom of the island here. Current took 'em quick enough after that. Swept 'em right off into the fog. The aunties and me had to go underwater to find 'em, but it's even harder to see under a fog than it is through it. Uplake, downlake, it's all the same in mist like that. Didn't know where we were half the time. I got turned around chasing a pup that turned out to be a school of brownies, and found myself right back at Bottle again. That's when I found out what was really up."

"Which was?"

"Stealing pups." Icer's eyes narrowed. "That's what it always comes down to. Pups have softer fur than bachelors, or aunties even. I guess Wizards still like nokken fur even if you humans don't. But he didn't see me. I guess he thought he'd chased us all away. Had a pup in his arms, though. One o' the bigger ones. Rollby, I think. So I squirted him hard, right in the face. He dropped the pup in the water and started spluttering. But that wasn't enough for me. Got myself a good swimming start and shot up onto the island to really get him. Don't think I've made a jump like that in years, but I was that mad. Only he saw me coming and hit me with one o' those fire balls. That's how I got this." Icer patted his bandages gently with a flipper. "Now I know why you humans are always so careful with your fires. That stuff hurts."

"So then what happened?" asked Berrel.

"Why, he disappeared. *Phfft!* Not another sign of him. Not that I was looking. Just wanted to get down to the water to soak my side. Which is where I was when you came by. And why I sent you out after the pups. Didn't know if anyone had found young Rollby yet."

"We took one of the ones we found over to Spinner's," said Berrel. "Don't know if it was your Rollby or not. He's got a burn like yours on his shoulder. Not as bad, though"

"That's not Rollby," wheezed the old gray nokken. "That's Longfin. Rollby'll be an auntie when she grows up."

A sudden shadow passed overhead, causing more than a few of the Home Guard to duck. A large, red-brown eagle swooped wide around the island, then swung back to land on the taller rocks at the north end.

"Redburr!" exclaimed Ferris as the fat bird settled its wings.

A wave of relief settled over the small company. Even Icer felt things would be better now the Shaper had joined them.

"Morning, Berrel." The bird cocked his head to look at the crowd with one bright eye. "Icer, you look like you ate too many mussels."

"Weren't mussels, Shaper. I was fightin' Wizards. Feels a lot better, now Ferris patched me up."

"Wizards?" Redburr riffled his wing feathers, but didn't look entirely surprised. "Which ones?"

"Just one," said Berrel. "We don't have any idea which."

"I do," said a voice that seemed to pop out of the ground at their feet. "He left me to inform you which one, I'll have you know."

"Who's that?" Berrel glanced nervously around the beach, his hand on the hilt of his knife. The Home Guard shuffled back toward the canoes.

Ferris found herself staring at the rocks on the shore. There was something familiar about that voice, especially its patronizing tone.

"Durk?" she asked, not believing she could possibly be right. And not wanting to be right, either, because of what it might mean. Neither Ossdonc nor Fornoch would have bothered to bring a talking stone to Valing. Her fears about Reiffen rushed back, stronger than ever.

"At your service, my lady. Though I should never have recognized your voice had I not heard your name. You don't sound anything like you used to."

Ferris studied the beach more closely. "Where are you?"

"On the ground, naturally."

"Where on the ground?"

"How should I know? It's not as if I can see."

"Well, keep talking then. We'll try to find you by your voice."

By this time everyone was moving around carefully and lifting their feet to stare at the stones underneath. Memory had overcome their initial surprise: the story of how Avender had found the talking stone in Ussene was a local favorite. To tell the truth, more than a few folks were disappointed that the talking stone, which had done so much to help Ferris and her friends escape the Wizard's fortress, hadn't been with them when they returned.

"Keep talking?" said Durk. "I think I can manage that. I am sorry I didn't recognize your voice at first, Ferris, but I imagine it's been a long time since we last met. You must be a charming young woman by now. I'm reminded of my fair Elinora, whom I met when she was just—ouch! Watch where you're stepping, sir. You might have shattered me into a thousand pieces."

"Who did that?" Ferris looked around quickly. "Who stepped on him?" The farmers and fishermen shrugged blankly and looked back at the ground. Almost at once there was a second squeak from the stone.

"Ferris! I implore you, please call off your brutes. By the time they're finished I shall be trampled so deeply into the stone not even the good Nurren would be able to find me."

"Here he is. I think." One of the Eastbay farmers stepped back gingerly and peered at the pebbles at his feet. "Not that I can see the difference. Just looks like stones to me."

"I assure you, my good man, I couldn't be more different."

Ferris got down on her knees and picked through the suspect stones. Even with a smaller area to search, it took her a minute to find the one she was looking for. After all, she had never seen Durk in sunlight before. He kept up a steady stream of commentary and complaint until she found him, a small, pale gray stone, not unlike the larger pebbles scattered on the lakeshore.

"Ahh," he said finally. "You have me now. I do say, Ferris, it is good to feel your hand again."

"So," said Berrel, as his daughter held Durk out for all to see. "Who brought you here? A Wizard?"

"Well, yes and no."

"What's that supposed to mean?" demanded Berrel.

Ferris thought she could guess. Her throat tightened at the notion, and her fingers curled around the stone. Even if it was true, it wouldn't be his fault, she told herself. It couldn't be. Not if he was under the Wizards' control.

"We could wait," she said. "Durk could tell us what he has to say back at the Manor."

"And leave all these good men who've come out to help us hanging? You know we can't do that, Ferris."

"That's right." The farmer who had stepped on the stone nodded impatiently. "I didn't leave my milking to go home empty-handed. Let's hear what the rock has to say."

Ferris took a deep breath. Uncurling her fingers, she held Durk out in the palm of her trembling hand. "All right, Durk," she said, her courage near to failing. "Tell them what you know."

"Are you sure? You won't like it."

"I'm sure."

"Very well then. It was Reiffen."

"It couldn't have been Reiffen," she snapped the moment her fear was confirmed. "Reiffen would never harm a nokken."

"He would now," replied the stone.

14

The Battle of Backford

The next morning Avender searched the sky from his window as soon as he woke, but the only birds he saw were the waterfowl in Backford Pool and some pigeons patrolling the wall. Five days had passed since the Shaper had left; if the bear didn't hurry, the war would start without him.

Ossdonc, however, had arrived with his army during the night and camped in the rough hills north of the watchtower. Avender went out through Nurren's tunnel before breakfast to have a look at them.

"Big fellow, ain't he?"

One of the soldiers on duty pointed his chin at the Wizard swaggering enormously across the field.

"Yeah, but he makes a big target," said a second. "If we had a catapult we could end all this right now."

"Not on my watch. I wouldn't want to get him mad. And there's his beasties to worry about, too."

Avender had heard the Wizards were huge, but his first sight of Ossdonc strutting among his soldiers made him think twice about how confident everyone in Backford was about the coming battle. The Black Wizard looked twice as tall as Redburr, and broader, too. Avender didn't see how the Dwarves, or anyone else for that matter, stood a chance against him.

The manders were even worse. Two of them lay chained in a small hollow out of sight and smell of the army's horses, the ground smoldering around them. Their tails flicked lazily back and forth across the burnt grass like waves on a beach. Black claws furrowed the earth.

"Gribbs told me the baron got a special sword from the Dwarves last night," said the first soldier. "And arrows, too. He'll take care of 'em, Wizards and beasties both."

Although he studied the camp closely, Avender found no sign of Reiffen among the thousands of soldiers and sissit milling about their master on the plain. Only Ossdonc was large enough to stand out at that distance.

Returning to the castle, he discovered Duke Arrand had arrived with two hundred pikemen from Rowanon. Boys pelted out from the stables as the duke passed through the gate, accompanied by two of his captains.

"Hello, lads," he called. "Ready to pluck a few nomads' feathers, are you? That's the spirit. Fine fighting lads, all of you."

Despite his long march, the duke's golden hair hung in glossy curls around his broad shoulders; his armor shone like something out of a song. On his shield two fierce wolves stood with paws together, but they were less menacing than the man who bore them. Even taller and broader than Avender, he looked the part of a hero far better as well.

Avender stood to one side as Lady Breeanna, tugging at her trailing veil, hurried out through the press of maids and pages at the castle door. The duke, with the assistance of two stable boys and a portable stair, dismounted. Plumed helm cradled in the crook of his arm, he advanced to greet the baroness. His mail shirt jingled like a bag of coins without the bag.

"Duke Arrand!" she exclaimed. "We are so delighted you have come! And so quickly!"

"I led my men out of Rowanon Keep the moment I received your husband's call," he replied, bowing deeply.

"But where are they?" The baroness peered past the duke and his captains at the empty gate behind them.

"In the village, milady. No need for them to tire themselves trudging up one last hill when the battle will be fought below. I only came up myself when I heard the baron had called a council of war. And to pay my respects to your ladyship, of course."

Gallantly, the duke offered the baroness his mailed arm and escorted her into the keep. Avender followed. The council of war had already assembled in the great hall, where shafts of sunlight illuminated little more than themselves as they slanted across the chamber from the high, narrow windows. Advancing to the long table, Lady Breeanna introduced the duke to the Dwarves.

Avender found himself an inconspicuous spot near the cellar door and leaned against the cold stone.

"Findle was just telling us about the manders, Duke," said Sir Worrel when the introductions were complete. "We're told he's hunted them more than any other Bryddin."

"A hunter, eh?" The duke's mustache wagged as he studied the smallest Dwarf. Accepting a cup of ale from a footman, he asked, "Can they swim? That's the main thing, when defending Backford. The river is always the key."

Findle shook his head, his neck and shoulders hardly moving. "Manders don't swim. But they can walk across the river bottom if they want to."

Duke Arrand rubbed his chin with one large hand; the Backford officers exchanged concerned glances. "That is not good," he said. "Still, there must be some way to deal with them. Everything has its weakness."

"I hadn't finished." Findle remained silent until he was certain he had everyone's attention. "If these manders are anything like the smaller sort, they'll stay well clear of the water. Nothing drains them faster. What they like is heat, which is why the Wizard has them basking. That way they'll be at full strength tonight. Which is when the attack will come, if you ask me."

"But how do we slay them?" inquired Sir Worrel. "Will it require the weapons you gave us?"

"Stone and steel will cut a mander," answered Nurren. "If your arm's strong enough."

"Take our advice," said Garven, "and let us handle the manders. You worry about the sissit and the soldiers."

"And who will take care of the Wizard?" asked the duke.

"We will." Findle slapped the pommel of his sword. "After we're finished with his beasts."

Duke Arrand regarded the smallest Dwarf with surprise and admiration. "You are like no Bryddin I have ever met, sir. You sound as martial as I."

Findle bowed. "Thank you, Duke. Usually I only hunt manders, and the occasional rockworm. Or giant spider. But I'll hunt anything that threatens Bryddlough, and that includes Wizards. They broke Finlis, you know."

"Yes, they did. And many others, on the Rimwich field. I look forward to standing beside you on Backford Bridge, friend Findle. Together we shall slay a host of enemies."

"We shall certainly be facing a host," said one of the baron's lieutenants. "I've never seen so many sissit, or Keeadini. If the Wasters force the crossing while we're fighting the Wizard and his army on the bridge, they might well carry the day."

The duke folded his arms on his broad chest, obscuring the jaws of the rampant wolves. "A hundred Keeadini are not the equal of one Banking knight, sir. Let them come."

"We may not have to face the tribesmen at all, if we defeat

the Wizard first." Sir Worrel turned to a sergeant at the wall. "Gribbs. Fetch the scout."

"Another scout?" asked the baroness as the grizzled soldier ducked out the door.

"The last to arrive, milady," replied the captain. "His mother married a farmer from Countinghill but, since she is Keeadini, the tribes allow him to come and go."

Sergeant Gribbs returned with a small, sun-worn man, who looked more Keeadini than Banking despite his farmer's shirt and trousers. His soft, wissundskin moccasins slipped silently across the floor.

"Tell us what you learned in the Keeadini camp, Osee." Sir Worrel gestured toward the officers around him. "Not all here have heard your report."

Osee bowed to his baron and the duke. "The tribes ain't made up their minds yet, your lordships. Wizard's bribes are enough to bring 'em here, but they won't join Him till He's crossed the Tumbling. Some of the young hotheads are on His side already, but the rest want proof that this time'll be different. They'll answer His call soon enough if He takes the town. No one wants to miss the sack of Malmoret."

"Sack of Malmoret! What nonsense is this?"

Osee blinked before the duke's sharp tone and glanced toward the baron, who nodded for him to continue. "It's what my mother's people told me, Sir Duke. The tribes think they'll have a free ride all the way to Far Mouthing if the Wizard beats your lordships here. It's not the fighting they're looking forward to, it's what they can loot and steal."

"So, if we defeat the Wizard, we have nothing to fear from the Keeadini?"

The scout nodded.

"Hold them a week," said Sir Worrel, "and the Wizard's army, as well as the tribes, will be forced to leave. What food they carry will have run out by then. The wissund are on the Easting, too far away to hunt."

From the nodded agreement around the room, Avender could tell the captain had voiced the general understanding.

The scout was dismissed, the final placement of the Banking troops determined, and the council drew to a close. All agreed the best course was to wait at Watch Hill and the river for the Wizard to make his next move. Time was on their side. Defeat Ossdonc and the other threats would melt away.

The rest of the day dragged. Afternoon shimmered into evening; a still summer night settled across lake and town. The thickening moon rose, bright enough to wash away the neighboring stars. Having been instructed by Lady Backford that he wasn't yet ready for the fight, Avender prowled the castle walls.

On the high cliff of the battlement, he felt as if he were back home on the Neck. Except for the sentries pacing their posts, the scene felt very much the same. Behind him the shoulders of the Blue Mountains rose almost as close to Castle Backford as the Low Bavadars were to the Manor; before him Backford Pool stretched off into the darkness like Valing Lake. The torches and campfires in the meadow between gleamed like Eastbay in the evening. But the stars to the east stretched away into the night in ways they couldn't in Valing, where mountains cupped the lake on either side. And there was no pulse and throb of crashing water, either.

"You wouldn't have a plug o' tobacco on you, would you?"

Avender recognized Sergeant Gribbs as he came up and leaned on his long spear.

"No? How 'bout a flask?"

"Sorry."

The older man sighed. "Only a pup would come out here

without a chew or sip, Hero o' the Stoneways or no. Here, have some o' mine."

Grinning crookedly, the sergeant offered Avender a tug on the flask he pulled from inside his mail shirt. Avender blinked at the fiery taste, and coughed behind his hand.

"Fine stuff, eh?" The sergeant winked in the moonlight. "My brother's recipe. He makes it south o' here, at his farm. My name's Gribbs. Sergeant Gribbs, if that sort of thing matters to you. We only keep up the spit an' polish for the baroness, you know. A rougher lot, we were, before she came. Another pull?"

Avender shook his head. The stars were already sharper than before. Gribbs rolled his head back for a second swig, then thrust the flask beneath his shirt. Patting the bulge in his jingling chain mail, he said, "The baron gave me this himself. He knew I'd like it better than a medal."

"You must have done something very brave." Avender tried to pick out the line of the dike below Watch Hill, but only the end of the lights jeweling the meadow marked Banking's first line of defense.

"Oh, it wasn't nothin'. Just a little matter o' stolen sheep. You'll probably get one in the next few days yourself. Baron's handy with presents, he is. To a fault, some say. But I say there's no fault in him at all. I'd follow him to Ussene itself, if he asked."

Avender remembered the look on Keln's face when he realized the baron had brought the lancers out to rescue them on the Waste, and the love in the baroness's eyes at the sight of her husband's safe return. An odd, silent baron, but a definite leader of men.

A flicker, as if from a fresh star, gleamed from the top of Watch Hill. It brightened and grew larger before Avender realized the light was a signal from the tower. Sergeant Gribbs straightened.

"Something's up," he said, peering into the darkness. "Can't tell what, though."

Avender wondered if there was a system, with different beacons to signal different sorts of danger. Dropping his eyes to the meadow, he searched the fires for any sign of activity. Beside him, Gribbs gripped the stone and leaned forward. A bat swept across the sky, its darting flight more remembered than seen.

"Here." The sergeant nudged Avender toward the stair. "Run on down to the lieutenant and tell him what's up, lad. I know you're a hero an' all, but your young legs'll do it faster'n mine. Better I stay up here on the wall in case there's another signal. Go on. I'll give you another sip o' my nighttime when you come back."

Avender set off quickly. On the rest of the wall other soldiers had also stopped their pacing and turned to the tower. But Avender was the first to reach the small alcove just inside the gate.

"A beacon, Lieutenant," he reported to the officer on duty. "From the watchtower."

The officer's eyes narrowed. "What sort of beacon?"

"A bright, steady light."

The officer tugged at his lip. "I guess it's come, then. About time, too. Let's tell the baron."

Without seeming to hurry, but still walking quickly, the lieutenant led Avender into the castle, up the stairs, and back to the apartment of the baron and baroness. The page dozing in front of their door scrambled to his feet as Avender and the officer arrived. At the lieutenant's urging, the boy turned and knocked loudly. The second rap was quickly answered.

"What is it?" The baroness's voice boomed through the heavy door. "I told Marietta not to bother me about any of the cows till morning!"

"It's not Marietta, milady!" The lieutenant raised his voice to be heard through the thick oak. "I must inform the baron the beacon has been lit on Watch Hill."

"The beacon! Oh dear! Did you hear that, Baron? He says the beacon's been lit! Yes, yes, I know. Look to yourself, sir. I need nothing. Your slippers are on your side of the bed, where you left them. I shall dress as soon as you're gone. There's a bit of duck I can have ready in an instant before you go, if you'd like."

The lieutenant and the page fastened their eyes to unimportant spots on the wall. Avender followed their lead.

"You may open the door now, Murrow. Sir Benerel, please enter."

The baroness's bedchamber was larger than Avender's, but only slightly better furnished. Thin summer curtains draped the bed, and a pier glass in a gilt frame ran from floor to ceiling along one wall. Beside the bed the baron was just buckling his sword to his side. Lady Breeanna pushed her head out between the pale curtains, her hair half in and half out of her nightcap.

"Is there any other news?" she asked breathlessly.

"No, milady." Lieutenant Benerel bowed in her direction, but kept his eyes on the baron. "I expect a messenger shortly. I thought it best to inform the baron at once."

"Of course. You are a marvel, Lieutenant. I wish I had you on my staff."

"Thank you, milady."

The baron crossed the room, buttoning the top of his tunic. Two soldiers joined him when he reached the main hall. Avender thought about trying to go off with them, but only three horses were waiting in the courtyard outside. Chains rattled at the castle gate, followed by the hollow clop of hooves echoing in the night. Avender hurried back onto the battlement just in time to see the baron and his officers round the first turn in the road and hasten toward town in the moonlight. The sound of their galloping dimmed as they passed between the wooden houses; the night went quiet again.

From the top of the wall Avender had an excellent view of the bridge and beyond. Though it was dark, the crisscrossing of torches through the meadow and town was easy to follow.

Nothing happened for a long while. Sergeant Gribbs went off to check on his squad along the wall, leaving Avender alone. Again Avender wondered what had happened to Redburr, and had to remind himself that, if the war with the Wizards had truly come, the Shaper would be wanted everywhere at once. His presence at Castle Backford would be comforting, and worth even a few Bryddin in the fighting, but he might be needed more in other places. King Brannis would have to make a stand somewhere if Ossdonc's army broke in through the back door of his kingdom. And Avender, unlike Keln and the rest of Backford, wasn't so certain the castle would hold. Even with Dwarves to help them.

A line of fire appeared in the narrow road below Watch Hill. Avender found himself wishing he was down there with the soldiers at the dike. Then he would at least have the expectation of bloodying his sword rather than watching anxiously from the walls of the castle.

More marching lights filled the darkness beyond the edge of the hill. Fresh torches approached the wall from the meadow as well, massing behind the strip of darkness that marked the earthen wall. Slowly the farther gleam approached the nearer. Small lights like grounded stars arced across the wall to start fires in the meadow. Silent as a puff of wind rolling across the lake, the torches of the enemy surged forward.

Avender stared transfixed as the fight raged in the darkness. From a distance, the battle at the edge of the hill looked like a pair of flames licking at one another from opposite sides of a log. Small sparks pierced the gap, leaping the blackness between. Others were thrown back upon themselves, curling like paper in a flame. The clash of metal drifted faintly atop the shouts of besiegers and besieged. The night brightened, as if the sky reflected the ferment below.

More lights flickered on in the town; the distant clamor took on a new tone. The shouting hoarsened and no longer seemed eager; groans and pain crept in beneath the din. Avender remembered the look on the man he had killed in the hills, but surprised himself by wishing he were still in the middle of the battle. He felt useless standing on the castle wall. If he was going to have to fight, better to get on with it. Waiting was even worse.

The knot of flame thickened on both sides of the far-off fight. Gradually the shouting died down until only the clash and groans remained. A flock of birds rose up in a mass against the speckled sheet of stars; for a moment the honking of geese was louder than the battle. The waterfowl streamed across the lake, taking their tumult with them. The sounds of swordplay resumed.

The enemy line parted. Several large, dark shapes passed through. Even at that distance Avender made out Ossdonc's giant figure against the torchlight. With him were his manders, their tails lashing the night. Avender leaned anxiously over the parapet, his hands gripping the rough stone as he remembered his own terrible encounter with a mander seven years before. Eyes and tongue like fire, teeth as sharp as knives. Redburr and Nolo had not been enough to destroy it, and Redburr had been in a blind, killing rage. What could simple Banking men be expected to achieve? Were the Dwarves out fighting with them?

Apparently not. The line of fire at the wall held briefly as the manders snarled and surged at the ends of what appeared to be leashes. Then Ossdonc released them. The creatures slithered forward like snakes across a furrowed field. Lights went out wherever they passed. Behind them, Ossdonc strode to the top of the wall, his tall shape silhouetted against the torchlight. Someone attacked him; the Wizard swept the man aside without even drawing his sword. Avender wondered if Keln was out there and whether he was safe.

He reached for his own weapon. Perhaps he should go down to the town and join the fighting, despite her ladyship's orders. Sergeant Gribbs, back from his rounds, wagged his head.

"No need for that, lad. There'll be plenty left for us tomorrow. The baron still has a trick or two up his sleeve."

"Where are the Dwarves?"

"Guarding the bridge. That's where the real fight will be."

The Backford line fell back. Thin lines of torches streamed across the plain, coming together at the bridge like a second, red-gold river. Behind them another wave of torchlight flooded forward. The lines at the bridge thickened quickly as they jammed together, a glowing eddy pressed against the river. Stragglers were swept away by the yellow tide behind them. Ossdonc and the manders remained at the wall, dark pools in the swelling flood that pressed wide around them.

A horn sounded above the din, the same clear horn Avender had heard when the baron had ridden out to rescue Sir Worrel's troop on the plain. The rushing horde paused. A second note sounded, closer than the first; Avender noticed a troop of horsemen gathered in the meadow on the other side of the river, close to the hills. His eyes straining in the dark, he guessed the first horn had come from a similar troop by the lakeshore.

Like black clouds, the mounted troops poured toward the middle of the meadow. In the face of two wings of charging cavalry, and without the manders or the Wizard to force them on, the tide of sissit and northerners retreated. The lancers galloped across the enemy line, moonlight silvering their helms. The front of Ossdonc's army collapsed, falling beneath the spears of the Banking charge, or scrambling back across the bodies of their comrades. Hooves thundering, the two troops met in the middle of the plain, wheeled to the south, and rode back to the bridge.

"Ah," said Gribbs. "They fell right into the trap." Reaching into his shirt, he brought out his flask to celebrate the change of fortune.

The enemy's withdrawal stopped at the back of the meadow, where the manders roared and whipped their tails. Ossdonc cuffed any who tried to flee back toward the open plain. It was some time before the chaos on the enemy side was calmed. Meanwhile, the last of the Banking soldiers crossed the bridge safely. The gate was shut behind them. New lights burst forth along the southern bank of the river as the baron's troops took up fresh positions. Behind them the streets of the town were as thick and lively as market day at the end of summer.

Avender looked back at the plain. The northern army appeared too disorganized to mount any fresh attack that night and, as long as Ossdonc and his manders were about, it was unlikely there would be any counterattack from the town.

His eyes lingered on the field, spotted as it was with the gleam of fallen torches and the black shadows of the dead. Was Reiffen out there? Not among the dead, of course, but somewhere among the sprouting flames as the invading army built fresh fires against the the dark.

The night passed sleeplessly, castle and town as busy as if it were broad day. When morning rose, Avender saw dogs from both sides of the river quarreling in the trampled grass; broken weapons and fallen bodies littered the ground. Plumes of smoke striped the morning air. Ussene's army was drawn up at the other end of the meadow, out of bowshot from the river. Ossdonc had disappeared, presumably into the enormous black tent that covered the far end of the field like a crouching spider, the two manders lazing at the entrance like dogs.

Behind the tent a swarm of sissit had cut a wide gap in the dirt wall. They buzzed over what was left of the berm, shovels flying, and around the tower and hill above. Banking soldiers fired the occasional arrow among them from high on the watchtower's stone walls, but, beyond their missiles' reach, Keeadini scouts roamed unchecked. With the bridge the only place to cross the river in force, no one worried about attack from that direction. The real danger was through the meadow.

Knowing Lady Breeanna was too busy tending the wounded to stop him, Avender grabbed a loaf of bread and a dry sausage from the kitchen and headed down the hill. Though he hadn't slept at all the night before, the dread and excitement of the approaching battle were more than enough to spark him through the day. Even his wound only bothered him when he paid attention to it. Today he would find out what a real fight was like, whether he wanted to or not.

It was a beautiful morning. The air was crisp, and butterflies hovered above the heather on either side of the road. At the bottom of the hill Avender found troopers and pikemen in the colors of Backford and Rowanon mingling on every porch and street. The inn overflowed with the wounded, their cries hushed as morning brought an end to the worst of their nightmares. Boys brought beer to the lounging soldiers, blood splashed across the men's shields like rust.

Moving on to the river, he joined the defenders at the bridge. The baron was there and Duke Arrand, and Wysko with his stone-tipped arrows. Avender felt self-conscious as the only unarmored man at the wall, but now was not the time for him to start learning how to wear chain mail. The officers allowed him to pass: for once it was a good thing to be known as the Hero of the Stoneways. Defending the bridge was exactly the place they all expected him to be. But Avender felt like no great warrior as he looked out upon the ruined meadow from the top of the wall. The blow he had struck in the darkness underground had been a lucky one, to pierce the mander's eye. He doubted very much he would be so lucky again.

The sweet morning passed. A hot afternoon simmered the

lake and meadow by the time Ossdonc, dressed in night black armor, finally emerged from his tent and whistled for his beasts. His companies of sissit and northerners assembled around him; his manders' long tongues and tails flicked like snakes as they strained on their leashes. Avender settled nervously against the stone and looked for signs of Reiffen.

In long lines that stretched across the meadow, the Wizard led his army forward. The clank of their weapons broke like a wave across the trampled field. A flock of crows rose from the western trees and wheeled above the valley. Avender and the Banking men stared at the approaching host, their faces grim, their hands gripping the hafts of their spears. The horses tethered on the bridge behind them in hopes of a sortie pawed the ground, scenting the sissits' stench.

Up close, in the strong light of day, the army of Ussene looked much more fearsome than it had during the night. Where before Avender had seen only their torches flickering on the plain, now he saw their faces. The sissit trudged, lumpy and pale, their armor seemingly borrowed from the grave, the humans even nastier because Avender could recognize the murder in their eyes. He wondered if they were just as scared as he.

Ossdonc raised a mailed fist. The rumble of steel and leather ceased as his army halted beyond bowshot from the farther shore. The Wizard approached. He wore a black breastplate and greaves, and a helmet with a black plume rising from the top. A long black sword was belted at his side, and over his shoulder he carried an enormous log. In his other hand he restrained his manders, each the size of a low barn, on iron chains. They scuttled forward close to the ground, their thick tails waving, their scales as black as the Wizard's armor. Their eyes and tongues were red, and the slaver that dripped from their jaws was gold. The ground smoked where their breath and spittle brushed the grass. Behind the Wizard, a man in black armor rode a black horse at the head of the army, his face hidden behind his helm.

"Bankings!"

The Wizard's voice boomed across the river with the vehemence of a storm. The circling crows scattered.

"It is I, Cuhurran, come to lead you once more. Lay down your arms and I shall spare your lives. Fight, and all will die, from your children to your dogs. Ask your fathers—they know no one has ever mastered me. This time will be no different. I have brought my own hounds to hunt you with, should you defy me."

He ended with a gale of laughter. Despite himself, Avender looked away. The Wizard's amusement felt like fists pummeling his shoulders. Around him one or two men dropped to their knees. Steadier hands helped them to their feet.

From the wall, Baron Backford answered Ossdonc's challenge. His voice seemed thin at first beside the Wizard's, but as he spoke it strengthened, until all along the riverbank heard him.

"Wizard! You are not wanted here. I rode with you of old in your wrongful wars, but I will make no such mistake again. Take your carrion back with you to the north. Between death and slavery you leave us no choice. Sow our fields with bones, we will not surrender. Our sons and daughters will fight you, and the earth we love as well. Return to your spells and spying. You get no passage here."

As the baron finished, a bow twanged close beside him. Wysko had shot one of his heartstone shafts. His aim was true, but his strength not enough to drive the arrow home. The shaft quivered in Ossdonc's neck, just above his black chest plate, barely piercing his skin.

Astonished, the Wizard looked down. For an instant he seemed not to know how to react. Then, with a roar of rage that scattered every bird still paddling on the lake, he pulled the arrow from his neck and cast it to the ground. Red blood, as red as any human's, oozed from his wound.

Wysko fitted a second arrow to his bow; the Wizard took something from a pouch at his side. With one quick motion his arm whipped forward. Wysko tumbled back from the wall as the missile struck him in the face; he landed heavily on his back on the bridge below. A crimson smear seeped out beneath his helm. Avender ducked behind the parapet; the Wizard threw several more stones. Two more men went down before the third was fast enough to angle his shield in front of him. The stone clanged hard enough to knock the man down, then arced into the river with a splash.

The archers on the wall fired a volley, but not a single arrow pierced its mark. A thin stream, blackening as it flowed, ran down Ossdonc's chest, but all the shafts that reached him rattled harmlessly to the earth.

With another booming laugh, the Wizard loosed his manders. In response, the Dwarves appeared atop the wall. Like gigantic, armored rats the lizards struck swiftly, their adamantine claws scrabbling on the stone. Findle met one attack, Garven and Nurren the other. Thinking to catch them off guard, Ossdonc launched another round of missiles. Findle caught his in one quick hand, but the others exploded in bursts of dust as they smashed against the Dwarves' hard hides.

The Dwarves swung their axes at the rearing beasts. The creatures bellowed as the blades struck home. Golden spittle sprayed across the wall; stone sizzled and wisps of black smoke rose toward the sky. The wall shuddered as the manders tore deep rents in the rock that blocked their way. Twice more the foul beasts tried to scale the barrier, and both times they were beaten back by the blows of the Dwarves. On the last attempt Findle buried his ax in his mander's steaming nose. Rearing up on its short hind legs, the creature clawed the air. Quickly, Findle seized a second ax and, hurling it over his head with both hands, sank the weapon deep in the creature's chest.

Black blood sprayed the wall, bursting into flame. Tongues of fire danced around the Dwarf, who flickered like firestone in a red-hot hearth. Writhing, the mander fell back to the ground. Avender and the other archers fired at the creature's dark belly, but their arrows had no more effect on the beast than they had on its master.

Ossdonc raised his club and stepped forward. The mander's fire died. Avender shot for the Wizard's eyes, but his arrows glanced away. Reaching the wall, the Wizard struck a great overhand blow with his log. Splinters of wood and shattered stone shot out in all directions. Several defenders fell backward onto the bridge behind them. Baron Backford, who had remained safe behind the parapet while the Dwarves fought the manders, slashed with his stone sword as the Wizard lifted his massive club for another blow.

His weapon too unwieldy to quickly fend the baron's blade, the Wizard braced himself for the cut. Behind him the black knight raised a hand. A bolt of fire shot from his fingers over Ossdonc's shoulder. The baron cried out as the flame caught his sword midstroke. Flying from his hand, the heavy weapon fell to the ground beside the dying mander.

Ossdonc's log descended. The baron crumpled, his back and legs crushed beneath the giant trunk. The wall trembled.

"Reiffen!" cried Avender with sudden insight. The knight in black showed no sign of recognition.

Findle leapt over the wall. Nurren followed, stumbling as he landed. Several soldiers carried the baron down to the safety of the bridge. Duke Arrand clanked forward to take his place. Avender had an easy shot at Ossdonc's eye, but again his arrow seemed to sheer off at the last second and pass harmlessly by the Wizard's ear.

At the bottom of the wall, Findle retrieved the baron's sword. The remaining mander attacked before he could strike the Wizard, but the mander was no match for Findle and the long Inach blade. The Dwarf's first swing severed the creature's reaching claw; his second removed its head. Another gout of flame splashed against the stone. Findle charged out of the black fire, the white sword held high.

The Wizard swung the log like a scythe. Findle dodged nimbly and hacked at Ossdonc's leg as Nurren attacked with his ax from the other side. The Wizard knocked Nurren's blow away, but he was too slow to stop Findle. Only by twisting his leg at the last minute was he able to catch the Dwarf's stroke on his greave. The sound of the blow rang out across the plain. Ossdonc howled in rage. Findle raised his sword for another strike. Several sissit leapt forward, swinging a pair of heavy nets above their heads. Avender and the archers poured arrows into the attackers, but not before a net had settled over each Dwarf, tangling them so thoroughly they couldn't move. Before the Bryddin could cut themselves free, other soldiers rushed up to throw more, heavier chains across them. The Dwarves vanished beneath twin piles of iron and rope.

Garven jumped down to save his brothers. Ossdonc swung his club again. A loud knock rang out above every other sound on the battlefield as the log caught Garven like a frog being swatted with an oar. Up into the air he shot, and out over the river. He landed with a hollow splash, like the stones Avender had thrown in Valing.

The Banking soldiers hushed. Nurren and Findle were dragged away, like bound flies reeled in by a spider. Their prizes secure, Ossdonc's army rolled forward. Avender fired until his arrows were gone. "For Backford and the baron!" cried the duke. Behind him Sir Worrel led fresh troops up onto the rampart to replace those who had fallen.

Grimly, the Banking men held their posts. There was no time for fear or courage. Already the enemy were raising ladders against the wall. Sissit rushed forward, while human archers supported them from behind. For every ladder Avender and his fellows pushed away, two more took its place. Arrows rained around them, the shafts clattering on the stone. Avender ducked and pressed his shoulder against the wall, kicking at the ladders. He pushed another to the ground, then stabbed a sissit in the throat who had managed to reach the top of the wall.

For a while the Banking soldiers held their own. Duke Arrand charged back and forth across the parapet, always appearing where the fight was heaviest, his sword slashing in the sunlight. Blood smeared his cheek and stained his wrist. The sissit had their ladders in place, but could get no one onto the battlement. Avender stabbed at each pale, slack face as it appeared above the stone. The crunch and scrape of his blade sickened him. Once it was a man he killed, a soldier from Ussene. The fellow bellowed as he reached the top of the wall, but his ferocity turned to a grimace as Avender ran him through the shoulder with his sword. The soldier fell backward; Avender yanked his blade free with a snap of muscle and bone.

He was beginning to think they might hold the bridge after all, when Ossdonc, forgotten in the first crush of fighting, returned. Crushing his own unwary soldiers beneath his feet, the Wizard put aside his log, grabbed the parapet just above his head, and pulled. Duke Arrand and the soldiers around him hacked fiercely at the Wizard's hands. Thin cuts and welts appeared across the fingers, but Ossdonc paid his injuries no mind. With a sudden crack, the front of the wall crashed down in rubble around the Wizard's ears.

Another roar went up from the northern army. Arrows and slung stones answered from the town. Retrieving his log, Ossdonc swept part of the rampart clean. The duke and the soldiers scrambled away, some falling onto the broken stones below. Reaching among the sissit around him, Ossdonc lifted two up to the wall. Avender drew his sword and slew one before the awkward creature caught its balance. A soldier bearing the wolves of Arrand on his shield killed the other. Two more took their place, and then two more again. Despite his own strength, Avender was soon pushed back by the weight of the enemy facing him. He found himself panting with fatigue. Sissit and soldiers in the black leather of Ussene poured through the gap at the top of the battlement, climbing ladders now.

The wall shuddered as a section near Avender crumbled beneath the Wizard's hands. Ossdonc's wrathful face appeared on the other side, spots of blood speckling his cheeks and chin. Avender dodged back before he could be swept aside, and fell over the edge of the bridge.

The cold of the river stunned him. An old nightmare rose up as the current swept him away, but Skimmer wasn't around to save him this time. Other bodies thrashed around him, the river thick as a spawning stream. A hand grabbed his arm, tugging him downward. The water churned as weighted men struggled to rid themselves of helms and mail. Avender tore himself free from the drowning man's grasp and kicked to the surface.

The battle's din seemed louder when his head broke through to air. He gasped for breath. Missiles ripped the water around him with a sound like tearing pillows. Beyond the bridge the river widened: the current had already carried him past the reach of stabbing spears. But he still needed to reach the other bank. Filling his lungs with air, he dove back deep beneath the water. His boots dragged him down, but he was a strong swimmer, with years of practice in Valing. The next time he returned to the surface, he had crossed half the river's width. The pock of arrows around him lessened.

Helping hands reached for him as he gained the far shore.

Everyone recognized the Hero of the Stoneways, beaten and bedraggled though he was. Exhausted, he stood dripping on the bank and watched as the Wizard smashed the wall of Backford Bridge to pieces with his bare hands.

Soldiers retreated along the span, sissit and northern men harrying them from behind. At the end of the bridge Duke Arrand rallied those with only minor wounds and, more men joining them from the shore, turned to make a final stand before the town. In an ordered rank they met the first wave of charging sissit and slew them all. A second wave attacked, and a third. The row of defenders thinned.

Ossdonc threw down the last of the wall and advanced to the middle of the bridge. A look of joy suffused his face as he drew his black sword, reminding Avender of how Redburr had looked when battle lust had overwhelmed the Shaper.

The Wizard attacked. Behind him his army paused. Duke Arrand and the Banking soldiers raised their blades to fend off the black sword, but all their weapons were shattered at Ossdonc's first sweeping swing. With one stroke the Wizard disarmed half a dozen; with the second he cut Duke Arrand and his comrades in half.

Ignoring the sudden panic started by the death of the duke, Avender attempted to push through the rows of men ranked by the river and return to the bridge. But the crowd was too thick. He slipped instead into the open doorway of the nearest shop, a chandler's, from the smell of beeswax and tallow. Bursting through several doors he came to the backyard and an empty henhouse. One of the mountain crows cawed from the top of a cherry tree, unripe fruit dripping from its beak. Avender clambered over the fence at the back and found himself in another deserted yard. Breaking a window to unlock the back door, he hurried through the empty house to the street.

Wounded men leaned against the buildings in the crowded

avenue beyond. The stink of blood and sweat was thick. Several soldiers loaded a stretcher onto the back of an empty cart. Avender recognized the baron's face above the bloody sheet.

"Avender!" Keln loomed out of the bloody crowd. "We thought all on the bridge had died. Help me take the baron back to the castle. You drive. I'll ride in back with my lord."

"I want to keep fighting."

"You've lost your sword." Keln scowled behind the blood that streaked his hands and face. "The fight at the bridge is over. We'll have our chance to kill plenty in the keep. Now drive!"

Before Avender could point out there were more than enough dropped swords lying on the ground around them, the trooper pushed him forward. From the side of the cart he saw the baron's eyelids flicker.

He jumped up to the seat. With a slap of the reins, horse and wagon started forward. The ancient animal trotted eagerly up the road, more than ready to leave the noise of the fight behind, but it turned reluctantly up the hill toward the castle a minute later.

Men skulked in the streets, heading south.

"Lice," cursed Keln.

Avender agreed, but he saw the wisdom in the cowards' flight as well. The way Ossdonc had smashed through both Dwarves and stone to take the bridge left little doubt the keep's fate would be the same, now that the Dwarves were gone.

They drove up the hill, passing other wounded soldiers headed the same way. Looking back, it was easy to measure the progress of the fight. The Wizard loomed large on the main street, already near the spot where Avender had found Keln and the baron. Elsewhere the ragged lines of sissit were held back by the more disciplined Banking soldiers. But there was no stopping Ossdonc. Men poured through the streets before him like water from a burst dam.

At the top of the road Avender looked farther out across the river. The army of Ussene crowded over the bridge like ants swarming a comb of honey. Beyond them, waiting perhaps for the sight of the town in flames, the Keeadini sat astride their ponies.

"Where's the baroness?" demanded Keln the moment they passed the castle gates.

"On the wall," said the guard.

Keln turned to the nearest wide-eyed page. "Fetch your mistress. You there. Give us a hand."

With the help of several guards, Keln and Avender carried the baron up the steps into the great hall. The only sign of life was the fluttering of his eyelids as they lifted him from the cart. Still in his armor, he was very heavy. They laid him on the same table he had hosted not two nights before. Blood, both fresh and dried, covered Avender's hands.

A scream pierced the gallery above. The baroness, her veil trailing like a ghost, rushed down upon them. Marietta followed behind.

"My baron!" cried the stricken baroness.

Her husband's eyes opened. Weakly, he raised his hand. She clutched his arm to her bosom. "My baron," she sobbed, collapsing to her knees at his side.

The baron smiled for his lady and died.

Avender's anger rose. Seeking fresh enemies, he seized a sword from the wall and returned to the courtyard. His fury burned at the thought that Reiffen was the cause of so much hurt, certain his old friend had been the one to burn the baron with a bolt of fire. Hurrying to the top of the wall, he watched the guards shut the castle gate after the last few stragglers. Two massive bolts planed from the trunks of trees slid home.

Plumes of fire lifted above the town, but the smell of smoke was smothered in the steaming fumes of oil boiling in vats on the wall. Guards levered stones into position. The road below was already spotted with bodies, the battle's fever having reached the hill. Sissit and black-clad soldiers waited halfway up the slope, beyond the range of the archers on the wall.

Ossdonc waded through the last of the town, sweeping his club before him. Buildings shattered and collapsed, timbers splintered. Twice the Wizard passed through the ruined buildings, leveling them to feed the hungry flames, before he started for the castle. His club over his shoulder like a harvester's scythe, he climbed the road with giant strides. More soldiers crept behind him. At the castle gate he stopped, but this time he made no speech. Blood stained his boots and black armor. Smoke smeared his handsome face, but his teeth flashed whitely as he smiled like a greedy child. Only the keep was left to finish his very fine day.

Unshouldering his club, he swung it forward like a great ram. A shivering boom filled the courtyard. Above the gate, the soldiers tipped their oil. The end of Ossdonc's club burned like a roaring hearth. Tongues of fire licked his giant legs. Paying the singeing heat no mind, he rammed his club against the gate in another blow. The great doors splintered, but didn't give. The walls shuddered on either side. Burning oil trickled down the hill, setting the heath on fire.

On the third stroke the Wizard's ram crashed through. The soldiers on the wall rained arrows and stones upon him, but they might as well have attacked a bear with gnats. Ossdonc thrust his head through the hole in the door and grinned like a drunkard in the stocks. Flexing legs thicker than the tree trunks barring the gate, he forced the heavy doors open with an explosion of stone and wood. Behind him his army shouted in triumph. Swords raised, they charged up through the dying flames.

Avender had seen what came of fighting the Wizard from above. The stair to the courtyard cut off, he turned and raced along the top of the parapet to the keep. Others joined him, some in fear and some with determination. Inside, they dashed through corridors gone dark with evening, following the path the baroness had taken not long before.

They came out in the gallery above the hall. The Wizard, enjoying his sport on the wall, had left the inner keep to those who had followed him up the hill. A few had already forced their way inside. Keln lay in a pool of blood by the door, his mistress facing their enemies with a broom while Marietta wept behind the table.

Avender raced to the baroness's defense, the other men behind him. But the sissit and northerners struck first, three of them lunging forward with their swords. Lady Breeanna knocked them all flat with one thumping swing. She caught two more on the backstroke before Avender reached her side.

Sensing reinforcements, she rushed her attackers. "For Backford!" she cried, buffeting the villains before her. Avender had no choice but to charge as well. With the chain-mailed guards soon joining them, they forced the sissit and northern men back through the door of the hall. Lady Breeanna would have chased them on into the courtyard had Avender not called her back.

"Baroness!" he cried. "Do not leave your baron. Your men and I will hold the door."

Together, Avender and the castle guard slew many, but more enemies flooded in through the broken gate. Fires burned along the wall, the Wizard laughing as he smashed everything with his smoking club.

In the doorway Avender stumbled back from a heavy blow. Another guard took his place, but there weren't many of them left.

Someone tugged his arm from behind.

"Please, Sir Avender. Help me with the baroness."

Avender looked at Marietta wildly, not understanding her question at all.

"Help you? Help you how?"

"The baroness is with child." Tears wet Marietta's cheeks as she spoke. "It's not fitting she throw the babe's life away with her own."

"With child?" Avender was too weary and dismayed to understand.

"She should at least try to escape. Into the hills, perhaps. Please."

"Escape?"

As Avender asked the question, his mind came back into focus. The baroness sobbed by the body of her baron, her broom discarded on the floor. At the doorway the next man who fell would be the last.

"There is a way," he said quickly. "Through the cellars. If you go now you can escape."

"Please." Marietta pleaded with sad, dark eyes. Avender sensed she was only just holding back from throwing herself on the body of her own lover. "You'll have to bring her yourself. My lady won't listen to me."

"Go to the cellar stair."

Without looking to see if the woman had obeyed, Avender darted toward the long table. "My lady." He spoke as firmly and as kindly as he could. "You must come with me."

Lady Breeanna looked up with tear-stained eyes, her face swollen with grief. "Excuse me, sir? Leave my baron?"

Avender knew he couldn't force her. Nor could he carry her off. "Yes, my lady. For the sake of your child."

"For the sake of my . . ." Anger swelled in the baroness's eyes. "Sir, you presume greatly to speak to me of such a thing."

"My lady, I presume greatly for Backford. And for your baron. It is what he would have me do."

As gallantly as he could manage, knowing the defense at the door might break at any moment, Avender bowed and held out his arm toward the doorway under the stair. The baroness gazed at him strangely, a light of understanding lifting in her eyes. She looked back at her baron. Avender thought the moment was lost. Gently she kissed her dead husband's hand.

"My baron," she said softly, dabbing the corner of her eye with her torn veil.

She rose from her knees as Avender was about to despair. "Lead on, sir. If you think we can escape, for the sake of my baron's heir, we must try."

"Through the cellar, my lady."

They ducked into the dark stair as the last man fell behind them. Marietta led the way down into the guttering darkness.

"There is no escape this way, Sir Avender." Breeanna's voice filled the chamber around them.

"There is, ma'am. Nurren showed me the back door."

"We will only be captured in the hills. But I suppose it is worth the attempt."

"We'll flee to the Stoneways. Down the Backford Way, if we can find it."

"I know the place." The baroness stooped low to enter the tunnel entrance. "My baron showed me himself."

"You know it?" For the first time real hope rose in Avender. He hadn't been sure he could find the spot on his own despite the Dwarf's directions.

"I do, Sir Avender. But it doesn't matter, as we haven't a key. Nor do we have a light to see in this filthy tunnel."

"I have both." Avender pulled the pouch out from inside his shirt and poured the lamp into his palm.

Lady Breeanna's face shone in the sudden pale light. Real hope came into her eyes.

Heavy boots sounded behind them. Avender cupped the lamp in his hand. "Quickly," he whispered. "Down the tunnel. If we're lucky, they won't see our light and will miss the hidden door."

They emerged on the hill above the castle confident no one had followed them. Orange curtains flickered in the windows of the keep. Beside the river the town burned like a broken forge. Breeanna led the way as they scrambled up through the covering trees. Three hundred and seventeen paces, Nurren had said, but fewer for Avender's long stride. Lady Breeanna's was just as long. Avender wondered if he should have asked Marietta to do the counting.

Sooner than he expected, the wood broke around them to expose a scar in the side of the mountain. Breeanna led them up the steep scree to a short cliff. The sun had set behind the mountains, leaving all but Backford Pool in shadow. Avender held Uhle's gift up before the wall. Slowly a pale line emerged, running across the stone like milk spilled in a narrow gutter.

The square closed, outlining the door. Avender moved his lamp across the rock.

"Where's the lock?" he asked impatiently.

"Right there. Right where my baron showed it to me the last time." Rubbing her damp eyes fiercely, the baroness pointed out a small hollow glowing in the rock.

Avender placed his lamp in the keyhole. From behind the stone came a sharp click. The door shivered and edged forward within its frame.

"Now what?" asked Avender.

"Push," said Lady Breeanna. "That's what Garven did."

Avender pushed, his legs slipping on the uneven footing.

"Someone's coming," said Marietta, her face white.

Avender looked down the rocky slope. A squad of northern soldiers filed out of the trees.

"Help me, Baroness!" he cried. "The stone's too heavy."

Lady Breeanna placed her broad shoulder against the rock. Marietta helped, too. The stone lurched forward. A thin crevice opened in the cliff.

"More," gasped Avender.

The stone slid forward another foot. Marietta slipped inside, followed by the baroness. There was no time for Avender to follow; the men below were only a lunge away. He rolled Uhle's gift into the tunnel.

"Run!" he called, drawing his sword. "I'll hold them off as long as I can."

Countering the first attacker's slash, Avender caught him a kick in the jaw that sent the soldier tumbling down the slope. The second ran his sword through Avender's chest.

He gasped. The Dwarven door snapped closed. Loose rock sliding beneath his feet, Avender crashed into the man below. The sword twisted in his chest, slicing along the rib. He felt his body open. The other soldiers jumped out of the way as he tumbled down the slope. His slide stopped at the edge of the trees.

High above, an eagle soared. The sky domed blue through rock and leaves. Much closer than the bird, a man in black armor loomed. Ossdonc, thought Avender dimly. His blood pooled on the stones around him. No. He recognized the face, though it had changed over the years.

It was Reiffen.

15

Ferris's Tears

lone with her father and the talking stone, Ferris paddled home. Icer they had sent ahead in one of the Eastbay canoes. Above their heads, Redburr winged heavily across the bright blue sky.

Durk did most of the talking. More than once he gushed on about how wonderful it felt to have finally escaped Ussene. Ferris concentrated on not crying. Tears for Skimmer and the pup were one thing, but public wretchedness over Reiffen was another matter entirely. Gripping her paddle till her fingers turned white, she fought to keep her eyes dry even as the growing breeze tried to tickle them to tears.

She wanted very much to hear what Durk had to say about Reiffen, and hoped the stone wouldn't be able to prove his claims about her old friend's new cruelty. But Berrel wouldn't let Durk talk about what had happened yet. He wanted Redburr and the others to judge what the stone had to say for themselves, so Durk told them the story of how Reiffen had found him instead. There was something about bats, and guano, and a slave named Spit, and more about Reiffen not being very nice anymore. Ferris found herself wishing Durk had stayed lost, if it meant her heart could remain unchanged.

"He cast me in the fire the very first time I opened my mouth after he found me." The stone's voice drummed off the planking on the bottom of the canoe. "All I did was ask how long it would be before he could take me outside. Believe me, nothing is worse than being thrown into a fiery pit, especially if you can't be consumed. All I could do was scream. When I finally came out, you can be sure I thought twice about arguing with him again."

"How could Reiffen take you outside if he wasn't allowed out himself?" said Ferris, drawing some small measure of satisfaction from the thought that Durk was already proving himself wrong.

"That's just it," replied the stone. "He was allowed out. All the time."

"He wasn't a prisoner?" asked Berrel.

"No. And he often brought things back with him, which was how I knew. Once he returned with a small wolf. At least that's what it sounded like. I'm not sure what your friend did with the poor creature, but the racket was awful. All that squealing and whimpering. He dumped me in the fire that time, too, and all I'd done was suggest he take his cruelty elsewhere."

"Sounds like you spent a lot of time in the fire."

"For more than I deserved."

Ferris kept paddling. She knew exactly what her father was thinking. If Reiffen could come and go from Ussene as he pleased, why hadn't he come home? The answer was obvious. He hadn't wanted to. Which meant Durk was right. Reiffen really had tried to steal the nokken pups on his own, and wasn't just following orders from the Three.

Glad she was in the bow where her father couldn't see, Ferris finally lost the struggle with her tears.

She rubbed her eyes dry as the canoe coasted into the lower

dock. The Home Guard had left Icer on the stone quay with Old Mortin, who had set out a bowl of ale. Icer's whiskers twitched as he sniffed at the sour but interesting smell; the two of them looked to be well on their way to forming a fast friendship.

Upstairs, Ferris found Redburr on the kitchen table gulping strips of bacon, his sharp claws scoring the wooden edge of his perch. The fact that the Shaper hadn't changed back to a bear suggested he intended to be taking wing again soon. Accompanied by the smell of frying butter, Hern flipped flapjacks on the stove, dishing out orders as well as helpings to those members of the Home Guard who had shown up hoping for a meal.

"Ferris." She waved her flat spoon at her daughter. "Go change out of those filthy clothes. I'll come get you when everyone's here for the meeting."

Her mind in a jumble, Ferris climbed the back stairs to her room and tried to sort through the horror of the morning. Her body felt empty, as if her insides had washed down the gorge with the nokken. Nothing was left for tears. Reiffen had murdered a friend, and tortured a wolf pup, and tried to steal nokken, most probably for reasons far worse than their fur. She had been wrong, and everyone else right; the Wizards had turned him after all.

She had been such a fool. All those times she had thought Reiffen was coming to her in her dreams, because maybe he thought about her the way she thought about him, and maybe thinking about her would keep him safe and sane through the long, terrible days and nights of Ussene; all those times she had been wrong. She had hoped that Reiffen nursed some memory of her deep in his heart, far from Wizards' prying. A memory to help keep him alive, to help keep true the part of him that would always be Reiffen. The part he would never allow to change, no matter what.

The part she might love forever.

Her tears burst through once more. Beside the bed, the curtains bellied in the breeze. Ferris hugged herself tightly. Plainly, Reiffen had never held her in his heart the way she had held him. Why should he? She had never said a word to him about how she felt. He had left before she was old enough to understand it herself. Now she had to teach herself not to care.

But it hurt so much to let go of her dreams.

By the time Hern knocked on the door, Ferris had stopped crying but still hadn't changed out of her bloody clothes. At the second rap she told her mother to go away. For once she wasn't interested in councils.

The door opened. Hern bustled into the room. "You know you can't sit around sulking like this. You don't want everyone downstairs guessing your secrets, do you?"

Opening the wardrobe, Ferris's mother pulled a plain work dress off a peg. Her daughter sighed.

"I know. It's hard." The bed creaked as Hern sat beside Ferris and gave her a loving squeeze. Flecks of flour speckled her arms below her rolled-up sleeves. "But now's no time to be heartsick, dear. You should have prepared for this day a long time ago. We all knew it was coming."

Ferris didn't look up. "He killed Skimmer, Mother. And a pup."

"And most likely he's going to kill a lot more. But you can't dwell on the might-have-beens, only the here and now. Redburr says there's war in the north and we all have to do our part. Otherwise a lot more nokken will die, and people, too."

Ferris stared at the floor, where just last night Reiffen's ghostly presence had flustered the shining moonlight. "What can I do? I can't use a sword. I don't know magic."

Hern snorted, refusing to believe her daughter could say such a thing, no matter how disappointed she was. "You can cook. You can sew. You can bandage wounds. Your father says Icer's already doing much better, thanks to you. It's not all about sw____ ___u know, no matter what some men might say. Except for A\ you know as much about the way Reiffen thinks as anyone. . sure the prince will listen to your counsel every bit as much as he does Redburr's, to take back to his father."

Ferris raised her face and looked at her mother. "Brizen's here? He's not in Bracken?"

"He rode back as soon as he heard. Nearly killed his horse, he was in such a hurry." Hern waved her hand impatiently, trying to get her daughter to start undressing. Ferris unfastened the top buttons of her blouse. Her mother got up off the bed and returned to the hall.

"We'll be in the Map Room when you're done," she said before closing the door. "There'll be plenty of time for grief when Redburr and the prince are gone."

The latch clicked closed. Ferris pulled off her dirty shirt and caught a glimpse of her puffy eyes and red nose in the mirror. Before putting on her dress she splashed cold water across her cheeks and toweled her hands and face dry. At least Brizen wouldn't see how hurt she was by Reiffen's defection. And, if anyone was going to pass judgment on what Reiffen had become, she at least would be present to listen to the sentence, no matter how crushed her heart.

Durk had already begun telling his story when she arrived, but she hadn't missed anything she hadn't already heard. The stone lay on a black velvet pillow on the long table in the middle of the room, everyone except the Shaper seated around him. Berrel occupied one end, a large map of the world covering the wall behind him, from the Toes to the Great Forest, the Blue Mountains to Cuspor. Hern sat opposite, by the door, with Prince Brizen, the chief forester, and the Mayor of Eastbay between her and her husband. Redburr perched in the open window behind Ranner and the mayor, his claws gripping the sill.

Ferris slipped into the empty seat between her mother and the prince. Hern patted her hand. Brizen offered a glance of deepest sympathy, his long face as somber as she had ever seen it.

"I consoled myself," the pompous stone was saying, "with the thought that, if ever I was lucky enough to return to the world of sunlight and polite conversation, I should dictate a play about my travels underground. *Done in in Darkness*, I'll call it. Or maybe *A Stone's Throw.*"

"Get on with the story," squawked the Shaper, scratching at the sill with his claws. Ferris felt her mother wince. "We have other important matters to discuss besides your confinement."

"If I'm to give you a true sense of how our old friend Reiffen has changed," replied Durk in an injured tone, "you must allow me to set the proper mood. As I was saying, after I fell to the bottom of that crevasse, and really, it would have been better for all concerned, as I suggested on more than one occasion, if Nurren or one of the other Dwarves had carried me. Too much responsibility for a boy. And he would have been more sure of defending himself, too, without having to worry about my safety. I suppose he's off doing a bit of farming, or maybe herding cows, now that he's home?"

"Actually, he's patrolling the north. Or at least he was. Isn't that right, Redburr?" Ferris turned guiltily toward the Shaper, ashamed she hadn't thought to ask about Avender before. "He is all right, isn't he?"

"He was fine when I left, girl. But we'll talk about the north later. If Durk here ever gives us the chance."

"I could go a lot faster if you didn't keep interrupting," said the stone.

"Then, please." Berrel glanced around the table. "No more interruptions."

"Thank you, Steward. I shall try to be as brief as possible. Just don't blame me if I'm unable to convey the subtler terror of the tale. Anyway, there I was, lost at the bottom of the world. For a very long time, I might add. Only rarely did I hear even the rustle and click of vermin, let alone the grunts of passing pasties, or the swearing of sissit. Finally, however, one of the slaves stumbled over me. I think she was a guano-picker, which, I'll have you know, is the very lowest of the low in that place. Better even to be a stone than a guano-picker. A nasty job, though I suppose somebody has to do it. She kept muttering about stinky, slippy bats, which is how I know what she did. I didn't say a word, because everyone knows guano-pickers never get any higher than the very lowest levels of the dungeons, but she spotted me right off. 'What a pretty stone,' she said, which didn't surprise me at all. It wasn't the first time my trim, smooth shape has prompted someone to pick me up. The only trouble was there were holes in all her pockets, which meant I kept slipping through her filthy rags and tumbling back to the ground. She remembered to pick me up the first few times, but finally the inevitable happened, and she didn't. I was lost again. And probably somewhere even worse than the first time. Luckily, I have lost my sense of smell completely since my transformation.

"After that it was another eternity before anyone came near me again. Finally, one day, I heard footsteps approaching, one pair booted and the other bare. You get very good at perceiving that sort of thing when the only sense you have left is your ears."

Ferris started to say something about how anyone could tell the difference between bare and booted feet but her father hushed her with a finger to his lips.

"They didn't speak until they were quite close." The stone's voice became more dramatic as he crept deeper into his tale. Given an audience, Durk always returned to his past as an actor and unbridled ham. "Then one of them said they had gone far enough. I guessed he was the one with the boots. The other stopped without a word. There was a moment's silence. Real life is never as interesting as a good play, you know. Then I heard the sound of a knife being drawn from its sheath. 'Oh no, my lord,' the second person cried. 'What are you doing?' That's when I discovered she was a woman. And what's more, much to my surprise, the same slave as had found me the first time. Though I suppose it's only natural for her to have had some sort of regular rounds she followed in her nasty business, no matter how drawn out.

"'I'm afraid I have to kill you,' the man with the boots told her.

"The woman moaned and sobbed. I made up my mind to remain mute, knowing there was no telling what a murderer might do to a talking stone. But her next words overwhelmed my prudence. 'Reiffen!' she cried. 'What have I ever done that you should want to kill me?'

"'My masters want it so,' he replied.

"I was astonished, to say the least, to hear her call him Reiffen. After all, how many Reiffens could there be? Especially in *that* place? Of course, it came as no surprise to me at all that Reiffen was still alive. It was the rest of you I thought were dead. Obviously the Wizards would have saved their prize captive after going to all the bother of catching him in the first place.

"At any rate, I was so astonished I couldn't stop myself. 'Reiffen!' I exclaimed as soon as I heard his name. The sobbing stopped. The darkness went absolutely silent. Then Reiffen called out, 'Who's there? Show yourself! If you know who I am, you also know I speak for the Three, and I hold their magic as well. Show yourself, or it will go much the worse when I find you.'

"Of course no one showed themselves. I debated whether I should do something to try and save myself, and the poor woman, too, of course, but I didn't think the trick I had used to fool the guards would work on Reiffen. Especially as he had been there the first time.

"But your old friend is a clever one. After his threat went unanswered, he quickly came up with the truth. 'Durk?' he asked. 'Is that you? There's nothing else in the tunnel I can see.'

"He began to scrabble among the rocks. I heard his boots scraping toward me. The woman, whom I later discovered had the singularly unattractive name of Spit, didn't move a muscle, though I heard her breathing near the wall. Knowing he would find me eventually, I made my presence known. I may not have been as persuasive as Ferris remembers I was that time with the guards, but I think I might have had some small effect. At any rate, he didn't kill the slave.

" 'You're right, Reiffen,' I told him. 'It is indeed I, Durk, lying here on the cold, hard stone. Given the cowardly way you are threatening this poor woman, I can no longer remain quiet. Remember, sir, should you insist on your dark intent, your crimes will not pass unheard.'

"He softened his tone at once and asked how I had come so very far from the place I had fallen. I told him some slave had found me, only to lose me again. I thought it just as well not to let either of them know that Spit was the one who had brought me, and asked instead what he intended to do with the poor woman.

" 'Why,' he replied, 'I shall have to let her go. It would never do to kill her before such a convincing informant.'

" 'Oh, my lord, thank you,' she gasped gratefully. The floor scuffed as she fell to her knees.

" 'Or I could just leave you both down here,' he went on more nastily. Spit began to sob again. 'Maybe her ghost will enter a stone like yours to keep you company.'

" 'Two wrongs don't make a right,' I said sagely.

" 'No,' he answered. 'Nor would I have the pleasure of your interesting company if I did. But, if I do take you Upstairs with me, I run the risk of you telling my mother what almost happened.

Stand up, Spit. I didn't really want to kill you, anyway. You were Ossdonc's choice, not mine. This way will be much better. Fornoch and Usseis would rather meet a talking stone than lose another slave to Ossdonc's caprice.'

"He had found me by then. Picked me up and put me in his pocket. Once he mentioned the Wizards I wouldn't have said another word, unless Spit needed my help again, of course. And that's how I was found. There are many more details I have left out, but that's the gist. You asked I be brief."

"So we did," said Berrel. "Thank you for your restraint."

The breeze outside the window ruffled the feathers on Redburr's back. "Did you ever meet the Wizards?" he cawed.

"Of course," answered the stone. "The Gray used to examine me regularly every time he visited Reiffen's workshop. Once or twice he even plucked me from the fire after Reiffen threw me there."

"And Usseis?"

"I never met the White. Or the Black. I think Reiffen and the Gray wanted to keep me for themselves. Once, the Gray told Reiffen that the White would be most impressed if he could unlock all my secrets. But nothing else Reiffen tried was ever as bad as the fire."

"What about Giserre?" asked Hern. "How is she? Did you meet her?"

"Sadly, no," the rock admitted. "Until he brought me here, our friend Reiffen kept me locked tight in his workshop. I think he was afraid I would tell his mother what a complete villain he had become. Mostly I was alone. Sometimes he brought the Gray Wizard with him, to talk about magic and war, but I stopped listening to their conversations after a while. It was always the same thing. Two teaspoons of batwing and a pinch of someone's blood. It gets boring fairly quickly, you know."

"This is all very well, but we still need to hear why Reiffen brought you here." Berrel tapped a finger on the dark table, its polished surface reflecting the sky above the pines. "You said before he brought you deliberately. How do you know that?"

"He told me so, that's how."

"He told you?" asked the Shaper.

"He did. He planned on leaving me here all along."

"Why?"

"He said he wanted to be certain everyone knew he was the one who stole the pup."

"Why would Reiffen want everyone to know that?" Brizen looked wonderingly around the table. "You'd think he would prefer just the opposite."

"He didn't say. He just told me he wanted to make sure you knew."

"Rubbing our noses in it," squawked the eagle.

"But why would Reiffen even want to steal a pup?" asked the mayor.

"Experiments," said the stone.

"Experiments?" The mayor's face pinched in confusion.

"Not having ever seen them, I couldn't say. But if they're anything like what I heard him do to that wolf cub, it wasn't pleasant."

"Reiffen never tortured an animal in his life," scoffed Ferris, unable to keep from defending her old friend even now.

"I hear he used to be friendly with the seals, too."

It took every bit of Ferris's self-control to keep from grabbing the stone off his soft pillow and hurling him out the window.

"That's enough," said Berrel. "You've made your point, Durk. Reiffen isn't the boy we knew any longer." The steward turned to the Shaper. "Now then, Redburr, you've been waiting patiently. I think it's time you tell us your news."

The bird picked at the feathers on his shoulder with his sharp beak. "As I said before, it's war. While Reiffen was visiting us this morning, to show what comes of spending seven years in Ussene, Ossdonc's army was marching south across the Waste. For Backford."

"That's why Reiffen acted so openly," said Brizen. "And why he wanted to make sure we knew it was him. By having Reiffen strike at Valing, the Three show us no place is safe. Have you told my father?"

"I was in Rimwich two nights ago. One of my reasons for flying on to Valing was to find you. If it's going to be war, the king wants you at his right hand."

Brizen nodded. "I shall not disappoint him. Hern, Berrel, if I might trouble you for a fresh horse. I'm afraid mine is completely blown by the gallop from Bracken."

"We'll give you any horse you need," replied Berrel. "But I'm guessing the rest of your escort will need fresh mounts as well, and I'm not sure we have enough for all of you. Besides, you might want to wait till we've decided our course of action in Valing. That way we won't have to send an extra messenger to the king."

The Shaper stretched his long neck, ruffling the soft feathers along his throat. "There's actually not much for you to decide. You won't send troops, because you don't have any. And it's unlikely, despite what happened today, for Valing to need to prepare itself for war. The Three won't come after you until they've conquered everyone else. Brizen's right. This thing with the nokken was just for spite."

"What would you have us do then?" demanded Hern. "Watch our cows and sheep as usual and ignore the rest of the world?"

"You know exactly what to do, Steward. You'll watch the pass and send extra patrols into the mountains. And, should the Three, with Reiffen in the lead, conquer Banking and Rimwich, they'll find Valing's farmers and fishermen more dangerous than

they think. But that's not what I want you to do now. The Bryddin need to be told what's going on."

"Issinlough's a long way from the Bavadars, Shaper," said
Ranner. "You'd be better off to fly there yourself, if you want the
message delivered quick."

The prince and the mayor nodded at the wisdom of the chief
forester's suggestion, but the stewards looked more thoughtful.
Ranner, sensing there was more to Redburr's suggestion than he
knew, waited for Hern or Berrel to respond.

"Is this the time for telling secrets, bird?" asked the latter.

"It's why the secret was made."

Everyone but the Shaper stared at the stewards. Ferris wondered what they could possibly be talking about. Valing held no
secrets. Even when the Sword had been hidden here, the only secret had been where.

"It is the fastest way." Hern looked at her husband. "Nolo said
to use it if there was any sudden need."

"Well, we certainly have sudden need." Berrel nodded briskly
as they made up their minds. "All right, we'll do it. There's a tunnel in the lower levels of the Neck that leads straight to the
Stoneways."

Had he said the tunnel led straight to Ussene, he would not
have caused greater surprise. Ferris's first reaction was to be out-
raged at the thought that she could have visited Issinlough any
time she felt like it, had her parents only bothered to tell her
about the secret passage. But, when she thought about it for a
moment, she realized that was impossible. Issinlough was still far
away, underneath Grangore, hundreds of leagues to the south-
west. Even if this new passage led straight to the Abyss, it would
still be a long trek through the dark to reach the mansions of the
Dwarves.

Brizen nodded to himself, as if he wasn't entirely surprised by the new development. Ferris wondered if there were other hidden routes to the Stoneways, with the Sun Road the only one everyone was aware of. It made sense. When she thought about how quickly the Dwarves had built secret tunnels through the Wizards' dungeons, it was only natural to think they might carve other ways to the surface of the world as well. Other ways they would want to keep secret from the Three.

"I see what you're suggesting." Brizen leaned forward on the table. "One of us needs to descend this passage to warn the Dwarves. For all we know one of the other Wizards is leading a second army against Issinlough at the same time Ossdonc attacks us on the surface."

"That's not quite it," answered the bird, "but you're close enough. Whether there's another army or not, the Dwarves need to be warned. At the very least they might be able to help us."

"Very well. I'll go."

Redburr flapped the prince's offer aside. "I already told you. Your place is with your father."

Hern sighed. "I suppose I can go. Berrel has to stay in case there's any fighting, but Sally can handle the housekeeping perfectly well on her own. She did fine the last time I went to Malmoret."

"The task isn't for you, either." The Shaper fixed Hern with a steady eye. "Except for Nolo, the Dwarves don't know you. Persuasion may be required to get them to move, and they might take it better from someone they know. Besides, I have the feeling Valing needs both its stewards at a time like this. And Ranner, too."

"Then who's your choice?"

"Ferris. She's the one who's been before. And we all know how persuasive she can be. Right, Ferris?"

Ferris's heart lifted. A long journey was just the thing to help her forget about Reiffen.

"I think it's an excellent idea," she said.

"Of course you would." Hern frowned, but said nothing to contradict Redburr's plan.

"I think it's brilliant," said Brizen. "A much better choice than I would have made."

"As long as no one asks me to go," said the stone from the middle of the table.

"There's no chance of that," said the Shaper.

"You're safe with us," said Berrel. "Hern'll find a lovely spot for you with plenty of sunlight."

"Actually, now that I'm here, I think I prefer the kitchen. That's where the best conversation is. As long as I'm not too close to the fire."

The council ended with Ferris in a hurry to be off. Valing held too much bitterness for her just now. Later, after she had been away for a while, perhaps she could bear to return. Then maybe every time she saw the lake glinting sweet and blue between the mountains she would see something other than Icer's raw wound, or Skimmer following the pup into the white crush of the gorge. In the meantime she would choose a more sensible course than the one she had been following. Castles built on solid ground were much more practical than those erected in the air.

She couldn't leave as quickly as she wished, however. Berrel and Brizen had to write letters for her to take to Dwvon and Uhle, and Redburr wanted to make sure there was nothing else to be done before he let her go. Ferris returned to her room to pack and change into warm clothes for traveling underground, then retreated to her favorite spot among the pines to wait for someone to show her the way to the new tunnel.

Brizen found her a few minutes later. Ferris scolded herself for not remembering the prince had found her at this spot before, but, to tell the truth, she was glad he had come. At least some people stayed true.

"If I am imposing," he said with a trace of his old hesitancy, "please bid me leave."

"You're not imposing," she told him.

For a while they didn't speak. Ferris sat on her flat rock; Brizen stood a little behind her, his hands crossed patiently behind his back. Beside them a squirrel swayed out over the side of the cliff on a low pine bough, its bushy tail brushing the long green needles as it tested the buoyancy of the branch.

"I'm sorry," said the prince kindly. "You've always been Reiffen's most loyal friend."

Ferris made no answer at first. She didn't want to defend herself, though she knew that wasn't what Brizen was asking. It really wasn't fair to let him stew, however. He had come to comfort her, showing how good and faithful he could be. He had said he wouldn't give up until he knew she loved someone else. Maybe now he would never know.

"Please don't talk about Reiffen," she said. "It's too sad."

"It is very sad," the prince agreed. Plucking a bundle of needles from the tree beside him, he spun them between his fingers. The branch waved like a long, languid arm as he released it.

"You won't start till tomorrow?" she asked.

"No. The horses need rest, and we'd only have to spend the night in the pass if we left this afternoon. And you?"

"I shall leave as soon as Redburr's ready for me to go."

"I wrote my letter." Brizen pulled his needles apart one by one and watched them dribble to the ground. "Redburr wanted me to remind Dwvon of the recent friendship of our peoples and how we need to face the Wizards together."

"That doesn't sound like much."

"That's what I thought. But Redburr says that's the sort of thing princes have to do. I must say, sometimes I wish I wasn't a prince. Then I could go with you."

"Everybody always wants to be something they're not," said Ferris. "I'm sure I'd love to be a princess."

Brizen's foot scuffed closer across the brown needles. With a bit of shock, Ferris realized what she'd said.

"You can be a princess a lot easier than I can not be a prince," he told her.

"I don't love you, Brizen," she replied, trying to recover what she hadn't even known she might let slip.

"I know." He sighed quietly and looked at his empty hands. "I love you, though. Very much. If I thought you could at least learn to love me . . ."

Another silence drifted among the trees. The squirrel dropped a broken pinecone to the ground.

"I do like you," said Ferris.

"I know that. I hope you'll—"

Brizen stopped in the middle of his sentence as a new thought entered his head.

"Are you saying . . . ?" He looked at her with a slight sideways twist. "Not that I'm complaining or anything, but why are you willing to listen to me now? It was only two days ago you told me there was no hope. The only thing that's changed since . . ."

He saw it all. Understanding spread across his face. "You were in love with Reiffen," he breathed. "Oh, Ferris. I'm so sorry."

It was the best thing he could have said. Ferris's heart climbed another step up out of the deep well it had fallen into. How wonderful that Brizen's first thought had been of her own sorrow rather than his new chance.

He made a little bow, the same sort of bow Giserre had taught Reiffen to make when apologizing. "I did not understand," he said. "If you can possibly forgive my obtuseness, I will take my leave of you now."

"Don't go." Ferris turned, half reaching out to him. Losing

two lovers in one day would really be too much. "I feel like such a fool."

Brizen maintained his formal manner. "No, my lady, it is I who have been a fool."

Ferris shook her head. "I'm no lady, Brizen. Just a simple woman from Valing. In that much, at least, you're wrong. But I am a fool. You came to me honestly, offering to lift me up beside you. Like a silly girl, I was unable to appreciate your offer, or your generous heart. Honest love, and not the foolish fancy of childhood. I've been clinging to my dreams like a little girl. It's time I grew up. I'm just sorry I didn't recognize your gifts earlier."

"I love you, Ferris. I always have, from the first time I saw you. I just wish you loved me."

"I do like you, Brizen. More and more all the time. And you've liked me all these years, even when I didn't treat you well at all."

"I think you have treated me very well, moon-eyed schoolboy that I have been."

She gave a deprecating laugh. "I treated you terribly that time I made you show me the hisser, and you know it."

Brizen brushed her confession aside. "That? That was my fault, not yours. I was trying to show off. To show you I could be as brave as Avender."

"And I was trying to be mean, because you weren't Reiffen. Because you had all the things I thought should have been his. His kingdoms. His titles."

"I would give them all to him in a minute," said Brizen, "if you would love me. Only, I doubt that would be a very good thing to do right now."

"Yes," Ferris admitted. "It would be the wrong thing to do now."

She looked up at the prince, who stood several steps back from the edge of the cliff. The lower branches of the pines graced his shoulders like a green mantle. He wasn't as handsome as Reiffen, but he was kinder. And more noble, too. He would be a fine king, if Reiffen and the Wizards left him any kingdom to inherit. Kindness softened his face, where in Reiffen there was only fierce pride. Brizen would want always to do the right thing, the good thing, without any thought for himself. Reiffen might once have done the good thing also, but he would have done it for his own sake, not others'. She had been such a fool not to see it. Such a fool to turn down the good things offered her, for the excitement of first love.

The prince looked back and saw her studying him. She turned her face away, not wanting him to see her disappointment.

"Ferris," he asked. "Do you think you might really love me some day?"

She whispered her answer into her dress. "I don't know. I would certainly try, Brizen. You're the finest man I know." Gaining strength, she added, "If I didn't, it would be my fault, not yours."

She raised her face toward his as she spoke. His eyes sparkled, his mouth curled in joy. In a fit of boldness he bent forward to kiss her. Their lips grazed. Ferris had never let anyone kiss her and felt a little ashamed. Her kiss she had saved for Reiffen. But that was stupid, there was no Reiffen anymore. Taking Brizen's face in hers, she kissed him back as fiercely as she knew how.

When she let him go, she was surprised at how her heart leapt and her blood raced. She could scarcely catch her breath. Brizen looked as if he might stumble off the cliff. Ferris pushed him gently to safety.

"You mustn't speak of this to anyone," she said. "Now is not the time for secret betrothals. We know the trouble it caused for Reiffen and Giserre. But, if things come out all right at the end of this war . . ." She looked down at the soft brown needles brushing the stone at her feet and almost blushed. "Maybe we can try again."

"I adore you, Ferris," he said.

"I know," she answered. "Thank you. Now please go. We both have things to do."

He kissed the hand she held out to him. Around them the trees stood solemn as courtly barons.

She sat alone on the rock after he left and thought about what she had done. Despite the kiss, and the desire she had felt, she still didn't love Brizen. She loved Reiffen. Or she thought she did. It was all terribly confusing. She loved what Reiffen had been, the boy who dared anything, who dreamed great dreams, the same as she. The boy she had thought more exciting than anything in the world. So often, when she and Reiffen and Avender had come to this place, to look out at the White Pool and the river charging off through the valley, Reiffen would tell them what they would do when he was king. How they would drive the Wizards from the world and live in a golden age. Avender would frown and tell him not to brag. And Ferris would tell Avender to mind his own business and let Reiffen have his dreams. Dreams she told neither of them she shared.

But she was older now, and understood that excitement grew less attractive with age. War had come, and it wasn't exciting at all. It was horrible.

What Reiffen had become was even worse.

For the third time that day Ferris bowed her face to her hands and wept for what she had lost. Above her head the squirrel leapt among the branches like a nokken racing through the waves.

BRIZEN

Aunties say there is a place
is a place, is a place
Just beyond the fog's thick face,
fog's thick face, fog's thick face
Where the graylings, sweet and plump,
sweet and plump, sweet and plump
Swim like ducks and never jump.
never jump, never jump
Where the rock is always warm,
always warm, always warm
Where the sky will never storm.
never storm, never storm
Where no boat has ever come,
ever come, ever come
That is where Whitespray has swum.

—"WHITESPRAY'S FALL," A NOKKEN SONG

16

Stinky, Slippy Bats

hat makes Spit so special?"

Giserre look up from her work. "Excuse me?"

"I'm wondering why the Three chose Spit to be your servant, milady." The thimble on the bard's left little finger clinked as he lifted the bottle of dark red Ankley from its place on the lunch tray. "Out of all the slaves in Ussene, why pick a woman from the woods? No one's a servant in the north. They know nothing about it."

"Someone had to be chosen." Giserre shook her head at Mindrell's offer of wine, and returned to her crucibles and powders. With Reiffen gone, she had to prepare her own ointments and draughts at the makeshift worktable he had arranged for her in the sitting room.

The bard set the bottle back on the tray. "Did you ever think there might be a reason?"

"What possible reason could anyone have for choosing Spit?"

"She could be a spy."

"Reiffen and I have always assumed she is. What difference does it make? Everyone is a spy in Ussene."

Her ingredients measured, Giserre began stirring the flask

with a tiny whisk of oleander twigs. Mindrell admired her slender hands from his seat on the couch; it was always so agreeable when pleasure and self-preservation followed the same course. There were definite advantages to being the personal bodyguard of the most beautiful woman he had ever seen. Some time ago he had decided he really didn't want anything to happen to her, for his own sake as much as Reiffen's. Perhaps one day he would thank the young wizard for saving him from domestication.

"What makes you bring this matter up now?" she asked.

"She's taken to disappearing. At night. Stealing something out of your bags and going off for several hours. I've spotted her at it twice."

"Stealing from my medical bags?" Giserre started across the room toward the satchels she used to carry her tonics and balms.

"She put it back. I made sure of that the second time. Though you might check for poison. It was one of the larger jars, about as round as my palm and a finger deep."

"If Spit wanted to poison me, she would have done it long ago."

Returning to the workbench, Giserre poured the contents of her beaker into a jar not unlike the one Mindrell had seen Spit borrow. The liquid oozed slowly from one pot to the other, like melting cheese.

"What's that you're making?" he asked.

Giserre tapped the edge of the beaker against the lip of the jar to encourage the last sluggish gob to drop into the smaller container. "A salve for rashes and inflammations of the skin. We are running low."

"The jar looks like the one I saw Spit take."

"I was thinking the same myself. It is not a cream I ever use on my own skin, however, which should put your poisoning theory to rest."

"I still think she's up to something. Slaves, or servants, shouldn't have business of their own in the middle of the night."

"She was a proper-enough slave when she first came to us, fearful as a whipped cur. I like her better now."

"We all improve in your presence, my lady." The bard dipped his head modestly.

"Perhaps. Spit still has her moments, however, especially around the Wizards."

"She should be afraid of more than Wizards."

"She fears you, if that improves your opinion of her. But, if you are so worried about Spit's nocturnal ramblings, I suggest you follow her. See what she is up to. I confess, you have piqued my interest. Nothing is ever as it seems in this place."

"Your ladyship won't mind if I leave you unguarded for an hour or two?"

"I am perfectly safe on my own, now Ossdonc and his soldiers have left the fortress. Really, there was no need for Reiffen to leave you behind to guard me."

"It's a duty I cherish."

"I prefer my guardians vigilant, not reverent, sir. And Reiffen might have prepared my finger just as easily as yours, which would have allowed you to cherish your duty with him, instead of with me."

"I doubt that very much, my lady. Attaching the thimble was a nasty bit of business to which your son, I hope, will never subject you."

How much further into her son's magical practices Giserre was now willing to go was left unsaid as Spit returned with the lamp oil her mistress had sent her to fetch from the kitchen. Mindrell selected a book of poetry from the volumes on the table at his elbow and, while the women busied themselves with their potions, settled down to read.

Later that afternoon Fornoch beckoned to him from the doorway.

"A moment of your time."

"I'm on duty, Your Eminence. Her ladyship is taking her afternoon nap."

"I assure you, nothing will happen to her while you are gone. Come with me."

Mindrell followed. He had made it a rule of life never to disobey a Wizard. In the Library the spider danced on its web while the books in the shelves showed their backs primly.

"Usseis asked me to speak with you," said Fornoch. "He has a task for you."

"It will be my privilege to fill some small function for his lordship."

"You do not care to hear first what it is you are asked to do?"

"I presume neither you nor Usseis would bother asking me to do something I can't."

Amusement clipped the corners of Fornoch's mouth. "How wise of you. And yes, you shall find no difficulty performing this task. You have already decided on the course of action yourself, I believe. With your mistress's permission."

"I have?"

"Yes. You are not the only one to have noticed Spit's midnight wanderings. Usseis and I have felt them as well. Apparently she has been doing something with magic. In a small way, of course, but enough so my brother and I have been brushed by her incantations. Since you have already taken it upon yourself to investigate the matter, we ask that you report your findings to us as well."

Mindrell inclined his head obediently. "I only wish all the Three's requests were so easily obliged. May I ask why you aren't looking into the matter yourself?"

"I have more important tasks. As does my brother."

At supper the bard studied Spit closely, wondering where she had found the courage to try casting spells. He wasn't surprised she could: he had cast a spell himself once, though it had been given him by Ossdonc. If Spit really was doing magic, the source of her power was probably the potions Reiffen had mixed for his mother, or those he had taught his mother to mix. Otherwise, if she really had picked up magic somehow during her time in Ussene, why hadn't she used it to escape? That was what he would do.

It was long past midnight when, watching from Reiffen's bedroom, he saw Spit filch from its bag the jar Giserre had prepared earlier and slip from the room. Her footsteps pattered lightly, like mice scurrying in an attic, as he followed her through the empty tunnels. Down they went, till she turned left at the level of the Main Gate and headed toward the dungeons. Mindrell hoped it wasn't so late the password had been changed.

Vermin rustled along the walls; jeering laughter sounded from the darkness ahead. Mindrell stole forward, not wanting anyone to notice him against the guttering illumination of the candles. Though he wasn't close enough to hear the exchange between Spit and the guards, he knew exactly what would be said. More than once he had fought soldiers who had not shown Giserre the proper respect, and he had accompanied Spit often enough to know the rudeness was far worse for her, despite her age.

Eventually the sentries allowed her to pass. The slave descended the ramp to the dungeons, a fresh torch in hand to light the way. Quickly Mindrell followed. There were too many choices at the next level; he knew he had to be close enough to see which path she took. If he fell too far behind her light he would lose her at once.

"Solace," he snapped as he entered the checkpoint. The guards jumped to attention. Sometimes he wondered if the officer who set the passwords was a poet in his spare time. The choices were so often ironic.

Hurrying, he caught sight of Spit's yellow torch as he followed her down the ramp. The walls opened out on either side until he was in an enormous room, the dark mirror of Usseis's audience chamber. The ramp descended to the floor. Mindrell watched carefully to see which part of the gallery Spit disappeared into, then sprinted down the incline and leapt after her to make sure he found the right tunnel before the glow of her torch disappeared.

Shallow puddles splashed beneath his feet. The passages yawned darkly except for one, its mouth still brushed with yellow light. Mindrell peered around the edge of the opening: it wouldn't do to come stumbling into Spit a short way down the passage. But he need not have feared. Just past the entrance the tunnel began to descend, torchlight wobbling along the ceiling.

A faint reek reached his nose as he started down, the odor deepening with every step. Halfway along the stair he thought he was actually inhaling the stuff through his ears. Cold air burned his skin and eyes; more than once he coughed. Ordinarily he didn't like dirtying the handkerchiefs her ladyship had embroidered for him, but he really didn't want Spit to hear him sneeze.

A sissit appeared at the bottom of the stair and swung open the bullet lantern in his hands. The bard blinked at the brightness and masked his eyes.

"What's this?" the sissit said. "Another one?"

"I'm with the woman."

"I don't care who you're with. Me'n the boys here keep slaves in, not out. Go on with ya."

Covering his light, the sissit stepped back into the chamber behind him. Mindrell plunged on into the stink, arriving after a few more paces at what felt like a large cavern. The stench, heavy as a wind, almost pushed him backward. The only light glittered from a torch on the nearest wall. Mindrell guessed the torch was Spit's but had no idea why she had left it behind, unless she wanted to keep her hands free.

Wiping stinging tears from his eyes, he peered farther into the gloom. A gray slope descended into a darker distance. Shadows moved against the floor of the vast hall, wading stiff-legged like herons in search of frogs. But it wasn't water they slogged through, or even sand. With a start, Mindrell realized the source of the smell was the floor of the cave, which was covered in a thick carpet of bat droppings. Glancing upward, he found a few odd shapes clinging to the high, rocky ceiling, brown wings folded across their bellies. The rest of the bats would be outside, he reminded himself, where it was night on the surface of the world.

Wanting to get out of that disgusting place as quickly as possible, he began his search. Unfortunately, in the dim light, the stooping shadows all looked the same. Mostly they kept to the center of the cavern, filling the sacks they dragged behind them by scooping up the filth with their hands. Those whose burdens were complete followed a twisting trail deeper into the dark. Noting a path that began in the bare rock at his feet, Mindrell set off into the pungent darkness, a handkerchief to his nose.

The torch at the mouth of the cave had grown dim and distant when he finally found what he was looking for. "There, there," he heard Spit say from the gloom to his left. "This will make it feel better."

She chanted:

"Stinky, slippy, bats so ickly,
Save my friend from being sickly."

The bard cringed. If that was magic, any fool could do it. Harpers had been thrown out second-story windows for less offensive couplets. He wondered if he could scare the slave into teaching him what she had learned.

"Thanks," said a second woman's voice. "It feels better already. Who'd o' thought magic could do that?"

"It can. I'll keep coming then, till those nasty sores on your legs are all healed."

Mindrell smiled as he heard Spit imitating her mistress. Still in a hurry, he stepped off the path directly toward the slave and her patient. His foot sank several inches into the goo before settling on hard ground; small things wriggled away across the ooze. He hesitated, but to follow the path would have meant traveling for some distance in the wrong direction before doubling back, breathing the foul stink all the while. A nearby digger watched with interest as Mindrell took another reluctant step farther in.

Halfway between the two curves of the trail his feet found no bottom. Warm muck dripped over the edges of his boots, not wet enough for mud, but not dry enough for sand, either. He shifted his weight to pull his front foot free, but that only managed to sink his back foot in deeper. Awkwardly, he sat back on the glop, both legs already buried to midthigh.

"Spit. I think I need your help."

His voice echoed. A few of the lingering bats dropped from the ceiling and skittered away. Around him the soft shifting of legs and hands through guano ceased.

"Is that you, Mr. Mindrell?" whispered Spit.

"It is."

"What are you doing here?"

"Following you."

"Following me!" Spit's whisper turned fearful. "You won't tell milady, will you?"

"Of course I'll tell your mistress. Why wouldn't I?"

"Oh no! Please, don't tell milady!" Bats scurried along the

ceiling a second time as Spit's fear rose. "She'll want to come herself, and that would be terrible. It's not safe here at all!"

Mindrell looked at his legs, which were still sinking. As was his backside. "So I've discovered."

"You should never leave the path, Mr. Mindrell."

"I see that now, Spit. But we can fix it easily enough. I'll just take my cloak off and, after rolling it up like this, toss it over to you. Then you and your friend can pull me to firmer ground. Unless you'd rather use magic."

"Magic! What makes you think I know magic, Mr. Mindrell?"

"I just heard you. 'Ickly-sickly'? I think you can do better than that. 'Ickly' isn't even a word."

The slave's voice sank to a whisper. "That's just a charm, Mr. Mindrell, sir. Reiffen taught it to me. He said it would help my friends."

"All right, Spit. We can talk about what you know later. Right now I need to get out of this mess." Mindrell made a note to himself to talk further with Reiffen about what charms he might learn.

"Let him sink."

Mindrell looked back at the digger who had watched him leave the path without saying a word. "I'd suggest you keep your nose out of this, slave. My affairs are no concern of yours."

"Let him sink," the slave repeated. "No one'll ever find him once the worms are done with him. What do we care if one more o' them's gone? None o' them lifted a finger for young Bill that time he fell in."

"I'm no more one of 'them' than you are, friend." Mindrell had no intention of telling either the speaker or Spit that he was down here on a Wizard's errand as well as his own. "I warn you again. This isn't your affair."

"I'll help you, Mr. Mindrell. But you'll have to promise not to tell milady."

"I assure you, Spit. Once I describe this place to her ladyship, she won't want to come here any more than I."

"You still have to promise."

Mindrell couldn't tell in the little light that shone this deeply into the cave, but he was fairly certain Spit had screwed her courage to the uttermost in order to defy him. There was just that hint of frailty behind her firmness. And it was this sort of display of strength that had made him wonder what she was up to in the first place. But she had the upper hand at the moment, and he had the feeling that bullying wouldn't work. Not with that troublemaker egging her on. It was too bad, though, she wasn't younger or better-looking. Then there might have been a better reason than magic to blackmail her once they were out of this disgusting cave.

"Very well." The slime had gained another inch and his legs were starting to sting along with his eyes and nose. "I promise not to tell her ladyship. You can keep your midnight missions of mercy to yourself. Now, take the other end of my cloak and haul me out."

It took a while, and Mindrell had to let himself be dragged on his belly through the nasty mess before he finally found fresh footing, but eventually he reached the far side of the path. The slave Spit had been ministering to retreated as he climbed from the dripping ordure, and even Spit took a step backward. But now was no time to be offended. Bowing elegantly, he thanked them for their help.

"You shouldn't have followed me like that," Spit replied, still nervous.

"And you shouldn't go sneaking off. You forget my job is to guard your mistress. You've been acting very suspiciously these last few nights. Now come on. I've wasted enough time in this foul place. Let's get out of here."

Spit's voice still quavered. "I haven't finished my rounds."

QUEEN FERRIS | 311

"Stay then. Just be sure you get back before Giserre wakes up. Otherwise I'll have to tell her where you've been." He saw no reason to explain that he would have to tell Giserre anyway, any more than he had explained about the Wizards.

Without another word he retraced his way along the path. The slaves he passed made certain they were hard at work by the time he reached them. Even the troublemaker was elbow deep in the muck and paying no attention at all when Mindrell gave him a kick that sent the fellow flying face-first into the filth.

Back upstairs he went straight to his quarters in the officers' barracks and ordered several slaves to prepare him a bath. "Don't wash those," he ordered when they bent to pick up his dirty clothes. "Just put them in a basket." Clean and freshly dressed, he carried his filthy laundry to Giserre's apartment, where, with particular enjoyment, he dumped it in with Spit's washing for the day. Then he removed both baskets to the hall so as not to offend Giserre.

She was standing at her door when he returned, her gown pulled close.

"So?"

"Apparently Spit's decided her work with you isn't enough. I found her dosing her old friends in the pits."

Giserre nodded approvingly. "That is most gratifying. I told you she had changed for the better. Even here, if you treat someone decently, they will in turn learn decency themselves."

"I still think a slave ought to act like a slave, milady. Otherwise there's no telling what they might do."

Usseis summoned him to the throne room the next morning. Gathering his wit, Mindrell followed the messenger back through the dim halls. Of the Three, he found the White Wizard the most difficult to deal with. Unlike Fornoch, who seemed almost genial sometimes, or Ossdonc, who loved flattery as much as blood, there was nothing human about Usseis.

He arrived to find the throne room occupied by the White and Gray Wizards. The vault of the ceiling soared above their heads like an immense overturned bowl, as if some giant even larger than the Three had trapped them all inside like mice.

"What have you learned?" Usseis leaned forward from his tall bench atop the dais. Fornoch sat on the bottom step.

Mindrell bowed deeply. In addition to obedience, working for Ossdonc had taught him never to show disrespect, or fear, either. "Very little, my lords. The slave apes her mistress by going among her old friends in the guano pits to cure them."

"And the magic?"

"Charms taught her by Reiffen. And not very good ones, either."

Usseis raised an eyebrow skeptically. His voice coated the room like the thickest ointment in Giserre's bag. "Since when have you become a judge of magic, harper?"

"I'm no judge of magic, my lord, but I do know rhyming. I can't imagine bad verse is any better for magic than it is for poetry."

The Gray Wizard folded his hands deeper into the sleeves of his robe and addressed his brother. "It is as I told you. The slave adores her mistress."

Usseis's face remained dark as his eyes. "Reiffen should not be passing our gifts on to others."

"What he has done is no worse than what Ossdonc has done before. We gain the advantage in the end, I might add, as her leeching will make some of our wretched servants live longer. We shall be less dependent on the Keeadini to bring us new recruits."

"We shall not be dependent upon them at all, once our vassal occupies the New Palace." The White Wizard turned his boot black eyes again to Mindrell. "Tell me exactly what you found her doing."

"I didn't stay long enough to find out, my lord, but I think she was curing your guano-diggers' sores with one of Giserre's good lotions and a bit of bad rhyme."

"That was all?"

"Yes, my lord."

"What else could it be?" asked Fornoch.

Usseis's voice strengthened as he came to his decision. "Nothing. I felt no stronger magic. Still, I shall speak to Reiffen when he returns. Even charms should not be given lightly."

"It is good he should dispense small favors," replied Fornoch. "A king cannot be too beloved by his people. Especially one who comes to them with the weight of fire and sword at his beck."

"Well said, my lord," declared Mindrell, playing up to the Wizard's vanity. "You would make a fine bard."

Fornoch fixed the human with his shining black eyes. "Do not be mistaken, harper. I am the father of bards. And of lovers whispering into their sweethearts' ears, and mothers singing to their babes. Your gift is given from me."

"Then I thank you for the honor, my lord, and will treasure our kinship dearly."

The White Wizard laughed, his amusement thin as a lizard's eyelid, but Fornoch accepted the bard's tribute like a sovereign from his fool.

17

Backford Pool

A vender woke in a small white tent. His first thought was to wonder how the Wizard's black pavilion had managed to change color and shrink. His second was why he was still alive.

Eyes half open, he sniffed the sun-baked canvas. What felt like a narrow camp bed lay beneath him; a pillow cushioned his head. Beyond his feet the tent flaps had been tied back to reveal a band of bright blue sky edged at the bottom by the tops of tall cattails. Dimly, as if from a far-off part of a large house, he heard the shouts and jingling harness of men and animals at work. Behind the odor of canvas the air itself smelled burned.

A wave of pain in his chest pushed him back down on the bed when he tried to sit up. Whatever else had happened, his wound was still there, though it didn't seem as crippling as it should have. He found that, by bending his waist as little as possible and pushing against the edges of the cot with his elbows, he could sit up without feeling like he had torn himself in two.

Carefully he examined his bandages. His shirt had been removed and his chest bound in clean white cloth. Looking around the tent, he discovered a heavy rug covering the ground and a field desk and small folding chair set up in the corner, which suggested the owner was someone important. Several books and small jars stood neatly on the desk's shelves.

Reiffen appeared outside.

"Looks like you're recovering well," he said, leaning with one arm raised against the tent pole at the entrance. His black armor was gone, replaced by ordinary traveling clothes, dull and dusty as Avender's own.

"What day is it?" Avender was still too numb for any greater confrontation. The last thing he wanted was for Reiffen to have rescued him, not after his former friend had helped Ossdonc destroy Backford so utterly.

"You were wounded yesterday, if that's what you're wondering."

"Did you capture the others, too?"

"Others? Oh, you mean Lady Breeanna and her friend. No, they escaped. Your heroics gave them just the time they needed. Very clever of you, to give them your lamp."

"They would never have gotten anywhere in the tunnel without it."

"It also prevented me from using it to reopen the door. Though I did have to save you first, anyway."

"Thank you so much."

"You don't think I went through the last seven years just so you could die, do you? If I'm to get any payment for what I've done, you and Ferris have to remain alive."

"I'm sure Ferris will be just as grateful as I am."

"More, I hope."

Reiffen moved away from the entrance. His face was narrower than it had been when he was a boy, as if the years in Ussene had honed him to a sharper focus. Avender watched closely for signs of the Wizards' compulsion but, truth be told, Reiffen looked better and more like himself than he had when they had rescued him years before.

Reiffen understood the look on Avender's face. "I'm under no spells, if that's what you're thinking. At least none that I know of."

"I'd kill you if I could, you know."

"I don't doubt you'd try. Maybe you'd even succeed. You used to beat me at everything in the old days, but this time I'm the one who's rescued you. Now you'll be able to ride with me into Malmoret, just as we always planned."

Avender grimaced. "How can you think I'd ever do that now?" Then he remembered how, even when they were small, and Avender had caught Reiffen in some trick or small deceit, Reiffen had always been prone to ignore what he had done and continue on as if nothing had happened.

"There is that, I suppose." Reiffen acknowledged his part in the previous day's fighting with a slight nod. "Though I have tried to make it all as easy as possible. I won't make you do anything you don't want to, you know."

"I don't know that at all."

"Well, I won't."

There was an awkward pause. Reiffen smiled reassuringly, delighted to be reunited with his oldest friend. Avender tried not to wince every time he breathed.

"How did you do it?" he asked to change the subject. "How did you save me?"

"My art gives me power for healing as well as death."

"So it was magic?"

"Yes, though other factors are involved as well. Here. Let me show you. It's time you had another draught, which is why I looked in on you in the first place."

Reiffen busied himself among the bottles on the desk, his

hands clicking whenever they touched a glass. Avender noticed the iron thimbles on both his old friend's little fingers. Evidently the one left behind on the balcony of the Tear had been replaced.

Selecting a clean tumbler, Reiffen added something to the glass from each of three different beakers. The mixture bubbled and foamed, but stayed within the cup. A faint smell of ground walnuts and ice drifted past Avender's nose. Pricking his index finger with the point of a knife, Reiffen pressed the tiny wound with his thumb and dropped a single spot of blood into the glass. The mixture sputtered a second time.

"Drink this." He handed the cup to his prisoner.

"I'm not drinking that. You bled into it."

"There are certain properties in my blood which will help your healing."

"Or poison me."

"Really, Avender. Why would I go to all the trouble of rescuing you just to poison you later? After all the years of you out-wrestling me in Valing, you could show a little more grace the first time I finally beat you."

"You didn't beat me. Ossdonc and his soldiers did that."

"True. But it was my plan. Now really, I insist you drink this. If you don't, you'll most likely die, and then you'll never get the chance to kill me."

All the old contests of will the two of them had ever had tugged at Avender's memory as he met his former friend's gaze. He didn't suppose this challenge was one he could possibly win. Even without the wound in his chest, the advantages were all Reiffen's.

"What is it?" he asked by way of compromise.

"That's a fair question." Reiffen settled comfortably in the chair beside the desk. "I wouldn't trust me either, if I were you. It's a concoction of my own invention to help you heal. The most appetizing ingredient is mold. A rather more complicated

318 | S. C. BUTLER

medicine than what Hern used to dose us with back in Valing. But I don't know why you should mind a drop or two of blood. It's not like this is something new."

The memory of the oath, when the two of them had pledged eternal friendship in what they thought was the best Keeadini manner, rushed back to Avender. After visiting their fathers' graves, they had cut shallow slits in their thumbs with a knife and pressed the wounds together. Later they told Giserre they had cut themselves while playing at scouts among Hern's rosebushes. She had never said a word about the peculiar similarity of the scratches, which Avender suspected meant she had known the truth all along.

"How's your mother?" he asked as he took the cup from his former friend.

"She's fine. I expect she'll be glad to see you."

Drinking the mixture, Avender found the taste thick and salty, the way he imagined clay would taste if mixed with day-old cream. But it wasn't any worse than most of the medicines Hern had made him drink as a boy.

Sneezing, he handed the glass back to Reiffen and wondered if there was anything he might say to get under his former friend's skin. As a boy, Reiffen's sore spots had always been as obvious as bruises on an apple. Now he appeared to have more self-control.

"Do you think you can walk?" Reiffen asked.

"How far do you want me to go?"

"Just across the meadow. Ossdonc will want to meet you, now you're awake. It will be better for us both if I'm present. His temper will surely come out with someone as stubborn as you."

Breathing deeply, but not so deeply as to stretch his sore rib, Avender stood. He felt better than he thought he would: apparently the sitting had been good for him. Or maybe Reiffen's draught had helped more than he supposed.

From a chest beneath the bed, Reiffen found his old friend a clean shirt and helped him put it on. His first steps halting, Avender came out of the tent into bright sunshine. Two soldiers standing guard bowed as Reiffen emerged behind him. Past the cattails, Backford Pool lay still as an empty mirror. A muddy path led through a gap in the tall stalks on the left, a watering spot for the horses that had galloped the meadow two days before.

Avender was nearly sickened as he looked back over the long, wide field. His nose recoiled from the acrid odor only hinted at inside the tent. Except for a few charred timbers standing like lightning-blasted pines, Backford was a smoking ruin. Plumes rose from dozens of sluggish fires, sissit and crows picking through the rubbish. Up on the hill the keep smoldered like a skull on a badly doused pyre. Its walls still stood, but greasy ropes of black smoke staggered from the shattered windows, the thick fumes almost too heavy for the air. Carrion birds feasted on the corpses of the manders next to the river, which were given a wide berth by the camping army.

Through that burned and trampled meadow they crossed to Ossdonc's tent. Sissit and men, wearing dresses, rich cloaks, and bangles stolen from the town, bowed to the young wizard as he passed. But, as Reiffen and Avender neared their goal, they were forced to give way before a Keeadini war band galloping for the bridge. Ossdonc had proven his power now, and the young tribesmen were rushing to join him. Even if they didn't follow the Wizard faithfully to war, their ravaging would cause the countryside as much misery as any sustained attack, now that Backford's stout shield had fallen.

The Keeadini passed. Reiffen and Avender arrived at the black pavilion, its flaps hanging dead in the windless air. Ignoring the guards, Reiffen lifted a corner of the heavy curtain. Avender followed him into thick darkness greased with a few stains of yellow illumination. The dense, gritty scent within reminded him of a barn. Reiffen dropped the flap; the sounds of the outside vanished.

Large cushions filled the interior, some as tall as Avender's waist. Pillows plump enough for a Wizard to lounge upon, he realized. Between them stood a few high tables, again set for a Wizard's height, at the level of Avender's nose. Several held burning lamps, thin wisps of brown smoke dirtying the tips of their flames. Others were piled with meat and drink, the joints and flagons looking like toys amid the massive furnishings.

Reiffen stood on tiptoe to take an apple from the largest table. "Would you like something to eat?" he asked.

"No."

"You had better come further into the room all the same. Away from the entrance. Otherwise Ossdonc might trip over you when he arrives."

Remembering the way the Wizard had crushed his own soldiers underfoot in his haste to attack the bridge, Avender moved deeper into the room. The animal smell thickened. Incense in the lamps, he thought, or maybe the smell of the beasts forced to cart all of this down from Ussene. He examined the rest of the room and noted it was smaller than it had seemed outside. Perhaps there were other apartments behind the dark fabric drooping from the ceiling.

"Where are the Dwarves?" he asked

Reiffen gestured toward the curtains. "In there. Wrapped in several hundredweight of chain. It's a pity we didn't catch them all. The netting worked exactly as planned. If Ossdonc had thought for a moment, instead of showing off his strength, we would have had all three."

A slight tremor rolled through the earth. Reiffen turned to face the entrance. Sudden brightness swept the room as the flap was thrown entirely open. Ossdonc stood outlined against the meadow and sky, his shoulders broad as a double gibbet. His voice roared through the tent, battering Avender's and Reiffen's ears as thoroughly as the daylight singed their eyes.

"What have we here!" he boomed. "Another prisoner? The third Dwarf, perhaps, or maybe the baroness?"

Stepping farther into the tent, Ossdonc dropped the curtain. His black armor vanished into the sudden dark. Seizing a large punch bowl from the center table, he raised it to his lips and swallowed greedily. The odor of strong wine filled the room as the excess slopped down the Wizard's stained and crusted armor to the floor. Puddles formed on the elegant rug, darkening as they settled into the weave. Ossdonc dropped the empty bowl to the ground with a rolling thud.

"So, what have you brought me?" He wiped his mouth with one of the smaller pillows and settled down on several of the larger.

"Avender of Valing, Ossdonc. The Hero of the Stoneways, as the Bankings call him."

The Wizard pressed the wine from his beard. Despite his wild thirst and battered armor, he remained a handsome rogue.

"Avender," he mused. "One of your friends from the little country."

"My closest friend."

"I'm no friend of yours any longer, Reiffen," Avender declared. "You killed my friends yesterday, and helped capture the Dwarves. If I weren't wounded, I'd show you how much a friend I am."

"Oho!" Ossdonc's colossal laugh sent the tent sides billowing. "A bold friend you once had, Reiffen. Shall I slay him?"

"No." Reiffen weighed the apple in his hand. "It is not his fault he does not understand. I would keep him alive so he can see how wrong we all have been."

Ossdonc shrugged. "It is no concern of mine. A cowherd from the mountains. You may have a dozen such. What of my other prisoners?"

"They remain on the other side of the tent."

"Fetch them."

"May I remind you we must still plan our next course of action?" said Reiffen. "Your troops await your orders."

"Pleasure first."

The lamps shook as the wizard got back to his feet and disappeared behind the draperies. The sound of dragging followed. Ossdonc reappeared pulling a pair of clanking bundles at the end of short chains. With a rattling crash, he dropped them at the center of the room. Only because he knew what the chains were wrapped around was Avender able to recognize the glimpses of a Bryddin arm or leg he saw inside. Otherwise the two Dwarves were swathed from head to foot in heavy iron, a second layer of thick rope to bind the chains tight against them. Neither could move a toe.

Ossdonc seized the bundle on the right and propped it against one of the large pillows. With a few swift twists, the Wizard unwrapped the Dwarf's outer covering of rope, then loosened the chain. Nurren's face appeared above the iron links. Avender couldn't quite tell in the dimness, but he thought the Wizard was gloating.

The Dwarf caught sight of Avender and smiled. "Hello, Avender. Come to rescue me and Findle, have you?"

"Not this time, small one," said Ossdonc.

Nurren frowned. He didn't look particularly afraid. "Not this time what?" he asked.

"No rescue, this time. Or triumph." Ossdonc's eyes flashed. "This time you are the ones caught off guard. Your human friends were slaughtered without you. My sissit and I have greatly enjoyed our sport."

The Black Wizard lifted something from one of the tables. Baron Backford's Inach sword. In his hand the long, heavy blade looked like a stabbing knife, gleaming palely. Judging its balance, he lowered the point against Nurren's beard at about the place where the Dwarf's throat might be.

"You know what this is?" Ossdonc rasped the sword's tip along a link of the black chain.

"Of course. It's one of the Inach swords."

"One of them? There are others?"

"Two in Rimwich, one in Malmoret—"

Avender leapt forward, ignoring the sharp pain in his chest. "Don't tell him anything more, Nurren! He's trying to find out what you know!"

A dark cloud stormed across Ossdonc's face. Reiffen positioned himself in front of his friend.

"Remember what I said, Ossdonc. This one is mine."

"Then curb him or face my wrath yourself."

Reiffen turned to Avender. "It is important you not interfere," he urged. "I cannot always answer for what Ossdonc does. His temper is worse than Redburr's."

"I don't care about his temper. He can't do anything to me I'll regret."

"Yes he can."

Reiffen pushed Avender firmly back onto one of the smaller cushions. His thimble clicked against a button on his friend's shirt. Avender sat rubbing his sore ribs, his mind filled with sudden visions of what the Wizard might do if he really put his mind to it.

Ossdonc's irritation passed. "Please continue," he said, returning to the Dwarf.

"What Avender said's right." Nurren pursed his mouth stubbornly. "I'm not saying another word."

"And this?" Ossdonc waved the sword in front of Nurren's eyes.

Nurren grew puzzled. "Why would an Inach sword make a difference?"

"It was an Inach sword that broke Finlis. You remember Finlis, don't you?"

Nurren's eyebrows rose, but it was a look of comprehension, not fear. "You're right. I hadn't thought of that. Do you intend to break me, too?"

"Only if you refuse to tell me what I want to know."

Nurren set his mouth firmly. "You might as well go ahead, then. I won't say another word."

Admiration for the Dwarf swelled in Avender. He knew Dwarves were stubborn and independent, unwilling to take orders from anyone, but he had thought that simple obduracy would have evaporated before the threat of breaking.

Evidently Ossdonc had thought so as well. His eyes narrowed impatiently and he leaned closer to the Dwarf. "I do not think you understand, small one. If I break you, that will be the end. You cannot be rebuilt."

"I know," answered Nurren seriously. "I was there when we tried to put Huri back together. It didn't work. The Breath of Brydds was gone. Without it we might as well be rocks in the dark."

"Knowing that, you still defy me?"

"Breaking me won't change anything. You'll never learn what you want then. If you don't break me, there's always the chance I might slip and tell you what you want to know by accident. I'm only a rockreader, you know."

"Your life means so little to you?"

"It means a great deal. But it won't be my life if I start doing what other people want instead of what I want."

"You could live forever, under the right circumstances."

"I guess these aren't the right circumstances."

"So be it."

Ossdonc lifted the Inach sword above his head and brought it down swiftly on the trapped Dwarf. Reiffen raised a hand to stop him, but it was too late. A loud crack, as sharp as spring ice splitting on a Valing Lake, burst across the room. The floor shook and the sword snapped in two as Nurren's face exploded in a shower of splintered stone. His chains sagged and settled; shards of rock spilled out between the links.

Avender choked back tears.

"What have you done?" Reiffen stepped between the Wizard and the second bundle of chains.

"A threat means nothing if not executed in the face of defiance. Now the other will be more amenable."

"Will he? Who knows if he even saw what happened?"

"He certainly heard it."

Reiffen shook his head in exasperation. "Do you think we are going to capture any more Bryddin as easily as this? We were going to bring them back to Usseis. We certainly cannot kill the other one now, and he knows it."

The Wizard's eyes narrowed to black slits, as if the Abyss were locked behind his face. "Do not tell me what to do, human."

Reiffen picked up the end of the sword. Ossdonc tightened his grip on the half still in his hand.

"I certainly will tell you what to do when you have done wrong," said Reiffen. "We have not begun this war for your pleasure. There are other aims. Destroying opportunities to further our knowledge is not among them. The Dwarf did not know anything we cannot learn easily from my friend. You were just looking for the chance to slay a Bryddin. To do what Fornoch has already done."

Ossdonc's malice curdled the air, but Reiffen didn't back down. Avender felt a reluctant admiration for his former friend. Despite the Wizards turning him, much of the old Reiffen remained. Avender wondered if Reiffen would use magic if the Wizard attacked him, and whether it would matter if he did.

"You remind me of your cousin," Ossdonc said finally, his

face and shoulders relaxing. "Loellin also used to defy me occasionally. I killed her in the end."

"As I remember the tale," said Reiffen, "it was Fornoch who killed her, and everyone else as well. Your blow only knocked Nolo into the gorge. But you've bagged your Bryddin now, so we will keep this last one for Usseis."

Ossdonc shook his head peevishly. "I have no stomach to send him back now. My brothers will have finished with him by the time I return. I prefer not to miss the play."

"Then take him with us."

Ossdonc discarded his half of the broken sword. "And risk his escape? All it would take is the promise of a lamp, and every Keeadini in our train would set him free. The only answer is to kill him."

"That is not true."

"You know another way?"

"Tonight, before the moon rises, I shall take the Bryddin out to the deepest part of the lake and drop him in. Still wrapped in his chains, of course. The Bankings will have no idea what we have done with him. When Malmoret and Rimwich are ours, we can return to retrieve him."

"Good. Remember to kill the soldiers who do the job."

The audience over, Reiffen led Avender back to his own tent. His earlier cheerfulness had faded to a more somber mood.

"It must be difficult," he said, "finding your oldest friend so changed. Even if I did just save the Bryddin's life."

"Save him? You let Nurren be killed."

"I was too late for Nurren, that's true. But I saved the other."

Avender snorted in disgust. "For what?"

"That is the question, isn't it? But not one we have to answer yet. Here. I think we both need some cheering up. I brought something special to eat."

"I'm not hungry."

"Perhaps I can tempt you."

The only thing tempting Avender was the urge to take a swing at Reiffen as the latter got on his knees in front of the bed. His chest still stiff and sore, Avender moved awkwardly aside instead. Wood scraped and buckles rattled as the young wizard dragged a wooden trunk out from under the cot. Avender wondered what sort of food Reiffen could possibly have in his trunk that would tempt him.

"Here it is." A small paper parcel in hand, Reiffen regained his feet.

Avender recognized the plain brown wrapping at once. "Where did you get that?" he demanded.

The barest frown creased Reiffen's forehead. "I was in Valing recently. You'll hear about it soon enough."

"But why—"

"I said you'll hear about it later. Now isn't the time. When I heard you were in the Waste with Redburr, I saved these for you. Even Ossdonc doesn't know I have them."

Reiffen spread the bag open on the desk. Avender caught himself almost reaching for a piece. He and Reiffen had spent half their waking hours in Valing scheming for ways to get at Mother Spinner's maple candy. Obviously it was much easier with magic.

"I can't eat that," he said.

"Suit yourself," Reiffen answered. "Just means there's more for me if you don't. It's not magic, if that's what's bothering you. I may have used magic to get there, but the candy is Mother Spinner's own."

Avender's thoughts shifted anxiously. "What were you doing in Valing? Did you see Ferris? Did you hurt her?"

Reiffen frowned, offended. Avender was glad he had finally found something that could throw his former friend off balance.

"Of course I didn't hurt her," Reiffen said. "I didn't hurt you. Why would I hurt Ferris?"

Avender gestured toward the meadow and the town beyond. "You hurt them. You don't think that hurts Ferris and me, too? It hurts us all."

"True." Picking up a sweet between forefinger and thumb, Reiffen took a thoughtful bite. "It couldn't be helped, though. No matter which way I look at the question, someone has to be hurt. I may not like it, but there was never any other alternative."

"You seem to like it fine enough as far as I can tell."

"You can accuse me of many things, Avender, but you can't accuse me of that." Reiffen spoke wearily, as if he had been through this question so many times it no longer troubled him. "You've seen Ossdonc kill, more than once, I imagine. Is that who I remind you of? Is it really?"

Avender didn't answer. He had been speaking from anger only. When Ossdonc had broken Nurren he had seen the difference, and it had made him ill. The Wizard's delight had been immense, like a child with a new toy.

"You could have stopped him from killing Nurren," he said.

"Could I?" Reiffen took another small bite from his candy. As a boy he would have eaten the entire piece at once. "Sometimes you have to give Ossdonc his head, if you want to manage him."

"Is that what you're doing? Managing Ossdonc?"

"Right now, yes."

"Then why don't you manage him back to Ussene? Then I might begin to believe you."

"I'm afraid that's not possible." Reiffen finished his candy with a third bite, then looked briefly at the ones he hadn't touched. "I have to finish what I've started, and sending Ossdonc home, even if I could, would only make things worse in the end."

"So you admit you're responsible for all this, for all the people who died today?"

The accusation slid off Reiffen's shoulders like snow off firs. "Not them, perhaps. Baron Backford and his people knew this day would come sometime. This ford between mountains and swamp has fallen before. This is just the first time it's happened since the bridge and lake were built. Not many people remember there's a dam at the other end of Backford Pool. I tried to persuade Ossdonc to smash it and pass through the old ford, avoiding the town completely, but as you saw, Ossdonc wanted to have his fun. No, I don't hold the deaths here to my own account, but there might be others elsewhere."

"I hope your efforts to manage the other Wizards are more successful," said Avender bitterly.

"I don't even try with them. Ossdonc's the only one who's manageable. His preferences are obvious. Fornoch and Usseis are much more subtle. Especially Fornoch. Be happy they're not all here, or I'd have no chance with Ossdonc at all."

"How lucky for us."

"No, not lucky. Usseis prefers his workshops, and Fornoch dislikes the risks of fighting. They'd rather leave that to Ossdonc. Believe me, when they think their final triumph is at hand, they'll be present."

A soldier arrived with a meal: a pitcher of wine, two loaves of black bread, and a wedge of hard cheese. Reiffen poured two glasses of wine. "It's not as lavish as Ossdonc's table," he said, "but it is filling. You can't starve yourself to death, you know. I won't let you."

Avender found himself accepting the food, his hunger, after a long and trying day, overcoming his reluctance. The bread was coarse and dry, the cheese surprisingly tasty. Before he knew it, the meal was gone.

"You want dessert?" Reiffen glanced at the candy still spread out on the desk.

"I said I won't touch that."

"No sense wasting it then." Reiffen carried the bundle outside to the guards. Avender thought they looked more than a little surprised by the gift.

"I have some things I must take care of," Reiffen told Avender from the entrance. "I suggest you rest while I'm gone. You'll heal faster. Whatever you do, don't leave the tent. This is the only place you're safe."

Avender didn't expect to sleep after Reiffen left but, after lying down on the bed to think, he only woke when he heard sissit shouting close by. Sitting up, he saw the reeds beyond the tent vanishing in the dusk. A pair of ducks sliced a corner off the sky as they flew deeper into the marshes.

The sissit were with Reiffen, who was directing a dozen of them as they guided a rattling cart to the lake. The solid wheels bit deep into the soft turf; something heavy jangled inside. A pair of flat-bottomed boats floated bow to stern in the narrow cut in the reeds like a pair of headless swans.

"Enough!" The sissit stopped at Reiffen's command and allowed the wagon to sink deeper into the mire. "Now unload him."

The axles creaked as half the sissit climbed into the back of the cart; the others waited at the open end. With muffled clanks and panting groans, the ones above handed something heavy wrapped in dark cloth to the ones below. Avender couldn't quite make out the details in the darkness, but he could make a good guess. The bundle was the right size for Findle, and the clanking within was clearly from thick chains.

He joined Reiffen as the sissit, their shoulders straining, squelched toward the lake through the mud.

"Put him in the second boat," Reiffen ordered.

In two rows, the sissit passed on either side of the skiffs, Findle suspended between them. One of the ones in front slipped in the weeds, dropping his burden against the stern of the second boat. Nervously the sissit looked back at Reiffen, expecting to be blasted for their clumsiness.

"Go on," he said. "Put him in the boat. Just watch not to drop him through the bottom."

Carefully the sissit lowered their burden. The skiff settled into the lake. Still cautious, the pale creatures let go and stepped back. The rowboat floated with barely a hand's breadth of clearance, lolling deeply.

"All right. Back to your mice and beetles." Reiffen dismissed the work detail with a wave and headed toward the tent. "Avender, you take the empty dinghy. I'll row the Bryddin."

"I'm coming with you?"

"Yes."

"Why?"

"So you'll know where I sink him."

"Aren't you supposed to kill whoever helps you?"

"Only if they're soldiers. Ossdonc was specific."

"Do you think I can manage it?" Avender patted his bandaged chest.

"I think you'll find you're feeling much better," said Reiffen. "I'll be doing the heavy work. Go on. I'll be back in a minute."

Removing his boots, Avender waded into the lake. Soft mud seeped between his toes. Colder than he expected, the water came only to midcalf. In the boat, he unshipped the oars and took a testing stroke through the air. His chest twinged, but not so much that he couldn't row. Whatever Reiffen had put in his potion had worked remarkably well. At this rate he would heal fully by morning.

Softly the boat drifted against the reeds. A bullfrog croaked in the darkness. Campfires flickered in the meadow as Ossdonc's army settled down for the night. Reiffen emerged from his tent, a glow at the top of the long walking stick in his hand.

It was an odd sort of light, brighter than a Dwarven lamp, but not seeming to burn naturally at all. No matter how hard Avender looked, he couldn't find the source of the illumination. It simply clung to end of the wooden shaft like a fallen star, or a bubble without sides.

Reiffen waded out to the second boat and pushed the bottom of his staff deep into the mud at the edge of the reeds. Next he threw something small and heavy into his skiff. A hand ax. So heavily loaded was the craft it didn't rock at all as Reiffen settled in at the bow.

They rowed out of the cut together, the wizard-light marking their progress from the shore. Avender's chest stung slightly with every pull on the oars, but it was no strain to follow Reiffen's sluggish pace. Avender hated being so cooperative, but he did want to know where Findle was sunk, in case he ever had a chance to rescue him. A Dwarf could last forever at the bottom of a lake, no matter how long he had stopped breathing.

To his left, the town glowed like a dying hearth, a thin line of red to match the last light of the sky beyond the mountains. Smoke haze dulled the stars to the south, but the north and west were clear. The Hawk swept low across Keeadin's hills, up too early for the moon.

They rowed until the sky was dark except for stars. Reiffen's staff glowed like a single, tiny eye in the reeds along the shore. Blind in the featureless night, Avender wasn't sure how far they had come, but he guessed it was at least halfway.

"This is far enough."

Avender shipped his oars. The edges of the two boats shimmered indistinctly in the blackness of lake and sky. Water swirled as Reiffen sculled his craft closer to Avender's, the skiffs jarring slightly as they bumped in the darkness. A loon called from the farther shore, its high, lonely cry ringing the night in an eerie noose.

"Hold the boats together," said Reiffen. His skiff's bottom scraped as Reiffen retrieved his hatchet.

Groping in the dark, Avender found the prow of the other craft. He listened as Reiffen whispered in a low voice: some spell to increase Findle's misery, no doubt. A heavy knock sounded in the darkness, followed by a throaty gurgle. Reiffen's boat shivered under Avender's fingers as the knock was repeated; the gurgle deepened. Reiffen tossed the hatchet into Avender's skiff with a loud thunk and followed it aboard. The skiff rocked; Avender let go the other craft. He was thinking about the hatchet lying somewhere on the wooden bottom just in front of him.

The murmur of the lake grew louder, almost bubbling. A soft gulp followed as the other craft went down. Crude laughter from the Wizard's camp rang distantly across the darkness.

Avender bent forward. Luck was with him: he found the hatchet right beneath his fingers. Reiffen sat silhouetted against the smoldering town. Glad of the cloaking dark, Avender gripped the handle and raised the weapon quickly. There was no way he could miss. He swung the hatchet hard and fast, hardly believing Reiffen had made such a mistake.

The blow crunched against the gunwale, chopping wood instead of flesh. Avender's chest burned at the jarring shock.

"You can't harm me," said Reiffen, his voice mild in the darkness.

Avender gritted his teeth. "Why not?"

"The potion I gave you did more than heal you. You're no longer entirely your own master."

Reiffen picked up the oars, though he would have to row backward. "I'll teach you the spell, if you like," he went on. "That's the best way to understand it. It's all about the blood. Mindrell made me drink a similar potion that night on Nokken Island."

"How long will it last?" Avender flexed his arm in the dark, trying to see if it would still obey him.

"A day or two. I'll have to give you another dose tomorrow."

"What if I won't take it?"

"You will."

Without giving himself time to think, Avender pulled the hatchet from the side of the boat and tried to strike Reiffen again. This time his hand opened in the middle of the blow and the hatchet flew off into the darkness. The water plopped softly.

"You can try all you like," said Reiffen, his manner still unconcerned. "I've tested the spell thoroughly. You won't find any holes. You'll have to keep drinking that potion for a while, though, until you stop wanting to kill me."

Avender set his jaw. "That will never happen."

"We'll see."

Far away across the water Reiffen's staff gleamed, unwinking as the lights of Issinlough.

18

The Pickerel

ere it is."

Berrel raised his lantern. Hern and Ferris peered into a large, round hole halfway up the wall on the right-hand side of the tunnel. They were deep in the stone passages beneath the Neck, deeper even than the drowned ways around Pittin's cave, where Fornoch had murdered Avender's and Reiffen's fathers.

"That's the way down?" asked Ferris. In the distance she saw a small circle of blackness that made her think she was staring into a long tube.

"It is," said her father.

"You can ride on this." Hern pulled a small rug out of the sack she had brought. "Nolo told me he got the idea from sledding on Baldun. Otherwise you'd never make it to the bottom without skinning yourself to the bone."

Ferris fingered the ragged sheepskin. "Isn't this the rug from the bath?"

"You don't expect me to send you down to the Abyss with anything good, do you? Who knows when I'll get it back."

While Berrel held the lantern, mother and daughter unrolled

the skin wool-side-up on the polished stone. Hern kept tight hold of it, or the rug would have slipped away on its own.

"Now, before you go, you're sure you have nothing to tell us?" Hern cocked an eye at her daughter in a way that had caused more than one young thief to hand over her slice of stolen pie. "You and Brizen spent an awfully long time together this afternoon."

"There's nothing to tell, Mother." Had her father asked Ferris the question, he might have shamed the secret out of her, but not Hern. Her mother's constant prying had long since worn thick calluses on Ferris's conscience. Besides, if she told her parents what she had done, there would never be any going back.

Kissing them good-bye, Ferris fastened her Dwarf lamp to the thin silver circlet Nolo had given her on her eighteenth birthday and climbed into the tunnel. Shining at her forehead in the proper Dwarven fashion, the gem's soft glow revealed even less of the passage than her father's fish-oil lantern.

The sheepskin began to slide the moment her parents released it. Quickly Ferris picked up speed, the edges of her cloak flapping like sheets hung out to dry in a high wind. The air whipped past her face. When her eyes started to water, she lay on her stomach, her head at the back of the sheepskin. With nothing to see, there was no way to tell how fast she was going. But she was certain she was going very fast all the same.

The ride was so smooth she might have slept, but her excitement kept her wide awake. A slight, but constant, push on her left side made her think the tunnel turned in a long spiral like the Sun Road. To pass the time she thought about what life would be like in Malmoret, whether it was all grand balls and tiresome dinners. She wondered if princesses were allowed to take sailboats out on the river and decided, if they weren't, she would certainly have something to say about it.

Later, when she had been descending for what felt like hours, she tried not to think about how dull the climb back to the surface would be once she reached the bottom.

Finally she coasted to a stop in a long, narrow cave. Picking up the sheepskin, the bottom of which felt nearly as hot as an oven, she climbed the steps to the doorway at the far end. On the other side she found a round chamber with a wide well in the floor, a second stair disappearing up into the stone on the other side. The well looked just like the one she and Avender had found at the bottom of the Uhliakh, through which they had caught their first glimpse of Issinlough. The only difference was this one had a narrow guardrail running around the edge, probably in deference to the humans who would use it at least as much as the Dwarves.

Assuming the second set of steps led the long way back to Valing, Ferris approached the well. Hanging below was the frame of a long, hollow unneret, fashioned of metal girders rather than the usual rock. From its tip a dim glow cast a soft gray radiance across the endless black Abyss, a small pupil of brightness in the center. A thin blumet staircase wound down the sides of the unneret toward the light.

Something moved at the bottom. "Ahoy! Is that you, Ferris!"

"Yes! Who's that?" Ferris leaned out over the guardrail, but the speaker was too far away to discern against the darkness of the undernight.

"It's Atty!"

"Atty Peeks?"

"That's right."

"I thought you went to Lugger!"

"That was Nolo's idea. Come on down and I'll explain."

Despite its frail appearance, the blumet stair neither swung nor swayed as Ferris descended. The light below grew steadily, until she was able to make out Atty smiling up at her from a trapdoor in the top of a small shed, his thatch of blond hair as wild and unruly in the windless Abyss as it had ever been in Valing.

Her boots boomed on the metal roof as she followed her host down to a room that looked like a sheep wagon with the sides rolled up. Low walls rose halfway to the ceiling, the bottom of the shed suspended on thin blumet rods from the top. Outside, the vast darkness of the Abyss was tempered only by the strange gray glow spreading across the nearer undersky like thin paint spilled on black canvas. Sheepskins, cloaks, bundles of food, and collections of odd-looking tools cluttered the walls. A half-eaten wheel of cheese sat atop an upturned barrel, a knife thrust into the top of the yellow rind. From the middle of the ceiling a Dwarven lamp cast a dim glow. A second trapdoor was set in the floor directly below.

"Welcome to the Valing Lamp." Atty spread his arms wide to encompass his small domain.

"The what?" asked Ferris.

"The Valing Lamp. You're standing on it."

"What are you talking about, Atty?"

Atty cleared his throat and stood up straight, just as he used to do when reciting lessons in the Manor schoolroom. "The Valing Lamp is one of a chain of lights Dwvon and Uhle have built across the bottom of the world. The first idea was to use them as beacons to guide airships across the Abyss—"

"I remember that," said Ferris. "Redburr had the idea during our first ride on the *Nightfish*."

"Well, later he figured out we could use the lamps to send messages, too. That's why I'm here. You can't send messages unless someone's there to see 'em."

"Why would anyone send messages to you?"

"So I can send them on to Valing, of course."

"How on earth would you ever get a message up to Valing from here?"

"Mistrin." Atty pointed toward a corner of the roof, where several small bats hung like leather pouches from pegs in the ceiling. "We use 'em like pigeons."

"Is that how you knew to expect me?"

"Nope." Atty scrabbled through a pile of sheepskins and came up with a large stone ball. Unscrewed, the rock revealed a hollow center. "I've got the note in my pocket if you want to see."

Ferris shook her head. "I'll take your word for it. I still don't understand about this signaling, though. Where do you get your messages? Who do you send them to?"

Atty pointed off into the dark. "It's four Lamps from here to Issinlough, not counting Issinlough itself. At more than forty leagues between Lamps, that's about five hundred mile. But any message I send gets to Issinlough faster'n a nokken can swim the bay."

Following the direction of Atty's finger, Ferris saw a point of light shining far off in the darkness.

"Bavadar Lamp's closest," he went on, "but it's not as good a post as this. There's no way to the surface. All you can do there is pass along the news."

"Shouldn't you be sending them a message to say I've arrived?"

"The *Pickerel*'s already on the way. Bavadar Lamp sent me the message hours ago after I told them you were coming. But it'll still be half a day before they get here."

"What's the *Pickerel*?"

"Grimble's new airship. It's a lot smaller than the *Nightfish,* so human's can fly it. Faster, too."

As they watched, the Bavadar Lamp blinked on and off in the darkness.

"Time check." Atty busied himself among his strange tools. Retrieving a thin sheet of blumet, he pushed it through a narrow slot in the floor next to the trapdoor, on the side of the lamp that faced its neighbor in the darkness. Twice he raised and lowered the sheet. A moment later the Bavadar Lamp replied with two more blinks. Atty answered with two of his own. Eight more winks followed from the point in the darkness; Atty signed off with a final pair.

"Eight o'clock on the surface," he announced as he tossed the metal sheet clattering back to the pile. "Time for supper."

They shared Atty's cheese and ale with Ferris's fresh bread and cold chicken, while Atty explained how Nolo had recruited him to secretly join the Lampkeepers. In return, Ferris told Atty what had happened since he left Valing, including Reiffen's attack on the nokken and Skimmer's death.

Atty's cheerfulness fell away at the news. "Why would Reiffen kill Skim? I thought he went off to be king of Banking."

"It doesn't make any sense. Redburr thinks he had to do something really nasty to convince the Wizards he was on their side."

Gloomily, Atty flipped the cheese knife in his hand. "Does that mean there's going to be war?"

"Yes. That's why I'm going to Issinlough."

Atty's frown deepened. "And here I thought I had the best job in the world. Now I'll miss everything."

Thinking of the raw wounds on Icer's side, Ferris made no reply.

The *Pickerel* arrived shortly after breakfast. Ferris had slept restlessly, her dreams filled with falling: nokken and the Tear and Valing Lamp. More than once she got up to make sure the bottom of the world was still safely overhead. Atty snored beside her.

He spotted the airship first, a tiny glow to the left of the Bavadar Lamp, like a firefly at the edge of the woods. Gradually the small speck grew, until finally the flying ship itself loomed out of the darkness in the powerful wash of light from the Valing Lamp. Though nearly as long, the *Pickerel* was slimmer than the *Nightfish* and had a shallower draft. Ferris felt a brush of wind from its propeller as the ship swept past. A fin popped out on the near side; the *Pickerel* circled back toward Atty's shed and slowed.

A man appeared on deck; Atty tossed him a rope. The man fastened the end to a cleat on the front of his ship. The *Pickerel* drifted upward as its motion slowed, the nose dipping lower than the tail. The man in the bow fended the ship from the bare beams of the unneret as Atty reeled it in.

"Ahoy, Jacks!"

"How are you, Atty? Got a passenger for us?"

"Here she is."

Ferris and Jacks nodded in greeting across the narrow gulf. He was a thin man, with a large ring in his ear and a peaked cap on his head. Ferris thought he looked exactly like the sailors she had met on *The Other Side* when she and Avender had crossed the Inner Sea.

A second man popped up from below, as wiry as the first. "I'm Gill," he said. "Glad to see you're wearing pants. Want t' come aboard? Dwvon told us we're supposed to hurry."

"Um, if you show me how, I'll come aboard at once." Ferris turned to Atty and whispered, "Why's he glad I'm wearing pants?"

"I think he hopes you'll help with the pedaling. Here." Handing Ferris a length of short rope, he pointed her toward the ceiling. "Tie this around your waist, and the other end to the unneret. The easiest way to board the *Pickerel* is from the roof. It's not much of a jump, but there's no sense taking chances."

Ferris climbed the ladder to the top of the shed. Five or six fathoms long, the *Pickerel* hovered in the air a stride or two away. At the stern the propeller revolved slowly, just beyond the cross-shaped tail. Trying not to look down, Ferris stepped close to the edge and tied herself off to the nearest girder. Rope or no, she didn't imagine the fall would be pleasant. Not to mention embarrassing.

She jumped. The sailors caught her arms; her feet scrabbled on the canvas hull. The airship began to sag.

"Best get that rope off, miss," said Jacks.

Ferris untied her makeshift belt and threw it over the side. Jacks was already unwinding the mooring rope as she clambered into the narrow deck that ran waist deep across the top of the ship below the hull. Behind her Gill dropped back into the hold.

"Have a good trip," called Atty. "If you see my mother before I do, tell her I'm fine."

"I will." Ferris waved good-bye to her friend. The airship, no longer tethered to the Lamp, continued to drop slowly.

"Watch your eyes, miss," warned Jacks.

Ferris turned away from Atty and the shed. The top of the airship filled with light. Every detail came sharply clear, from the grommets on the canvas to the bags of gas bulging beneath the grated deck. At the same time a familiar whirring started up and the ship began to tremble. The long blades of the propeller began to spin. Still drifting downward through the bright flood of the Lamp, the *Pickerel* glided forward through the night. A growing wind brushed Ferris's cheek and hair.

"I need to go below," said Jacks. "Starting up's the hardest part. Once we build up to a fair pace the rest is easy."

"Is there room for me to come watch?"

"If you don't mind bein' squashed tight as a hold full of plangels."

Belowdecks gas bags squeezed against the blumet mesh that held the balloons in place. Rather than working a hand crank like the one that had powered the *Nightfish*, Ferris found Jacks climbing into a seat beside Gill on a strange machine that faced the starboard side. Each pumped his legs furiously at a pair of revolving pedals, the pedals attached to a series of gears below the seats. Thin metal chains rattled from the gears down through two holes in the deck to turn a long shaft below. Since it was pointed back toward the stern, Ferris assumed the shaft turned the propeller. For balance, the two sailors held on to a metal handle attached to the blumet mesh in front of them.

"Switch!" called Jacks as he flipped a long lever between him and Gill. With a short rattle, the chains slipped to a smaller gear. The sailors' pumping slowed slightly, but the whirring of the mechanism rose to a higher, faster whine.

Twice more Jacks called, "Switch!" before Ferris decided she would rather ride upstairs. With both men laboring like sprinters on a hill, the small room had grown extremely stuffy. It was obvious why they were both so thin and wiry. Wondering how long they could keep up such a difficult pace, she went back up on deck for a breath of fresher air.

The wind streamed past, more rapidly than anything she remembered from the *Nightfish*, though not so rapidly as during her slide down the tube from Valing. The other, larger ship had been shaped more like a fat grayling, while the *Pickerel* was more like a darting pike. Naturally the *Pickerel* was faster, even with humans propelling it rather than sturdy Dwarves.

Once they reached top speed only one man was needed on the pedals at a time. When Jacks took the first break, Ferris learned he and Gill had both been sailors before settling underground.

"Hunted leviathans, we did," he told her. "But the price of oil went down when the Dwarves started trading their lamps, so Gill an' me decided to take a try at mining. Didn't like it much, though. Too dirty. We missed the sun and wind. So, when Mr. Dwvon offered us the chance to man the *Pickerel*, we jumped right on it. At least this way we can get a breeze."

They let her have a try on the pedals, since she was wearing pants, and though the pumping was easy at first, she was soon winded.

"You get used to it quick enough," said Gill. "It's a whole lot easier than crankin'."

They pointed out the beacons to Ferris as they passed: Bavadar and Rimwich, Malmoret and Sprucel. Otherwise there was nothing to see until the lights of Issinlough blossomed in the darkness after hours and hours of flying. The glistening curtains of the Seven Veils, the long stone finger of the Halvanankh ringed by graceful unnerets, the Bryddsmett dangling beneath: the Bryddin city looked more beautiful than ever to Ferris, a dab of brightness in an empty sky.

Jacks came on deck to steer as they approached the outer ring of the Veils. By pulling on various knobs and levers in the bow, he was able to raise or lower the fins on either side of the airship to make it turn. Slicing between two of the shimmering waterfalls, the *Pickerel* glided toward the hanging city.

"What's going on in the mett?" Ferris pointed toward the shallow silver dish that hung from the three inner unnerets, the tip of the Halvanankh poised above. "It looks like it's full of people."

Jacks peered at the Bryddsmett as well. "So it does, miss. Must be a meeting. Looks to be breaking up, though."

He steered the ship carefully forward, braking with the side fins as he came. Gill poked his head above decks for a quick look round, then retreated to the pedals to make sure the airship had steerage. Through the tangle of catwalks and upside-down towers, Jacks threaded the *Pickerel* toward one of the central unnerets, which Ferris soon recognized as the Rupiniah from the glassed-in Bryddis B'wee at the bottom. The Bryddin on the silvery paths paid them no attention, but most of the humans in sight stopped to watch the landing. Leaving his controls, Jacks hopped to the bow and leapt onto a blumet bridge, a coil of rope in his hand. With a few deft twists he looped the mooring line around a stanchion. The ship drifted upward. Gill appeared in the stern and also jumped onto the catwalk to fasten a second line. Ferris stared down at them from a height of about a fathom, the curve of the airship's hull bumping lightly against the silver-blue metal.

"Ferris, dear!"

Ferris slid down the side of the airship as Mother Norra bustled out from the unneret to greet her.

"My, you've grown." Holding Ferris at arm's length, the gray-haired woman examined every inch of her younger friend. "What's it been, three years since you last visited? And so pretty, too! Why aren't you married yet, dear? Turnips and toast, I know you've been asked. More than once, too, I'm sure!"

Behind her Jacks and Gill were already untying the airship. Ferris bowed deeply in the proper Bryddin manner and thanked them for bringing her to Issinlough. The sailors told her it was nothing and scrambled nimbly up the side of their ship. The *Pickerel* floated upward, but soon the propeller was spinning once more and, with Gill steering this time, the small craft slipped away like a lazy fish in a deep pool.

Ignoring Mother Norra's question, Ferris asked one of her own. "Where are Nolo and Dwvon? I need to talk to them as soon as possible."

"Corn and cukes, dear, what's your hurry? They're at the mett, which I think just ended. We'll have ourselves a cozy cup and you can tell me all the gossip while we wait for them. But tell me, is it true what I hear? Has Prince Brizen really asked you to marry him?"

Following Mother Norra into the Rupiniah and through its winding passages to the kitchen, Ferris did her best to persuade her friend that, though Brizen had, indeed, proposed to her, nothing more had happened.

The old woman clucked and poured the tea. "Mash and mush, I've heard that before. A girl likes to feel she's having her say, but you'll take him, my dear. 'Less there's someone else, of course. I never had any prince ask me to marry him, not even a baron, but it's always the same in the end. Love's a good start, but you need a patch of garden, too. I never would have married my

Bob if he hadn't known how to bend a barrel, and sell it at the right price. All the love in the world won't ever fill your stomach. Not that it isn't too hard to find both. Here now, I think I hear the boys on the stair. They'll be wanting a late supper, I think, after all that talking."

Their bare feet clomping on the stone, Nolo and Dwvon rumbled into the kitchen. Uhle and Angun followed close behind. Ferris started to bow but Nolo cut her off.

"Ferris, lass!" he cried delightedly. "You're a sight for sandy eyes! Welcome back to Issinlough!"

Ferris had learned long ago that hugging Dwarves wasn't a good idea, but for a moment it looked as if Nolo was going to do it just the same. Luckily he stopped himself at the last moment. Behind him, his three brethren joined him in a bow. Solemnly, Ferris returned their greeting.

"Yes, welcome to Issinlough, Ferris." Dwvon came forward, grinning from ear to ear. The usual drift of powdered rock fell from the oldest Dwarf's shoulders as he clasped her hand. "It's hard for me to remember how you keep growing and changing."

"Hopefully I've stopped that for a while." Ferris wiggled her fingers to get the blood flowing. "I saw your meeting in the Bryddsmett when I arrived."

Dwvon sighed, his beard fluttering around his mouth. "You humans can be very difficult sometimes."

"What do you mean?"

Angun frowned. "We caught two men trying to steal lamps in Vonn Kurr. There used to be a time when illumination stayed in place until it was needed elsewhere. Now everything must be guarded."

"We can't make them fast enough to keep up with the pilfering," grumbled Nolo.

"Which is why humans should be banned from Bryddlough."

"Enough." Dwvon raised his hands wearily. "We've just been

QUEEN FERRIS | 347

through this at the mett. Let's not start it all over again. You won your point, Angun. Now's the time to hear the news from Valing. Sit, Ferris, and tell us the tale. Redburr's message sounded urgent."

Taking her place at Mother Norra's stone table, Ferris handed Dwvon the letters from Berrel and Prince Brizen. The Dwarves settled on the benches around her and listened as she described Reiffen's attack on the nokken and the Black Wizard's expected assault on Backford. Though she had only told the tale once before, to Atty, she found herself already weary of it, especially Reiffen's part. It took all her strength to keep from breaking down.

"Here now." Mother Norra handed round bowls of flinny stew. "Can't you see the poor girl's exhausted? Think of what she's been through these last couple days. And Reiffen her old friend, too."

Ferris laid a hand on the old woman's arm. "Thank you, Mother Norra, but I'm all right. This is no time for tears." She turned back to the Bryddin. "Redburr sent me to Issinlough to ask for your help."

"That's what the prince and Berrel ask in their letters, too." Dwvon laid down the pages beside his bowl of stew.

"As usual," complained Angun, "the humans ask for much, while offering nothing in return."

Uhle plucked at the notes on the table, glancing quickly at what was written. "We all know the Shaper's way is to suggest the best fault in the rock and leave it to others to judge where they want to strike."

"The best fault for humans," insisted Angun.

"And for us. It wasn't humans who broke Finlis. Wizards did that. Which is why we should help the humans fight them now."

"And who will be broken this time?" Angun fumed. "The Wizards only broke Finlis because he and Nolo shined their lamps where they didn't belong. Humans offer us nothing. They're like their children, interested only in themselves. I've seen their cities and harbors. There's nothing they can do we can't do better."

"That's not true." Ferris slapped her knee impatiently; Angun wasn't helping things at all. It was time to take matters into her own hands. "When was the last time you planted a tree? Or brewed a cask of ale? Is there any one of you can do what Mother Norra's doing right now?" The old woman looked up from her pot by the fire at the mention of her name.

"Do any of us want to?" Angun eyed his fellows, certain they agreed with him.

"I do." Nolo raised his hand like a schoolboy. "But it always turns to mush when I try. The materials are all so soft. Mother Norra, what you do is a wonder."

Plucking the edges of her skirt, the old woman dropped a tiny curtsy. "Thank you, Mr. Nolo. Would you like thirds?"

"Yes, ma'am." Nolo offered up his bowl.

"Hmph." Angun crossed his thick arms stubbornly. "One day you'll regret your taste for human craft, Nolo. As we all will, if we don't separate our world from theirs. I have no need for ale or flinny stew, and my furnace heats as well as Abben. If I wish to see its brilliance, there are places I can go on the surface where there are no humans. But, if we follow this vein to the end, all our projects will be theirs. And for what? Trees? Uhle says we act against the Wizards now, or regret it later. I say, separate ourselves from humans now, because we already regret it."

"Maybe if you looked at living things once in a while instead of rock you'd understand," answered Ferris. "You build in stone and metal, not flesh and blood. We humans, for all our faults, add as much to the world as you do. Do you know how long it takes to grow an orchard? You compare us to our children, but our children are what make us what we are. We can't spend a hundred years trying to figure out the best way to shape a piece of rock. We have to make our plans right now."

Angun leaned forward, a thin smile splitting the middle of his trim beard. "Children aren't the only difference between humans and Bryddin. Don't forget your fondness for war. What Bryddin ever raised a hand against another? Even now we choose to discuss what you humans would long since have come to blows over. I've seen you fight over a cup of ale, or an accidental elbow. What good will come to us from your fighting?"

"You fight manders, don't you? And rock eels. You kill them because you know sooner or later they'll attack you. Well, that's how it is with Wizards, too."

"This is all very interesting."

Uhle's companions fell silent as he unfolded his long fingers on the table. Dwvon looked troubled, but Nolo winked at Ferris encouragingly.

"It is time to decide our course," Uhle continued. "Angun. Nolo and I understand why you oppose us, but you must understand our position as well. You must allow us to do as we see fit."

"Not when the shaft you sink is likely to undermine my own. Your course will end with every Bryddin broken."

"It's the Bryddin way. Each chooses his own rock."

"Yes," sighed Dwvon. "It is our way. And yet, I wish we could all agree on this. So much is at stake."

"Call the mett," urged Angun. "Let us all decide."

"There's no time," said Nolo. "And spies would tell the Three our decision."

"Better to leave, then, and start new somewhere else than run the risk of breaking."

"Bryddlough is wide and deep," replied Dwvon. "There will always be wild cave."

"I like it here." Stone mugs and empty bowls bounced as Nolo slapped the table loudly. "And I like Valing and Rimwich, too. Mark my words, the Wizards will try to take Issinlough away from us some day, just as they're trying to take Banking and Wayland now. Better to help the humans in their fight than fight alone later."

"I agree," said Uhle.

Angun's face remained set. An earthquake wouldn't change his mind.

"Do as you wish," said Dwvon with a sigh. "I won't stop you."

"Then it's settled." Nolo wiped his mouth on the back of his sleeve. "I started packing as soon as we got Redburr's message. All that's left is sending out the mistrin."

"Where will you meet?" asked Dwvon.

"In Usslough, in ten days."

"Ten days?" Ferris's shoulders slumped. "I can't possibly walk all the way to Ussene in ten days."

"You can follow later, lass. On the *Nightfish*. With the late arrivals."

Being Dwarves, there were no long good-byes when the meeting ended. Even Mother Norra barely bothered to look up from her hearth. Ferris decided to escort Nolo to the top of Dwvon's unnerets; it had been months since he last visited Valing and she was unwilling to let him go so quickly now they had met again. Issinlough would be lonely when he left.

"By the way," she asked as they crossed a stone balcony in the side of the unneret. "Whatever happened to the humans Angun caught stealing lamps?"

Nolo stopped, his face somber. "Angun wanted to drop them into the Abyss, but Dwvon stopped him. Then a delegation of humans convinced them to let them deal with the matter. That's what the mett was all about."

"What did they decide?" A stone rail, carved like a flock of streaming bats, separated the side of the terrace from the long darkness at Ferris's feet. Potted mushrooms bunched along the walls.

"That was the oddest part." Nolo scratched his chin. "They

did just what Angun wanted. They threw the thieves over the side."

Shuddering, Ferris gazed down into the deep darkness. She couldn't imagine a more horrible way to die, tumbling forever through the undersky until thirst and hunger finally did you in. She was surprised Angun had even thought of it.

"Maybe Dwarves and humans aren't so different after all," she said.

Nolo flicked a spot of dust from the rail. "Could be that's what Angun's most afraid of, lass."

19

Prince Gerrit

ssdonc's host left Backford with all North Banking summer-rich before them. Larks darted up from the golden fields like cinders against the hot sky; cows swished their tails in ash heaps of lazy shade. But once the army had trampled through the verdant land, only the distant hills remained lush, and even those were marred by plumes of smoke where villages and farms had slumbered peacefully until the Keeadini found them.

Reiffen and Avender traveled apart from the main column as much as possible, but they couldn't completely escape its devastation. More than once they found themselves picking their way through smoking fields and bone-strewn yards. On the third day after leaving Backford they came to a farm where an ox lay in the duck pond, its black blood thickening the mud. Dogs shredded chickens outside a blazing barn. While Reiffen's small escort of northern soldiers led their horses to the pond, Reiffen himself rode into the middle of the crowd of Keeadini surrounding the farmhouse door. The tribesmen, though inclined to shove back as the horse pushed in among them, gave way sullenly when they recognized the rider.

Inside the cottage Avender and Reiffen found themselves in a low, crowded room. Tribesmen jammed the space between thatched roof and dirt floor. Hard laughter filled the dimness, the smell of blood and men overpowering the normal odors of hearth and straw.

Reiffen raised his arms: "Open high to sun and sky!"

As if they had been pushed, Avender and the Keeadini staggered back against the walls. The roof blew off the top of the cottage, straw swirling. Light and air replaced the gloom.

"Much better," said Reiffen, advancing to the middle of the room.

The chief of the war band pushed forward. Red lightning branded his cheeks in jagged streaks; a pair of rippling black lines dressed his forehead. Behind him the farmwife cowered in front of the hearth, arms wrapped around her small daughter. It was a moment before Avender spied her husband's body where it had been kicked into a corner.

"This is ours," claimed the leader, recovering his dignity despite the sudden removal of the roof.

Reiffen answered in the man's own tongue. The chief scowled; his war party grumbled from the edges of the room. Reiffen's voice turned peremptory. Jerking his head for his men to follow, the chief stalked out the door.

The farmwife shrank farther back against the wall as Reiffen came close, her daughter's face buried in her shawl.

"Softly." Reiffen raised his hands in peace. "I will not hurt you."

Avender had heard no rhyme, but the woman calmed all the same. Her shoulders settled; the wildness in her eyes dimmed.

"Tell me," Reiffen asked, "why did you linger?"

"It's all is ours," the woman replied. Dirt and tears streaked her face. "Tug thought none 'ud notice, hidden up here in the hills."

"The Keeadini can find an ant in the prairie, if that is what they seek. Do not look there."

Reiffen caught the woman's gaze with his hand as she turned toward her husband's body. Gently he brought her eyes back to his own.

"Do you have anywhere you can go?" he asked.

The woman shook her head.

"No family?"

"West and north. We can't go there."

"You cannot stay here, either. I will not be able to protect you when I leave. You must go south. Prince Gerrit approaches from that direction. The Keeadini will not venture that way without the Wizard."

At the mention of the Wizard, fear poured back into the woman's eyes. She clutched her daughter tightly.

"Don't worry," Reiffen soothed. "The Black One is not coming this way. If you go south you will be safe. I will give you what protection I can, but you must leave."

Reaching into the cold hearth, he pulled out a handful of ashes. Tossed into the air above the woman's head, they fell across her shoulders, glittering like shattered sunlight.

"Dust of forest, twig, and tree,
Cloak this woman.
Let none see."

Avender expected the farmwife to turn into a tree or, at the very least, a thorny rosebush, but nothing happened.

"Go." Reiffen waved toward the back of the cottage. "Speak to no one who isn't a friend."

The woman led her daughter out the broken door into the garden.

"That's a horrible trick." Avender waited for the Keeadini to grab her. "Why not just murder her yourself?"

"They won't see her," said Reiffen.

Woman and child disappeared into the trees without the Keeadini noticing them at all.

"You saw me cast the spell," Reiffen explained. "That's why you could still see her. As for the Keeadini, as long as she doesn't blunder into them, they won't notice her. Full invisibility would have scared her half to death."

"You're really letting her go?"

"Yes."

Avender shook his head. "You sack Backford, burn every village and farm you pass, then turn around and let some farmwife you don't even know go free?"

"Ossdonc sacked Backford, Avender, not I. Do not confuse me with Ossdonc. He and I have different ends entirely."

Avender followed Reiffen out of the cottage, wondering about what had just happened, and what Reiffen's ends might be if they really were different from Ossdonc's. He was learning this new Reiffen was much harder to understand than the old.

In camp that night, as red flames danced behind him in the village he had set ablaze at dusk, the Black Wizard tossed a half-gnawed hoof into the fire and called for a song.

A harper jumped to his feet. "Something light and amusing, my lord?"

"Yes. With blood." The Wizard emptied a barrel of Southy down his gullet, but the wine had no more effect on him than lemonade.

The minstrel plucked his harp.

"The rivers ride along the rocks,
The seas slide over stone,
The winds weave wild among the flocks
And blades still batter bone . . ."

Reiffen nudged his companion. "Let's sleep somewhere else tonight," he said.

The song faded as he and Avender moved off into the darkness. Despite the fires of the Keeadini dotting the nearby countryside like sparks kindling a dried-up plain, they found an empty beechwood. The din of the army was muffled by distance and trees. Reiffen's guard posted themselves unseen in the darkness.

"How's your wound?" With a touch of his finger, Reiffen started a warm blaze in the kindling at their feet.

"There's a scar along the rib," said Avender, "but that's about it. I don't even feel it anymore."

Pulling his knife from his belt, he made several short, chopping strokes through the air, stretching the muscles in his chest. Reiffen hadn't insisted he take his daily dose of medicine and magic that morning, which left Avender wondering if it would now be possible for him to slay his old friend. Perhaps he would try that night, only there was this new matter of Reiffen saving the farmwife and her daughter to consider.

"What was that you said today about Prince Gerrit coming up from the south?" he asked as he put the knife away.

Reiffen pushed a blazing branch deeper into the fire. "The prince is gathering the flower of Banking to meet us. It's why we're in such a rush."

"They're marching north?"

"Some are. The main force is coming by galley. If we reach Rundel before they do, we'll catch them coming ashore and drive them back into the river."

"Why would you attack your ally?"

"My ally?"

"Redburr and I saw you," said Avender. "That night you visited your uncle in Malmoret."

"Did you? Then I guess pretending there's going to be a battle in Rundel isn't necessary with you."

"Redburr always assumed Gerrit would turn traitor."

"Who else did you tell?"

"No one." Avender felt himself wishing Reiffen were a bit more discomfited by his news. "Redburr said that to move without proof might cause a rebellion at the wrong time."

"Wise in great matters is our Redburr, however foolish he might be in small." Reiffen held Avender's eyes with his own. "But some might say Brannis is the rebel."

Avender didn't look away. "That was before you joined the Three."

"Let me show you something."

Reiffen retrieved a small, unframed mirror from his cloak. Its gleaming surface caught the yellow glint of the fire and swirled with reflected smoke as he slowly passed his palm across the glass. Or at least Avender thought it was smoke until the cloud writhed and disappeared. In its place another image emerged, a picture from far away. Avender saw a sitting room filled with rich furniture and rugs that reminded him of Prince Gerrit's palace in Malmoret.

"Mother? Are you there?" asked Reiffen.

Avender watched the glass.

"I am here, Reiffen. Where are you?"

Giserre's worried face followed her voice into the mirror.

"In Banking, Mother."

"Is there fighting?"

"Not right now. There was fighting, in Backford, but that is finished. Now we are three days' march from Rundel."

"Rundel? I had a friend from Rundel when I was a child. Baron Rundel's second daughter, Renore. I suppose she is married and long gone by now."

"Let us hope so." Reiffen tilted the mirror toward Avender. "Look whom I found in Backford."

"Avender!" Giserre's face opened in pleasant surprise. She

didn't look as if she had aged a day since leaving Valing. "I am so glad Reiffen has found you. I shall sleep much better, now I know you are there to keep an eye on him."

"I shall do what I can, my lady." Avender nodded stiffly, not wishing to insult Giserre by telling her what he really thought of her son.

Reiffen twisted the small glass back toward himself. "You should know, he did try to kill me, Mother. He may not be the best person to watch over me."

"You appear to have forgiven him. So shall I."

Giserre leaned forward and to the side, looking for Avender around the edge of the mirror. Reiffen shifted the glass back toward his friend.

"It is difficult to understand at first, Avender," she said. "I had a hard time accepting the change as well. My own son, cooperating with the Three? I assure you, everything would be much worse had he not."

"Death is no dishonor, ma'am."

"Some would disagree with that," said a new voice.

Giserre twisted her mirror until a second face appeared behind her own. Avender recognized the bard at once.

"Apparently you turned out to be a better swimmer than I thought," said Mindrell, his eyes twinkling.

Reiffen turned the mirror back to his own face before Avender could think of a reply. "Everything is well in the fortress?"

Mindrell shrugged. "The place is empty, but that's not such a bad thing, given the manners of those who've gone. Your mother and Spit have less to do, now the slaves have fewer folks around to be cruel to them."

The glass shifted back to Giserre. "It has been quiet," she agreed. "I have not seen Fornoch since you left. I must confess, it will be a great pleasure to finally leave this dreary place and see

Banking again after so many years. Half my life has passed since I last saw Malmoret."

"Soon, Mother. We meet Gerrit in three days. Unless Brannis has amassed an army of Bryddin, it will all be over quickly."

"Take care, my son. My heart is with you."

"And mine with you, Mother."

Smoke swirled again as Reiffen brushed his fingertips across the mirror. The curling currents faded, replaced by reflections of the night.

"Mindrell?" demanded Avender, as dismayed by Reiffen's and Giserre's apparent acceptance of the bard as by anything else he had seen in the last few days.

"He guards my mother well."

"How can you trust him?"

"Would you rather I had called upon you to perform the task?"

Avender had no answer to that. He would have guarded Giserre with his life, but he doubted his life would have lasted long in Ussene. Perhaps the bard was better suited for that particular chore.

Later, when the fire had broken up into orange crumbs and darkness fogged the trees, Avender fingered his knife. If the magic really had worn off, it would be easy to kill Reiffen now. No guard was close enough to stop him. But talking to Giserre had made him think twice about murdering his old friend. Giserre had said once she would kill her son herself if it ever came to that. Only it had, and she hadn't. There had to be a reason Giserre had stayed her hand; she hadn't appeared to be under any spells. Maybe his best course was to wait and discover that reason, however much he might prefer to do something now.

In three more days they reached the river. Ossdonc halted his army around the burned-out shell of a once fine farm. Lifting a dead heifer by its hind legs the way a man might hold a slaughtered lamb, he called Reiffen to his side.

"Perhaps I shall raid Rundel Keep tonight," he said. His teeth gleamed between his black Wizard's eyes and his collar.

"I would rather you not," Reiffen answered. "I wish a country to rule, not an ash heap. You promised Usseis I would have my chance with my uncle."

"So you shall." Blood from the heifer's neck sprayed Reiffen's and Avender's trousers as Ossdonc waved his arms magnanimously. "Though my own pleasure be diminished by your success, I shall permit your attempt. But remember, lordling. If you fail, I will have my sport."

"You will get your sport at Rimwich," Reiffen replied. "And revenge for your defeat twenty-one years ago. But not here. The barons are our allies. Fornoch and I have assured ourselves of that."

The Wizard dismissed them with another wave; Reiffen led Avender off to a high bluff above the Great River. West Wayland rose on the far side in a series of forested hills above a broad bend where small boats tacked across the water like gliding birds. To the south, the bluff pulled back from the water in half a league of meadows and farms. Rundel stood on a stretch of high ground at the far end, a score of galleys moored like islands in the current offshore. Hundreds of tents marked the fields beyond the walls on the other side of the town, from the dirty gray tarps of the poorest knights to the large orange and black pavilion at the center of the encampment.

Reiffen scanned the dull brown river in both directions. "My uncle's scouts will tell him we're here soon enough, but nightfall is no time for what I have in mind. Tomorrow morning at first light, you and I shall ride down to meet him."

"What about the Keeadini?" asked Avender. "How are you going to call them off once you've made your peace with the barons?"

"The Keeadini will be taken care of once matters between Brannis and myself are decided. In the meantime, their presence will help ensure the barons don't go back on their word. I admit, too many honest farmers and villagers will lose their homes, but, as long as they stay in the towns, they'll be safe. Barns can be rebuilt."

Before dawn they led their horses down a steep path through the woods. Reiffen's face showed hard and pale as stone in the gray light filtering through the branches, his mouth drawn tightly closed. Thick mist rolled in to hide them from the town as the sun rose, the smell of the river heavy in the cloud.

At the bottom of the bluff they swung into their saddles. Reiffen handed a large white handkerchief to a soldier, who tied it to the tip of his sword and raised it as a pennant. Though the mist began to thin as soon as they rode into the fields, they were well in among the farmhouses before the first dogs sniffed them out and began to bark. Farmers raised the alarm. A goodwife hurried back to her cottage, hens scattering like tenpins. Along the town wall, night-dull sentries stiffened and peered forward. The Banking army came to life.

Reiffen halted at the entrance to the camp. A line of pikes faced him, a double hedgerow of long thorns. Beyond the spears several officers waited quietly on horseback to hear what the parley had to say. The colored plumes of the officers' tents curved gently above their helms in the still morning air: Walking and Ankley, Illie and Far Mouthing. Avender's horse whinnied and pawed the ground.

"My name is Reiffen." Reiffen's voice rang clear across the early morning. "I am your proper king. Giserre is my mother,

Ablen my father. Enneria was my grandmother, sister to King On-allai, who was father to Queen Loellin. Through Enneria's father, King Alani, lies my claim to the throne of Malmoret.

"My uncle in Rimwich can lay no such title to the Banking throne. He is Wayland born and knows nothing of our land. Not for him the vineyards of Ankley and the granaries of Emess. Eddstone Harbor is a fishing village to Far Mouthing's great port, and Rimwich a cold stone castle compared to the grace and beauty of Malmoret, greatest city in the world. For twelve years Brannis allowed me, his kin, to languish in Valing. When I was taken by the Three, he did nothing to rescue me. He laughed at my mother, his nephew's wife, when she asked for aid.

"Despite him, I have returned. My army camps upon the ridge above, but I come alone, as is my right. With me I bring as well great power learned from the Three, who have taught me their arts, not to conquer, but to lead. Arts that will fill our land with knowledge and wealth, fattening our wisdom and our purses. Your king should have your blood running through his veins. I am that king.

"What say you to my claim?"

Silence greeted Reiffen's speech. It wasn't for pikemen to resolve such questions. A sergeant barked an order: slowly the martial hedgerow thinned as soldiers shuffled to either side. Through the gap that appeared an officer in shining silver plate rode a white warhorse, orange and black plumes in his helm. His armor gleamed so brightly Avender was forced to slit his eyes to see the three crossed swords upon his shield, but it wasn't the armor that caught Avender's attention. Sheathed along the flank of Prince Gerrit's stallion was a long, heavy sword, kin to the stone blade Baron Backford had been given by the Dwarves.

Halting before Reiffen, Prince Gerrit removed his helm. Behind him waited a line of equally resplendent barons.

"Welcome, Reiffen," said the prince. The incline of his head suggested graciousness but not submission. "If that is truly who you are."

"I have anticipated your doubt, and have brought one whose word you may believe."

Reiffen turned toward Avender. Gerrit followed his nephew's gesture, but it took Avender a moment to understand why the prince was pretending not to recognize Reiffen. They had never met during the years Reiffen had spent in Valing, and to know one another now would be to admit they had met secretly since.

"My friend is older than when last you met," said Reiffen. "Perhaps you remember him."

"The Hero of the Stoneways," replied the prince. "I know him well. He has guested in my house. Sir Avender, do you ride willingly with Reiffen and his Wizard?"

"Not willingly, Prince Gerrit. I was taken at Backford."

"Were you? By Ossdonc himself, no doubt."

"By a pair of plain soldiers, my lord. They wounded me dearly, but Reiffen healed my hurt."

"Then you vouch this is, indeed, Prince Reiffen?"

"I do."

"And how do I know you are not under some magic of the Three?"

"You don't. I don't know myself. But he seems like Reiffen to me."

"You lack the look of one ensorceled, Sir Avender. And your companion does have the look of my sister about him." Gerrit laid his right hand on the weapon at his side and looked back at Reiffen.

"Do you know this sword?" he asked.

"It is a sword of heartstone," Reiffen answered.

"Know then, Prince, that I come to you not in weakness, but in strength. This is no frontier uhlan I lead, but the king's own horse from Malmoret, and all the gathered power of the southern and western barons as well. We do not fear Ossdonc, especially not with this weapon in my hand."

"You should always fear Ossdonc, Uncle."

"Respect, perhaps. But never fear."

Reaching forward, Gerrit drew the sword. His arm strained with the weight until he could grip it with both hands. As he lifted the blade upright, the cold stone gleamed dull beside the shining brilliance of his armor.

"Prince Reiffen, I offer you this sword, a gift of the Bryddin to our house. As my liege lord, this honor is properly yours. I offer as well my fealty, and acknowledge in you the true king of Banking."

A few of the soldiers gasped, but none said a word of censure. Reiffen accepted the sword, his arms bending under its weight. Gerrit turned to the soldiers behind him and cried, "Hail Reiffen, King of Banking!"

Spears rose in salute. A shout rose from the ranks. Their allegiance had been completed without a drop of blood. The barons echoed the soldiers' shout with one of their own. Avender decided, at least for the barons, it had all been planned. How else to explain so many of them up so early in the morning, their armor polished? Reiffen and Gerrit had left nothing to chance. Avender didn't know whether to admire his friend's thoroughness, or curse his cold-bloodedness. Now all that was left to stand against him was Rimwich and King Brannis.

A herald was sent to Rundel to proclaim the advent of the true king, while Gerrit led Reiffen, his escort, and the barons back to his pavilion. Those who had not been part of the plan dressed hastily in their tents, astonishment on their faces at the sight of northern soldiers in the camp. Avender recognized Baron Sevral among them, his stern face chafing in displeasure.

Food and drink were laid out in Prince Gerrit's tent, fruit and bread and flagons of wine on tables between the chairs. A pair of sleek greyhounds rose to greet their master, their tails whipping at his touch.

"You have appeared more quickly than anticipated." The prince offered his nephew a choice of upholstered seats, the backs of which were embroidered with scenes of hunting dogs and their masters.

"We marched quickly and lightly." Reiffen declined to sit, but accepted a glass of wine. "However, I am afraid we left our mark on the land."

Gerrit pursed his lips. "Regrettable, but necessary. I would have preferred to meet you at the border, to avoid such blood-shed."

"As would I. But there is only so much I can do with Ossdonc. Before we cross the river, you might send one of your best captains to harry the Keeadini back into the Waste, or they will burn everything."

The late arrivals pressed around the tent. Some were like Baron Backford, stiff as pokers and staunch as hounds; others seemed more like chimney smoke, willing to be guided by the wind. All stood aside as Sevral, his chin quivering indignantly, came face-to-face with Gerrit.

"What is the meaning of this?" the baron demanded. "Prince Gerrit, have you lost your mind?"

"Not at all, Sevral." The prince sipped from his cup and met the baron's reproof with condescension. "I would think you, among us all, would leap at the chance to welcome the true king. You have ever been a champion of justice."

Baron Sevral straightened at this challenge to his own strict sense of right and wrong, and looked the prince in the eye. "I have sworn an oath to Brannis, Your Highness. We all have, otherwise we would be wasting in the Rimwich dungeons or cowering in the Toes. It is not fit we break our oaths without first allowing the king to state his case."

"We all know what Brannis's case is," scoffed Gerrit.

"Brannis has no case." Reiffen swept Baron Sevral's objections aside. "Either join us, or remain here as our prisoner. I have no intention of pleading my suit before my Wayland uncle."

Baron Sevral straightened his back another inch. "Then I am your prisoner, sirs. I cannot condone oath breaking. But I warn you both, our very way of life shall turn to dust if you insist on this course. Honor is all that separates us from brutes."

"Very well, Baron. If that is your choice."

As Reiffen turned away to set his wineglass on the nearest table, one of the northern guards stepped forward. Before his master could stop him, the guard drew his sword and slashed the baron's head from his shoulders. His strange, black blade swallowed both sunshine and blood as it struck.

Booming laughter followed. The tent flaps cracked in a sudden wind. Like a swiftly filling wineskin, the guard swelled up to a Wizard's full size, his head grazing the canvas at the top of the tent.

"Did you really think I was going to let you attend this meeting unaccompanied, Your Majesty?" Ossdonc roared. His bottomless black eyes bored hungrily around the room.

For the first time Avender saw Reiffen flinch before the Wizard. His old friend's jaw clenched and his eyes flashed. Avender prepared himself for a burst of temper like the ones he had seen so often when he and Reiffen were boys, but somehow Reiffen held himself in. Evidently not all the changes he had undergone in Ussene had been for the worse.

"That was not necessary," said Reiffen, his eyes still angry.

"Oh, but it was, Your Majesty." Ossdonc grinned broadly, reminding Avender of how Mindrell had once mocked Reiffen in exactly the same way. "If I may contradict your uncle, fear is the order of the day in Banking now. Respect is done with entirely."

20

The Greenbank

ater that morning, Reiffen and Avender sailed downriver alone. Ossdonc, accompanied by his army of sissit and northerners, was to follow them to the Greenbank in the galleys the following day. In the meantime the ships would ferry Prince Gerrit and the barons across the Great River to West Wayland. The two armies would advance on Rimwich from west and south, trapping Brannis between them like a mouse between a cat's paws.

Avender, however, had more on his mind than the coming campaign. Finding himself in a small boat with Reiffen at the tiller was a bit too much like old times, as far as he was concerned.

"I still don't get it," he said, poking at the packs in the bottom of the boat with his foot. "You looked honestly upset when Ossdonc killed Baron Sevral. If I hadn't seen you kill Baron Backford with my own eyes, I'd almost think you're on our side."

"I didn't kill Baron Backford. Ossdonc did that." Reiffen steered the boat around a drifting snag; three egrets stared out at them from the dull green leaves.

"It might just as well have been you. If you hadn't used magic to stop the baron, he could have killed the Wizard."

"Baron Backford could never have killed Ossdonc. He could have wounded him, but that would have made everything worse. A wounded Ossdonc would have been a disaster. I'd never have been able to manage him at all."

"Really? And how do you plan to manage him now that you've left him behind?"

"He'll follow us."

"Why?"

"He has to come up the Greenbank," answered Reiffen confidently. "You can't attack Rimwich from the Wedge without first occupying the east bank of the river to guard your crossing. Everyone knows that."

"Yes, but it takes a lot longer to march up the Greenbank than it does to cross the Wedge. Prince Gerrit will get there two days early. Brannis can catch him on the west side of the river, then be back in Rimwich before Ossdonc arrives."

"Ossdonc won't be marching up the Greenbank."

"How else can he come? The current's too strong for rowing."

"Not with a stiff wind from the south."

Avender lifted his cheek to the breeze. "This wind's from the north."

"Then I guess I'll have to make certain it shifts tomorrow."

"You can control the wind?"

"I can control a lot of things. Except Wizards, unfortunately."

It was late afternoon when they met the Greenbank advancing from the east as a sheet of blue against the thick brown of the Great River. Reiffen filled a small vial with the clear, cool water from the spot where the two streams joined, then guided the nose of their skiff up the smaller stream. For a while they ran with the wind abeam but, looking ahead, Avender saw the river turned to the north, directly into the breeze.

"Are you going to cast your spell now?" he asked.

Reiffen shook his head. "Summoning a wind is not something you can just do. It takes time and preparation. And we have to get a lot farther upstream before it will do any good."

"Why not just use that thimble trick of yours? It would be a lot quicker than sailing. You've got a pair of them right there on your hands."

"A traveling spell only works if you're going somewhere you've been before. You can't just shift yourself to someplace new. Even Usseis can't do that."

"So how do we get upriver?"

"We walk."

They pulled the skiff into a clump of tall reeds and splashed ashore. Untying a walking stick from one of the bags, Reiffen said, "I'll take this pack. You take the other."

"What's in them?"

"Tools in mine. Food in yours."

Avender could guess what sort of tools. His was the lighter of the two knapsacks, which meant Reiffen wanted to keep what was in his close to hand. In the old days, Reiffen had always tried to palm off the heavier load.

"How far are we going?"

"To Boatsend. It's ten leagues, and we need to be there by morning."

Bushwhacking through the woods, they came to a narrow track beside an open field. The corn stood taller than Avender on either side, golden tassels fluttering like pennants in the evening breeze. A large crow feasting on early ears squawked and took flight as they came out of the thick woods, its black wings clutching at the sky.

Reiffen set a brisk pace. For the first few miles they followed the river. Wheel marks in the mud proved the track wasn't entirely deserted. Beyond the fields they saw the occasional brush of smoke from unseen farmhouses, and once they passed straight through a farmyard, ruffled hens dancing off at their approach. Reiffen smiled amiably and nodded at the farmer as they passed; the Waylander dipped his chin curtly in reply.

A wide creek forced them up to a bridge on the highway as the first bats of evening swept the air. Beyond the bridge they came to a village. Avender and Reiffen drew stares as they passed down the dusty main street, but no one stopped them. On a low hill to the east, the thane's house loomed like a watchful shadow.

Darkness had fallen by the time they returned to the fields. The moon wouldn't rise for several hours, and even then the clouds would mask its light. Reiffen raised his walking stick; an inch or two of handle protruded above his fist. Like a coal in a breeze, the top began to glow; pale yellow light buttered the road.

"I thought you had to speak to cast a spell," said Avender.

"Not always." The top of the walking stick brightened. "Illumination isn't difficult, as spells go. If I taught you, you could easily do it yourself."

"No thanks."

They walked on. Despite his recent wound, Avender didn't feel in the least fatigued. Frogs piped in the trees; small things rustled through the edges of the fields. Without stars or moon, the night seemed stuck in timeless darkness, like the Stoneways. Avender thought about Ferris and wondered if she had heard the news from Backford. It might take weeks for reports of war to reach Valing. Would she guess Reiffen had left Ussene? Probably. Avender wondered if they would find her at Rimwich; Ferris would know where Reiffen was going as well as anyone. And she would want to see for herself whether he was actually as awful as everyone said. Only the evidence of her own eyes would ever change her mind.

Avender wished he could make up his own mind so easily, but then things always were simpler for Ferris. And for Reiffen, for that matter. Sometimes he felt as if his friends were older than he, and that he had a long way to catch up. They knew what they wanted and asked for it, while he stood awkwardly on the side. Even now he couldn't decide what to think about Reiffen, but trudged along beside him like a prisoner, kicking at the dirt.

Dawn was rising when Reiffen finally led them off the main road and back toward the river. In front of them rose a short hill, smooth and round as a bent knee.

"Gather as much firewood as you can," said Reiffen as they entered a narrow strip of woods at the bottom.

At the summit Avender dropped his bundle of sticks and looked around. To the north the Greenbank rose in a series of rapids, long white gashes tearing the water brightly in the dim light. Below the race the stream broadened, before sweeping in a tight curve around the hill, the town of Boatsend tucked out of sight on the eastern shore. Mist on the water drifted southward with the river around the hill, where the Greenbank opened out again in a second broad sheet. Beyond the reeds that poked through the mist at the foot of the southern slope, the bank stretched in a long sandy beach.

Reiffen had already started a fire on a rocky shelf at the crest of the knoll. A thin plume of smoke trailed southward before the breeze.

"We're going to need more wood," he said.

Avender dropped his knapsack to the ground and started down the hill. Bells jingled on the cows grazing the meadow above the trees.

It occurred to him that, if he wanted to escape, now was the time to try. Once he reached the woods he would be completely hidden. Surely someone in Boatsend would help him get to Rimwich to warn the king.

Trying not to hurry, he crossed the last few strides to the trees. The cows paid him no mind. Once inside the wood he took three steps, each quicker than the one before, and broke into a run. Dry leaves crackled underfoot; patches of gray sky fluttered among the branches above his head. For a while he ran as fast as he had ever run in his life, faster than he and Ferris had run through the dungeons in Ussene. The forest grabbed at him; his cloak tore as he bulled his way through brambles and snags. Reiffen loomed behind him, a dark smoke from the hilltop writhing forward with grasping hands. Avender's heart pounded, his breath rasped. The forest blurred.

He stopped, panting. What was he so scared of? Turning around, he leaned against a tree and looked back. A bright red cardinal flitted through shafts of morning light strung like gossamer in the forest. Nothing had followed him. His terror eased, along with his thumping heart. Catching his breath, he realized he didn't want to run away at all. The sudden sense of freedom was what had sent him flying as soon as he was out of Reiffen's sight, like beer fizzing out of a barrel. No longer a prisoner, he finally saw clearly what he had to do. Running off to Rimwich would change nothing. Redburr already knew Ossdonc and Reiffen were on their way. What could he tell the Shaper except that the Wizard's army was going to arrive a day or two early? Rimwich would be besieged all the same.

He snapped a dead branch off the side of a tree. No matter how things turned out, whether Reiffen was playing a deeper game or was truly the Wizards' creature, Avender understood he had to remain with his old friend till the end. Reiffen was the focus, as he always had been, and Avender's place was at Reiffen's side, as it had always been, regardless of whether he helped or hindered him. He would just have to wait until he knew which it would be.

He began to gather wood.

"That took a while," said Reiffen when Avender finally returned. "Where'd you go? Rimwich?"

"I thought about it." Avender laid down his armload of fuel a safe distance from the fire.

"Saw leaving wouldn't help much, didn't you?"

"You know, if you didn't act like Mindrell so often, this would be a lot easier."

"Sorry." Reiffen finished laying objects from his pack on a cloth beside the fire. "It's just that I've found Mindrell's way of not seeming to care about anything is very helpful in Ussene. I haven't meant to offend."

"Does Giserre let you act like that around her?"

"I'll try to be easier on you."

"Thanks. I don't suppose you'd start by telling me what it is we're doing."

"I've already told you. I'm summoning the wind." His pack empty, Reiffen began adding Avender's wood to the fire. The dry branches caught quickly, adding to the dance of heat in the air.

Avender kept well away from the blaze. "I don't mean what you're doing now. I mean what's going to happen next. Are you with or against Ossdonc? You didn't give me a straight answer the last time I asked."

"I won't this time, either."

"Why not? Don't you trust me? I came back, didn't I? I didn't run away."

Reiffen added the last and largest of Avender's branches to the flames. "I don't trust anyone. Not with Wizards about. Even Giserre doesn't know my plans."

Kneeling beside the fire, the young wizard reached for the first object set out on the cloth. Avender recognized the wing of a hunting bird, a hawk perhaps. Fresh blood stained the ends of the hollow bones. Holding the feathered lump in both hands, Reiffen lifted it, palms up, above the flames.

"Hawk and lark and wind and breeze,
Fly to me across the trees."

The wind from the north freshened. Avender looked upstream, not knowing what to expect, but there was nothing to see. It was a north wind, anyway, which wasn't what they wanted.

Next Reiffen held a small vial above the flames, the same one he had filled from the river. Avender sneezed at the stench of roasting feathers. With a flick of both wrists, Reiffen unstopped the bottle and flicked the contents into the smoke, where they disappeared with a sharp hiss.

"Lake and pond and sea and spray,
Rise to me from far away."

This time there was no answering puff of wind. Carefully Reiffen placed the bottle back on the cloth and picked up the next item, an oak leaf. For each and every object beside him he repeated the process, each act accompanied by a verse spoken in a plain, strong voice. Avender waited for the wind to strengthen again but, if anything, what little was blowing from the north actually died away. Except for the crackling of the flame and the reek of the motley junk Reiffen had dropped into it, the hilltop seemed utterly desolate. To the east the sun rose fully above the edge of the world.

Reiffen leaned forward, his chin bearded in smoke.

"Heart and throat and mouth and tongue,
Areft's breath to me be swung."

The fire belched. A thick column of gray smoke spiraled into the sky. Bits of feather and leaf swirled inside the rising plume like flotsam in a swollen stream. Reiffen's hair blew upward over his ears as he pulled his face back away from the rush of air.

A gust of wind stirred Avender's cloak from the south.

Eyes fierce with satisfaction, Reiffen joined his friend on the windward side of the fire. The breeze strengthened.

"It's working," he said, his arms and legs akimbo. Cloak and hair streamed out behind him in the quickening wind. "Feel how strong it is."

The wind grew. Small waves kicked dark shadows across the river. Copses swayed in the gale. Below them, the cows lumbered toward the shelter of a low tree growing sideways from the hill like a stunted arm.

Avender leaned into the wind, his own cloak flapping. It was a hot, heavy blow, not at all like the sudden, cooling rush of air that comes before a summer storm. Clouds gathered in the south like fat white galleys, piling together from east and west. Lightning burst across the distant sky, too far away to hear.

Avender shouted accusingly above the noise of the gale. "Looks like you've called up more than wind!"

Reiffen's eyes flashed. "I must be stronger than I thought, eh? Come on, let's get out of the storm. Ossdonc should be here by noon."

Avender supposed they would have to descend to some sheltered spot on the north side of the hill but, as soon as they passed the fire, the air grew still. In amazement he looked at the land behind them: the Greenbank was already throwing up long plumes of spray, the trees along its banks shaking like mops out a window. But, on the other side of the hill, what little breeze there had been before had dropped entirely away. A horsefly buzzed along the grass, flew into the edge of the odd south wind, and careened drunkenly away.

"How did you do that?" Avender was even more impressed by the limits of the wind than by the strength of its conjuring.

376 | S. C. BUTLER

"It's in the magic." Reiffen nodded toward the fire, his pride evident for all his pretended nonchalance. "I called a wind to the fire from the south, where I took water from the river. So the wind ends at this spot. It's easier to call a wind over water than over land. Wind and wave are old companions."

Avender looked at the blaze, which should have been blown to bits by the gale. Instead the fire burned hotter, orange as a forge. The smoke had disappeared but the column remained visible all the same, the burning air shimmering as it swept upward. A few of the larger logs glowed red as molten metal in a Dwarven furnace, but the rest of the fuel had disappeared in the brightness against the stone. At the edge of the flame the short-cropped grass bent sideways toward the fire. Carefully Avender reached into the wall of wind and felt his fingers pulled sideways toward the heat. The power was incredible; he couldn't imagine how Reiffen had done it. A hawk's wing, a handful of leaves. Was the power in the magic, or in Reiffen?

"I can teach you. As Fornoch taught me."

For one brief moment Avender saw what Reiffen's life in Ussene must have been like. Foul pits on one side, the power of earth, sea, and sky on the other. But what had Reiffen given up in return? Did his heart remain intact? Had he accepted power in exchange for what had made him human?

A pair of pigeons, dancing upward along the north side of the hill, sheered off as they met the wall of wind and bolted back for the trees.

"What would I want with all that power?" said Avender.

"Better to ask why you wouldn't want it." The passion faded in Reiffen's eyes as he realized Avender wasn't quite as eager as he in the matter of magic. "Once we get this difficulty settled of who is king in Rimwich, there will be much to teach."

"Is that what you're going to do? Teach?" Avender walked a few paces farther from the wind, just in case something changed.

"I'll have to be careful whom I teach, of course. We can't have magic falling into the wrong hands."

"Like Mindrell's, I suppose."

Reiffen's mouth curled thoughtfully. "No. Mindrell would not be someone I would want to teach. Too selfish. But you and Ferris will make excellent students."

"What about the Three? What will they say when you start spreading their power around? Won't they object?"

"I'm not worried about them."

"No?" Avender frowned suspiciously. "Just the other day you told me you could only control Ossdonc, and him only so far. I'm guessing that teaching magic to Ferris and me might be on the other side of so far."

"Ossdonc doesn't worry about magic," said Reiffen, too confident for worry. The first flush of his success still carried him forward past any possible obstacles. "And you don't see Fornoch or Usseis lurking anywhere about, do you? Fornoch's too cautious, and Usseis can't tear his mind away from his fiddling with life and death. You'll see, Avender. The three of us will do great things."

But Avender didn't smile. Reiffen had as yet said nothing to convince him he wanted to learn about so much power. Better to let breezes blow of their own accord.

With the wind howling beside them, they took the bread and cheese from Avender's pack and enjoyed breakfast in the sun while the cows huddled against the storm. Small whirlwinds twisted along the edge of the road, spraying handfuls of dust through wood and field. More than one farmer and his wife came up to examine the edge of the tempest; a farm boy stepping into the wind lost his hat. Avender guessed he would have been knocked bowling into the fire had he tried the same thing at the top of the hill.

Rain came finally about an hour before noon, though only on the southern slope. The wind had grown so strong by then the river seemed to be running the wrong way. Below the rapids, the water looked higher than it had earlier in the morning; the few boatmen who had been on the river had long since rowed their craft to shore. Like the farmers, they gathered along the bank to examine the strange gale.

"There they are."

Avender, who had been watching the boatmen from the northern slope, walked back to the top of the hill. Following Reiffen's gaze, he saw several large black dots gliding upriver. Around them a small storm raged, but the wind stayed steady and strong. The sails swelled wide and full. Faster than Avender could have imagined, the galleys rode forward before the gale, their sails beginning to show as streaks of color through the rain. Red and blue, yellow and green, they rose like flowers from a summer shower, except for that of the lead ship, whose sail was black as Ossdonc's sword. The Wizard himself stood in the prow like a second figurehead pressed close behind the first.

Sissit and men showed on the decks as the craft grew near, their cloaks whipping. A hundred yards from shore the oars of the lead ship came out like a centipede's and dragged in the water to slow it down. The black sail wrinkled as the stays were loosened, then bellied out again in a narrowing band as the yard dropped to the deck. Men struggled to fold it away in the teeth of the ripping wind, but even after the canvas was stowed the ship plowed on.

The last few yards passed in an instant. The bow of the black-sailed ship crashed into the shore and rode high up the sand. Reiffen chanted behind the wall of wind.

"*Hawk and river, wind and breath,*
Now turn all as still as death."

The wind ceased. Ossdonc leapt down from the first ship and drew his hungry black blade. The rain seemed to swerve around him as he strode up the beach and disappeared into the trees. Avender turned to see Reiffen standing beside a patch of blackened rock, no other trace left of fuel or fire. Raindrops pattered across their shoulders as the storm passed north across the hill.

Other galleys followed the first. Soldiers and sissit poured over the sides of their ships to follow Ossdonc into the wood. Sergeants lashed them on, their cries harsh in the sodden air. Slick with rain and mud, the pale sissit lurched across the beach like freshly dug up corpses. Out on the river the flood surged forward, no longer held back by the wind. One galley, lagging behind the others, washed downstream despite the desperate rowing of its crew, caught in the current like a speck of spinning driftwood.

Reiffen turned to his companion as the last ships ground their way up the flooded shore to spill their swarming cargo.

"It's time to go."

Avender shouldered his knapsack. Reiffen packed away his cloth and started down the hill. Below them, at the bottom of the slope, Ossdonc led his army out of the woods and onto the road, ignoring several figures fleeing across the fields. The soaking rain, set free from Reiffen's magic, followed.

21

Dwarves and Molten Stone

very morning Mother Norra marked off the new day at breakfast on a slate beside the fire while Ferris waited restlessly for her trip across the Abyss to begin.

"But how can you know it's really a new day?" she asked. "You don't even have an hour-glass."

From one of the many pockets in her apron the old woman produced something Dwarven that fit neatly in her palm. Round and flat as a skipping stone, one side was smooth gold, the other clear glass. Dwarven runes from one to ten circled the white enamel face, a pair of black needles revolving around them from the center. The longer needle pointed toward the number three, the shorter toward the five.

"If you hold it to your ear," said Mother Norra, "you can hear it tick. Mr. Dwvon gave it to me as a present in honor of my long and distinguished service."

Ferris lifted the piece gently to her ear. From somewhere inside came a sound like half a cricket's chirp repeated over and over. "What is it?"

"A wenwick. Mr. Grimble made it."

"What are the numbers for?"

"To tell the time, dear."

"Then why are there only ten instead of twenty-four?"

Mother Norra raised her hands helplessly. "Don't ask me. I just know three-thirty is breakfast time. Mr. Dwvon told me Mr. Grimble invented it so he could figure out how fast he was going in those airships of his, but I don't understand a word of it. . . . Crayfish and crumbs, my eggs!"

Even without a wenwick, Ferris still needed ways to pass the time before she started on her journey to Ussene. Since Uhle's workshop was easily her favorite in all Issinlough, she visited him the most. Unlike the other loughs, Uhle's wasn't filled with heat and dust and noise. Instead, light suffused every inch of the chamber. Rows and rows of lamps of all shapes and sizes and colors lined the walls: lamps built into mirrored boxes like smaller versions of the one Atty cared for below Valing, lamps that turned off and on at the touch of a finger, lamps that flickered and blinked in failure. And piled on tables and spilling out of sacks were stored enough gems to make the wealthiest merchant in Malmoret weep.

Uhle bowed from behind his desk as she arrived. Through the wide opening in the wall behind him, the city gleamed like the Old Palace in Malmoret set for a midnight ball. Offering Ferris two lamps from among the ones he had been working on, he asked, "Can you tell the difference between these?"

Gripping the stones delicately between the tips of her fingers, Ferris held them up to the light. Both were small and clear, their points sharp against her skin. Handing them back to Uhle, she said, "I don't see any difference."

"None of you humans ever do." The Bryddin rolled the gems backhanded across his desk as casually as a dicing soldier. His reverence for his work wasn't quite the same as Ferris's. "But I keep hoping I'll meet someone who does just the same."

"What was I supposed to feel?" Ferris tapped one of the gems gently with her finger.

"That one," Uhle nodded toward the other stone, "is made from fire. The one beneath your finger is filled with Abbeniss."

Nolo had tried to explain to her once about how Bryddin could feel light. "It's like the spark you get when you rub your hands against a piece of wool, then touch an iron poker. We Bryddin get that spark with light as well, only it's much stronger. We think it's because Brydds remembered making the sun when he created us. They're the same thing, you know, that spark from the wool and the spark we get from light."

He had tried to describe it further, but Ferris had only shaken her head at all his talk of waves and particles smaller than grains of sand. It had been hard enough the time Grimble had attempted to explain how "nothing" was lighter than air. Nolo's lesson on light was even worse. The fact was, a Dwarf could cup a drop of light in his hands the way Ferris could cup a drop of water. And, after catching it, squeeze it inside a gem.

"Come." Uhle rose from the table. "Perhaps it will help if you see how it's done."

He led her through tunnels in the rock, past rooms where daisies and small oaks drooped under the light of glowing stones, through a chamber where they had to cover their eyes with goggles to protect them from the glare of a single diamond the size of a small cottage, and another where green insects glowed on unlit walls, before they passed into a low, dark passage. Ferris felt her way along the stone as several quick turns plunged the tunnel into darkness.

"Don't touch anything," said Uhle when they stopped.

The sound of a pumping bellows followed. Leather creaked and air whooshed. Heat pushed against Ferris's face. Soon a faint light began to glow in the front of the room. A red light, so low and deep it resembled darkness gleaming. Uhle took shape as a shadow on the right; the glow grew from red to orange.

When her eyes grew used to the dimness, she made out Uhle standing beside a stone forge working a bellows with his hands. The orange glow came from the molten stone heating on top of the forge, its fire concealed below. The more Uhle pumped, the brighter the molten rock became. Small chunks of crusted black stone sank below the bubbling surface one by one.

"Watch yourself," said Uhle as the heat thickened in the room. "I have to seal the doorway."

Tucking herself into a corner, she watched the Bryddin remove a stone bar from the wall above the entrance. With a rattling slam, a heavy slab crashed to the floor, sealing them in. Ferris's throat tightened as she felt the closeness of the dark room and the weight of the rock around them.

"There can be no other light," explained Uhle as he returned to the forge.

Ferris remained in her corner as the Bryddin took a small metal lamp from a hook on the wall and placed it on a ledge beside the furnace. To light his lamp, he dipped a finger in the bubbling pool and brought up a drop of molten rock. The wick sprouted a small flame as soon as it touched the burning stone.

Uhle reached into one of the pockets of his leather apron. "What color lamp would you like?"

"You're going to give me another lamp?"

"I don't need any more."

Ferris's forehead glowed with the heat, making her regret lamps couldn't be made in shady forest glades. "How about green?"

"Green it shall be."

Without looking, Uhle pulled a gem the size of a robin's egg from his pocket. Rolling it between thumb and forefinger, he held the jewel in the low flame of the metal lamp, washing it in the light. The stone winked and sparkled like a gaudy green star. With his other hand, he stroked the flame. Around the gem the light swelled and grew, as if Uhle were wrapping transparent yarn around a tiny ball.

Slowly the Bryddin drew his hands out of the light. More like taffy than yarn, the lamp flame followed the stone. It stretched thin as yellow hair and sagged in the middle, as if the light itself had suddenly picked up weight to go with its shape. Ferris wished she could pluck the string but remembered Uhle had told her to touch nothing. Two, three, four times he rolled the stone in the lamp's yellow flame and pulled it away. Each time the haze of light grew denser. His fingers no longer touched the gem at all. Instead they rolled and pressed the light itself, gathering and packing it close around the stone.

The fifth time he pulled his hand away more quickly. The thread of yellow light stretched and snapped with a crack like tiny thunder. The flame returned to normal. Uhle tossed the ball into the air with a flick of his wrist. Like a tiny sun, the yellow globe rose in a short arc before dropping into the bubbling stone with a soft plop, where it glowed like an eye in the midst of the molten fire.

Using both hands, Uhle thrust the gem deeper into the burning stone. Ferris winced as the nirrin hissed against the Bryddin's skin. With his hands buried to the wrists, it looked almost as if he was washing them in the rock. His forearms flexed, the tendons standing out like granite ribbons. Smoke rose from his sleeves where drops of nirrin splashed. The smell of burning leather drifted across the room.

After what felt like hours, but was probably less than half a minute, Uhle lifted his hands from the fire. Gobs of molten stone splashed back into the bowl. The brand-new lamp gleamed green, the wrapping of yellow light gone. Carefully Uhle wiped away the nirrin on his hands. When he was done only a little stone remained crusted to his fingers, like clumps of clay on a potter. The green gem cast an emerald light across his face and beard.

"It has to cool, and could use a little polishing." Blowing on the stone, he rubbed it against his apron. The smell of burning leather returned. "After that it's yours."

Ferris stared at the lamp, hardly believing that ten minutes before its light had been burning at the end of an oil wick. Everything, from the way the Bryddin had played with the light, to the hiss of the stone against his skin, was remarkable. She had known Nolo all her life and had seen him squeeze sand into glass and shape granite between his fingers, but nothing he had ever done was nearly as impressive as what Uhle could do with light and stone. Uhle might protest all he wanted about how there was no magic in what he did; she would always think it was as wonderful as anything any Wizard could accomplish.

Dousing the wick with his fingers, he heaved the stone door back into place and shot home the bolt that held it open. Fresh air plunged across Ferris's face. The orange forge cooled, its dull light dying.

"How do you do that with sunlight?" she asked when they had come back to the main workroom.

Uhle lay the new lamp on his desk. "The principle's the same, but it still has to be done underground. Otherwise the light is too overwhelming. There's a cave in Granglough with a hole in the roof that allows just the right amount of light. You can do it with moonlight, too. You don't get much of a lamp, though."

"Can I see one of those?"

The Bryddin crossed the room to a stone chest whose sides were carved with images of unnerets pointed toward the floor. Opening a drawer, he rummaged through a large selection of soft leather bags that clinked heavily as he pushed among them.

Finding the one he wanted, he untied the top and poured the contents into his palm.

"These came out the best." The rounded stones clicked against each other and Uhle's hard skin as he rolled them in his hand. "It was even worse when I tried cut stones. Then the gems just looked flawed. But, rounded like this, the moonlight at least fills the entire sphere."

The moonstones shone like large, dull pearls. Ferris plucked one from her host's hand. A flicker of color spun across the surface; each milky orb was veined with crooked lines, red and yellow, green and blue, thin as hair but bright and sharp against the solid whiteness. A flash of red tore through the one in her hand like lightning through the belly of a cloud, the crooked line swirling across the surface faster than Ferris could turn the moonstone. Quivering, it bolted back into view from the other side, having circled the polished rock completely.

"They're beautiful," she breathed. "What makes the lightning?"

"Starlight." The Bryddin frowned. "There's no way to filter it out."

"I wouldn't think you'd want to." The thin twist of red swept once more across the tiny globe before disappearing into the pale background. "It's like looking at clouds from the top of the sky. I can imagine a whole tiny world underneath."

"I can assure you, there's no such thing." Uhle missed the romance of the idea entirely. "I've cut several open. There's nothing inside but light and stone."

"Why haven't you traded any of these? Think of the necklace they'd make!"

"I hadn't thought of that." Returning most of the moonstones to their bag, he held one up to study thoughtfully. "The lines fade when the gem's broken. But it might be possible."

With some reluctance, Ferris carefully laid the stone she had taken in with its fellows. Peeping into the bag, she saw the gems jumbled together at the bottom like tiny birds' eggs. The jagged colors flashed brighter and more fiercely than ever in the dimness of their pouch.

Swallowing hard, she closed the top. One moonstone would make a fitting gift for any king or queen. She could just imagine what an entire necklace would look like on a moonlit balcony. Undoubtedly Uhle would give them to her for the asking, but it would never be right to ask.

He smiled, the fire in his eyes turning briefly mellow. "A gift for your daughter one day, perhaps. Though why anyone should want presents after receiving the joy of a child, I'll never understand. You humans have no idea what a gift it is to carry time from parent to child in small, manageable pieces. We Bryddin have to deal with the immeasurable in its entirety."

That night, her freshly washed hair spread out on Mother Norra's clean pillows, Ferris found it hard to fall asleep. A distant pump whistled and wheezed. A pipe *drip-drip-dripped* until she realized she hadn't closed the tap in her room tight enough. The cold stone floor at the edge of the tub chilled her bare toes; she rubbed them for a moment before tucking them back under the covers.

She comforted herself by thinking how Brizen would make a good father, better than his own had been. Their children would live splendid, happy lives, in Rimwich and Malmoret and Valing, adored by all, at home everywhere in the world. Her daughter, radiant in moonpearls, would be beautiful beyond belief.

A tear trickled down beside her nose. Fiercely, she smudged it away. She had made up her mind. There was no going back now. Besides, there was still much to accomplish before there could be any real thought of marriage, let alone a child. Did she really want to bring children into a world where Wizards could steal people's souls? Better to defeat Reiffen and the Wizards first, then

there would be nothing to stop her giving her heart to Brizen.
Who deserved it so much more.

The pump stopped wheezing. In its place a soft weeping crept
across the long night like wind from a faraway sea.

Three more times the short needle on Mother Norra's wenwick circled its enameled dial before Ferris, along with a
dozen Bryddin, boarded the *Nightfish* for the trip across the Abyss.

Gammit accepted his passengers with his usual sour manner.
"I could be studying ballast densities," he grumbled as Ferris
came aboard. "But no. Nolo and Dwvon want me to go flying
around the bottom of the world instead. I ask you, does that
sound like fun?"

Knowing that Gammit, like all Dwarves, only did what he
wanted, Ferris didn't bother to answer. Instead she busied herself
constructing a corner berth on the narrow deck with blankets
she had brought for just that purpose. Around her the Dwarves
talked about some large bit of excavation they had planned for
the near future, completely ignoring the coming battle. Ferris
wondered how even Bryddin could be so unconcerned.

Two days later, after the *Nightfish* had docked once again beneath the Stoneways, she was too busy to worry about the
Dwarves. They soon outpaced her on the endless stairs leading
up to Ussene, their short legs handling the steps much more easily than her long ones. Finally one named Groff lagged behind
the others to make certain she didn't get lost. Ferris, accustomed
though she was to hiking in the mountains around Valing, plodded steadily as a donkey, too weary to notice anything other than
the occasional flat stretch in the endless ascent despite the new
green lamp gleaming at her forehead.

Eventually Groff noticed Ferris couldn't keep up even her

slow human pace forever, and allowed her to rest. She fell asleep the instant her cheek touched the hard stone. Stiff and chill when she woke, she barely had strength enough to wolf down a cold breakfast. But twenty minutes later, with another thousand stairs behind her, she had warmed up enough to almost feel fine.

Groff wasn't talkative, and Ferris was too tired for conversation, so mostly they climbed in silence. They found little of interest along their path. Ferris had seen the marvels of wild cave before, and had too much on her mind for sightseeing this time. The closer they came to Ussene, the more its terrors rose up in her mind, and she didn't want to talk about those.

"Did you hear that?" she whispered, certain something had slapped softly against the stone nearby as they entered a stretch of wider and more level passages.

"Yes," Groff answered over his shoulder and continued on.

Despite the Dwarf's unconcern, Ferris's fear increased. "What was it?"

"Pasties."

"Pasties!"

"Don't worry. They're almost tame. But if we don't ignore them, they'll want us to feed them. Just like mistrin."

The shuffling increased as they went on, but only when the passage widened into a large chamber did Ferris catch her first glimpse of the odd creatures. Several lurched like slow shadows just beyond the arc of the lamps, pale, passive things that skittered after her like termites trailing their queen. Groff swung to the left as one loomed into the light before him; Ferris caught a glimpse of shredded clothing and scraggly hair dangling from pale, thin limbs like moss on a dying oak. What was it Durk had said? Usseis took what he wanted from everyone: sometimes the body, sometimes the mind. Now that she had seen both, Ferris decided taking the mind was the worst. She would much rather be Durk than some slobbering, mindless carcass, no matter how much the talking rock had to depend on other people to carry him around.

Then again, what had been done to Reiffen was probably the worst of all.

Stumbling with exhaustion, she finally reached Usslough. The cave was the same as she remembered: the hearth, the little waterfall trickling over the stone dam at the edge of the small pool. This was where they had camped with Delven and the other Bryddin the last time she had been to Ussene. Without even pausing to wash her face, Ferris wrapped her blankets around her and collapsed on the floor. Pale figures hovered at the edge of her sleep, their fingers fluttering toward her like tattered rags. Silver-lined and rippling at the touch of wind and moon, another soulless creature urged them on.

When she woke the cavern was filled with more Bryddin than she had ever seen before in one place. Scores of them milled around the cave, talking, eating, fiddling with their hands. But something was missing, though at first she couldn't say what.

Nolo appeared, a grin splintering his granite face. "Good morning, lass. Enjoy your sleep? We're about ready to go."

Ferris realized what was missing as she glanced at the tools hanging from Nolo's belt. "Where are your weapons?" she asked. "Where's your ax?"

Her old friend's craggy brows wriggled in surprise. "What do I need my ax for?"

"You're going to fight Wizards, aren't you?"

Nolo shook his head. "Not fight them. Destroy them."

"It's the same thing."

"No. Fighting would produce a much less sure result."

"But how can you expect to destroy the Wizards without fighting them?"

"Easy, if you look at the problem as a miner instead of a

soldier. Question: How to destroy Ussene? Answer: Pull the bottom out from under it."

Ferris stared at Nolo in disbelief.

"We're going to dig the bottom out from underneath the fortress," he went on, "and bring it smashing down. We expect the Wizards will be killed in the general structural collapse. They aren't Bryddin, you know."

"And you think the Three are going to let you walk right in and do that?"

"They won't even know we're there. We've already done most of the job over the last six years. No one's caught us yet. Why should it be any different this time? The stone beneath the fortress was already a maze of caverns and passages before we got here. All we had to do was finish the process."

Ferris couldn't believe what she was hearing. "And that's your plan? To just let the whole place crash down a few feet into the earth?"

"It is." Nolo smoothed his beard proudly. "The whole mountain will collapse once we pull out the last supports. Plus there's a large bed of nirrin underneath that will melt a lot of it, too."

Before Ferris could ask another question, their old friend Delven climbed to the top of the hearth and announced it was time to start. Without any discussion, the stocky crew filed out of the cavern. Nolo started to follow until Ferris caught him by the sleeve.

"Wait a minute," she urged. "You've forgotten one important detail."

The skin around the Dwarf's deep-set eyes crinkled. "What's that?"

"Did you ever think what would happen to the people inside when the fortress comes crashing down?"

"They'll all die, I suppose." Nolo scratched his chin. "They'd die if we attacked them, too. Can't say I see the difference."

Hands on her hips like Hern, Ferris gave the Dwarf a withering look. "You forget, not everyone in Ussene's an evil Wizard. What about Giserre? And the slaves?"

"Giserre? Do you think she's still alive?"

"I'm sure of it. Whatever kind of monster Reiffen has turned into, he didn't bring Giserre to Ussene just to kill her. Most likely the Three have her hidden away somewhere to make sure he behaves."

The Dwarf pulled harder at his beard. "You know, you're right. I should have thought of that. All the same, we can't possibly find her in time. Shortly after Abben rises, most of the mountain up there is going to collapse." He pointed toward the stone roof over their heads. "The only reason it's going to take even that long is we have to do it carefully. So we don't get smashed ourselves."

"What time is it now?"

"Now? Why, I suppose about an hour short of supper."

"That gives us all evening and night to find Giserre." Ferris grabbed Nolo's arm again. "Come on. We have to hurry if we're going to have any chance at all."

"Lass, you can't really mean this." Nolo permitted Ferris to pull him a few steps toward the exit. "You know it's impossible."

"Everyone said rescuing Reiffen was impossible, but we did that."

"For about a month."

"That wasn't our fault, especially now we know he was in league with the Wizards all along. Come on. We can do this. We have to do this. The fortress is probably empty because of the war. No one will catch us."

Nolo made one last attempt to dissuade her. "But we don't even know where to look, lass. Remember how long it took us to find Reiffen? And that was with Redburr helping, disguised as a bat and a guard. We'll never find Giserre on our own."

"Yes we will. This time I have you, which is even better than Redburr. I'll bet Delven's cut a hundred secret passages through Ussene."

"He has, but—"

"Good. We'll look for that Front Window Reiffen told us about. Giserre won't be too far away from light and air." With a final heave, she pulled the stubborn Dwarf forward.

Nolo sighed. "It won't be easy, lass. Delven didn't dig the new ways with humans in mind."

"I'll get through," said Ferris firmly.

Without another word, she led Nolo off briskly into the darkness. Having no idea where they were going, she soon made him switch places. Their lamplight, white and green, swept across the walls. Nothing was as Ferris had feared, no bugs, no burning lake, no bones. Just tunnels twisting through rock like knotted rigging. Only a Dwarf could keep from getting lost in such a place.

Despite her bold front, she wasn't as confident as she sounded. She guessed they had a better chance of finding Giserre than they had of actually getting out again, the same as when they had rescued Reiffen.

Apparently Nolo was thinking the same thing. While shimmying through a long, narrow tube, he asked, "Have you thought about how we're going to get out once we find her? What if we run out of time?"

"You'll think of something."

"Lass, I'm not sure you understand. The entire mountain's coming down."

"Can't your stone sense help you find a safe place for us to ride it out?"

Nolo grunted and muttered something about not knowing he had brought Hern along with him. Ferris thought it best to ignore the slur.

394 | S. C. BUTLER

Beyond the narrow tube they emerged into a low passage where Ferris had to bend sideways to keep from banging her head. The air grew warm. The rock grew warm as well, unlike the usual cold stone. Ferris was sure Nolo, with his bare feet, had noticed the change as well, though it was sometimes hard to tell what Bryddin did and didn't notice with their stony skin.

"Why's the rock hot?" she asked.

"I told you the passage was difficult. Just wait a bit more and you'll see why."

Ferris wrinkled her nose. In addition to warmth, the air had picked up the sharp, bitter smell of a struck flint. Both heat and odor increased as she followed her guide through a series of tight, narrow bends to an opening in the side of a vast, hot chamber.

They stood on a ledge overlooking an enormous nirrin-filled cavern. Five or six fathoms down, the molten surface bubbled. Dark patches spread across the orange fire like duckweed on a pond, slowly breaking up as fresh gouts of golden heat boiled up from below. Here and there across the room black pillars rose to the ceiling from small islands.

Nolo pointed toward the nearest column. "That's where we're going," he said.

Ferris gestured at the boiling lake. "I can't cross that."

"There might be another way."

Thoughtfully, Nolo stamped on the ledge with his broad feet. Ferris withdrew to the relative cool of the tunnel and waited to see what her companion had in mind.

He wasn't long. Examining the rocky outcrop closely, including a short climb out of sight over the edge, he reappeared nodding optimistically.

"Stay back, lass. We can't have you falling into the nirrin if I'm off on my measuring. Good thing I have my tools with me rather than my ax, eh?"

Ferris retreated a second time; Nolo removed several iron wedges and the hammer from his belt and began thumping away at the stone. He worked near the back of the ledge, along a fissure in the rock, burying the wedges deep with sure strokes. Once, unhappy with his placement, he wriggled his hand into the stone and retrieved the tool. More than once Ferris felt the shiver of his blows in the rock beneath her feet, though she stood a good three paces deep in the tunnel.

Scurrying over the edge again, he banged away at spots where the crevice ran along the wall. Returning to the top, he knelt on Ferris's side of the fissure and hollowed out a small hole on the edge of the stone with two fingers, like a potter working in stiff clay. When that was done he pulled a coil of rope from his pack and tied it off through the opening, the line looped on the cave floor beside him.

"Ready?"

Ferris nodded.

"We have to be quick. The bridge I'm about to make won't float long. If it works at all. Dwvon would do it much better."

Taking the last, and biggest, wedge from his tool belt, Nolo smashed it home. A large crack ripped the air. The fissure widened abruptly, and the ledge seemed to hang suspended above the pool before it fell, grinding against the wall. Nirrin splashed in fountains of red and gold. Globs of molten stone spattered the entrance to the cave.

"Come on!" Nolo brushed off a lump that had landed on his shoulder and kicked the rope over the side. His shirt smoldered. Below him the fallen wall formed a bridge across the burning lake. Nirrin licked at the edges, devouring the cooler stone. At the far end a narrow gap gleamed like a red gash between the end of the bridge and the black column.

Feeling as if she were descending into the mouth of an open oven, Ferris followed him over the wall. By the time she reached the bottom her hands and face felt burned. Nolo was running across the bridge, though Ferris had no idea where he would go once he reached the other side. The black column had no openings that she could see.

He leapt the gap at the end. But Bryddin don't jump well, and he didn't make it all the way. One foot slipped up to the ankle into the glowing lake. Nolo's trouser leg burst into flames before he pulled his foot free and patted out the fire. Ferris winced, but it didn't look like a hard jump for her at all.

Pulling himself up onto the narrow island at the base of the pillar, the Dwarf removed his lamp and pressed it against the stone. Though Ferris could see nothing in the black rock, he was soon pushing hard against it. That he had opened something became clear when he tumbled through the gap and waved Ferris forward.

She sprinted as fast as she could down the bridge and jumped. The heat below her feet as she passed over the gap nearly peeled her skin. Then Nolo caught her in his arms and the two of them fell back into cool cave. The Dwarf swung the stone door closed behind them.

"Are you okay, lass?"

"I think so." She rubbed her face where she had scraped herself on the Bryddin's rough hands. "How's your foot?"

"My foot's fine."

Ferris checked for herself. Aside from his trouser leg being burnt to the knee, his foot did look fine. For that matter, it looked a lot cleaner than the other.

She examined the new cave. A tight tube led straight up, though she couldn't tell how far. Beyond the glow of her light the tunnel overhead was as dark as the back of a throat.

"We're in Ussene's chimneys now," Nolo explained, "though this one was never used for ordinary smoke. It used to bring molten nirrin up to Usseis's workshops. Lucky for us the passage was blocked up long ago."

"How do we get up?"

"We climb. After I tie you to my back."

He strapped her on with the last of his rope, her arms around his chest. Despite several layers of clothing between them, Ferris felt as if she had been bound over the back of a boulder. Wishing she were younger, she wriggled into a slightly more comfortable position.

Hanging over his shoulder with both their lamps shining on the rock, Ferris had a clear view of Nolo's hands gripping the stone. Like thick mud, the black rock dimpled beneath his fingers. But, unlike mud, it didn't give way as the Dwarf applied his weight to his handhold and pulled them upward. From the way his weight shifted every time he reached for a new grip, Ferris guessed he was doing the same thing with his toes.

The bottom of the shaft disappeared. Ferris tried not to think what would happen if they fell. If she closed her eyes she could almost imagine she was being hoisted up the side of the Neck. Nolo's progress was in short, slow jerks as he went from hand to hand, the same motion the long crane made when Berrel wanted something heavy brought up quickly from the lake to the Manor.

"How tall is this chimney, anyway?" she asked, her eyes still closed.

"Thirty-two-point-oh-five fathoms, according to the map."

"And at the top?"

"More chimney."

They climbed. Nolo's stiff, dirty hair tickled Ferris's nose. She passed the time trying to remember everything she could about her last trip inside Ussene, hoping to recall something to help them find Giserre.

Eventually the stone changed to rougher rock, where the

Dwarf could climb more quickly. Later the passage elbowed into an ascending angle, at which point Nolo had Ferris crawl up the rock behind him, though he kept them lashed together. Her knees and fingers quickly became scratched and bruised. Snags in the stone tore her shirt and trousers. When the tube went straight up again, the way had grown too narrow for Nolo to carry her any farther. Tired as she was, there was nothing for it but to keep on climbing. She slipped once, but Nolo's noose around her arms and shoulders caught her before she had fallen far. Loose stones clattered into the long fathoms of darkness beneath her dangling feet. Sighing, she reached for fresh handholds and started up again.

Gradually she became aware that the smell of dry, dusty stone had been replaced by the thicker odor of something burned. Black dust filled the tight passage, rubbed away from the rock by Nolo's passing. Ferris rubbed her nose and wondered just how awful she looked. Giserre would think she had been crawling around in a coal bin.

She sneezed, sending soot swirling through the air.

"Shhh!" Nolo's lamp gleamed downward. "We're almost there. Stay where you are. I'll go ahead to make sure the way is clear."

The rope between them dropped free to hang from Ferris's shoulders. Nolo scuttled away, his toes sending a fresh cloud of grit settling down the back of her neck. Ferris felt a moment's panic at the thought she was suspended over who knew how long a drop below. Wedging herself as tightly as she could in the tight passage, she took long, calming breaths and waited for the Dwarf's return.

His light soon reappeared. "Come on up," he whispered. "The fire's out and the cave's empty."

As quickly and cautiously as she could, Ferris ascended. Nolo disappeared again soon after she started, but Ferris reached the spot where he had been not much later. A new, impossibly tight tunnel continued into the darkness overhead. Below shone the clear gleam of Nolo's lamp. With a start, Ferris realized she was looking down the inside of a chimney at a hearth. A curved grate stood on the stone directly below her, the light seeping in from the opening to the room.

Nolo pushed his head in beneath what had to be the mantel on the other side, his lamp gleaming at his forehead. "Hurry up. We don't have much time."

Her hands slipping on the filthy flue, Ferris half climbed, half slid the final few feet. The room beyond held a bare bed against one wall, a metal trunk beneath. Ferris considered rifling the trunk for a disguise, but remembered there was no disguising a Dwarf.

Opening the door slowly, they peered in both directions down the dim hall. Low candles burned along the walls.

"Which way?" she whispered.

Nolo pointed left. "There's fresh air that way, though it's a ways off." Soot puffed from his beard as he spoke. Behind them a trail of dark dust led back to the empty room.

"Too late to start worrying about that," the Dwarf added, seeing Ferris had noticed their trail. "We'd better take off our lamps, though."

Ferris led the way, Nolo passing directions from behind. Filthy as she was, she could easily pretend to be a slave if someone spotted her, while Nolo hid around the corner in the rear. Surprisingly, she found she wasn't as scared as she had been seven years before and wondered if she had had more sense as a child. More than once they passed empty barracks, the stacked beds in much greater disarray than the first room they had found. Had the fortress been at full strength, they would have been caught long ago. But, though the upper levels spread out farther than even the New Palace in Malmoret, it was the dungeons of Ussene that were deep and endless, not the Upstairs. Eventually Nolo stopped before a heavy wooden door. Ferris's heart lifted.

"There's no one on the other side," said the Dwarf, "but this is one of the places I'm sensing fresh air. There's another further on down the corridor."

Ferris opened the door on a finely furnished sitting room, a woman's needlework discarded on the couch. Two more open doors in the far wall led to bedrooms. "This has to be her apartment," she declared.

Soot cascaded on the cleanly swept floor as Nolo scratched his beard. "Maybe we should check the other window, in case she's there. And there was that library Reiffen told us about."

"I think we should wait here. I doubt Giserre spends much time in any other part of the fortress." Ferris went into the bedroom on the right, where the last pale gray of night shrouded the view outside.

Nolo went straight to the window.

"How much time is left?" she asked.

"Three hours and seventeen minutes. Barely enough to return. But this isn't as bad as I thought. It might be easier to go this way. If we can get over to the next ridge we'll be all right. I'd better go see if there's any kind of path up above. Hold on, I'll be right back."

"What about warning the slaves?"

Nolo was already gone. Leaning out the window, Ferris looked for him without success. When she turned back to the room she found a woman staring at her from the doorway, mop and bucket in hand.

Ferris spoke first, though even *her* tongue was tied during the first few moments of surprise. The other woman was about her height, with gray hair in a long braid and a dress that had been patched many times. Ferris remembered what she had said about warning the slaves.

"Do you know where Giserre is?" she asked.

The slave nodded, her eyes brimming with fear.

"Can you bring her here?"

The slave nodded mutely again.

"Then do it. As quickly as possible. And warn all the other slaves as well. Everyone has to get out. The fortress is about to be destroyed." Ferris searched her mind for a description the slave, who didn't seem intelligent, might understand. "It's going to be like a giant avalanche. There won't be anything left. But tell Giserre to come here first."

For a third time the slave nodded, but still didn't move. Ferris thought she understood what was required.

"Go!" she commanded, pointing toward the door in what she imagined to be the overbearing manner of a Wizard. "As fast as you can! Now!"

The slave bolted. Her mop and bucket spilled to the floor. Ferris leaned back out the window, calling up to Nolo that she had sent a slave to fetch Giserre, but heard no answer.

When she pulled her head back into the room, the Gray Wizard stood in the doorway instead of the slave.

22

Holes in Water

eiffen's storm faded into a steamy afternoon as Ossdonc's army marched north, but rain and wet clothing had left their mark on the Wizard's troops. By the time they reached Rimwich, half the column was coughing. Sissit sneezed and rubbed their rheumy eyes; soldiers spat gobs of greenish phlegm along the road.

"It's not as if Ussene is the healthiest place in the world," explained Reiffen as he and Avender tramped beside the wheezing column. "And the way the army's been gorging itself all week, I'm surprised they're not already dying in droves."

In Rimwich, Wayland's soldiers bristled along the high wall, the keep rising on the hill above like the tail of a strutting tomcat. Despite the sound of Gerrit's axmen attacking the trees on the far side of the Greenbank as they set about building rafts, Avender couldn't help but feel it was the well-defended town waiting to pounce on Ossdonc's army, and not the other way around. Redburr was probably behind those Dwarf-strengthened walls, counseling Brannis on the best way to defeat the Wizard. Fingering the knife at his belt, Avender glanced at Reiffen and wondered again which way his friend would try to lead him.

Outside the walls not a single cow or goat grazed the pastures beside the river. The army, used to easy feasting at the end of every day, grumbled. Ossdonc waved several companies forward to rush the empty outer town; the defenders on the walls met them with a rain of rocks and arrows. The northerners replied by setting fire to everything they couldn't carry off and, laden with plunder, dashed back out of the archers' range. Dark smoke thickened the air as the flames leapt from the buildings to the golden fields.

The Black Wizard laughed. "Torch it all!" he shouted. "Tomorrow we dine in Rimwich!"

Reiffen led Avender to the river as the soot and cinders quickened the coughing among the Wizard's troops. Cool water swirled past the grassy bank, the mere sight of it a welcome relief after the smoke and heat in the fields. Avender took a deep breath, then coughed himself as something thickened in his throat.

A small boat, rowing crabwise across the current, set out from the far shore. Reiffen frowned. "I told Gerrit to keep to the other side until tomorrow."

Avender squinted through the dying light. "I don't think it's Prince Gerrit."

Reiffen signaled the boat. The rowers continued at an angle upstream until the current slackened, then swung round toward the two men standing on the shore. Reiffen waded out to meet them. Water whirling at his knees, he caught the bow in both hands as they rowed in close to the bank.

"I told Gerrit to send no one across the river," he said.

"Please, Your Majesty." The officer in the stern eyed the water nervously as he attempted to stand. "With Prince Gerrit's compliments, he invites you to join his camp for the evening."

"Tell my uncle I thank him, but choose to remain where I am. Someone has to watch the Wizard."

The officer nodded, but his glance toward the smoke and flame suggested he didn't understand why anyone would willingly remain on the Wizard's side of the river. Pushing the bow of the boat back toward the current, Reiffen sent the messenger on his way.

"I wouldn't mind spending the night on the other side," said Avender.

"You won't be spending it here, if that's what's worrying you." Reiffen waded back to shore. "It's time you earned your keep."

Sensing Reiffen was finally going to reveal his purpose, Avender scrambled down the bank. His heart pounded; now maybe he could make up his own mind as well. But, before he could say a word, a curl of smoke caught his chest and set him hacking again.

"Here. Try some of this." Reiffen offered Avender a small silver flask. "Just a sip."

Whatever was in the flask, it cleaned Avender's mouth and throat like a swallow of vinegar. His nose itched, and he thought he was going to sneeze. But the catch to his throat disappeared.

Grimacing, he returned the bottle. "What was that?"

"A tonic. Something I made for my mother to administer to the slaves in Ussene. Now is no time for you to catch cold."

"What is it you want me to do?"

"Go to Rimwich." Reiffen nodded toward the part of the wall that ran out into the river, securing the snug harbor on the other side.

"Do you want me to call a parley?"

"I want you to sneak in."

"Sneak in? Aren't you afraid I might stay there once I get inside?"

"No. Which side you choose isn't going to matter much longer."

"You're that sure of winning?"

"Yes."

Avender clenched his fists. Not since they first met had he so wanted to knock his old friend down. But they weren't little boys any longer and wrestling in the river wouldn't solve anything. No matter how much he didn't want to, he would stick to the decision he had made in the woods that afternoon.

"What if I'd rather stay with you?"

Reiffen's eyebrows rose. Avender felt a certain satisfaction in having said something his smug friend hadn't expected.

"What, so you can kill me when I turn out to be evil after all?" The young wizard shook his head with a condescending smile. Avender knotted his fists in frustration a second time. "You'll have to stab me in the back to do that, even without the compulsion, and I don't think you can. Which makes you luckier than I, old friend. No, this is your opportunity to get away from here, on the off chance my plan fails. Go to Rimwich. See Redburr."

"I don't have to sneak in to do that. All I have to do is go up to the front gate with a flag of truce and Redburr will tell them to let me right in."

"I don't want Ossdonc to see you."

"That'll be a nice trick."

"You'll be invisible."

"Invisible?" Avender's face pinched in disbelief.

"Yes." Reiffen pulled a small, oiled pouch from inside his shirt, just like the ones they had used to bring salt to the nokken, and thrust it into Avender's hand. "Give this to Redburr when you reach the city."

"How am I going to do that? Being invisible won't help me climb the walls. And I can hardly ask them to open the gate if they can't see me."

"You still know how to swim, don't you? It's dark enough no one will notice you floating around the embankment to the docks on the other side. Then you can sneak in through the river gate. Once inside the walls, find someplace safe and change back. Invisibility is more trouble than it's worth most of the time, especially in a crowd."

"What if I'm caught?"

Reiffen clapped his old friend on the shoulder. "That will work just as well. Demand they take you to Redburr. Even Brannis won't ignore the Hero of the Stoneways."

"What's in the pouch?"

"A letter. I can't tell you what it says, though. It's still not the right time. You're just going to have to keep trusting me till Redburr reads it. Or not."

Before Avender had a chance to respond, Reiffen stepped away. He checked the top of the bank to make sure no one was close enough to see what he was up to, pressed his hands together in front of his chest, and spoke.

"Shadow lost,
Shadow found,
Shadow bend the light around."

As he finished, he let his hands fall forward, fingers pointing at Avender.

Avender looked down, but there was nothing there. No legs. No hands or stomach, either. Where his feet should have been he saw instead the impression of his boot heels in the moist earth. He moved slightly: the mud squished clearly and new prints formed. Something small bounced off his shoulder, a moth hurrying toward the flames behind him.

"Won't someone see me in the water?" he asked. "I'm going to make a fair-sized hole."

"That's why we're doing this at dusk." Reiffen spoke as if Avender were standing to the right of where he actually was. "At this time of day, you'll just be another shadow."

"How do I get rid of the spell?"

"Say the word 'see.' But I suggest you only do it when no one's looking. Otherwise you might cause a real commotion when you pop back into view. And I remind you, a crowded town is about the worst place to be invisible. Someone's always about to bump into you, and most dogs trust their noses more than their eyes, so they won't have any trouble finding you at all."

"You sound like you've had some experience at this." As he spoke, Avender stepped into the river. His legs made holes in the water that went straight to the bottom.

"A little. And don't try looking at your feet. Not being able to see them will make you stumble."

Wading farther into the cold stream, Avender thought about how some things never changed. Once again Reiffen had talked him into doing something he hadn't wanted to.

"Only Redburr can read the letter," called Reiffen softly from the bank. "Good luck."

His words tattered away behind the cautious swish of Avender's legs through the shallows. The town loomed through the smoke a quarter of a mile away, but only one northern picket marked the shore in between. Across the river bright fires glowed among the trees to light the Banking soldiers at their work. Axes thunked heavily, reminding Avender how far sound carried across water in the dark. Slowly he slid through the stream, feeling carefully for safe footing before moving forward.

Beyond the picket he quickened his pace. A splash wouldn't matter as much now. A long bowshot separated him from the battlement, where Wayland sentries patrolled between flickering torches. None of them noticed as Avender slipped deeper into the stream. Soon the current was tugging him along, his boots dragging in the mud. He thought about taking them off, only he didn't want to be wandering Rimwich barefoot in the dark. Besides, he was a strong swimmer. And who knew when he would find another pair of boots that fit?

A floating branch bumped his shoulder, giving him an idea. Wood always collected in slack water, and there would be plenty of slack water by the wall. He stopped swimming toward the middle of the river and worked his way back to the corner where the embankment left the shore and jutted into the stream. Despite the failing light, he soon found what he was looking for: an old, weathered trunk, its bark stripped away by the rapids and falls upstream. Looping one arm around it, Avender pushed both himself and the log out from the wall and into the river.

The current forced him immediately back against the stone. There was no way he could swim against it, especially not holding the log. He would have to work his way along the wall instead. His boots slipping on the slimy rock, he managed to creep steadily forward. Waves slapped at his face as he moved into deeper water. Coughing, he looked up at the sentries on the wall, but the night had grown quite dark. He saw no one and was certain no one saw him.

The gurgling water took on a thicker, swallowing sound as the stream swept him round the edge of the wall. Now the challenge was to keep from being carried too far too fast. Lights blazed in the darkness, both from the town on the hill above and the lanterns along the docks. Guards paraded back and forth along the wharves and walls. Kicking silently, Avender pushed his float toward shore, steering for the gate in the middle of the wall.

The town disappeared as something loomed above his head, the log ramming whatever he had run into with a loud *thwock*.

"What's that?"

Several lanterns snapped toward Avender. Footsteps barked above the high shadow of a long stone dock.

"Sounds like a snag."

"I told you that flatboat was too far out in the stream."

"And I told you there's nowhere else to put it."

"Well then, maybe you should be the one goes out there to free it."

Avender let go of the log, hoping that would make the sentries leave. The long timber bumped once more on the side of the boat, then disappeared downstream. Avender gripped the boat's gunwale tightly to keep from drifting off himself.

"See?" crowed the first voice. "She's fine where she is after all."

"Oh yeah?" His companion didn't seem convinced. "Maybe we should check and make sure the snag was the only thing that got hung up. Come on. Lend a hand here with the rope."

Setting their lanterns down, the two men pulled the boat in to the dock. Avender hung on for the ride. Even with their lights shining full upon him, they couldn't see him. By the time one of them held the painter fast and the other clambered aboard, Avender had moved from the boat to the dock. Back in still water, the swimming was easy now despite his boots. All the same, he kept close to the stone wharf, feeling for a ladder or some other means to climb up. Other boats were moored bow-in against the pier, but there was plenty of room beneath their curved hulls for a swimmer to pass between them and the stone.

He encountered another problem once he found a ladder. Starting up the stone rungs, he had to drop back down almost as soon as he came clear. The water pouring from his clothes had revealed his presence more certainly than any torchlight. Crouching with his lower half in the water, he waited as two pairs of feet slapped toward him on the stone above.

"I tell you, Lon, you keep hearing things. If you're gonna get this spooked the first night of the siege, I'll tell the captain I'm not standing watch with you anymore."

"I know I heard something."

"You know old Grimjaw likes to hunt around the docks at night. Probably caught himself a rat."

Avender hoped he was too big to interest Grimjaw. Then again, he was probably as invisible to any pike or turtle as he was to the sentries.

"All the same, I think we oughtta search these boats. And warn the guard as well. Captain! There's somethin' makin' noise out here."

Avender swam to the front of the pier as a squad filed out to check the alarm. This time he slipped slowly from the river, letting the water run down his clothes before finally scooting up and onto the quay as quickly as possible. The noise from the search covered his squelching footsteps as he crept along the wharf. In fact, with most of the watch scurrying around the docks, he was able to slip easily past the two guards left at the gate and into the town. Not that he would have been able to do any of it without Reiffen's spell.

He had to dodge quickly as he came out on the other side. Another line of guards was marching down the narrow lane toward the gate. As it was, one of them tripped over Avender's foot as Avender threw himself against a wall.

"Here, watch where you're goin'!"

"Watch yerself! Not my fault you fell down!"

Avender held his breath as the column filed past. Reiffen had told him he should reverse the spell as soon as he got inside the town, and here he'd nearly been caught already. As the end of the column disappeared through the gate, he crawled into the deepest shadow he could find and softly whispered, "See."

Hands, feet, and the rest of him reappeared. He examined himself for a moment, just to make certain nothing had changed in the time his body was gone, then started rapidly up the cobbled street. Around him the town was strangely silent, taverns locked, cats patrolling the lanes. Above the dark storefronts, shuttered windows leaked yellow lamplight. Unlike Backford, Rimwich seemed to have finished its preparations well before the battle. All that was left was the waiting.

He headed uphill, knowing he would reach the castle eventually as long as he kept climbing. Zigzagging through crooked alleys, he found a steep flight of steps that passed through a short, black tunnel where restless pigeons cooed against the ceiling like sleepless ghosts. Emerging at the top into the square outside the castle gate, he was challenged immediately.

"Halt!"

A young officer strode forward, followed by a pair of pikemen, their spears pointed straight at Avender's chest.

"Don't you know everyone's confined to quarters tonight? State your business!"

Relieved at no longer having to sneak around, Avender snapped to attention. "Avender of Valing, Lieutenant. I'm here with an important message for Redburr."

The lieutenant eyed him carefully, youthful curiosity contending with his sense of duty. "Avender of Valing? The Hero of the Stoneways? You don't look like a courier. What's the password? And where's your horse? Don't tell me you came all the way from Valing on foot."

"I haven't come from Valing." Avender decided the truth would make the most compelling story. Though he might have decided to trust Reiffen for the moment, it wouldn't be fair to expect others to make the same choice without hearing the facts. "Actually I'm from the northern army."

Astonished, the lieutenant stepped backward. The guards stepped forward, their spear points between Avender and their commander.

Avender eyed their spears warily. "I've been sent with a special message for the Oeinnen. I was captured at Backford, but before that I was with Redburr in the Waste. Since then I've been Oss-donc's prisoner."

"Ossdonc sent you with a message?"

"No. Reiffen sent me."

"Reiffen! The traitor?"

"Traitor or not," said Avender, "I think Redburr should see the message. He'll know what to do."

The spears pushed closer. The lieutenant, feeling his reputation might be injured were it to become known he had let his men-at-arms protect him from an unarmed and bedraggled spy, even if he was the Hero of the Stoneways, pushed the shafts aside.

"We'll see about that. If you really are Avender of Valing."

Walking briskly, Avender managed to stay between the officer and the spears as they escorted him into Rimwich Castle. Though the streets were deserted, inside there was plenty of activity. Torches blazed along the walls, thanes and barons talking in small clumps or sharpening swords beneath the light. Boys bounded in and out of the central keep, their faces flush with important errands. Hammer blows from the armorer's forge rang louder than the Banking axes on the other side of the river.

Sir Firnum met them at the entrance to the tower. His eyes narrowed as he recognized Avender, but he was looking at the officer when he spoke.

"Report."

The young lieutenant saluted. "We found this man outside the keep, Sir Firnum. He claims to be Avender of Valing, and that he brings a message from Reiffen."

"For Redburr," added Avender.

Reiffen's name had no effect on Sir Firnum. "Did he say how he got in?"

The young lieutenant blinked. "He didn't get in, sir. I stopped him outside the gate."

"Into the town, Lieutenant. Past the walls."

The young officer's back stiffened. "I—I didn't think to ask, sir. I thought I was only guarding the keep."

"And so you are." Sir Firnum waved the officer back to his post. "I'll take the prisoner from here."

"Well, Avender," he said when the lieutenant and his men had left. "How did you get past the walls?"

"I'd rather not say. Not until I've given my message to Redburr."

"That might prove harder than you think."

"Redburr isn't here?"

"Oh, he's here, all right. I think he's on the walls with Prince Brizen. But King Brannis commands in Rimwich, not the Oeinnen."

"Reiffen told me the message is for Redburr."

"Still defending your friend, I see, despite the army camped outside our walls."

"I won't defend him, Sir Firnum, but I have seen enough to make me wonder what he's up to. With any luck, Redburr will know what to do."

The officer led him into the main hall, a tall round room on the ground level of the central tower. Groups of men filled the chamber, half a dozen Dwarves among them. At the far end, the king sat on a simple wooden chair in the midst of a group of arguing thanes. Their discussion ceased as Sir Firnum led his prisoner to the foot of the dais. Avender's boots squeaked wetly on the stone floor.

"Avender of Valing," said Brannis in answer to the young man's bow. "Redburr told me he left you in the Waste. How have you come here?"

"I was captured at Backford, Your Majesty. Reiffen brought me with him. To bring Redburr a message."

"Redburr?" Brannis's face hardened. "Are Redburr and Reiffen in league, to send each other secret messages?"

"I came openly, Your Majesty. You can ask the officer at the gate."

"Did you? And how did you get past the outer walls?"

"He wouldn't say, sire," said Sir Firnum.

"Magic, perhaps?" mused the king. "I suppose Ossdonc cast a spell allowing you to fly."

"Actually, I was made invisible, Your Majesty." Avender thought it wisest not to mention by whom. "After that I swam around the wall. Your guards almost caught me sneaking in through the river gate, even though they couldn't see me."

Brannis turned to his captain. "Pass the word, Firnum. All sentries are to pay careful attention to anything that seems odd, no matter how innocent."

"Perhaps we should bring out the dogs as well, sire."

"Excellent suggestion. Do it."

Brannis held out his hand to his prisoner as Sir Firnum strode away. "Give me the message," he said.

"I'm supposed to give it to Redburr, Your Majesty."

"The Oeinnen is not here. I shall take it instead."

"I'm sorry, Your Majesty. I can't."

The king snapped a finger. Two guards seized Avender's arms, while a third quickly discovered the pouch in his shirt. Avender ignored them, watching stoically as Brannis extracted a slip of paper from the oiled bag. As he unrolled it, the king's eyes narrowed. He turned the page the other way and frowned.

Confronting Avender, he said, "Reiffen has chosen to communicate with his old friend in code. I cannot read it. What does it say?"

"I have no idea."

Brannis nodded to one of the guards; the guard cuffed Avender across the face. The king leaned forward, his eyes harsh. "Out with it, boy. We're at war. We need answers now, not childish loyalty. For all I know, Ossdonc has placed other spies in the city. What is on the paper?"

Avender stretched his jaw and wondered if there was a side he really wanted to be on in this war. "I told you. I don't know."

He braced himself for another blow, but Brannis was known for hardness, not cruelty. "Take him downstairs," the king told the guards. "And someone fetch the Oeinnen. At the very least he can explain why he and the traitor are exchanging coded messages."

His arms still pinned, the guards dragged Avender out of the hall. When he showed no inclination to fight, they allowed him to walk, though they kept their shoulders pressed tightly against his. Torches flickered against the smoky walls as they descended into the keep. Past a small guardroom where a pair of jailers talked quietly over their pots of beer, Avender's escort dumped him in a small cell and locked the heavy door behind him.

It wasn't that bad. Much better than the dungeons in Ussene. The cell had a cot and a candle, and what looked like a window narrowing up into the stone beneath the ceiling. Though it was too dark to see what lay at the other end, Avender thought he smelled fresh air.

The door opened and one of the jailers brought in a bowl of stew and a mug of ale. Not having eaten since his picnic on the hilltop with Reiffen that morning, Avender cleaned the bowl. Thin, like the ale, but hot.

He wondered what Brannis planned to do with him. Surely Redburr wouldn't let the king keep him languishing in the dungeon. Not without a chance of defending himself. He supposed it all depended on what was in Reiffen's note.

All the same, once his dinner was finished and time began to drag, he found he couldn't sit still. For a while he paced back and forth, his boot heels clicking on the stone. When he grew tired of that he stood on the foot of the bed and, pushing the candle as deeply as possible up the embrasure, tried to see outside. The flame flickered in a breeze Avender couldn't feel, which at least proved it was a window. With any luck, he'd never see the view.

Pacing again, he told himself he ought to pass the time thinking of useful things to tell Redburr. What did he remember about Ossdonc's army? How had they fought and who were their best captains? But Reiffen had kept him away from the soldiers and sissit most of the time they had been together, and he couldn't think of much to tell. He had to make sure the Dwarves knew about the nets, though. That was important.

He was beginning to wonder if Reiffen had some reason for wanting him stuck in a Rimwich cell when the door burst open and Redburr, his furry shoulders almost too wide for the doorway, shoved his way in.

"Come on, boy! We've wasted too much time already!"

"Where have you been? I've been waiting for hours."

"If you'd just given Brannis the letter when he asked for it, he wouldn't have tossed you in the dungeon."

"Reiffen told me to give the letter to you."

"Do you always do what the enemy tells you?"

"He hasn't been acting much like an enemy lately," replied Avender.

"Really? I'm sure Lady Breeanna would appreciate you telling her that. Though she might almost believe you after you nearly got yourself killed helping her escape."

"How could you possibly know that?"

"I'll tell you on the way."

The Shaper backed out of the cell, but he still filled the corridor beyond. Avender followed the bear's massive haunches to the guardroom, where Brizen was waiting for both of them.

The prince shook Avender's hand. "Please accept my apologies for my father's hastiness, but he has a great deal on his mind. And you were acting suspiciously."

"So Redburr tells me. What did the message say, anyway? Was it worth all this?"

Brizen glanced uneasily at the jailers, who pretended to study their beer.

"Not here," said the bear.

Prince and prisoner followed the Shaper up the stairs. Avender asked if Ferris was in Rimwich as well. The prince looked uncomfortably at the bear.

"We'll talk about it all as soon as we find someplace private," Redburr told them.

At the top of the stairs the Shaper led them away from the main hall and into the kitchens. Though it was after midnight, every pot and pan in the place seemed to be in use. Undercooks rushed back and forth with trays of bread and tubs of beans; half the animals that would normally have filled the pastures beyond the walls turned gently on spits before the fires. Avender's mouth watered despite his bowl of stew. One particularly enticing roast lay on a platter near the door. Putting his forepaws on the table like a giant dog, the Shaper seized the juicy morsel in his gaping jaws.

"Stop that!" A white-aproned chef Avender recognized only too well bustled forward, cleaver waving.

Redburr growled. The cook hesitated. "That is for the king," he declared.

"Tell my father I took it, Gridlin," said the prince. "The Oeinnen has my permission."

"But it's my best roast, Your Highness." An undercook dodged nimbly as his chief waved the cleaver in despair.

"That's probably why he took it," said Brizen as he followed Redburr and Avender out the door.

They found the courtyard even busier than the kitchen, but

everyone gave way before the bear, who led them to a small shed near the smithy and against the wall. Light from the forge revealed a litter of stolen jam jars and clawed wood, proving they had reached the Shaper's den. Next door the bellows roared; odd bits of iron gleamed in the shadows.

Avender sat on a wobbly barrel eyeing Redburr's stolen joint. "So what did the message say?" he demanded.

The bear dropped his roast in the dirt and placed a proprietary paw on top. "I thought you wanted to hear how I know about Breeanna."

"First I want to hear about the message."

Brizen leaned against the wall by the door. Redburr snapped a rib off the roast with a loud crack, the chop dangling down his chin.

"It said, 'Do not leave Rimwich tonight for any reason. I will meet you in the fields an hour after sunrise.'"

"You knew the code?"

"It wasn't a code. It was Dremen."

"My father had a merchant who deals with the Dremen read it to make sure," added Brizen.

"What was decided?"

"Against my better judgment we're doing what Reiffen asked." Bones crunched. The bear's long red tongue flickered as he licked the inside of a split rib.

"It was what we had already decided to do before the message, anyway," said Brizen.

"So you're going to trust him?"

"No." Redburr dropped the bone on the floor and pulled a second chop off the roast. "We'll meet him like he asks tomorrow. Then I'll kill him."

"What?" Avender started up from his barrel. "You can't do that. The least you can do is listen to what he has to say."

"There's no listening to wizards," growled the bear. "That's the worst thing you can do."

"I agreed with you, Avender," said Brizen. "But I was the only one. Redburr pointed out our best chance to slay Reiffen will be when we first meet him. One of the Dwarves will be with us, so he won't be able to use his magic. At least not on all of us."

"Yes," said Avender. "And after we kill him, your claim to the throne will be secure."

Brizen stiffened. "I expect Reiffen will slay some of us before we slay him, with or without magic. I may die as easily as anyone else."

"It's the only solution." Redburr looked Avender straight in the eye. "We discussed it all, years ago. Killing Reiffen is the only way to avert a civil war between Wayland and Banking. You agreed then—you can't change your mind now. Reiffen is no longer Reiffen, he's been with the Wizards too long."

"But that's not true." Avender's voice nearly broke with desperation. "You haven't spent time with him the way I have. He's not like Ossdonc at all. He's been trying to save lives, not murdering."

"You see what he lets you see, boy. There have been other killings in places besides Backford."

"What do you mean?"

"He killed Skimmer." The Shaper's voice hardened. "And a pup."

"I don't believe it."

Avender felt his world unraveling. To find out now that Reiffen was, if anything, even worse than he had first imagined, was too much. And after Avender had all but convinced himself that Reiffen had some secret plan to turn on the Wizards and save them all. "Why would he do that? The nokken have nothing to do with Brannis, or the Wizards."

"That's what makes it so cruel."

"Did you see it?"

"No." Redburr's low growl leaked like spilled wine across the floor.

"Then how can you be so sure it was him?"

"The nokken saw it. Do you think they were mistaken?"

Avender wanted to say he did, but knew that would be wrong. Reiffen hadn't been difficult to recognize, even after seven years. Taller and thinner in the face, he was still unmistakably Reiffen. The uncombed brown hair was the same, and the too-clever eyes.

"He threw fire at the pups," the bear went on. "Skimmer went over the gorge trying to save one. Ferris saw that."

"I saw him save Findle," Avender whispered, trying hard not to believe.

"He saved Findle," replied the bear, "because Usseis must have ordered him to."

Avender threw up his hands in frustration. "How do you know he saved Findle? You know about Lady Breeanna, you know about Findle. How is that possible?"

The bear ripped another bone from his roast. "I know about Lady Breeanna because I was there. I told you I would return to Backford. I just didn't get there in time to do anything but watch. I was almost directly overhead when you fell down the cliff."

"And he knows what happened to me because I told him."

Looking up, Avender found Findle standing in the doorway, his low figure blocking the glow of the forge.

23

The Fight at Rimwich

Redburr's eyes gleamed as Findle entered the shed.

"That's right," growled the Shaper. "I forgot to mention that part. Findle escaped. He's going to help us with Reiffen tomorrow."

"Escaped? How?" Avender stared in astonishment as the open bellows roared on the other side of the door. Orange sparks snapped at the night.

"The chains loosened when I hit the bottom of the pool," Findle explained. "After that, it was easy to work myself free."

Avender remembered how Reiffen had whispered something just before smashing the bottom of Findle's boat. Perhaps he had voiced a spell to loosen the Dwarf's chains. But why free Findle after killing Skimmer? It made no sense.

"Findle walked day and night to get here," said Brizen. "Right across Banking and West Wayland."

"Crossing the Great River was harder than I thought," the Dwarf confessed. "Some of those oldfish lurking on the bottom are plenty big. Still, it'll be a long time before I trust a boat again."

Avender, stunned by the news that Reiffen had killed Skimmer,

422 | S. C. BUTLER

nursed his grief while the others discussed their plans. Plainly, what the good Reiffen had done in the last few days was nothing compared to the evil. He had only been trying to win Avender over to his side. For all Avender knew, the whole scene with the Keeadini and the farmwife had been staged for his benefit. The tribesmen could easily have butchered the woman the moment he and Reiffen had ridden away. The same as Reiffen had murdered Skim.

The Dwarf's voice caught Avender's attention; Findle was asking if he should challenge Reiffen to single combat. "His magic won't affect me," the Bryddin said. "The rest of you can stay safe while I take care of him."

"Ossdonc would love a challenge," replied the bear. "But not Reiffen. He'll run. He knows honor's just for songs. Brannis has always been right about that. We have to all go for him at once if we're going to have a chance."

Findle patted his sword. "He'll never escape the three of us."

In that moment Avender made up his mind. Killing Skimmer outweighed everything else. Even if Reiffen managed to save Rimwich and slay all three Wizards, it would never make up for his murdering a friend.

"The four of us," he said, rising from his barrel. "A long time ago I promised Giserre I'd forget friendship if Reiffen ever stopped being himself. Killing Skimmer's proof of that for me. He might as well have murdered Ferris."

"I'm glad you think that way, boy." The bear's heavy growl rumbled through the shed. "Makes me think I haven't failed completely."

Brizen stirred uncomfortably. "I for one would welcome the opportunity to forgive Reiffen. But I suppose he's gone too far for that."

"Much too far." The bear's teeth snapped sharply on the last of his roast, grinding gristle and bone.

The decision made, Brizen and Findle left to take their places on the outer wall. Avender would have accompanied them, only the Shaper stopped him with a heavy paw.

"Not you, boy. You look like you could use some sleep."

"Do you think Brizen will sleep tonight?" Avender protested.

"Brannis will see to it that Brizen gets a few hours' rest. Besides, I want you to tell me everything you can about Reiffen. The more I know about what he can and can't do, the better chance we have to defeat him."

Wearily Avender slumped back down on his barrel. His first surge of horror at Skimmer's death had ebbed; body and soul, he was exhausted. "I have no idea what he can't do," he said. "As far as I can tell, he can do anything. Summon storms, heal wounds, make people invisible. He offered to teach it all to me, too. But how he can think anyone can ever trust him after killing Skimmer . . ."

His tale broken up by yawns, he told Redburr everything that had happened since first waking in the tent by Backford Pool. For once the Shaper listened without interrupting, asking no questions and leaving Avender to longer and longer silences as the young man tried to remember every last detail. With each pause Avender fought harder to stay awake.

His chin dropped to his chest; the hammer blows from the smithy grew soothing as far-off thunder. "For a while tonight I thought it was going to be like the old days," he mumbled. "I was sure Reiffen had found a way to turn the tables on the Three."

"No one turns the tables on Wizards," said the bear.

More anvil blows woke them before dawn, the weary men still hard at work in the red glow of the forge. Darkness lay close about the rest of the keep, though from the courtyard the sky did appear lighter than the ground.

They saw no one on the streets except a company of the city guard, but there was more activity at the gate. Torches burned low along the walls to keep the light hidden from the Wizard's sharp eyes and expert aim. Above the massive wooden doors, two large caldrons squatted over a bed of glowing coals. Stones lay stacked close to the bottom of the wall, slings and cranes ready to hoist the rocks up to the parapet as soon as they were needed.

Brannis, Brizen, and Findle stood on the wall to the side of the gate, away from the heat of the fires. The slick scent of oil filtered the air, reminding Avender of Hern and Ferris cooking sinkers. It occurred to him that, however angry he might be with Reiffen, Ferris's disappointment would be worse. Her faith in their friend had remained undimmed.

Rearing massively on his hind legs, Redburr leaned on the wall beside the king, an arm's length taller than everyone else. "They've let their fires go out," he said, squinting at the shadows in the blackened fields.

"That began in the middle watches of the night," answered Brizen. His father wore a thick cloak against the early chill, but Brizen's back was bare of any covering other than his armor.

"No doubt they wanted to hide their movements," said the king.

"I still think we should send out a patrol," urged Findle.

"Not until there is light enough to see."

"Reiffen's message said to wait till an hour after dawn," Brizen reminded his father.

"We'll leave earlier than that," said Redburr.

Brizen turned to Avender. "There was a lot of coughing out there last night, but most of it stopped an hour or so ago. Was much of the army ill when you left?"

"Yes," Avender answered. "Maybe Reiffen's cured everybody's colds the way he healed my wound."

An officer appeared at the king's shoulder. "Sire, the cooks are ready. Shall I start sending the men to breakfast?"

"Yes, Captain. Start at the gate and work outward from there.

I want the fresh troops here first, where an attack is most likely to
occur."

Beyond the wall the gray dawn lifted to reveal a mist rolling
in from the river, but the inland fields remained clear. Dark lumps
speckled the burnt ground in the uncertain light.

"Where are their pickets?" asked Avender.

"I can't see that far." Screwing up his weak eyes, the Shaper
leaned farther over the parapet.

Concerned, the king glanced toward the river. "You're right.
They must be using the fog to mask some movement on the water. Brizen, go to the north wall and check with Sir Firnum. Make
certain the river guard remains alert."

The prince hurried off. In the east, the day's first color spread
from sky to ground. A songbird called from a lemon tree on the
terrace of a house behind the wall.

"I still don't see anything," said Avender.

"Nor I," agreed the king.

The charred fields, however, looked much more uneven than
they had the day before. The number of lumps thickened the farther they stretched from the wall.

Brizen came running back, his hand on his sword to keep
from tripping on the scabbard.

"Corpses, sire," he called, before he even reached his father.
"Dozens of corpses are floating in the river."

"Corpses?"

Avender realized at once that was what the lumps in the field
were as well. His gorge rose, though all he smelled was oil.
"Don't you see?" He swept an arm along the view. A large black
crow was already hopping toward one of the limp piles. "Those
black mounds on the ground, they're the pickets. And behind
them it looks like more."

"Of course." Brizen moved to the wall beside him. "Nothing's moving out there at all."

"I still can't see a thing." Redburr sniffed the air. "Can't smell anything, either. The breeze is wrong."

Findle shrugged. "Don't ask me what I think. We Bryddin have eyes for short work, not distance."

"Has there been a quarrel in Ossdonc's camp?" wondered the king. "Sissit and men at each other's throats?"

"Maybe Gerrit isn't a traitor at all." Brizen studied the mist. "Maybe he crossed the river and slew them in the night."

"We would have heard any fighting," said the Shaper. "This is something else entirely."

"Reiffen?" suggested Avender bitterly. Skimmer was still dead, after all. "Some new trick?"

"He has shown a penchant for murder," the bear agreed.

"This strikes me as more the work of a hero," said Brizen. "Those are our enemies lying dead out there."

More crows settled on the ground. No one shooed them away. A few pecked at specks of grain in the blackened grass, hopeful of better to come. Still more flew down from the trees.

Findle slid off the top of the wall to stand beside the others. "No more waiting. Who'll go with me, or shall I go alone?"

The king raised his eyebrows. "I will give the orders, Sir Findle."

Findle snorted. "It's not a matter of orders, Your Majesty, but speed."

"I agree." Redburr dropped back to all fours. "I can't see anything from up here, anyway."

"I'll go," said the prince.

"And I," said Avender.

Brannis scanned the fields one more time. Except for the mist along the river, the view was clear. "What about Ossdonc?"

"He'll show up eventually," said Redburr. "Whether he has an army or not."

The king turned to his son. "If the Wizard appears, return at once."

"I shall not be shepherded, Father. I carry one of the heart-stone blades, after all."

"It is not shepherding to be cautious in the face of a Wizard, Prince." Redburr turned back to the stone stair. "Brannis, make them open the post-door so we can leave."

Calling out the order, the king accompanied them to the gate. For a moment it appeared the small door inside the larger portal was too narrow for the Shaper, but with a final, determined grunt, Redburr squeezed through. Brannis embraced his son, then let him go. Avender and Findle followed, paying no attention to the clumps of reddish-brown fur caught in the wooden frame.

With Redburr leading, they entered the outer town. Smoke curled from the blackened beams of the ruined houses, the stench of burning much stronger than it had been from the walls. Behind them every archer on the parapet had an arrow at the ready, but no one challenged them. In the fields nothing moved but the crows.

Leaving the road, Redburr guided them across the burnt ground straight toward the closest body. Avender grew aware of a low, buzzing hum.

"Approach no closer."

The company stopped. A man stood to their right, a dark cloak covering him from head to toe. At the sound of his voice the buzzing thickened and a swarm of flies rose briefly from the nearest corpse. Findle and Brizen placed their hands on the hilts of their swords. Avender felt the Shaper tense beside him.

"Do not attack me, Redburr," said the stranger. "It is your death if you do. The same as Ossdonc's army's."

"It's Reiffen," said Avender. Strangely, he felt no fear as he recognized his old friend, though he knew at once all this death was the young wizard's doing. His anger surged.

Redburr raised a paw to take another step.

Reiffen's face remained hidden beneath his hood. "You will die if you come any closer," he repeated. "Whether you kill me or not. Better I should go to you."

"That will certainly make it easier," answered the bear.

"Safer, as well. But perhaps you will not want to kill me once you hear what I have to say."

His boots crunching on the seared earth, Reiffen approached. His hands he kept hidden within his sleeves.

"Show yourself," Redburr demanded.

Reiffen pulled back the hood of his cloak. Dark circles drained his eyes, and his brown hair stood stiff as the half-burned straw in the meadow. A far cry from a triumphant king, he looked more like a half-mad village fool.

"What is it that is so dangerous?" asked Brizen.

"The bodies of the men and sissit I have killed."

"Why should bodies be dangerous?"

"Have you ever heard of plague?"

His face ashen, Brizen took two or three quick steps backward. Growling in anger, Redburr also retreated. Only Avender, who felt oddly confident Reiffen had kept them far enough from danger, and Findle, who had never been sick a day in his life, remained where they were.

"Do not worry. I stopped you with room to spare." Reaching slowly into his cloak, Reiffen pulled out a small flask. Avender recognized it as the one he had drunk from the day before. "One sip of this and you will be safe, if you really think it necessary to examine the bodies of the dead."

Brizen's eyes narrowed. "Can we afford to trust you, Reiffen?"

"Not that I want to vouch for him, but I drank from that flask yesterday and feel fine." Avender took a step toward the closest corpse. "I'm guessing it's safe for me to look?"

Reiffen nodded.

Redburr's eyes glittered warily. "Be careful, Avender. Ossdonc is still about. Reiffen, you can't believe your poison had any effect on the Wizard."

"Of course not."

"Then where is he?"

"Sleeping. His evening was most entertaining. But he will be up and about soon, though we are not yet in any danger. We will hear him long before we see him."

Avender looked back; the Shaper signaled his consent. Findle followed as the young man advanced toward the nearest body.

"Tell us plainly what you've done."

Reiffen answered Redburr across the ruined ground. "I have brought sickness to Ossdonc's camp. Every sissit and human has died. And the dogs. Crows and flies are the only survivors."

Avender hesitated when he reached the corpse, but Findle poked it with his foot. Flies rose in a hazy shroud; the dead flesh sagged backward. Black scabs covered the face, a bloody crust coated chin and tunic. Avender's stomach rolled. He had seen dead men before, but there was something unnatural about this one, something wrong, almost as if the poor soul, however bad he had been in life, had suffered far more than he deserved before he died. No wonder Reiffen looked so ghastly. To do this to so many must have been horrible.

Not that that had stopped Reiffen from doing it.

"You did all this with a spell?" Redburr wagged his massive head in the direction of the feasting crows.

"A number of spells, actually. You saw what it was like at Backford. All that waste. Women and children killed. This struck me as a much better way. There are no innocents among these dead."

A shout rose from the forest, the crowing of an enormous rooster still delighted with his world. Avender retreated back to

Redburr and Brizen, his eyes on Reiffen, who gazed coolly toward the woods before joining them. Findle remained beside the body, flicking flies from the air with nimble fingers.

"Let's get back to Rimwich," said Redburr to his companions. "Ossdonc will be in a rare temper now, and we've lost our chance with this one."

"Now is not the time to leave," Reiffen replied. "You can deal with me later. When the Black Wizard loses his temper, that will be the best time to deal with him. Much the same as you, Redburr, when you are taken with the blood rage."

"Well, I'm not in one now. And I don't particularly want to get myself into one if it's only going to get me killed."

Reiffen's eyes gleamed, much as they had when he had offered to teach Avender magic. "We may never have a chance like this again, Redburr. Believe me, Wizards are a lot easier to handle one at a time."

"I'll stay," said Findle. "Fighting the Wizard is what I came for."

Brizen looked uneasily at the bear. "I would not want it said we left our companions to face the Black One alone."

Redburr stared hard at Reiffen before making up his mind. "You still have to answer for Skimmer and the pup, boy. No matter how many Wizards you kill."

"I know."

Avender's eyes blazed. "I'll always hate you," he said.

"I know that, too."

"Ferris will hate you even more."

Reiffen's jaw tightened.

"Here now," said Brizen. "There's no need to bring Ferris into this. I'm sure she'll let us know what she thinks in due time."

Reiffen's glare shifted to the prince. "As if you could ever know what Ferris might do."

Redburr growled. "It's not Ferris we're fighting about, boys. It's the Wizard. Reiffen, I assume you have a plan?"

"Yes. Stay out of the way until I cast my spell. Once Ossdonc is stunned, there will be a short moment before he recovers. Strike him then, before he gets back to his feet. Otherwise some of us are going to die."

Avender hoped it would be Reiffen. Though, with the rest of them doing the close-in fighting, that was probably the least likely result. Maybe it would be better if he hoped he died himself. At least then he wouldn't have to listen to the cheers Reiffen would undoubtedly receive as the savior of Rimwich if they won. Outside of Valing, no one was going to care much about what had happened to Skimmer.

He raised his sword solemnly, unable to resist declaring whom it was he might be dying for.

"For Ferris," he said.

"For Ferris," Reiffen and Brizen replied.

The Wizard emerged from the forest, dark as storms.

"He's normal-sized." Brizen lowered his weapon in surprise.

"Last night's pleasure required it," said Reiffen.

The prince's face crinkled, then turned to a frown as he understood Reiffen's meaning. "How soon before he changes back?"

"I believe he'll change as soon as he understands what has happened. It won't be long."

A second shout shattered the morning as Ossdonc discovered the wreck of his army. Every crow in the fields leapt for the sky.

"Reiffen!"

"I am here." Like birdsong, Reiffen's voice piped in reply.

Ossdonc raced forward, his figure growing. Trumpets rang out from the Rimwich wall.

"The king sounds the recall," said Brizen, bracing himself for the Wizard's attack.

"Go back," said Redburr. "No one will blame you for obeying the king's command."

"No one will blame me if I don't, either."

The earth trembled. The Wizard was nearly upon them, tall as a tree, wild as a boar. Arms lifted, Reiffen began his spell, his thin hands protruding like claws from the sleeves of his cloak. Avender and Brizen raised their swords. Avender recalled how useless his weapons had been the last time he fought the Black Wizard. At least Brizen and Findle had heartstone blades.

The Dwarf darted forward.

Reiffen's chanting faltered. Redburr snarled. "Cast your spell, boy—now! The Bryddin won't be affected."

"He's blocking my target."

Findle charged across the blackened field, much faster than Avender had ever seen a Dwarf run before. When he was directly in Ossdonc's path he halted, both hands thrust before him.

"Stop! I, Findle of Smales, challenge you to trial by combat! Let the blood of Nurren's murder be washed clean in my stone blade!"

Much to Avender's surprise, Ossdonc stopped, his boots carving great swaths in the burnt earth. Flecks of glee graced the corners of his eyes, and he made a great show of putting his hands on his waist and peering down at the Dwarf as if at an ant.

"A challenge, little one?" Throwing back his head, the Wizard laughed. The crows, who had settled in the nearer trees, left the field for good.

"You have to understand," answered the Dwarf, "I've never done this before. Manders and rock eels don't require challenging. I hope I followed the rules."

Ossdonc's leer broadened. "You have done well, Dwarf. And I see by your presence that Reiffen's treachery has been long planned."

"I freed myself, if that's what you mean. Reiffen had nothing to do with it."

"I doubt that. You Dwarves are an arrogant kind. I look forward to your comeuppance."

The bear called loudly to the two dissimilar figures standing alone in the field. "Yes, that would be something, Wizard, you slaughtering somebody five times smaller than yourself."

From the side of his mouth he added in a whisper to the humans beside him, "Reiffen, think of something. I'll stall him as long as I can."

Ossdonc looked over Findle toward the Shaper. "Patience, bear. After all these years, your time has finally come. Surely you can wait a minute longer."

"I have no intention of waiting any longer than I have to. When you're done I'm going to flee as fast as I can. I'm as old as you, remember, and I didn't get that way by taking foolish chances. But I had thought you might find the sport more amusing if you returned to human size. At the very least, it might last an extra minute or two."

Findle brandished his thin sword. "The Wizard must not reduce himself in any way. These contests are supposed to be fair, you know."

"Bravely spoken, Dwarf. You heard the challenge, bear. Far be it for me to deny this small one the death he wishes. I advise you to start running now and find yourself a deep hole to crawl into, or I shall be sure to find you."

Certain Reiffen was stalling deliberately, Avender grabbed him roughly by the shoulder. "Do something!"

Reiffen eyed his old friend coldly. "There's nothing I can do. The magic won't work correctly around a Dwarf. Findle will have to take his chance. Whatever you do, don't join him. With the rest of you out there, I'll never get a clear shot."

"If Findle dies, that's one more on your head."

"Fair enough." Reiffen straightened his cloak after Avender had let him go.

A second round of trumpets blared from the walls of the city, different from the first. "My father sends a sortie," said Brizen in a low voice. "Soon the odds will be in our favor."

"If the five of us fail to kill the Wizard," answered Reiffen, "no number of Wayland knights will do the trick."

"Then I suppose we have found ourselves in a song after all," said the prince.

Ossdonc drew his black sword. "On your guard, small thing. I have more work to do when I finish with you."

Next to the Wizard, Findle looked like a child about to receive a lesson in swordsmanship from his father. None of his companions believed the Dwarf had a chance. How could he, when he was one-third the size of his enemy and had only known of swords and swordsmanship for twenty years? Ossdonc had easily defeated Nolo years ago at the henge, and Nolo was larger than Findle.

Grinning, Ossdonc sliced at the Dwarf's head. Findle dodged easily, more nimbly than Nolo could have managed, and the Wizard's sword smote the ground. The earth shook. With a quick lunge Findle buried the point of his blade in the Wizard's wrist. Ossdonc grimaced and backed away, a crimson bracelet dribbling down his arm.

"The Inach makes you bold, small one," he declared. "Too bold, perhaps."

He swung his blade in a great, slashing arc, almost too fast to see. Findle ducked beneath the sweeping sword, but this time the Wizard had anticipated the move. At the last minute, with unbelievable strength, he dipped his blade. The sword caught Findle on the chin, knocking him backward and spinning him to the ground. Avender's heart rushed to his throat as Ossdonc cut savagely at his fallen opponent; he expected to see Findle shatter into a thousand pieces, but at the last minute the Dwarf managed to raise his own weapon to deflect the Wizard's blow. Once more Ossdonc buried his sword in the earth, deeper this time than the first. Iron rang against buried rock; Findle rolled to his feet and stabbed Ossdonc deeply behind the knee.

The Wizard went blind with rage. Blow after blow rained on the Dwarf, but somehow Findle caught them all, bearing the force with a wrist as strong as Inach. Sparks flashed above his head with every stroke. The clashing blades rang.

Hoofbeats thudded from behind. Brannis, accompanied by a squad of cavalry, halted beside his son. Half a dozen Dwarves lagged behind on stubby legs, still only halfway from the castle.

"What is going on here?" the king demanded.

"A matter of honor," said Reiffen without turning around.

"And who might you be?" inquired the king as another round of blows crashed across the field.

"That's Reiffen, Father."

"Reiffen!"

"Quiet," growled Redburr.

The fury of his attack spent, Ossdonc stepped back to catch his breath. Reiffen raised his arms to cast his spell. Findle, however, wouldn't let the Wizard rest, and sprang forward like a terrier worrying a boar. Scowling, Reiffen stopped his magic a second time. Grimly now, without boasting, the Wizard blocked the Bryddin's cuts. Bloody streaks appeared on his arms and legs, showing he couldn't stop them all. All the same, Findle was too small to press the Wizard as fiercely as the Wizard had pressed him. Realizing this, the savage brightness returned to the Wizard's dark eyes. His sword strokes became more careful. Clearly he was gathering himself for another rush. But once again Ossdonc's impetuosity was nearly his undoing. Findle ducked inside the Wizard's thrust and stabbed him deeply in the thigh, the Dwarf's sword point once again finding the gaps in the Wizard's armor.

This time Ossdonc didn't lose his temper. Punching his other knee forward, he caught Findle full in the chest. The Dwarf flew backward, but even as he was in the air Ossdonc swatted him with his empty hand. Once again Findle spun across the ground. Ossdonc fell on him immediately, beating Findle's head and shoulders with great blows before the Dwarf could regain his feet. Findle had fought boldly, and far more successfully than anyone had believed possible, but the end had plainly come. Each attack drove the Dwarf deeper into the ground, until he disappeared completely into the earth. Black dirt sprayed across the sky.

Reiffen began his casting a third time.

A dog barked from the wall. War horns called from across the river. Kneeling on the ground, Ossdonc raised his sword with both hands and brought it down with one last crushing blow, as if to rend the earth. A loud crack burst from the ground, the sound of stone breaking. Ossdonc struggled to his feet.

Six Bryddin rushed through Brannis's troop toward the Black Wizard as Reiffen finished his spell. Three bolts of lightning flashed from his fingers, striking the Bryddin as they darted awkwardly into the way. Five of the six fell like tenpins. The sixth stopped when he realized he was the only one still standing.

Laughing, Ossdonc plucked a stone from the pouch at his side. Avender ducked, remembering what had happened the last time he had seen the Wizard throwing stones.

"Wide," said Reiffen, not flinching. The stone sped past his ear.

Ossdonc laughed again. "You will have no further chance for spells, traitor. Drop your guard for a moment and I shall kill you." The Wizard turned his attention to the Dwarves, who were groggily picking themselves up off the ground. Avender wondered how the magic had been able to affect them at all. "As for you, small things, your brother lies in the earth, where I have planted him. Perhaps fresh stones will grow to take his place, since you can raise no new ones of your own. Come, let me bury the rest of you beside him."

The Wizard took a step forward. As he did so a small hand reached up from the ground to grasp his boot. Like a man stumbling over a root, the giant toppled. Findle crawled out of his grave. Clumps of dirt fell from his shoulders as he raised his sword and thrust it full into the back of Ossdonc's neck. The Black Wizard writhed; his feet beat against the ground. Findle's fellows stumbled up to help him, but there was nothing more to be done. The Wizard was dead. His spasms passed as a cold wind swept from south to north across the land.

Avender stared in disbelief. Humans and Dwarves shouted with joy. Reiffen's entreaties to keep back from the blackened dead were buried beneath their gladness.

"We thought you were broken," said one of the Dwarves to Findle as the tumult began to ebb.

"That's what I wanted Ossdonc to think." Dark wetness seeped slowly from the gouges on Findle's head and shoulders, but he paid it no mind. "He pounded me so deep he couldn't see what he was doing anymore. So I pulled a rock out of the ground and held it up as a shield. That's what broke."

Avender felt a hand on his shoulder and turned to see Reiffen still looking grim.

"We have to go."

"Go? Why would I go anywhere with you? I wish you'd died with the Wizard."

"Giserre is in danger."

"Giserre?" Being angry with Reiffen was one thing, but Giserre was another matter entirely. "Where?"

"In Ussene."

Avender's hands went cold. "How will we get there?"

"Get where?" Elated by the Wizard's defeat, Brizen beamed over Reiffen's shoulder. As Avender had expected, the prince had forgotten all about Skimmer. "What are you two talking about?"

"There are other Wizards yet to kill, cousin," answered Reiffen.

"Tell your father not to be too harsh on Prince Gerrit and the others on the far side of the river. It was me they joined, not Ossdonc. Besides, your father will need their help to drive the Keeadini from Banking. Give him this." He pulled a parchment from his cloak. "With this abjuration I renounce all claims to the thrones of both Banking and Wayland. Some day they'll be yours. I'm in too much of a hurry to stay."

Brizen's delight was replaced with confusion, though he held in his hand what should have delighted him even more.

Another voice, deeper and gruffer, growled at Reiffen's back. "I don't suppose that's it for the day, is it? What else do you have in mind, boy?"

"We're going to Ussene."

"So I guessed. Can your magic take me as well?"

"I think so. Though I've never tried with three."

"Let's see what happens. But remember, you're not out of the woods yet."

"What about me?" Disappointment creased Prince Brizen's face as he realized Reiffen meant to leave without him. "I also have the means of killing Wizards." Shoving Reiffen's proclamation awkwardly under his arm, he half pulled his Inach sword from its sheath.

"You have to stay and help your father." Reiffen spoke patiently, despite his hurry to get away. "He'll need you more than we will, even if you manage to avoid fighting Prince Gerrit. And make sure you and every man out here drinks from this flask before you return to town. It will be safe to walk these fields this evening, but until then keep everyone inside." Reiffen pressed the small flask he had shown them earlier into Brizen's hand. "Lastly," he went on, "I would consider it a great honor if you would allow me to borrow your sword, Your Highness."

Somewhat crestfallen that his sword was needed rather than

himself, Brizen handed over the blade. Bowing, Reiffen accepted the gift.

"Now then," he began. "Avender, I need you and Redburr to grasp my arms."

Reluctantly, Avender did as he was told. Things were moving too fast for thinking now. If only Reiffen hadn't murdered Skimmer, everything would be perfect. But he had, which meant, for Avender at least, that everything was worse instead of better. A murdering hero would be much harder to deal with than a murdering villain.

His yellow teeth bared, Redburr took Reiffen's other arm in his mouth. Avender found some satisfaction in the notion that, at the first sign of treachery, the Shaper would probably tear Reiffen's arm off at the shoulder. Reaching the arm Avender was holding across to the other, Reiffen took hold of the thimble in his right hand. "Return," he said simply, pulling the hard iron from his finger.

"So that's how it's done," mumbled Redburr through Reiffen's sleeve as the world disappeared around them.

24

Reiffen's Workshop

he moment the Gray Wizard took Ferris's arm, Giserre's bedroom vanished. There wasn't even time to scream. Instead, she found herself in the middle of an enormous, gloomy hall ringed by tall columns. Fornoch stood beside her at the bottom of a raised dais, a long stone bench at the top. Each step leading up to it was higher than her knees.

The Wizard regarded her with his all-dark eyes. Though her heart pounded terribly, Ferris returned his gaze, determined to show no fear. She wondered if Reiffen would come to gloat over her before she died.

"Who are you?" asked Fornoch, his voice as warm as steaming tea. "How have you come here? Through the chimneys, it would appear."

Ferris tilted her chin higher, but it was hard to look Fornoch in the eye when she couldn't find a pupil in all that blackness. "My name is Ferris."

"Ferris of Valing? Reiffen's lady love, come to rescue him a second time? Or have you finally thrown him over in favor of one of your other suitors?"

"I haven't thrown anyone over. Reiffen did that himself."

Though his eyes remained expressionless, a hint of sympathy peeked out at the corners of Fornoch's massive mouth. "Quite right," he said. "Your loyalty deserved far better. But it was necessary for Reiffen's education to make certain he cut himself off from everything he held dear. Murdering Molio was not enough."

Ferris had no idea who Molio was, but the knowledge that Reiffen had murdered more than nokken during his time in Ussene chilled her. She no longer knew him at all.

Fornoch went on in his low, soothing tone. "If you have come to rescue him again, I am afraid this time he would not have gone with you."

The fact the Wizard didn't know everything helped Ferris regain some of her courage. "We weren't rescuing Reiffen," she said rashly. "We were rescuing Giserre."

"Giserre? How interesting. All these years, and suddenly fresh interest in Giserre? Surely she prefers to remain with her son. What danger could possibly threaten Giserre as long as Reiffen is close at hand?"

"More than you'll—"

Ferris closed her mouth abruptly, realizing she had already said too much. Fornoch, with his soft words and pretended sympathy, had nearly gotten her to admit that Giserre, and all of Ussene, faced utter ruin. Clamping her jaw tight, she determined not to say another word.

Fornoch nodded, understanding everything. "Very well then. You need say nothing more, if that is your wish. But I hope you will excuse me if I leave you alone while I inspect the fortress for other signs of intrusion. I do not expect you have come all this way alone."

Bowing, the Wizard was gone. Ferris waved her hand through

the empty air, then looked around the room. A low gallery circled the hall behind the columns, reminding her of a similar chamber she and her friends had passed through deep in the dungeons seven years before. A fine, pale light drifted down from a ceiling too far away to see.

Doubting very much the Gray Wizard had left her a means of escape, Ferris began searching along the gallery for a door. Eventually she came to a pair of massive iron portals that, unfortunately, no amount of pushing or frustrated kicking could persuade to open. Time was rapidly running out and, if she didn't find an exit soon, her fate would be the same as everyone else's in Ussene.

She circled the room, but there were no other doors. Hope crushed, she slumped against the iron gates and decided she really had reached the end. Pressing her palms against the smooth stone, she felt for some faint sign of the Dwarves' labor far below, but the floor was still. The stone was as dead as she soon would be.

The doors boomed behind her. Before Ferris could think to hide behind one of the pillars, a small, stocky form appeared in the middle of the exit.

"Nolo!" She threw herself into the Dwarf's arms, bruising her hip and shoulder. Tears sprang to her eyes, but not from pain.

"Enough, lass. It may already be too late."

"But how did you find me?"

"A sissit told me where the Three like to bring their new prisoners. It was a lucky chance I ran into him."

Seizing the Dwarf's hand, Ferris felt something wet and sticky across the back of his knuckles.

"Let's go," she said.

He led her back through the doors. A soldier lay crumpled on the other side. Beyond him stretched a long corridor. Dwarf and human hurried to the far end. They had covered nearly half the distance when a gray shape appeared out of the air before them.

Nolo pulled up short. "The other way, lass! I'll hold him off while you escape."

"But there's no other way out!"

"Then go back anyway. I'll fight him better without you around to worry about."

Fornoch's calm voice filled the hall. "There is no need to fight, Bryddin. Your brethren are nearly finished. I find myself powerless to stop them."

"Then save yourself and let us do the same."

"I fear there is not time enough for you to do that." The Wizard's gray robes flowed across the floor as he approached. "The nearest exit is too far for you to reach. I, on the other hand, can easily save your friend. You, my magic cannot help."

Shouting defiance, Nolo swung his mallet. Fornoch dodged easily. Instead of bothering to strike a blow in return, he reached out a long arm and grabbed Ferris by the shoulder. Nolo swung blindly at the sound of Ferris's pained cry, catching the Wizard in the side. Fornoch grunted, but still didn't fight back. Something dropped from his robe and rolled across the floor: an egg-shaped stone as large as the Dwarf's head.

The floor opened. Walls and ceiling shook. Ferris drowned in crashing sound. Showers of dust and fine stone cascaded around them as the fortress began to fall apart. Desperately Nolo lunged for the edge as he dropped into the sudden chasm. His fingers dug into the rock. Another crevice gaped as a second shudder shook the hall. Clinging tightly to his chunk of falling stone, Nolo disappeared into the dark smoke below. The Wizard's egg-shaped rock tumbled in beside him.

Once again the room disappeared. Ferris caught a last glimpse of stones crashing down from the ceiling and fresh cracks opening in the floor before the Wizard whisked her away once more.

Mindrell replaced the mirror in his pocket and absently fingered the thimble on his left hand. His instructions were clear. Reiffen expected to return to Ussene by early morning and wanted his mother and Mindrell to be ready for him in the apartment.

The bard called to the sleeper lying on her pallet beside the dull glow of the hearth. "Spit. Wake your mistress."

Yawning, the slave rose and did as she was told. Mindrell lowered his eyes as Giserre appeared at her door, though his first instinct was to stare openly. Never did Giserre look more lovely than when her long dark hair was draped loosely around her shoulders in the morning.

"Have you heard from Reiffen?" she asked.

The bard nodded. "He plans to return in the second hour after sunrise and wants us ready to meet him."

He was toasting bread at the hearth when Giserre returned, dressed and gripping her healing satchels in her hands. Spit had already gone off to start her morning chores.

"No time for breakfast," commanded the lady. "I have to make sure the last batch of medicine gets Downstairs. I knew we should have done this last night."

Deftly Mindrell plucked his half-cooked slice of bread from the toasting fork and tucked it in his pocket. "If I might suggest, milady, it might be better to wait here. What if Reiffen returns early?"

"This must be done first. We still have plenty of time. We shall be back before Spit has even finished the mopping."

Bowing, Mindrell made no further argument. Giserre accepted his presence much more easily when he did as he was told. Hefting the heavier of the two bags, he followed her out the door.

They were on their way back to the upper levels, their satchels empty, when Spit found them.

"Mistress!" The poor woman collapsed miserably in the filth in the passage as she threw herself at Giserre's feet. "Save me! Save us all!"

"Save you?" Pulling her skirts out of Spit's grasp, Giserre glanced quickly at Mindrell. "What is there to save you from? All the soldiers are gone."

"An avalanche!" The poor woman scrabbled forward till she was clutching Giserre's ankles once more. "Snow and ice! It's going to bury us all!"

"Snow and ice? Calm down, woman." Giserre lifted Spit to her feet. "This is summer. There is no snow. Nor avalanches."

"But that's what the woman said, my lady!"

"Please, Spit. What woman? And why would you believe her?"

Her hands trembling like leaves, Spit made some effort to do as her mistress asked. She pushed her hair back from her face and rubbed her fingers across her eyes.

"A terrible creature, milady, covered in black like Him! And her face and hands as black as her clothes!"

"Who was she?"

Spit shrugged.

"Where did she come from?"

Spit shrugged again.

Giserre pursed her mouth impatiently. "What, exactly, did this woman in black tell you?"

"That the fortress is going to be destroyed in a terrible avalanche and everyone has to get away. And she wants you, milady, to come meet her first. In the sitting room."

It was Giserre's turn to be surprised. "Meet her! Why?"

"She didn't say, ma'am. Only that you should hurry."

"A trick, my lady." Mindrell turned to the servant. "Did this woman in black mention Reiffen?"

Spit shook her head.

The bard rubbed his thimble. "Wild talk of the fortress being destroyed, counsel that's the opposite of what Reiffen gave me an hour ago. I think it's time to follow the course Reiffen set out if I ever thought you were threatened."

"I agree," said Giserre.

Mindrell held up his little finger. "I don't know where this will take us, but Reiffen assured me no one could follow."

"Can I come?" asked Spit.

"Of course," Giserre assured her.

"I have to warn the slaves first." Spit set her mouth firmly as she spoke, in a way Mindrell thought she had learned from her mistress. "The woman told me to do that."

"What this woman told you is most likely false," said Giserre. "You might not return to us in time."

"I can't let myself be afraid, my lady, not if there's any chance I can help my old friends. You taught me that."

"Go then. But know we cannot wait long."

Dropping a quick curtsy, the servant vanished down the dim passage. Mindrell wasn't sorry to see her go. She would have made an uncomfortable encumbrance, and Giserre would have insisted he guard her as fully as herself.

"She won't make it back, you know," he said.

Giserre laid her hand on his arm. "We can wait a little while."

"Can we? What if the White Wizard catches us? Reiffen won't be happy if I fail." He clasped the hand on his arm with his own.

Giserre withdrew her touch. Mindrell waited beside her, his nervousness growing. The dark minutes crept along. Finally he said, "My lady, I must insist. Your danger increases with every moment."

Frowning, she returned her hand to his arm. Fatigue and worry faulted the corners of her mouth. Mindrell took the little finger of his left hand in his right.

"I would we could have saved her," she said.

"Return," he answered, removing the thimble as Reiffen had taught him.

Avender ducked as a roof replaced the sky. The black fields disappeared, and Ossdonc's body as well. On the other side of Reiffen, Redburr's fur stuck straight out the way it sometimes did just before a thunderstorm.

They stood in a woman's bedroom, the three of them crowding the stone chamber tightly. Avender recognized the needlework on the pillows as Giserre's.

Frowning, Reiffen poked his head out the door into the next room. "Giserre was supposed to meet me here."

"Well, there's no time to look for her." Redburr sniffed underneath the bed.

"Why not?"

"This place isn't safe."

"We knew that before we came," said Avender.

"I'm not talking about Wizards, boy. Nolo and the Bryddin have mined the bottom out from under the fortress. For all I know they're about to bring it down around our heads right now."

Reiffen broke into a smile. "Really? That will save me a lot of trouble. I hadn't expected to accomplish much more than slay Ossdonc and escape this time around."

"What about Giserre?" asked Avender. "We can't just leave her."

"My mother will be safe," answered Reiffen. "Her escort has strict orders to flee at the first sign of trouble."

"How're they going to do that?" Avender leaned out the window and studied the long drop to the valley below.

Reiffen raised his hand, displaying his second thimble. "Her escort has one of these. Moreover, it will take them to the same place as mine."

"Then let's get on with it," growled the bear. His teeth showed wickedly yellow against his black muzzle. "This place isn't healthy for me. And there's no sense waiting around for a Wizard to find us."

"Very well." Reiffen gestured for his companions to grasp his shoulders. For the second time they watched as he took one hand in the other and spoke the word "Return."

This time Avender tried not to blink as Reiffen swept them across the world, but he wasn't sure he succeeded. One moment they were in the sitting room, the pale morning light washing across them from the window; the next they were in the shadows of a much darker cave, the only light coming from a blazing hearth.

Two figures stood on the other side of the fire. Avender's hand went to his sword.

"Mother. Are you all right?" asked Reiffen.

"I am fine, my son."

Reiffen bowed to the man standing beside Giserre. "Thank you, Mindrell. You have done everything I asked. I release you from my service."

"A bit soon for that, Your Majesty. I think I'll wait till we get back to the surface before accepting your offer."

The bear padded into the light, his claws clicking on the stone. "Reiffen, you've certainly picked your friends strangely these last few years, but the harper is right. Let's get out of here."

"That will take some time."

"I already told you, we don't have a lot of time."

"This place is far from Ussene. What the Dwarves do there will not affect us here."

"What makes you think Usseis and Fornoch won't follow us as soon as Ussene is destroyed?"

"Ussene is actually going to be destroyed?" Giserre glanced quickly at the bard. "Then the woman Spit saw told her the truth."

"What woman?" asked Reiffen.

"Spit saw her, not I. She wanted me to meet her."

"Who's Spit?" asked Avender.

The bear tossed his large head impatiently. "None of this matters now. We have to get out of here as soon as possible. Come on, Reiffen. Chant the spell, pull the secret lever. Let's go, however you do it."

"It's not that simple. To cast a traveling spell without a link requires preparation. And even then I may not be strong enough to take everyone at once. But I assure you, there is no need to hurry. Usseis doesn't know where this place is, and Fornoch is no fighter. There is more difference among the Three than you might think."

"Are you sure? What if Fornoch has told Usseis about this place? Will we be safe then? Do you trust the Wizard that much?"

"Very well." Avender thought Reiffen was simply humoring the bear. "Perhaps I should take some precautions, but the magic itself cannot be rushed. Mother, if you and Mindrell would arrange yourselves around the empty table."

Handing Avender the Inach sword he had borrowed from Brizen, he went on. "I shall be too busy for guard duty. And I am sure you are a better swordsman than I, anyway."

With his back to the center of the room, the young wizard sketched a square in the air and chanted.

"*Magic mine, and nothing more,*
May pass this line
From roof to floor."

The square Reiffen had traced shimmered with a faint silver light, as if Hern's best tea tray hung suspended in the air before him. Taking hold of each of the upper corners, he flung them left and right. The tea tray turned into a thin silver sheet that unfolded in the air. For a moment it hovered above the table, a shiver of tiny stars cascading from ceiling to floor at its edges. The stars winked out and all trace of the spell disappeared.

"Is it still there?" Mindrell reached out a tentative hand.

"It's there until I end it," replied Reiffen. "But it will only block magic, so take care if anything solid comes your way."

The first spell cast, Reiffen began the next. While Avender and Redburr guarded the ends of the empty table, Reiffen collected a variety of bottles, bowls, and beakers from a second bench. Ugly odors filled the room as he mixed the contents into a thick paste, which he poured into two small pots. With a pair of tongs, he plucked a dull red coal from the fire to light them. The nasty smell thickened.

"Now comes the tricky part." Reiffen set the smoking pots at either end of the empty table. "It might take fifteen minutes for me to find the precise memory I need. In the meantime everyone must keep touching me while I'm concentrating. My shins and ankles will probably be best."

No one dared speak as Reiffen lay down on the table between the smudges, for fear of disturbing his focus. Redburr snuffled, his muzzle drooping guiltily in response to his companions' reproving glares. The minutes passed, slow as mist beading on a pane of glass.

A white blur stepped out of the fire. Usseis's long shadow blackened the floor. Mindrell pulled Giserre around to the far side of the table while Avender pointed the heavy sword at the White Wizard's chest. His concentration broken, Reiffen came quickly to his feet and emerged from the protective barrier of his magic.

Flames from the fire licked the hem of Usseis's robe. "Too late I find that Fornoch was wrong to trust you," he said, "and Ossdonc foolish in his preference for pleasure and power. My way was always best. So it shall be henceforth."

Grandly, the White Wizard lifted his right arm and spread his fingers wide. Reiffen made a sweeping motion with his hand.

"Enough," he said. "Your will no longer has the strength to force mine."

The Wizard's black eyes gaped like night sky between bright stars. Sword in hand, Avender followed Reiffen out of the magic circle and felt himself drawn immediately into those hollow depths. The Wizard's eyes compelled him forward, the same way the Abyss sometimes beckoned when he turned his gaze downward too long from the heights of Issinlough. What was he doing, taking orders from Reiffen, anyway? Hadn't he bested his former friend in every contest they had ever fought? Crowns and power were one thing: Avender had never wanted those. But there were other prizes more precious, and Avender deserved them far more than any turncoat prince. All he had to do—

Reiffen stepped between his old friend and the Wizard. Avender blinked, as if a cloud had crossed the sky, and tried to remember what he had been thinking.

"You will not compel my friends, either," said Reiffen.

"So be it," said the Wizard. "We shall see how good you have become with cruder magics."

He raised a hand. Strength and power rippled across his dead black eyes.

"*Catch,*" answered Reiffen, though Usseis had made no rhyme.

The air burst in a clap of thunder; a slim dagger appeared in the air. Lightning blazed around the iron blade like waves on the rocks in Valing gorge. Avender staggered at the shock.

Usseis pushed at the air with his hand a second time.

"*Quench,*" said Reiffen.

Warm spray splashed across the cave. The fire in the hearth fizzled, but stayed lit. Despite the discomfort of being soaked, nothing worse followed.

Usseis raised his arms; the sleeves of his cloak fell to the floor like a white marble wall. His fingers clawed wide like sunbeams striking through dark clouds.

"*Form,*" he said, voicing his spell for the first time.

The walls began to writhe. Small creatures bulged from the stone. Like an army of ants sliding off a tilted tray, the things broke free of the rock and slipped scrabbling to the floor. Pincers clicked; stingers jabbed blindly.

"*Ground,*" responded Reiffen.

The floor swallowed the creatures as quickly as they were vomited from the walls.

Light and clamor and blood blasted the cave as Reiffen countered each of the Wizard's attacks with a single word. A rain of vipers was answered by a wave of cold; a choking fog by a cleansing wind; a cloud of wasps by a flock of darting blackbirds. But nothing the Wizard sent penetrated the barrier Reiffen had placed around Giserre and the others, and everything was dispelled before Reiffen or Avender was harmed.

But the strain of countering the Wizard's spells was showing. The hollow, anguished look in Reiffen's face that had greeted them that morning was now stretched thin as a starving mask. Nor was he able to attack in any way, but only defend, while Usseis's power had not diminished at all. Avender wondered how long his former friend could continue. Hate him or not, Reiffen was the only thing standing between them and the White Wizard. If someone didn't help him soon, they were all going to die. Or worse.

"*Sand,*" said Reiffen. A storm of jagged stones crumbled to stinging dust, but the force behind it remained powerful enough to knock the weary spellcaster to the ground. Avender leapt over his fallen friend and thrust his Inach sword at the White Wizard's broad chest.

Absently, as if Avender were less than a conjured wasp, Usseis raised an arm to ward the attack. Only when the sharp edge of the sword bit deeply into his forearm did the Wizard realize he faced no ordinary weapon. With a growl of anger and pain, he swung viciously at Avender with his other hand. Avender dodged, but Usseis still struck him glancingly across the chest.

Fields of stars burst across the young man's eyes. His chest felt as if it had collapsed against his back, but at least the pain reassured him he was still alive. Gasping for breath, he realized he had lost Brizen's sword.

He opened his eyes. Usseis was flailing away at Reiffen in the middle of the room, the Wizard's bloody arm scratching crimson trails through the air. Redburr worried his leg like a giant dog. But Usseis couldn't turn to deal with the Shaper because Reiffen had the Inach sword. Instead the White Wizard dragged the bear around the room, trying to knock the weapon out of Reiffen's hand, while Reiffen darted back and forth in search of an opening to stab and slash.

With a loud rip, Usseis pulled himself free from Redburr's sharp teeth and kicked the enormous bear across the room. Tossing the torn fabric to the floor, Redburr leapt after the Wizard again, but he was too late. In the short moment his legs were free, Usseis caught Reiffen a blow with his good arm that knocked the human to the floor. He landed on his back, his head twisted horribly to the side. The sword flew out of his hands.

The Wizard bounded forward. But Redburr had him by the leg again, so Mindrell was faster. The bard pounced on the blade, lifting it with both hands. At the same time Giserre, leaving the safety of Reiffen's shield, seized the scrap of the Wizard's robe. With the long practice of one who had made beds for years in Valing, she tossed the piece of fabric so that it billowed open like a sheet across the Wizard's face, blocking his view. As Usseis clawed the cloth away, Mindrell thrust the Inach sword straight through the fabric and up into the White Wizard's chest.

A line of crimson thickened on the cloth. Usseis dropped to his knees. His face contorted with disbelief, he toppled to the floor. Black blood welled out beneath him.

Giserre rushed to Reiffen's side. Bones crunched as Redburr made sure the Wizard was dead. Avender, hardly daring to breathe because of the pain in his chest, braced himself for Giserre's grief.

But Reiffen was alive. "Is the Wizard dead?" he asked as Giserre cradled his head in her lap, his voice far stronger than it should have been.

Tenderly Giserre brushed Reiffen's hair away from his face. "He is, my son. Mindrell struck the blow."

The bard bowed modestly, his preening confidence strangely absent. "With your help, my lady. It was your deft touch that turned the tide."

"It was all of us," said Reiffen. "Everyone had a part."

Avender struggled to draw a breath deep enough to speak so he could let everyone know that he, too, was still alive. However many ribs it turned out he had broken, his chest hurt more now than it had after his stabbing in Banking. It felt like he was slowly suffocating as well. But Redburr hadn't forgotten him and, after pausing for one last lap at the Wizard's blood, came over to give him a sniff. Avender tried to speak again, going so far as to open his mouth, but no words came out.

"Don't talk, boy," said the Shaper. Then, turning to the others, "This one's alive, too. Though I'm not so surprised at him as I am at Reiffen."

"Killing things is not all that magic is good for." Sitting up in his mother's arms, Reiffen twisted his neck. An ugly crack echoed across the workshop, but his head sat correctly on his shoulders again when he was done.

"If you're feeling that much better," growled the bear, "maybe it's time to try getting out of here again. I'd just as soon not be around if Fornoch shows up, too. I don't think we can survive another fight like that last one."

"I lack the strength for any magic right now," said Reiffen. "It might be some time before I recover."

"Then it is just as well I have arrived."

Fornoch emerged from the shadows at the back of the room leading a filthy Ferris by the arm.

"Redburr!" she cried, wrestling against the Gray Wizard's grip. "Help me!"

Wondering how Fornoch had captured her, Avender tried to push himself up from the cold stone but collapsed back, breathless and in pain. Rage at everything that had happened rushed through him, but there was nothing his broken body could do. First Reiffen, then Skimmer, now Ferris. It would be just as well if he received his death blow from the Wizards, too.

Holding his captive tightly, Fornoch stopped close beside Usseis's body. His black eyes flicked around the room like a pair of hovering bees.

"Quite impressive. You have killed both my brothers in a single day. I congratulate you, Reiffen. You have far exceeded my expectations."

"Expectations?" asked the bear.

"Reiffen didn't do this." Ferris struck at the Wizard's arm with her fist. "He's on your side."

Fornoch paid no attention to her. "Do you actually believe all this has happened without my allowing it?" he told the Shaper.

"I do. It would be just like you to claim authorship of events you had nothing to do with."

"It would," the Wizard agreed.

Reiffen struggled painfully to his feet, his hand on his mother's shoulder. "Hello, Ferris." Turning to the Gray Wizard, he asked, "So, this was your plan? To have me kill your rivals so you might have your way unopposed?"

"There was never any plan, Reiffen. Matters have found their own course, like water running to the sea. I have sought no one's death."

"Yet somehow you managed to reveal this place to Usseis. Despite assuring me you would not."

The Gray Wizard shrugged amiably, admitting his fault. "When he discovered I had placed a workshop at your disposal, he insisted on knowing its location. I had to tell him, otherwise he would have suspected us of concealing secrets. Fool that he was, his suspicions have led him to his own death. I followed as soon as I learned he was here. To help, one way or the other."

"In other words," said Giserre, "you thought to take advantage of whatever situation you found."

"That is Fornoch's way, Mother," said her son. "He knew some day it would come to this, for all his twisting words. Ossdonc was the easy one, but the outcome with Usseis was always in doubt."

Fornoch smiled, as he always did when Reiffen was being clever. "I admit, some such encounter was inevitable. Usseis's mistake was to underestimate others' strength. He did not understand that even a mere actor might cling to life so tightly he reemerges as a stone. Always Usseis has wanted too much control over things living and dead. And Ossdonc believed only in destruction."

"And you?" asked the bear.

"I seek only to suggest."

Giserre looked into Fornoch's hollow eyes. "You use words, Wizard, the way your brothers used spells and swords. Words whispered in the night like daggers tipped with poison."

"Words have many meanings, my lady. As I said before, I came to help." Fornoch smiled again, but this time his good humor reminded Avender of shopkeepers in Malmoret whose goods were worth less than their words.

"If you really want to help," growled Redburr, "do us all a favor and leave. Without the girl."

"I would be happy to leave," said the Wizard. "But you might want me to do the same for the rest of you before I go."

"Don't listen to him!" Ferris pulled again at the Wizard's iron grip. "Who knows where he'll take us? We might end up on top of High Enossin, or in the middle of the Outer Sea. He left Nolo behind in Ussene when it was destroyed and made me watch it all from the next mountain over. It was horrible."

"True, there is the risk I might be lying. Life has its uncertainties." With his free hand the Wizard reached inside his robe. Bear and humans tensed, fearing the worst and knowing they could do nothing about it. Instead Fornoch brought out a puppy, tail wagging, and set it on the floor. Not until it took a few delighted hops did anyone notice it only had three legs. The fourth was capped at the knee with a small iron cup.

"What have you done?" asked Ferris, aghast.

"Magic has its price," replied the Wizard.

"I see what you have fashioned," said Reiffen. "An interesting variation. May I ask where you placed the other limb?"

"In the barracks near the Valley Gate. They still stand, but you had better hurry. Some things escaped the general destruction. I assume they are hungry, and a tender young dog's leg is just the sort of treat they love."

"We don't need your help, Wizard," said Giserre. "We can wait for my son to be rested enough to cast his spell."

"Can you? With my brother's body rotting beside you? There is much magic in this room, and much in Usseis's flesh as well. Even I cannot predict how the two may interact."

As if on cue, a narrow split cracked the ceiling. Small stones pattered to the floor. Tail wagging, the puppy left off pawing a dead blackbird and tripped over to sniff the debris.

Reiffen looked angrily at the Wizard. "What's going on? You said this place was far from Ussene."

"It is." Fornoch folded his hands solemnly into his sleeves. "But Usseis is here and he is dead. There are repercussions."

"I suggest we leave," said the bear. Gently he picked up the puppy with his large yellow teeth.

"Why do you help us?" Giserre demanded. "What profit is yours?"

"Maybe I'm not as bad as I seem." Fornoch released his grip on Ferris's arm, setting her free to join her friends. "And maybe I'm not as good, either. What matters is your son return to the world with everything he has learned."

He disappeared.

25

Home

ry as she might, Ferris could find nothing wrong with the puppy's legs after they returned to the ruins outside Ussene. All four limbs wriggled in her lap as she scratched the dog's velvet throat; its pink tongue licked her soot-covered hands.

Declaring Ferris to be too dirty, Giserre tended Avender and her son. Reiffen rested awhile, then set his smudge pots at either end of the battered cot his old friend was lying in.

"One more trip and we're home," he said.

Mindrell poked his nose in through the doorway of the windowless barrack. A layer of fine dust had already covered his head and shoulders in the short time he had been standing guard with Redburr outside.

"I think I'll stay behind," said the bard.

"It is not safe," protested Giserre. "Fornoch said so himself."

"No, but I'd rather face manders and sissit than the good people of Valing. I don't suppose they'll give me much of a welcome, no matter how many Wizards I've killed."

"As you wish." Reiffen settled on the bed beside Avender. "I have released you from my service. And one less person to transport will make the magic that much easier. I might even be able to reach Valing on the first attempt."

Pushing Mindrell aside, the bear thrust his own stone gray shoulders into the room. "I think I'll stay as well."

Ferris's eyes narrowed. "Why? You didn't get into the beehives again before you left, did you?"

Avender, trying not to laugh, hurt his chest coughing instead. Giserre did her best to hold him still.

"There's still Nolo to find," said the Shaper. "The Dwarves will be up here soon to inspect their handiwork. Someone needs to tell them about Nolo so they can dig him out."

The puppy nipped Ferris's finger to encourage more scratching. "Do you think there's any hope?" she asked.

"Of course there's hope, girl. Nolo's fought manders, swum nirrin, been drowned by pirates. A little rockslide won't bother him at all. Why, he even went over Valing Falls that time fighting the Wizards—"

The Shaper stopped as everyone else went silent. "What? What did I say? Oh. Well, you can't ignore it forever, you know. Skimmer's gone and that's that. The sooner you all start talking about it, the better. In the meantime I'm going to go look for Dwarves. I don't suppose you're coming with me, harper?"

"No. I'll find my own path."

"Good. We'll leave when the spell's done. Until then we're still on guard duty."

"I'll come back to help look for Nolo when I can," said Reiffen.

"Finding Nolo won't make up for what you've done any more than killing Wizards," Ferris told him bitterly.

With a rumbling grunt, Redburr left the room. After a grand bow, the bard followed. Ferris turned away from Reiffen once her friends were gone, while Avender lay gloomily on his pallet looking as if he hoped he never healed.

Reiffen closed his eyes and rested his hands on his knees.

Following Giserre's lead, Ferris reluctantly lay a hand on Reiffen's arm, then helped Avender do the same while she balanced the squirming pup. She didn't know what to expect, but there seemed to be nothing else to the spell. No knives or potions, puppies or iron thimbles.

The room grew still. Even the pup curled up quietly when it saw no one wanted to play. Ferris imagined she could see the dust swirl in response to the beating of its young heart. Time passed. The world widened around her in a steadily growing circle: a fly buzzing in the doorway; a raven calling its mate as it picked through the rubbish left behind by the fleeing guards; the dull roll of the odd stone still tumbling down the fallen mountain. She wondered if that was part of the spell, her mind following Reiffen's in wider and wider spans across the world until finally they arrived in Valing. What would come next? A coyote howling in the Waste? A duck scrabbling in the Wetting weeds? The wind whistling through the summer ice in the High Bavadars?

"We're here."

She opened her eyes at the sound of Reiffen's voice. He had said once he would teach her magic: she couldn't wait to learn the traveling spell. To the right, rows of low benches circled down to a hearth; to the left, small, square panes of glass blurred with mist and rain. They were in the Tear.

"Reiffen," said his mother, "perhaps you and Ferris should go to the Manor to tell them we have returned."

"Perhaps."

"You have won great honor. It is fitting your first acclamation should be from the land that has shown you the truest friendship."

Angrily Ferris let the pup slip to the floor. "What's the matter with you? How can you think Valing will ever welcome Reiffen after what he's done? Wayland and Banking may not care, but Valing will never forget!"

"Never forget what, my dear? Reiffen has helped slay two Wizards and ended a terrible war. Why would they not honor him?"

Ferris gave Reiffen a brutal look. "Haven't you told her? Did you think I wouldn't? You may be a great hero elsewhere, but in Valing you'll always be a murderer and a beast."

"Reiffen?" Giserre turned to her son.

"I would not have kept this secret from you, Mother, but there has been little enough time to tell everything that has happened. I was in Valing several weeks ago, proving my fealty yet again to Usseis. Because of me, Skimmer was swept into the gorge."

"And a pup," snapped Ferris.

"And a pup," Reiffen agreed.

Giserre showed no reaction to Reiffen's revelation, but it was a moment before she spoke. "My son has been put to many trials, Ferris. More than you, or I, will ever know. I can understand how you might hate him. He has betrayed one of Valing's greatest trusts. I only ask you to learn to pity him. But please, Avender has done no wrong. He is in great pain. If you would go to the Manor, perhaps your mother and father will be able to make him more comfortable."

Ferris opened her mouth to say something sharp in reply, then decided Giserre was right. There would be a better time to let Reiffen know how angry she was. Picking the pup back up, she asked Reiffen if he was coming with her.

"I'll stay here for the moment, I think."

The dog's soft fur comforted her as she stormed away, but she set it down on the ground when she reached the top of the Neck. Sniffing at the wet grass, the pup followed her to the house, where she found her mother in the garden picking beans.

"We were wondering when you'd get back," said Hern.

"Why are you so filthy? You look like you've been sweeping chimneys. Did things go well in Issinlough? And where'd you get that dog?"

Ferris remembered her mother had no idea she'd left Issinlough for Ussene. Better to tell her that later. "Everything's splendid, Mother. More splendid than you can imagine. Usseis and Ossdonc are dead, and Ussene destroyed. But there's no time to talk about it now. Avender's in the Tear, terribly hurt."

Hern put aside her basket of beans and jumped to her feet. "Avender's hurt? Why's he in the Tear? You could at least have brought him—"

"Reiffen and Giserre are with him, Mother."

"Reiffen? Berrel will be glad to hear that. He's been on the lake every day since the fight trying to straighten things out with the nokken. Some of the bachelors have been tearing nets, you know. Maybe they'll settle down a bit after we have a trial."

"I don't think there will be a trial, Mother. Reiffen's a hero now. It's his doing that the Wizards have been destroyed. But I've already wasted too much time talking. We'll need a stretcher, and bearers. . . ."

By the time they returned to the Tear, Ferris had told her mother most of the story. Then Dennol arrived with two foresters and a stretcher, and Tinnet brought bandages and hot tea, and Anella came running up to throw herself in Giserre's arms, and all in all it was a while before Ferris noticed that Reiffen had disappeared.

"He changed his mind and went up after you," said Giserre. "Did you not see him? No? Well, I doubt he has left without me. He will turn up."

With many hands helping, it took perhaps a little longer than necessary to carry Avender up to the Manor, where he was established in the best bedroom. Durk chattered away from his pillow in the window while Hern bandaged her patient's chest tightly. So tightly, in fact, he couldn't take a deep breath no matter how hard he tried.

"I'll smother," he whispered.

"Discomfort's a good thing in a patient," she scolded in reply. "Makes you want to heal faster."

Things were finally settling down when Tinnet reappeared with Sally and a bright-faced bundle in a blanket. "We finally got our girl, Ferris." Tinnet's wife wiped the glad tears from her cheeks. "I hope you don't mind we named her after you. But all of us do love you so much, it only seemed natural."

"Of course I don't mind. Why, she looks just like her father!" Ferris pulled a corner of the blanket back to admire the babe's red cheeks and thick dark hair. "How terribly unfortunate."

Everyone laughed, including the parents. "Guess she won't be so lucky in love as you then," said Tinnet.

Ferris held her tongue. All the same, it was time to tell the world of her engagement. Perhaps when the room emptied she could start by telling her parents and friends.

When that time came, however, she found her mother had business of her own to take care of first. "Now then." Hern faced Giserre, hands on hips. "Where's your son?"

"Somewhere about."

"We don't want him here, you know."

"We know."

"Some folks might not take kindly to you staying long, either. I'm not one of them, mind you, and you'll always have a home here as far as I'm concerned. But I'm warning you, it might be difficult."

Giserre nodded, coldly gracious. "Your house has been the most hospitable of any where I have ever guested, and I thank you for renewing your invitation. Believe me when I say it pains me deeply to know my son has dishonored your trust. I assure you, we will leave as soon as possible."

"We'll be sad to see you go, my lady." Berrel slipped an arm around his wife's waist. Her stern face softened. "Both you and Reiffen, for the sake of the boy he was."

"Thank you, Steward."

Ferris decided she had waited long enough. It was Reiffen's own fault if he wasn't there to hear. "Since you'll be leaving soon, Giserre, I think I should tell you my news. Mother. Father. I have accepted Prince Brizen."

Berrel's jaw dropped. Hern leaned against the bed. Avender, despite the bandages constricting his chest, sat up straight enough to start coughing again. Only Giserre showed no emotion.

"My, my." Hern fanned herself with one hand. "This has been a day of surprises. Berrel, if you would pour me a cup of water from the pitcher on the bureau."

"An excellent choice," Durk assured Ferris from the window. "The prince is a fine fellow. As I told him whenever he was faint-hearted in his pursuit:

> *"What though the questing heart may quail and quake,*
> *Still love's reward will steadfast suitors wake."*

"When did you ever meet Prince Brizen?"

"I haven't met him? Hmm. I meet so many people these days. There are drawbacks to not having eyes, you know."

"If I may offer my congratulations as well, Ferris. You will make Brizen a fine queen."

"Thank you, Giserre. I'll be following your example, you know. I hope you'll tell me when I slip up."

A hint of fondness flickered briefly across Giserre's face. "Thank you, Ferris. Thank you very much."

Stepping forward, she took both of Ferris's hands in hers and kissed her on the forehead. Ferris felt like a girl of seven again, in awe of the great lady who didn't mind making beds.

Hern dabbed at her eyes with the corner of her apron. Berrel beamed beside her. "You know your father and I are delighted, dear heart, but what made you change your mind?"

"He loves me very much, Mother."

Then Hern held out her arms and Ferris rushed into them and mother and daughter had a terrific cry. And Berrel wept, too, and even Giserre allowed some dampness to glisten her cheeks. And Tinnet arrived with broth for Avender and asked what was going on and then of course the whole house knew, and Eastbay soon after. And then Bracken and Sothend and Low Spinney, too. And bells were rung and casks unstopped and mussels stewed as all Valing crowed that one of theirs would be a queen.

But no one noticed that Avender didn't say a word.

It was some time before Ferris managed to slip away alone. Although she knew he'd hear the news from his mother, she wanted to tell Reiffen herself. With the puppy trailing close behind, she went off to find him.

The first place she looked was the orchard, but Reiffen wasn't there. At the edge of the cliff she paused to take in the view she hadn't seen in weeks, and wasn't likely to see much more of once she became a princess. The puppy pounced at beetles and sniffed at things unseen in the breeze. To the west the sun had caught on the peaks like a peach on a picket fence, but the boats on the lake below still glided in bright sunlight. Nokken Rock and the Bottle glistened like pale green lily pads against the silver-blue water.

She couldn't find Reiffen anywhere. He wasn't in the pine woods on the north side of the Manor, nor in the room he had shared with Avender, nor in the Tear. He wasn't in the cellars or the stables or the Map Room. Finally, after searching every place she could think of, she trudged wearily up the long stair from the lower dock, where the sight of a nearly healed Icer lounging on the quay with Old Mortin had reminded her that Reiffen would never have gone there. Back at the cliff, the wind, strengthening as it did on a late-summer afternoon, tossed her skirts and hair.

"Where is he?" she wondered aloud, cradling the exhausted puppy in her arms. "Has he already gone back to Ussene?"

"No. I'm here."

Reiffen appeared in front of her as if he had stepped through a door in the breeze.

"Why didn't you show yourself sooner?" she asked suspiciously.

The puppy sniffed at Reiffen as he crossed the rock between them. "You didn't ask."

Ferris turned to the lake, knowing Reiffen would have to retreat or else let her windblown hair flick him in the face and eyes.

He stopped at the top of the cliff, farther away from her than he had intended. "Giserre always said you'd be the one who'd never give up on me. I guess she was wrong."

"She was." Ferris told herself the tear in her eye was from the wind. "How can you bear to look at the lake, knowing what you've done?"

"Do you mean the nokken?"

"Of course I mean the nokken. Did you think I was talking about the sheep?"

"No."

"That's good. Otherwise I might have thought you'd cast some kind of stupidity spell on yourself."

A smile crossed Reiffen's face like a kite in a high wind. "There's the old Ferris. If there's one thing you never could forgive it was stupidity. At least you can't hold that against me. I've done terrible things, but I've known what it meant when I did them. I was afraid you'd never forgive me for Skimmer."

"I won't. He was our friend."

"Yes. But would you rather it had been you? Or Avender? Because that's what I had to do to prove my fealty to the Three. Kill a friend."

Ferris stared at him in horror. "You mean you chose Skimmer deliberately? I thought they forced you."

Sadness drew Reiffen's face into long planes of weariness and pain. Leaning out of Ferris's arms, the puppy licked his hands. "That's what's so awful about Wizards. Even if they make you do something, they let you choose the way to do it. That way they show you the horrible things in your own heart."

"You've been spending too much time with Mindrell. I'm sure he has excuses for what he's done as well. Either you know the difference between right and wrong, or you don't. The Reiffen I was in love with certainly knew that."

Reiffen's eyebrows rose.

"Notice I said 'was,' " Ferris added quickly. "Besides, none of that matters anymore. The reason I came looking for you is to tell you I've accepted Brizen."

Reiffen's face turned to stone. Ferris had thought she would be pleased to see him hurt, but now she found she wanted to comfort him. Thinking of Skimmer instead, she kept her arms stiffly at her side.

"There's the old Reiffen," she mocked. "Getting angry whenever you can't have your own way."

"But Brannis's son!"

"He's a better catch than you are. Especially now you've saved both his kingdoms for him. And he's not a murderer, either. Fornoch told me about Molio."

"That was different. I didn't . . ."

"There's nothing you can say."

Reiffen's mouth pursed, as if he were struggling with himself.

His jaw tightened, his will as firm as hers. "No. There's nothing I can say."

They stood awkwardly at the edge of the cliff. The look of loss on Reiffen's face tore at her. She wished he could be what he had been. She had loved him so much. Childhood friend, and yet he had always been mysterious and different, strange and exciting and wild, like weather in high mountains. Like no one she had ever met. She had never thought about whether he loved her in return. They had never even kissed. And yet, especially after their first return from Ussene when he had been taken away from her again so quickly, she had understood how terribly she missed him. And how she believed in him so much more than anyone else. That fact alone had intensified her feeling as much as anything. If no one else could be true, then she would be even truer.

But no longer. The memory of Skimmer disappearing into the gorge, foam and clouds so mixed that sky and water were the same, would never leave her. It was hard to trust a lover who could murder his friends.

"You're a great hero now," she said, looking him in the eye. "You can have any maid in the Three Kingdoms, but you can't have me. That's the price you'll pay for what you've done."

"Do you love Brizen?"

"I don't love you."

"That's not what I asked."

Ferris swept her windblown hair back over her shoulder. The puppy scrambled into Reiffen's hands.

"Does it really matter?" she asked. "There's much more than love involved in marrying a king."

"Brizen isn't a king yet. Nor was Ablen when my mother married him. Love was all they needed."

"And look where it got them."

"I'm told they were happy."

"For a month. I'll be happy a lot longer than that."

His eyes probed hers. Ferris thought his irises were darker than they had been before he left, as if the gloom in which he had lived so long had left its trace upon him. He reminded her of Fornoch.

"I could compel you."

Anger flushed her face and throat. "You wouldn't dare."

"You're right. I wouldn't. But I often think there's nothing to any of what I've learned from the Three except compulsion and killing."

"That's not true. Avender told me how you cured his wound in Backford. And those travel spells, too, especially the quick one with the thimbles."

"Believe me, Ferris"—Reiffen shook his head—"that is not a pleasant process."

"You'd have died in your workshop without magic. Giserre told us about the Living Stones."

"Would you have preferred my dying?"

"It would have made everything simpler. But then who would teach me magic?"

Reiffen laughed. The puppy licked his chin. "You won't marry a murderer, but you'll let him teach you magic? I'd have thought my penalty would be much more severe."

Ferris looked him in the eye again. "There's no need for me to sacrifice everything. If you're going to pass on what you've learned, I certainly intend to be one of your students."

Reiffen's eyes brightened. "Sacrifice? What sort of sacrifice would be involved in not loving a murderer?"

"I never said that."

"No, you didn't, but you might just as well have. Perhaps I should have asked if you love me, rather than inquiring about Brizen."

"What I might want, and what I will allow myself, are two different things. The sooner you understand that, the easier it will be for both of us."

"I suppose you're right." Reiffen's eyes, however, still shone.

She gave him a narrow glance. "You don't look convinced."

He bowed slightly. "You'll forgive me if I allow myself some happiness over not having been banished forever."

"I'll forgive you when I see you actually acting that way and not just saying it. If there's one thing we've all learned these last few weeks, Reiffen, it's that you're not to be trusted. Even if it is in a good cause."

Bowing once more, he said, "I'll do my best to change your opinion on that score. In the meantime, if you'll excuse me, I think I'd better leave. My welcome is not what it was the last time I returned. And Uhle and Redburr might need me at Ussene."

"You're leaving just like that?" Ferris had hoped they might be able to start her lessons soon. "What about Giserre? And Avender?"

"I'll make my own good-byes to Avender. Giserre is coming with me as far as Rimwich. Will you invite me to the wedding?"

"I won't, but I can't answer for the groom. Politics is sometimes more important than good taste."

Bowing one last time, Reiffen walked away through the orchard. Tongue drooping, the puppy looked back at Ferris over his shoulder. She watched them go, her heart as sore as it had been the day she had decided to marry the prince.

Only this time she didn't cry.

26

The Wedding

ews of Ferris's betrothal traveled quickly. Presents from Brizen began arriving within a fortnight of her return: bolts of cloth laced with blumet and gold; a black mare from Dremen that galloped faster than a hawk could fly; pearls from the southern isles. All the same a month passed while Ferris waited for Avender's ribs to heal before she started south. She wouldn't leave for Malmoret without him.

"If I'd been thinking straight," she told her mother one morning while shelling peas, "I'd have asked Reiffen to heal him before he left, the way he did in Backford. Avender is so uncomfortable. And he's in a bad mood all the time."

"I haven't noticed you minding the wait."

"You know I'm going to miss Valing terribly."

"Are you sure that's the only reason you don't mind?"

"Yes, Mother. I'm sure."

Hern clucked patiently, the way she had when Ferris was a child. "You know perfectly well a young woman's allowed to change her mind," she said, regarding her daughter steadily. "In fact she's supposed to, if she thinks she's made a mistake."

"I haven't made a mistake and I haven't changed my mind.

It's not like I'm marrying Nod Woolson. Who's already gotten himself engaged to Renny Punter, I see."

"Hmm." Hern looked like she was about to say one thing, then changed her mind and said another. "You know dear, no one's been happier for you in this marriage than me, but if I pushed you too hard, I'll understand. Prince Brizen's fine and good, and that moonstruck on you I wouldn't believe it if I hadn't seen it myself, but if you can't bring yourself to love him, you should give it up right now."

"I'll love him, Mother. It might take me a while, but I'll love him. I'll be as good a wife to him as any wife ever was. You can be sure of that."

They were quiet for a moment, the only sound the pea pods snapping. Overhead the sky swung sharply from blue to gray to blue again as the sun played catch-up with the clouds. For the hundredth time since Reiffen had left, Ferris told herself might-have-beens were for moony farm girls, and she certainly wasn't one of those.

"We'll leave as soon as Avender can travel," she went on. "I've said that all along. In the meantime, I'm going to enjoy my last end of summer in Valing."

The lower slopes of the mountains had already turned from green to gold by the time Ferris finally started on her journey to Malmoret. Her parents and Avender went with her, while Durk rode in a mesh bag tied to Avender's saddle. The thanes and knights who accompanied them were delighted to make the talking stone's acquaintance and wouldn't let him shut up once during the entire trip.

"If everyone in Malmoret is like these fine cavaliers," confided the stone to Avender when they reached Lugger, "I shall surely make my fortune."

"But what will you spend it on?"

"Why, gems and jewels, of course. I've decided, if I'm going to be a stone, I might as well associate with the very best. No pebbly riffraff for me, thank you very much."

Because the preparations for the wedding were taking place in Malmoret, they sailed to Eddstone Harbor in Wayland rather than directly to Banking. Wayland would have a processional across the southeastern corner of the country as its share of the celebrations. At Lower Neeling, the first village inland from Eddstone, Ferris and her party were met by a large banner spanning the center of the street. **Welcome Princess Ferriss!** it proclaimed. Behind it the lane was crammed with tables bowing under the weight of the feast prepared for the princess's arrival.

"Look at that," said Avender. "They didn't even get your name—"

Ferris smacked his arm away before he could point at the banner. She had suddenly realized just how much of an ordeal this was going to be before they even got to Malmoret, and had no wish for Avender to make it worse. Boys and girls ran up and down the dusty street shouting, "She's here! She's here!" But the town elders had evidently received earlier warning and were already standing in front of the public house with various bundles in their hands as the rest of the village raced in from the fields. The thane and his wife stood at the very front, the largest bundle of all draped over the shoulder of the page beside them.

Durk, riding alone on a velvet cushion on a dappled gray pony, served as herald. "Fine people of Lower Neeling," he proclaimed, "thanes and swineherds, goodwives and farmers, grans and babes, tanners and lumberjacks, coopers and public men, barbers and weavers, tipplers and the infirm, it is my great honor and pleasure and privilege and delight to present to you Her Highness Ferris of Valing, Beauty of the Bavadars, Lady of the Lake, Mistress of the Manor, Virgin of the Gorge, and your future queen!"

The thane and his wife, and everyone behind them, bowed

low. Ferris nodded her head regally and made up her mind that Durk would not be her herald much longer.

"Welcome, Princess Ferris, to our humble village." The thane's ruddy face beamed. Beside him his wife, a large bouquet of flowers in her arms, could barely contain her excitement.

"You honor me, Thane." Ferris stared at Avender until he realized he was supposed to help her dismount.

"Oh no, Your Highness. It is we who are honored." The ends of the thane's mustache quivered in the full gale of his excitement. "In the name of the king, we welcome you to Wayland. Lower Neeling is proud to be the first stop on your triumphant tour through our fair land."

A stout young man standing behind the thane and his wife, whom Ferris suspected to be their oldest son, raised a thick hand. "Everyone! Let's give a cheer to Princess Ferris! Hip, hip, hooray!"

When the cheers finally died down the thane's wife stepped forward. "These are for you, milady," she said hesitantly, presenting her bouquet.

"They're beautiful."

"If you would care to join us, we have a simple meal set out for you."

The thane and his wife stood back to allow Ferris an open field at the food. If the formality was this bad when she was only engaged, she wondered, how much worse would it be after she was married? Popping a large black grape from the bunch at the head of the table into her mouth, she soon guessed that no one would follow her until she had made her way down to the far end. So she moved on, sampling a little of this and a little of that, fresh bread and roast pork and a steaming tub of buttered squash. Remembering that princesses weren't supposed to wipe their fingers off on their riding habits, she looked around for a napkin. Avender, quicker this time, was beside her in a moment, his handkerchief in his hand.

"Your Highness," he said gravely.

"Stop it," she whispered, "or I'll order you beheaded."

When she was finished, she turned and bowed to the expectant villagers. From the way they still restrained themselves, she decided they were waiting for something more.

"Thank you," she said grandly. "Lower Neeling is indeed blessed with the, um, bounties of the land. And such good cooking, too!"

It was the best she could do on short notice, but she was going to have to work on her speechifying if this was going to keep up.

"Do you think they're going to do this at every town we come to?" she asked Avender when they were resting for a moment under a large elm in the center of the village.

"I hope not."

"I'll run away if they do."

"Your Majesty must learn to accept her new responsibilities."

"Not yet, if I can help it. And stop calling me Your Majesty."

Not until she had opened her gifts was the company allowed to depart. While a pair of dogs fought over the last mutton bone, Ferris received a large pumpkin, two beeberry pies, a leather belt with all the houses on the village street worked into the design, and six embroidered handkerchiefs. The thane's gift, which the page had been lugging around all this time, came last. Unwrapping it, Ferris found a large quilt with a border the color of blooming heather and many brightly stitched panels.

"Every goodwife and maid in Lower and Upper Neeling helped make that," said the thane proudly, his red face even redder after his beef and beer. "See? There's a panel shows you meeting the prince that first time in Rimwich. And here's one of you traveling with the Dwarf and the bear. And this one has you finding the Talking Stone. Our girl, Willamette, did that one."

"It's lovely. They're all lovely." Ferris pointed at what looked like a giant black rat with an extra-thick tail being poked in the eye by a blue stick figure. "And this is?"

Mrs. Thane turned away with another blush. Her husband threw out his chest, the leather straps on his cuirass strained to their limit. "That's my wife's, that is. It shows the noble knight Avender slaying the mander." The Thane turned his attention momentarily toward the princess's companion. "Very brave that was, if you don't mind my saying, Sir Avender. And you still only a boy and all."

"You honor me, sir," said Avender with a bow.

Though the quilt's history was incorrect, Ferris thanked her hosts with a pretty speech she had been preparing ever since she saw this moment coming. Much later than originally planned, the party finally continued on.

And so it went, all the way to Nearside on the northern bank of the Great River. On the other side of the drifting current the towers and turrets of Malmoret shimmered brightly like damselfly wings at the edge of a pond. Galleys were drawn up at the Nearside dock and, after the town had put on its little show, all the smaller in the knowledge that Malmoret's far greater pomp was yet to come, Ferris and her company set off across the broad, slow stream.

Small boats bore down upon them, the occupants hoping for an early view of their new princess. From the middle of the river came the sound of hammering across the water. Ferris spied a long black barge moored midway between Banking and Wayland.

"What's that?"

"Begging your pardon, ma'am." The captain touched the edge of his gold-braided hat. "That's where the wedding's to take place day after tomorrow. That way no one on either side of the river can claim they were given preference."

"King Brannis is an astute ruler," observed Berrel.

"As Brizen will be one day," said Ferris.

They found Giserre waiting for them on the long stone quays of Malmoret, at the head of a gilded company. Her black dress matched her midnight hair, a golden girdle at her waist to go with the diadem at her head.

"Welcome to Malmoret, Princess." Giserre's clear voice rang out across the dock. A cheer went up from the workmen on the wharves around her. "Welcome to my city. As King Brannis and Prince Brizen are in the Old Palace, I have been sent to lead you to the New."

"Giserre," Ferris exclaimed. "We hardly expected to find you here."

"Malmoret is my home," she replied. "Now that Reiffen is acclaimed a hero, it is my privilege to return. Besides, you would not expect me to miss your wedding, would you?"

They rode together, Ferris and Giserre, in a gilded coach with tall wheels pulled by four snow white mares. Avender and the Valing stewards followed in the car behind. Cheering crowds packed the broad streets; girls in brightly colored dresses scattered rose petals across the cobblestoned road. Some in the crowd waved the black and orange of Banking, some the brown and green of Wayland. Not a few sported white flags, which some court official had decided was the proper color for frosty, snowbound Valing. Ferris smiled and waved to them all, though she couldn't quite shake the feeling she was being led into a world from which she could never escape. The thought of endless processions, and balls and receptions and afternoon teas, chilled her as much as Fornoch's touch.

"Is Reiffen here?" she asked, her eyes on the happy crowds around her.

"He has been gone this last month," replied Giserre.

"He said he would come back to teach me magic."

"He will. When the time is right."

Finally the horses stepped into the courtyard of the New Palace, where flowers graced the walls and windows like lamplight in Vonn Kurr. A beautiful woman with blond hair and a charming smile curtsied deeply at the door. "Welcome to your new home, Lady Ferris," she declared warmly. "I hope you will find everything satisfactory."

"Lady Wellin is to be chief among your ladies-in-waiting," explained Giserre.

"I hope we'll be great friends," said Ferris.

Lady Wellin inclined her head. "Your friendship will be my honor, my lady."

"Please call me Ferris. And I'll call you Wellin, if I'm allowed." She glanced nervously at Giserre.

Giserre smiled. "You are allowed. But try to keep your affection to the privacy of your own apartments as much as possible. Certain displays must be maintained before the world."

Wellin led them inside, where they were met by the rest of Ferris's noble attendants and taken on a tour of the palace. In awe, Hern trailed dutifully behind her daughter, Avender and her husband at her side. When they were done, the majordomo inquired what time her ladyship would like dinner to be served. Ferris glanced helplessly at Giserre.

"Her Highness would like very much for the palace staff to maintain their normal routine as much as possible, Sir Nevis. Please serve dinner at the regular hour. The stewards, Sir Avender, and I shall join the princess for the meal in her apartments."

Ferris's apartment turned out to have more rooms than she remembered to count, with ceilings as tall as the Great Hall back home. Paintings of all kinds filled the walls, from miniatures no larger than her outspread hand to panoramas of ancient battles that stretched from wall to wall. Three full-length portraits dominated the drawing room, one each for Brannis and Brizen, an elegant woman in between. Ferris didn't recognize the middle figure at first, as the face was about ten feet off the floor, but, when she had stepped farther back into the room, she realized the woman was supposed to be her. The likeness wasn't very close, as if the artist had been working from others' descriptions, but the color of the eyes and hair was her own, and the general shape of the face. Judging from the heights of the two men on either side, the artist had made her a little taller, too. But the dress! Every detail was perfect, from the stitching in the cuffs and collar to the pale gleam of the pearls sewn in dozens along the sleeves. Ferris had never seen such a dress and, though she had spent much of her life preferring rough brown skirts and woolen sweaters, found herself hoping the painting might some day come true. The color was perfect, the pale yellow of autumn beech leaves, trimmed in deep warm gold.

"It is a lovely painting," said Wellin, mistaking Ferris's regard. "Mirim will come back to finish it, now you have arrived. I do hope you approve that I served as his model. You are only a little taller than I."

And a little thinner, thought Ferris, as she eyed the other's lovely figure. But the artist had apparently been told about that, too, and had made Ferris slim and elegant in the splendid yellow gown.

She found it impossible to dismiss the ladies-in-waiting, but with Wellin herding everyone off to another part of the apartment, she did manage to take her bath alone. The tub room, thankfully, was without portraiture, though the walls were painted with what looked like someone who had never been to Valing's incorrect view of what a late-summer day might look like on the lake. The fishermen more closely resembled gentleman anglers than men who made their living with nets and small boats, and the nokken, some of whom appeared to be carrying fat whitefins back to the fishermen, looked a little too much like dogs. Ferris would have snorted with disdain if the mural hadn' reminded her of Skimmer, and the reason she had decided to get married in the first place.

Closing her eyes, she sank into the tub and drove all memories of nokken from her mind. There were taps in the wall, just like in Issinlough, and the hot water splashed into the bath shortly after she turned it on. Despite the ladies-in-waiting and all the waving from carriages, she decided there might be some advantages to being a princess after all. She had always liked her baths, and now that taking one was so easy, she might be able to bathe twice a week at least.

She snuck into her dressing room when she was finished. Alone, she went through the wardrobes and trunks that filled the chamber, running her eyes and fingers along the silks and satins, linens and lace. Although she found all sorts of dresses, some of which looked almost as enchanting as the gown in the painting, she put on the plainest one she could find. Until she had actually earned that wardrobe, she told herself, it wouldn't do to get too carried away.

Someone had snatched her boots for cleaning, so, after finding the shoes and slippers provided all too small and tight, she reappeared in the drawing room in bare feet.

The ladies-in-waiting quailed. A conspiratorial smile dimpled Wellin's cheeks. "But Your Highness," she declared, "such a thing is just not done!"

Ferris rubbed her toes comfortably in the thick carpet. "It will be."

Giserre barely suppressed a smile of her own when she returned for supper with the others and saw Ferris's bare toes. "Really, Ferris. You could allow everyone a little more time to get used to your wild, northern ways."

"I say give it to 'em as fast as you can," said Avender.

"Don't listen to him," ordered Hern. "He's spent too much time with Redburr. Giserre is right."

"Remember your dignity," chipped in Durk.

They were admiring the view of the river and gardens through one of the tall, thin windows that opened onto the terrace when a large brown shape tumbled wetly over the wall. Paws slipping on instant puddles, Redburr scrabbled across the stone into the room.

Hern was aghast. "What's wrong with you! You can't come in here. You're dripping wet!"

Ferris fell back against a settee to avoid being flattened, but was up and after the bear like her mother in a moment.

"Don't you even think about shaking in here. I'll ban you from the wedding feast if you do. Don't think I won't. Avender, there's a year's supply of towels in the closet off my bath. Bring all you can. I swear, Redburr, if you get so much as a single hair on any of the furniture in this room I'll stuff you myself."

The bear looked up at her with a mournful gaze that suggested he had never misbehaved in his entire life. "That fool Nevis won't let me in the palace as long as I'm a bear. He says I have to change, otherwise he's making me stay in the stables."

"What did you do, swim here from there?"

"I did."

"Sir Nevis is no fool, Redburr." With thumb and forefinger extended, Giserre plucked a waterlogged muffin from behind the Shaper's ear. "Have you perhaps been visiting other sections of the palace?"

Redburr made a halfhearted swipe for the muffin with his teeth, but Giserre pulled it out of reach. "Well, I did make a couple of cooks unhappy. And I don't think they'll let me into the dairy again even if I do make the switch."

"What switch?" asked Avender as he and Berrel returned with the towels.

Another trip was required before they had the bear dry enough that he no longer threatened to flood the room. Then more towels were necessary before they finished mopping the floor. By that time dinner had arrived. The head cook brought it up himself as an excuse to meet the future princess, but he lost his composure completely as soon as he saw the bear. Trusting Ferris to protect him, Redburr began sniffing at the trays. Hern smacked him with a pillow from one of the deep, plush couches.

Giserre assured the cook that Redburr would make no more forays into the kitchen. "I will, however, speak to Sir Nevis about the necessity of allowing the Oeinnen into the palace. He needs to be informed that Redburr will be much better behaved as long as one of us knows where he is at all times."

With Redburr banished to a spot on the floor where the rugs had been rolled up and replaced with towels, they all sat down to one of the most delicious meals any of them had ever tasted. They were finishing the last of the cakes when a footman opened the door and announced a familiar shape.

"Dwvon!" Ferris flew up from the table to greet him. "Have you found Nolo yet?"

Dust drifted from the Bryddin's beard as Ferris pecked him on the cheek. "No, but we will. We've tunneled into the main hall. Now it's just a question of how deep he fell. Uhle's supervising the dig, so he sent me with a gift instead."

"And Lady Breeanna?" asked Avender.

"Garven found her on the Backford Way. Mother Norra's keeping her in Issinlough until she's fit to travel."

The mention of a gift brought Redburr out of his sulk. He padded forward from his bed of towels. "A wedding present? From Uhle? It's probably worth half of Banking."

From inside his cloak, Dwvon drew out a large wooden box, its dark wood polished to a deep glow. The swirls and knobs of the elaborate carving might easily hide any number of openings. Dwvon pushed on one and poked at another, then lifted the top off the container as easily as Hern might open her sewing box.

Redburr sniffed suspiciously at the flicker of movement inside. "They're alive," he said.

Ferris gasped as she realized what Uhle had done. "It's moonstones."

With trembling hands, she lifted the gems from the soft velvet of their container. Strung together on a thin loop of blumet, the largest in the middle and the smallest at either end, each separated by tiny blue or yellow sapphires, the stony pearls flickered and flashed in their own silent storms.

"Oh, Dwvon. It's beautiful. Please tell Uhle for me. And thank him, too."

Hern and Giserre came close to examine the gift. "Moonstones?" asked Giserre. "I've never seen anything like them."

"They're lamps made with moon and starlight," answered Dwvon. "Those two don't bind to stone as well as sunlight and fire."

"We need to see you wearing this, my dear." Gently Giserre lifted the strand of swirling gems out of its dark box and draped the stones around the younger woman's shoulders. "It suits you perfectly."

"It feels beautiful." Indeed, the necklace lay as easily on Ferris's shoulders as a summer shawl. She felt no weight at all, though some of the stones were larger than acorns.

"You can wear it at the ceremony," suggested Redburr. "Brannis will like that. A pretty addition to his kingdom."

"The gift is to the girl and not her husband-to-be," said Giserre.

"Do you really think I should wear it?"

"Of course. Let us hope it matches your gown."

"I need a mirror."

Her bare feet padding softly across the thick rugs of the New Palace, Ferris went off in search of a mirror to admire her treasure.

The next morning Wellin knocked on the door as soon as Ferris had finished dressing. "You have a visitor, my lady."

The Banking woman ducked away without announcing the guest. Assuming it was the prince, Ferris began composing herself at once. She hadn't seen Brizen since the time they had kissed, and she wasn't sure she would be able to start up again where they had left off until she worked herself up to it. So much had happened in between.

The door opened. Ferris curtsied. Her visitor wasn't Brizen, however. It was the king.

"I wasn't expecting you, Your Majesty," she said.

He returned her greeting with a nod and crossed to the windows, ignoring the wet towels still piled on the floor. Beyond the garden, bright sunshine made the brown river sparkle like the scales on a leaping fish.

"Although it is not customary," he began, "I thought you and I might meet at least once before the wedding."

"Yes, Your Majesty."

"We need to talk."

"We do, Your Majesty?"

Brannis turned to face her. Ferris knew she wasn't supposed to sit while the king stood but thought about doing so, anyway, just to prove he couldn't bully her. Only she was determined to be a good wife, and being a good wife meant paying the proper respect to her father-in-law.

"Don't play coy with me, miss. You know exactly what I mean." Brannis stepped around the couch, avoiding the wet spot on the rug without seeming to have noticed it. "Why are you marrying my son?"

Ferris drew herself up to her full height, imagining Giserre would have done the same. "I should think that would be obvious, Your Majesty. He asked me."

"That's no answer. I ask you again, why are you marrying him?"

"You expect me to refuse him?"

"Yes. You refused him before. Why accept him now?"

Ferris ran her fingers along the dark upholstery. "I changed my mind."

"Of course you did. That is why I am here. I believe I have a good idea of what your reasons were without your telling me. My informants have provided me with all the circumstances behind this summer's events in Valing."

"Then why are you here? Have you come to see if your spies told you the truth?"

"The truthfulness of my spies is not your concern. I am here to find out what I must give you, in order to persuade you to change your mind again."

"I am not one of your hirelings, Your Majesty, to be bought and sold."

"No, you are not. But I am convinced you can be persuaded to end this foolish engagement. I am not the only one to note you do not seem to love Brizen greatly."

"You have not seen us together for more than a year," replied Ferris proudly. "Much has changed. I now realize Brizen is the finest man I know. He loves me."

"Yes, he does. So much so, he has finally found his own legs beneath him. Never has he crossed my will in anything before. For that, I thank you. I like this new determination you have brought out in him. It is why I am not forbidding the marriage. With you, however, I need show no such restraint."

"I will not give him up."

"Are you sure you will make him happy? Will your eyes stay on home and hearth, or will they wander north? There are others who will take him, if you turn away. Valing brings nothing to my kingdom. Lady Wellin, however, with her holdings in the south, would bring a great deal."

"I should have known she was part of this."

"Wellin? She knows more than she ought, and no doubt understands why I am here, but she is not privy to my councils. And there is no plotting behind my offer, mind you. I only thought you should know, now that your former lover has returned the hero, if you wish to call this marriage off, I will not stop you. Just the opposite, in fact. I am prepared to reward you. Generously."

"What could you possibly offer me I would accept? Some dingy estate near Wetting? A barony for my firstborn? I have all I want in Valing, should I ever choose to return. I need nothing from you, or Brizen."

Brannis smiled. "Is that really true? Would you ever actually return to Valing? What sort of woman from that place would choose to fall in love with a prince? An ambitious one, I think. One even more ambitious than Lady Wellin, and more imaginative as well. You will make my son a fine queen, whether you love him or not, of that I am certain. But your dower is too small to be of any use to me. Wellin, at least, would bring the barons to my side, regardless of your fledgling wizard's promises."

Ferris's temper flared. "You can be sure Reiffen will keep his word. Which is more than you ever did."

Brannis's eyes narrowed. "Promises may be regretted, as you may discover yourself one day. In the meantime, I tell you plainly, it is better to break my son's heart now than later. Better for him, and better for you, too. Better even for me, perhaps, as I believe he will be more manageable in the matter of his next choice once you hurt him."

Ferris shook her head in disbelief. "You're even more horrible than I thought. How can you say such a thing about your own son? I'm going to be a wonderful wife for Brizen. You just watch me."

"Perhaps you will." Ignoring Ferris's anger, Brannis started for the door. "He will love you dearly for it, if you do. As will I. But it will be hard for you, not loving him. Think about what I have said. You can change your mind at any time. The choice is yours."

Ferris stared furiously at the door as it closed behind the king. But she was flattered, too, at the idea that Brannis thought she would make a good queen. Clearly he saw right through her. More than her mother. More than anyone, perhaps. But she would prove him wrong, she would prove them all wrong. She would love Brizen as no one had ever been loved before.

Sulking, and almost as angry with herself as she was with the king, Ferris flopped onto the nearest couch. None of this was working out the way she expected.

But the rest of the day was delightful. She had anticipated a miserable morning and afternoon of fittings and sittings, only to discover early on that the dress in the painting was the one she would be married in. That made the fittings much less annoying. Uhle's necklace went well with it, the topazes setting off the yellow and gold fabric nicely, and the moonstones going well with the pearls. Ferris found herself fingering both in amazement whenever she had them on. They seemed made for someone else; touching them was the only thing that made her even half believe they really were her own.

Exhausted by her long day, she fell asleep that night dreaming of moonbeams and storms.

The next morning dawned clear and cool. Autumn scraped down from the north, the wind chipping the river into ridges of white and steel blue. The pennants in the palace garden flapped crisp and stiff in the breeze.

Giserre and Hern arrived, a squadron of ladies-in-waiting behind them, with Wellin bringing up the rear. Hern tried gamely to take command, but in the end she had to defer to Giserre's and Wellin's vastly superior knowledge. Ferris submitted while her attendants performed their jobs. Getting into the dress was mystery enough, what with the hooks and stays and buttons the likes of which she had never seen before, but there were also the stockings and the powder and the rouge and her hair. By the time they were finished Ferris felt like a goose trussed up for a winter feast. She gasped as Giserre led her to a long mirror; for the first time in her life she thought she looked beautiful. Maybe her eyes were too small, and it would be nice if her hair were as dark as Giserre's, or her figure more like Lady Wellin's. Her heart beat rapidly: it was a heady feeling, looking beautiful. For the first time she truly understood what Giserre had given up by exiling herself in Valing.

The ladies-in-waiting nearly fainted when Hern brought out the moonstone necklace as the final touch. Even Wellin's eyes shone when she fastened the clasp at the back of her mistress's neck. Then, her ladies protecting her like an imperial guard, Ferris waltzed through the palace in her splendid gown. Servants gasped, curtsied, and bowed as she passed. The same carriage that had carried her from the dock two days before stood ready in the courtyard, four chestnut stallions stamping impatiently as they waited their turn to parade. Avender, arrayed in shining silver armor like a proper hero, tugged uncomfortably at his collar. Durk hung from a ribbon round his neck.

"How does she look?" asked the stone.

"Like a queen," answered Avender sadly.

"I wish I could see it."

"Where are Redburr and Dwvon?" inquired Ferris as her father helped her into the carriage.

"They had to go on ahead," he said. "Redburr was making the horses nervous."

On a gray gelding, Avender led the way. Pale gravel sprayed out behind the carriage wheels. Two more coaches followed: the stewards, Giserre, and Wellin in one, and the ladies-in-waiting in the other. A column of the king's own cavalry brought up the rear.

Ferris grew more and more nervous the closer they came to the docks. This time the crowds that lined the streets waved small yellow and gold flags as they cheered. At the riverside a small galley rested at the end of the longest pier, oars raised. Ship and rowers alike were draped in green and black. In the middle of the craft, where the mast would normally have been, stood a raised throne.

She stepped into the galley clasping her father's hand while Avender helped Giserre. A gull eyed the moonstone necklace greedily from the top of a stone bollard. When the last lady-in-waiting had been eased into the middle of the boat, the helmsman cast off. Lowering their oars, the rowers pulled the craft quickly across the flat water of the harbor, cutting the dark surface with long, clean strokes. Ferris shaded her eyes with her yellow-gloved hand and stared from her high seat out across the dark back of the river to the far-off smudge of the barge.

The sun was nearly straight up in the sky when they arrived. Sailors in the same green and black as the men who had rowed her ran a railed gangway directly to Ferris's chair. Crossing, she found herself at the top of an aisle between rows of guests. At the bottom Brizen regarded her from a raised platform with his father, a green-and-black canopy suspended over the stern to shade them from the sun. Ferris thought he looked terribly handsome in his uniform and sword, his face suffused with joy. Reiffen would never have looked at her that way, no matter how much he loved her.

Her father offered his arm. Redburr, his red fur brushed and combed, peered down the aisle at her from the spot up front where he and Dwvon had found choice seats. Determined she would be stronger than all the rest of them put together, but also afraid her knees would give out, Ferris marched forward.

Brizen's joy increased as she left her father and stood beside him. Trembling, she gave him her arm.

"Shall we begin?" asked the king, regal in his crown and robes of state.

A jet of water fountained up from the river behind them.

Like hoofbeats on a dry road, it cascaded heavily onto the canopy overhead.

"Hey, Ferris!" came a voice from the water. "Why didn't you invite me? I can't believe you're getting married without inviting me!"

Careful of tripping in her dress, Ferris stepped past the king and leaned over the stern. Brizen followed. A whiskered face stared up at them from the river.

"Skimmer?" Ferris felt a door open in the back of her heart. Sunlight streamed in. "Skimmer!"

The nokken answered with another jet of water.

The barge erupted. Brizen wanted to know how a nokken had come to Malmoret; King Brannis called for the guard. Avender shouldered his way forward to see the truth for himself, astonishment emptying his face.

Ferris went down on her hands and knees, no longer caring if she ruined her lovely dress, and leaned closer to Skimmer. The moonstones swung lightly at her neck.

"You're alive!"

Skimmer did a little roll along the side of the barge. "I am. I had a real adventure, just like yours."

"So Reiffen didn't kill you?"

"Not me. Or Rollby either."

Ferris's heart swelled to bursting. "But that means . . ."

"He says that means you can marry him. At least that's what he told me. So will you?"

"Will I? Of all the rotten, horrible tricks." Ferris clutched the sides of her dress, not knowing whether to scream or cry. "If he thinks I'm going to—of course I'll marry him."

The king's voice cut through Ferris's elation like an ax. "Archers, ready. At my command."

Ferris scrambled to her feet. "Don't shoot him! He's not hurting you. He's just a nokken!"

The Shaper growled at her side. Avender reached for his ceremonial sword.

The king's face grew black, but he gave no further command. His soldiers lined the back of the barge, arrows bristling. Skimmer eyed them warily, then disappeared into the water like a snake. A few heartbeats later he resurfaced farther away, spitting another fountain in the air.

"Would somebody please tell me what's going on?" demanded Durk.

Ignoring the stone, Ferris cupped her hands to her mouth in a most undignified manner and called, "Where's Reiffen?"

"Waiting for you!" replied Skimmer across the water.

Ferris turned back to the king and prince. As happy as he had seemed before, Brizen now looked even more unhappy. Brannis tugged at his lip. Guilt pulled uncomfortably at Ferris, but not enough to make her even think about changing her mind. Again.

"I'm sorry," she said.

"So am I," replied Brizen.

Avender opened a way for Giserre through the crowd of soldiers. Her piercing glance skipped from king to bride to groom and back again. "What has happened?" she demanded.

"Skimmer's alive. Didn't you know?"

Understanding rose quickly in Giserre's eyes. "No."

"Do you love him?" asked Brizen before anyone else could say a word.

At first Ferris thought he meant Skimmer, but she knew that was wrong. Only Reiffen mattered now.

"Yes. I love him."

The prince breathed deeply, trying to control his heart. Avender remained still as stone.

Hands clenched at his sides, Brizen spoke again. "Then you should marry him. I release you from your pledge. I have his kingdom. It is not right I take his love as well. Just do me one favor and marry him somewhere else, and not in front of me."

Tears welled in Ferris's eyes. Reaching in front of the king, she clasped the back of the prince's hand. Briefly he let her touch him, then pulled his arm away as if burned.

"And you, Your Majesty?" Giserre faced the king. "My son has given you your kingdom; will you spare him the hand of a penniless girl from Valing?"

"The choice is hers," said Brannis. "She knows that."

Another call from Skimmer brought their attention back to the water. Only now he wasn't alone. Behind him a catboat, its sail lowered, rested easily in the current.

"Are you coming?" cried the nokken.

"Yes, are you coming?" repeated Reiffen from the boat. Beside him the puppy, twice as large as before, barked eagerly, its paws on the gunwales.

The bowmen, having received no other command from their king, continued to aim their arrows at the water.

"Come closer so I can hop in," answered Ferris.

"I can't." Reiffen waved for her to come to him. Ferris thought it odd his boat hadn't blown closer in the breeze. "I'm not really here."

"Then how am I supposed to get to you?"

Skimmer shot another long stream of water through the air. "Swim!" he cried.

"I can't swim!" Ferris lifted the sides of her dress. "Look what I'm wearing! I'll drown!"

"I'll carry you!" Skimmer rolled in the water. He was as big as Longback now and could carry her easily no matter how heavily she was dressed.

Ferris kicked off her shoes.

"Oh no," exclaimed Hern. "You'll ruin your dress."

"The necklace will make it through," said the bear.

Just as if she were back at Nokken Rock, Ferris dove off the barge. The water was clean and cold. The ballooning fabric of the dress stopped her from going very deep, and pockets of air in the petticoats soon brought her back to the surface, but even so she was in no position to swim. Something large and sleek rose beneath her. Clinging to Skimmer's strong neck, she flew swiftly through the water.

Reiffen pulled her into his boat. The puppy licked her cheek. The moonstone necklace slid across her skin. Before she could say a word, Reiffen kissed her. She kissed him back but, before he was done, she pulled away and smacked him hard.

"What was that for?" he complained.

"For making me think you were a murderer. This would have been a lot easier if you didn't insist on keeping so many secrets."

"I had to be sure, before I could tell you Skimmer was alive. I hadn't seen him since the day I left him and the pup in the White Pool after rescuing them from the gorge. For all I knew, they died in the rapids beyond and I really was a murderer."

"But you're not." She kissed him again.

"No, I'm not." He kissed her back.

Some time later she thought to look around. She had only just noticed the air was colder than it had been. The river was gone, replaced by a pond surrounded by thick trees. Many were evergreens, their dark coats glistening in the noonday sun. Unshipping the oars, Reiffen began rowing the boat toward a small cabin. Gray smoke wound from the chimney.

"Where are we?" she asked.

"In the Great Forest. Close under the backs of the High Bavadars."

Skimmer leapt out of the water across their bows, then circled back to the boat. A pup popped up to the surface beside him. "Me and Rollby are hungry," he said.

"Go catch some fish," Reiffen answered.

"I thought we were having lunch with you?" The nokken's whiskers twitched in disappointment.

"Not lunch, Skimmer." Ferris hugged Reiffen tighter to keep from getting cold. "Maybe dinner, but not lunch."

"Maybe not dinner, either," grunted Reiffen as he pulled them faster toward the shore.

His thimbles clicked against the oars.